Acclaim for Isla Dewar:

'Dewar's gift is to pull you into the minutiae of her people's lives . . . few writers are so good at making the reader empathise' *Scotland on Sunday*

'Acute observations of small-town life . . . Magda is a wonderfully strong female character' Tom Shields, *Herald*, Glasgow

'Dewar's vivacious, bawdy portrait of life in a Scottish village is fresh, likeable and wincingly familiar' *Scotland on Sunday*

'Breathless . . . appealingly spirited . . . sparkiness, freshness and verve' *Mail on Sunday*

'Observant and needle-sharp . . . entertainment with energy and attack' *The Times*

'Genuinely moving and evocative' *Scotland on Sunday*

'A remarkable, uplifting novel' *Edinburgh Evening News*

'You'll love this enchanting, touchy-feely tale of small-town Scottsh life' *Options*

Isla Dewar lives in Fife with her husband, a cartoonist. Her novels *Keeping Up With Magda*, *Women Talking Dirty* and *Giving Up On Ordinary* are also available from Review.

It Could Happen To You

Isla Dewar

review

First published in 1998
by HEADLINE BOOK PUBLISHING

First published in paperback in 1999
by HEADLINE BOOK PUBLISHING

A REVIEW paperback

10 9 8 7 6 5 4 3 2 1

ISBN 0 7472 5551 2

Typeset by Palimpsest Book Production Limited
Polmont, Stirlingshire

Printed and bound in Great Britain by
Clays Ltd, St Ives plc.

HEADLINE BOOK PUBLISHING
A division of Hodder Headline PLC
338 Euston Road
LONDON NW1 3BH

For Rosa O'Keefe

Chapter One

Rowan loved Eileen the first time she saw her. She knew that. It wasn't any sort of physical passion, this love. It only needed the simplest of touches. But love it was. When it died, the fascination lingered. Years after they'd parted Rowan would be washing up, watching the suds flood over the side of a salad dish, daydreaming, and her thoughts would turn to Eileen. God, she'd think, Eileen. Wonder what she's doing now? Whatever happened to her, whatever dramatic turns her life took, Rowan knew she could never forget Eileen.

When she first met her, Rowan longed for Eileen's company. She was obsessed in the simplistic way tender and innocent people obsess about those they imagine to be endowed with all the attributes they believe they're lacking. She was starstruck.

People thought Rowan withdrawn. She shut herself away, could not come up with an emotion when she needed one. She forgave people anything when face to face. But later, when reconsidering an insult, a misdeed, she'd shake with anger. She never was any good at friendships. Brief all-consuming passions, yes. But camaraderie passed her by. She never could project the person she knew she was inside. The dreamer, the traveller, the stubborn sardonic wit.

In her mind, Rowan could always deal with awkward situations. But, when it came to the bit, when awkward situations horribly presented themselves, Rowan would disappear into her shell, say nothing. Later, and alone, considering the moment, she would take charge, say out loud to her empty room what she ought to have said. Oh, the tongue-lashings vented on sofas and cushions that ought to have been dished out to lippy shop assistants, surly doctors and pushy young voices on the telephone selling double glazing. Witty retaliations, crushing put-downs always occurred to Rowan too late. Eileen knew that. She could not resist taking advantage. Malice was not intended, she was just an opportunist. A fabulous, outspoken, extravagant, painted opportunist.

The first time they met Rowan was moving into her room in the house in Islington. She was climbing the stairs, two flights covered with a patterned carpet so worn she could see wooden steps beneath the strands. The wall she leaned against every now and then, resting from the strain of carrying too much, was covered with maroon and gold flock wallpaper. The thick smell of stale cooking – reheated vindaloos – and damp coated the insides of her nostrils. This house she had come to London to live in, once grand, was now slipping towards squalor.

Her legs were leaden with the weight of stuff she had tucked under her arms, in her hands, crammed into the pockets of her long leather coat. She was burdened with books, maps and a couple of cases, trying to bring up too much and, therefore, make fewer journeys up and down to the main hallway. Every few steps she dropped something, and turned awkwardly to watch it tumble and bump back the way she'd just come.

Eileen had the room across the landing. First she eased the door ajar so that she could peek out. Then she flung it open wide. 'Who's this?' She was wearing a black basque, suspenders, nylons, very, very high heels and a red Santa hat. A white bobble dangled drunkenly just past her nose.

'Only me,' said Rowan, trying to act cool about being confronted by a loud-mouthed person. A brazen tart, her mother would have said. Trying to keep her eyes steady, meeting Eileen's eyes. 'Sorry. Didn't mean to disturb you. Just moving in.' She thought she was smiling too much, her face was glistening shyness.

'My new neighbour.' Eileen stepped grandly onto the landing, offering a slight handshake. 'I'm Eileen. And you are?'

'Rowan,' said Rowan.

Eileen considered her closely. 'You do not look like a Rowan. You look a little lost. Bewildered. Alone in the wide, wide world. I shall call you Joe.'

Rowan suffered the name Joe for two months before she protested. 'My name is Rowan. Please call me that.'

Eileen shrugged. 'Whatever,' she said, the timbre in her voice rattled by disappointment. Rowan felt she'd betrayed her. She should have been grateful for the time and thought Eileen now imagined she'd put into finding Rowan an appropriate name.

It was 14 December, 1989. Christmas clamour everywhere. In the shops, streets, lights beaming out of the houses Rowan passed on her way down the street, old Slade and John Lennon Yuletide hits jangling on the radio. In every newspaper she opened, on discussion programmes on television, pundits earnestly appraised the glitz and greed of the decade she'd just lived through – and, she felt, missed.

In a series of news-clips and Top Ten hits, the decade cackled from a radio that Rowan set up in her new room. The Gulf War and Wham! Thatcher's rise, and rise, and Boy George. Live Aid and U2. The Communards and Billy Ocean. Filofaxes, shoulder pads, Ecstasy, networking, house prices rocketing, house prices falling and Kylie Minogue. As she came and went bringing stuff up to her room, Rowan listened. None of it, she said to herself. I had none of it. Not a shoulder pad, not a filofax. Nothing. She thought the reviews of the decade were tinged with a slight shame. The greed of it all. But she was ashamed she had nothing to be ashamed of. What had she done in the last ten years? Grown up. Left home. Had a few lovers, nothing lasting, nothing serious, nothing heartbreaking. Whenever lasting, serious or heartbreaking threatened, Rowan withdrew. They were not part of her plans. She had not networked, had not worked at moving up the career ladder. She had made few friends. She was neither mover nor shaker. She was, she thought, nothing. Yet she had her dreams.

Jive Bunny and the Mastermixers played *Let's Party* and the incessant, heartless cheeriness of it all turned Rowan's isolation into an ache so intense she almost relished it. She planned to spend Christmas Day alone, sitting in that squalid kitchen she had just passed, eating a single Marks and Spencer chicken breast and defrosted Brussels sprouts, slowly demolishing a bottle of Australian white. Her major celebration would be no Christmas pudding – which she hated. It sounded so dreadful she could hardly wait to get on with it.

She had resisted her mother's pleas to go home, saying it was too far to travel since she had to be back at work the day after Boxing Day. A lie. She had a fortnight's Christmas leave. But going home was not part of her plans. Rowan had two burning ambitions. One was to travel the world. The other was never to return to the dreary little town where she grew up.

Rowan longed to be considered cool. She did not know what the code of cool decreed on the matter of flouncing about before strangers, scantily clad with a limp Santa hat atop. But she did know that she was required not to remark on this, or even notice it. She was cool therefore she said nothing. Hell, she met women in deranged hats all the time, every day. Thought nothing of it. Just so long as she did not have to appear in such a state herself.

'Would give you a hand,' said Eileen. 'But I must fly.' She skipped back into her room, turned, winked hugely. 'Entertaining, if you catch my drift.' From inside came the greenish sensual waft of something herbal being smoked and the chokingly aromatic fug of musk joss sticks. 'Eileen. The hell are you doing flashing about in that out there? Get back in here. Shut the fucking door.' A male voice. Eileen shut the door.

Rowan went into her room, looked round. This was to be home till she raised enough money for her great adventure, her world trip. She was twenty-four. She'd been dreaming of travelling the world since she was twelve.

Mr Kinear her geography teacher had set her dreaming. He cycled to school winter and summer wearing a poncho. He was not a man who kept to the point. Trying to fill young uninterested minds with facts – a country's imports, exports, natural resources, population drifts – bored him. He would gaze across the rows of numbed, unformed faces before him, aware of how weary they were of the process of gathering knowledge they did not seek. He would see who was sucking a sweet and who was staring out of the window and who was passing notes to whom, and he could not bear that he was the cause of all these mindless escapes from tedium. So he would digress. He would tell his pupils about his journeys. His days of backpacking through Peru, across Australia, and from this little town he'd been born in down to London, across Europe to India. Nonplussed, his pupils continued to suck, gaze and scribble.

4

Only Rowan in her stiff new school uniform listened. She was enthralled. She wanted to do that, go places where she was not known. Travel the world with just a rucksack and a spare pair of shoes. She wanted away from this town, away from her parents and the routine life they led. Their strict mealtimes, breakfast seventhirty, lunch quarter to one, tea five-thirty, and their annual fortnight's trip to Southport. She wanted to spend years on the move till she found the place she was meant to be. In those days she would get excited just being someplace where the buses were a different colour. She was convinced there was a place out there somewhere where she would be completely happy. She would find it. She would one day walk into some strange little town, sit down at a table in a small cafe, look round and say, 'This is it. This is where I am meant to be.'

Looking for her place in the world, she wanted to follow in the footsteps of her heroes – Mr Kinear, Mungo Park (all the way from Dunfermline up the Niger to Bussa where he died in 1806; Rowan was determined to go one day, to take that journey), Burton, Speke and, lately, Martha Gellhorn whose *Travels with Myself and Another* Rowan had read till the book had fallen apart. She put her battered, Sellotaped copy on the little chest beside her bed. She planned to read it once more tonight. It would soothe the turmoil of nerves she felt at moving into a new home, and starting, next Monday, a new job.

Rowan's maps were old, waxed, cracked with time, pitted and bruised from the constant proddings of teachers' pointers. She had rescued them from a skip outside her old school, ten years ago. They were coloured pinks, greens, yellows, the seas and oceans a strange grubby pale turquoise. They were no longer relevant, these maps. The world had changed since they were printed. Elaborate copperplate recorded the names of places that had long been reinvented and renamed – Abyssinia, The Gold Coast, Mesopotamia.

Eileen, Rowan would discover, used her walls to pay homage to screen heroes and drugs. But Rowan's room was a shrine to her great longing. The routes she planned to take, following in the footsteps of other travellers, greater than she thought she would ever be, were carefully marked. One day, she told herself, she would visit the places on her maps. She would stand on lonesome railway platforms waiting for sometime trains to come heaving and steaming along, and join the clattering throngs already aboard, travelling to wherever the tracks took her. She would walk from village to village along the Niger, eating (when food was scarce), as Mungo had done, blossoms of maize stewed with milk or water. She suspected that most of the villages Mungo stopped at no longer existed, and that if they did, the people in them would drink Coke-Cola and eat Big Macs, but she denied this thought. Cast it out whenever it snuck up on her. Modern culture had no place in her yearnings. She wanted to stare down the well into which Mungo's horse had fallen at Wonda, watch wide, grey lakes turn pink with flamingos, trek the Australian outback guided only by ancient dreaming songs, under southern skies. She would join camel trains, wander with nomad tribes who had never before cast their eyes on a lone white woman, with only her wonder and her longing to travel with them to save her from their ravages. She would visit Patagonia and Peru. She would walk the Great Wall of China. She would sleep under canvas whilst beyond her tent a jungle lived and moved. Her worn and dreaming feet would wander the deserts of Sudan. She would do all that, and more. She would. *She would.*

She imagined a whole wide gorgeous world waiting for her to come tramp across it. Determined to fulfil her dream she did not notice the things that were going on around her, and denied herself all sorts of simple pleasures – booze, music, nights out. But that was before Eileen turned her head.

There were three little words that ruled Eileen's life – *it's not enough*. 'It's not enough,' she would cry, looking desperately round. She needed to be sated; whatever she was drinking, eating, smoking she needed to be sated. One bar of chocolate? 'Not enough. Run and fetch me more, darling.' (To Rowan who usually obliged.) One cigarette? 'Not enough.' She'd chainsmoke a packet. Then open another. One drink. Unthinkable. She drank and she drank. She moved about the room drink in one hand, fag in the other, dancing a little, singing a little, laughing a lot, shrilly and at nothing at all, pursuing happiness, drunkenness, a rash and headlong dash away from sobriety. Nobody could keep up with her. But everybody adored her. Or so it seemed to Rowan.

Within two days of meeting her, Rowan was Eileen's best friend. Or so it seemed to Eileen, who made and lost friends (especially best ones) easily. 'This is Rowan,' she'd say. 'You've just got to meet her. Isn't she gorgeous? So little. And look at her hair. All cropped and fluffy. Don't you just love her to bits? She's my best friend.'

'No, I'm not,' Rowan would protest, looking harassed. 'I hardly know you. Besides, my best friend is Claudia Rossi. I went to school with her.' She had left Claudia behind long ago, hadn't seen her in years. But she still thought of her as her best friend.

Everyone would laugh.

'Like I said,' Eileen would insist. 'Isn't she a sweetie?'

But Rowan didn't want to be a sweetie. She wanted to be an intrepid and daring traveller. Somehow, though, her irritation only ever amused people. She had come to London to work as secretary to James Frobisher, editor at Tingwell & Mason, publishers of educational books.

The style and dash of the eighties had passed him by, as it had Rowan. He was the grumpiest man she'd ever encountered. At least once a week, he would appear at her desk amidst clouds of pipe smoke demanding she wipe up the coffee he'd spilled. She'd go through to his room and stand in quiet despair behind his giant mahogany desk surveying the catastrophe – the soaked sheets of typed paper, the flakes of tobacco swimming in little caffeine pools, the tidal swill of Nescafé pouring onto the carpet. She would sigh at the flooded ashtray awash with coffee, ash, dead matches and tobacco. Then she would set about the mess with a box of Kleenex. Behind her, Mr Frobisher would dab ineffectually at his stained cavalry twills. Moving past him, she would toss the sodden sheets of paper into his waste-bin. 'It's all right, Mr Frobisher, I'll print these out again.' Then she'd fetch a damp cloth and clean the carpet. He would fidget, anxious to get on with his work. It was as if it were choreographed. They did not look at one another. They squeezed their bodies into the tiny space behind his desk. They rarely touched, but when they did they both shivered in slight alarm.

Eight hours a day she shared a pale-green-painted room with four other secretaries, clacking on her keyboard, watching Mr

Frobisher's long convoluted letters to his authors and memos to other departments – sales, rights, publicity – march up her computer screen. At ten-thirty and three-thirty she fetched Mr Frobisher's coffee, wondering if this cup was to be the disaster cup.

First thing each day Rowan filed Mr Frobisher's letters from the day before (he insisted on keeping hard copies of his outpourings). Then, since he refused to have an actual computer himself, Rowan would note Mr Frobisher's dictation in shorthand, making a play of listening to the toneless drone of his voice whilst staring out of the window. Daydreaming whenever he took off into his head, weaving and balancing his sentences. From eleven-thirty till four she typed Mr Frobisher's letters. And at four o'clock each day she put all the letters and memos she'd typed into an elegant leather padded folder and took them to him to be signed. Mr Frobisher unfailingly returned several to be re-typed. 'Re-do these, Miss Campbell,' he'd say, shoving the padded folder back at Rowan, complaining that she had placed a comma where he had not indicated a comma be placed, or that she had *not* placed a comma where he had indicated a comma be placed.

Every four weeks Rowan was on biscuit duty. She took money from the secretarial biscuit tin, went to Marks and Spencer and bought the week's supply. She always bought ones with soft fig centres or coconut cookies because she knew Mr Frobisher hated them. Once every four weeks, then, Mr Frobisher would storm into the typing pool waving a biscuit demanding to know who was on biscuit duty. 'I hate these,' he'd say. 'You know I hate these. Who bought them?' Rowan would shake her head. 'Dunno.' It was war. Only a biscuit war that Mr Frobisher was not really aware was being waged against him. But his protest and frustration made Rowan feel she was, in some small way, winning.

Every few months Mr Frobisher would come into the office a changed man. He would be stylishly dressed – expensive shirt, polka-dot tie – smelling of Givenchy aftershave. 'Meetings,' he would explain. 'Overseas agents.' The other secretaries wondered if he had a mistress, but Rowan dismissed this. 'Who would fancy him?'

The only contact Rowan had with home was with her mother.

They had a strict phoning routine. Without ever discussing it, Rowan's mother, Norma, had decided that Rowan should call her one week, and she'd call Rowan the next. It was a ritual, always performed around two o'clock on Sundays. If Rowan phoned late, her mother worried. If she missed a week her mother panicked that she'd been murdered or abducted. Yet she never phoned to check. If Rowan broke the ritual, her mother was hurt and worried. But she'd wait till it was her turn to phone before she let Rowan know how disappointed she was.

As soon as Rowan heard the ringing down the line, she could see the little table in the hall where the phone sat beside a small, flowering cactus and an African violet. She could see her mother walking purposefully over the brown and gold patterned carpet saying, 'Who's this now?' She would be wearing her green dress, black low-heeled shoes; she'd pick up the receiver: 'Hello. Four, five, double nine, six.' Looking in the gilt-framed mirror on the wall as she spoke. Fingering the double row of pearls round her neck. She always said the number when she picked up the receiver as she'd been told in the booklet (that was, after twenty years, still in pristine condition, and kept tidily inside the phone directory) they'd been given when they'd had the phone put in. She got upset if someone in the family didn't follow the correct telephone-answering procedure.

'Hello,' Rowan would say. 'It's me.'

'Who's me?' her mother would ask.

'Rowan.' Rowan always felt her shoulders slump when her mother said this. 'You know fine who me is.'

'You should always say your name on the telephone. It could save vital time in case of an emergency.'

Rowan always wanted to argue with her mother, accusing her of knowing who me was. Why couldn't she just relax and say hello? But she knew that if she did, they'd ring off still quarrelling and wouldn't make it up till the next call in a week's time. So she always changed the subject. 'Anything happening? Any news?'

'Your father's sleeping off his Sunday lunch. We didn't get any milk this morning. I don't think the forsythia is going to flower this year.' A short silence as her mother raked around in her brain for more news. 'Oh, and the County Arms Hotel went up

9

in flames last Wednesday. George O'Connell had to jump out a second-storey window. Broke his leg. Not that he noticed, he was that drunk. That's the problem with owning a hotel, the drink's too available. You should see the price of fish at Payne's this week. You'll never guess what I had to pay for two haddock.'

'No, I don't suppose I could.' Rowan would, by now, be slowly sliding down the wall.

'Yes. I've told the milkman if he forgets to deliver again I'll just cancel.'

'Right.' Rowan's bottom hit the floor.

'That George O'Connell is going to be in hospital for six weeks with his leg.'

'I expect he would be.' Rowan put her head between her knees.

'I said to your father, "We'll just have to have ham. I'm not paying that price for fish".'

'Too right.' Rowan put her free arm over her head.

'Do you remember Duncan Willis?'

'Vaguely.' Mumbling from the depths of her foetal position. How could she forget Duncan Willis? He had relieved her of her virginity in the back seat of his father's Toyota.

'Well, he has run away with Kathy Ross the plumber's wife. She's twenty years older than him. Got three children. I don't know what she sees in a young boy.'

Rowan thought she could fill her in with a few details there. But then again, perhaps not.

'Actually I think we should have had the haddock, after all. The ham was salty. So how about you? Are you fine?' Her mother asked this every week.

Surfacing, emerging from her defensive crouch, sliding up the wall again, Rowan would tell her she was well. Had made friends. Had settled in at work and loved her job. Then they would bid each other goodbye, till next week. Rowan would replace the receiver, aching to scream out loud. Once again she'd listened to those small stories from the town where she'd been raised. Once again she had nothing in her life to match them. Once again, she'd found them boring, frustrating and utterly fascinating. Why was she interested to know that the haddock in Payne's was over-priced? Aaargh! She wanted to scream, to rush from the house screaming, down the centre of the road, arms spread and still screaming.

What was really interesting about Rowan's conversations with her mother was not what was said, but what was *not* said. Their inane dialogues were conducted with an unaddressed undertow of mutual disapproval. Norma did not understand – didn't want to understand – why Rowan would want to backpack across the world alone; she feared for her daughter. Rowan hated her mother's complacent acceptance of a life filled with small routines. Wiping the same surfaces daily, seeing the same faces in the same shops where she bought the same food week in week out. So they lied to each other. Norma made a virtue of the little rituals she thought might make her scream if she let go and admitted how boring she found them. And Rowan told her mother her weekly lie – that she loved her job and had a fun-filled life – when the only person she knew socially was Eileen, and she hated her job, hated Mr Frobisher.

That didn't matter though, did it? This secretary business was not to be taken seriously. It was just a short stop on her way to the day when her real life started.

'You have your life all planned out, don't you?' Eileen said one night.

'Of course I do. You just have to decide what it is you want, then you go out and get it. What do you do, anyway?'

'Do? I don't do anything. I am.'

'How do you get money? Pay the rent? Buy food? All that boring stuff.'

'I live from day to day, get what I need by being me. I do not worry. I refuse to worry.' She lit a cigarette. 'Worrying's for the fools and drudges, the little grey people who do the dreary nine to five.'

She glanced over at her CD collection. 'There's a record, an early Dylan track that says it all for me. Who I am, and that. "She's got everything she needs . . ." I'll just find it.' She flicked through her albums. She had a track for every emotion, every situation. When words failed her, and they often did, she'd find a relevant track and put it on, demanding everyone present sit silent and listen. It saved her a deal of conversational effort. 'Can't find it,' she complained.

'But look at this.' Pulling out a battered four-year-old copy of the *Sun*. 'Look, that's me. I did that. Got enough cash for a week or so from that.' The centre spread showed a photo of half a dozen nearly naked women riding mountain bikes. 'Me,' said Eileen, rapping the page.

Rowan stared at it. She had not seen exactly which woman Eileen had been pointing to, and frankly, did not think anybody in the picture looked like her. But didn't like to say. 'Wow,' she said instead. It seemed appropriate. When she was with Eileen, Rowan said 'Wow' a lot.

'Then,' Eileen continued, 'I was in that ad. You know, Levi's? I was one of the women in the laundrette, looking wicked.' She smiled. 'Then I had a part in a film with Michael Caine.'

'Michael Caine,' Rowan's eyes opened wider, 'really? Wow!'

'Yes. He walked past me in the street. I was Disinterested Passer-by. That was what it had in the script. I looked into a shop window and ignored him. Then I had a part in a play on telly. I had actual lines. I had to say: "Mr Barker, the doctor will see you now".'

'Mr Barker, the doctor will see you now,' Rowan slowly repeated.

'No,' Eileen scolded. 'Not like that. *Mr Barker*, the doctor will see you now.' She got up. Wafted (her word, her description, she never just went anywhere – she wafted) across the room, long dark-red velvet caftan floating behind her. 'You have to live it. You have to make it sound chilling. Fill Mr Barker with apprehension. What is going to happen to him when the doctor sees him? What will the doctor say?' She came back to Rowan, clutched her arm. 'Who is the doctor, anyway? All that. You have to put all that into the line. It isn't as easy as it sounds. Then there's men.'

'Men? You don't . . . ?'

'No.' Eileen was tiring of this conversation. 'I don't do it for money. Of course not. Good heavens.' She clutched herself, shocked at the thought. 'Just men. They give you things, stuff. Pressies. Take you out to meals. Where would we be without them?'

'Dunno,' said Rowan. Men were not part of her great scheme.

12

Eileen despaired of her. 'Really. We have to sort you out. You've no men in your life. You don't drink. Don't smoke. What *do* you do?'

Rowan shrugged. 'Nothing.'

'Oh my. We absolutely must do something about you.' Eileen reached under her bed, brought out an old shoe box, rummaged amongst the letters and cards inside it and took out a Kodak film canister and a packet of Rizla papers. 'This'll sort you out.' She rolled a joint. Lit it. Drew on it several times gazing in abstracted bliss at Rowan, then, with a beatific grin, handed it to her.

'No. No!' Rowan shook her hands in front of her. 'I don't do any of that sort of thing.'

'Rubbish. Of course you do. You can't let it pass you by. You've got to try everything.'

'Everything?' Rowan said.

'Everything. Your life could pass you by and this moment will never come again. I am offering you the chance to see things as you haven't seen them before. I am offering you the chance to drift.' Eileen nodded.

Rowan considered this. It was true. What adventurer would turn down the chance of a little marijuana? *A chance to drift.* She took the joint. At first only the tobacco hit her. A nausea crept up from her throat, spread behind her eyeballs, across her scalp. Two more drags and she felt dizzy. She didn't like this. Handed the joint back to Eileen. The room smelled sweet, of hay. Rowan leaned back. Eileen put on a record. Sang along with some song Rowan did not know. The joint came back to her, and Rowan drifted into a silence in her head. She was staring at the floor, at the sad rush matting. Then she looked at the wall. She felt she was seeing it anew. The patterns, the thin strips of wallpaper visible between posters, a gold stripe, a vertical line of small sworls and a green stripe, seemed somehow crisper, clearer, more interesting than it had before. Wow, she thought. The wall.

Eileen's walls were completely covered with posters – one huge print of Aubrey Beardsley's *Lady in a Black Cape*, and bands, singers, guitar heroes. 'Had him,' Eileen said, pointing at someone Rowan had never seen before. 'And him.' Pointing at someone else. She took Rowan on a tour of her walls. 'Met him. And him. He's a bastard. Hate him. And he's lovely.'

And Rowan said, 'Wow.'

Chapter Two

Eileen had a cat, a heap of black fur called Elvis. Though the cat belonged to Eileen, he moved freely from room to room in the house, curling up with whoever it was pleased him most today. Eileen would leave notes in the kitchen. *Gone out. Be back sometime, who knows when. Feed Elvis, somebody.* Somebody was always Rowan. On her way home from work Rowan would buy cat food, lingering in the pet section deciding if Elvis would like chicken and duck flavour, or tuna and salmon flavour or maybe just plain beef flavour for his tea tonight. She didn't mind. Looking after something else took her mind off the loneliness of looking after herself. Though she knew if she was going to live the life she longed for, loneliness was something she was going to have to get used to. However, it was not long before Elvis decided that the person who pleased him most was Rowan. He moved in with her. The little cat arched his back when stroked, and answered her when she spoke to him with a tiny squeaking meow showing the insides of his mouth, soft and pink against his black body. Rowan was charmed.

Nights, when she had the house to herself, he would curl on her knee, purring. She would smoke (a new habit Eileen had encouraged in her), stare at her maps, listen to CDs borrowed from Eileen and lose herself in her great longing. Every now and then she would look down at the cat, gently scratch his head and murmur to him. His warm weight on her lap pleased her.

Sometimes Eileen would insist Rowan went with her to parties. They would bundle excitedly into Eileen's Beetle. Eileen never looked round checking the road before rattling off. '"I'm an artist. I don't look back",' she explained, quoting Dylan.

'I don't think he meant the Highway Code when he wrote that,' Rowan protested.

And Eileen answered, 'Pah.' She never signalled. She'd nose into the traffic blowing kisses at irate drivers. 'Toot, toot. Out the way. Party people coming through.' Winter and summer she wore her beloved cony coat, an Oxfam find. When they arrived at the party, before Eileen made her entrance – and she always made an entrance – she'd toss the car keys to Rowan. Rowan always drove home alone.

Eileen had strict rules about parties. A person must never arrive before ten-thirty. A person must never arrive sober. And if possible, a person must never go home that night. If they did, it must not be before four in the morning. Anything earlier was early. Only boring people went home early. For Rowan the worst thing about parties was arriving. Eileen was good at that. She burst into rooms, embraced the throng, 'Hi, folks,' and disappeared, squealing, into the arms of friends and cohorts. Party after party it was always the same friends and cohorts, and they always greeted one another as if they hadn't met up for years.

Rowan always arrived sheepishly, looking around, hoping nobody would notice her. She always ended up in the kitchen talking to the suicide. There was always one person at these parties who was contemplating it. 'Why?' she would ask.

'Because,' she was usually told, 'there is nothing to live for. I'm twenty-three and I haven't succeeded in anything. What's the point? If you haven't made it by the time you're twenty-four you're never going to make it. Too late for me.' This conversation – and she had it often – always chilled Rowan. She had never had any desire to make it. All she'd ever wanted to do was escape this life she was leading. Yet talking to the suicide made sure she avoided the party drama.

There was always one. Eileen was always in the thick of it. Women would weep and wail and disappear into the loo to sob about life, about love, about being misunderstood. Rowan would watch from her corner and plan her exit. After she'd talked to the suicide, Rowan would drift. And watch from a distance.

All round her people would be groping each other, smoking dope, dancing, drinking, laughing. Rooms would throb. Rowan would observe, trying to look interested. Or interesting. Whatever drugs were being handed round never came her way. She never knew if she was insulted by this or not. On the one hand it might be nice to be included, to be thought of as a cool and druggy sort of person. On the other if sudden rushes of absurd emotion was what happened to you, she was glad she appeared too sensible to be bothered.

At the height of the partying odd couples would disappear to the bedrooms, or to any corner they could find and return later, rumpled, flushed and grinning. Eileen would be joining in as much of it all as she could.

It took six weeks of partying for Rowan to decide that these heated, turbulent rooms were not for her. She had no place in them. After that she refused to go to another.

The only thing she'd enjoyed about Eileen's parties was the drive home alone. She loved city dawns. Streets that were chill and fresh and empty. Tower blocks, spires against paling skies. There were never many people about, revellers, with all the revelry knocked out of them, slouching home, policemen and milkmen. It was then she'd see urban wildlife. Once she saw three jays in a lime tree. Once a peregrine flew from its ledge on an office block and hovered, wings quivering, above the streets. What had it seen down there? A mouse? An abandoned burger?

Her most thrilling sighting was a fox. It was standing in the middle of a road, in the clean silence of the city morning, terraced houses, curtains drawn, either side. It looked as confused by metropolitan life as she was. It was scruffy and undernourished. She stopped the car, got out, leaving the door open, and walked towards it. 'Hello, fox.' It watched her approach. She held her breath, thrilled. How close was she going to get? 'Hello, fox,' she whispered, holding out her hand. It turned, sloped off up the street, into the dawn. Then it stopped, looked back at her. 'Hello, fox,' she said again, making a kissing noise. The noise she made to call Elvis the cat. The fox moved its ears. She saw it was shy, sly, unreachable and wild. She knew not to go any nearer. When it finally fled she noticed a raw wound on its rump. On impulse she ran after it. Feet pounding on the empty tarmac, an echoing rhythmic slap that silence made resounding. 'Oh don't go,' she called out. 'I can help.' But the fox leapt a fence and disappeared into a garden. She held onto the iron railings, catching her breath, bending over to ease the pain that running too fast, too far had caused in her side.

'I could've done something. I could've had it fixed,' she told herself before turning to walk the long way back to the car which she'd left in the middle of the road, door wide open, keys still in the ignition.

There were four other people in the house besides Eileen and Rowan. Danny and Fred had a ground-floor room each, Harry and Lou were on the first floor. Danny and Fred had the kitchen, Harry and Lou the lavatory. 'But,' Eileen said, 'we live on top. We may have to travel down a flight of stairs to the loo. But we have the view. And the view is everything.'

'Not when you're needing a pee in the middle of the night,' Rowan said.

They all came and they went. Wore loud clothes – a lot of orange and lime – played even louder music. They seemed to Rowan wonderful and wild, incandescent with their talk and their opinions. It was years before she realised they were transient souls who crossed her path on their way to being normal, respectable people. Ordinary. She rarely spoke to them. She kept her dreams to herself.

Danny, who supplied Eileen with her marijuana, warned Rowan about her. 'Watch out for her. She hurts people.'

'Why? She's my friend.'

'She's everybody's friend. She'll use you. She uses everybody.'

'She's not like that at all. She lends me her records. She shares her stuff all the time.'

Danny shrugged. 'She shares what she wants you to think she's sharing. But that's only to get you to share whatever it is she wants from you. You don't even seem to see how old she is.'

'I don't know what you mean.'

'Christ, the woman quotes Dylan. She's ancient. She's got to be way past thirty. At least.'

'She can't be. She doesn't look it. Nah. Anyway, so what if she is.'

Having an interesting older friend appealed to Rowan. It seemed sophisticated.

Danny lost interest in the warning he was giving Rowan. If she did not have the gumption to wonder what the hell a woman of that age was doing living the life she led, in a dump like they all shared, then what was it to him? He'd tried. He took his coffee across to the kitchen table, tapped his cigarette ash into the ashtray and started to read a newspaper, turning the pages swiftly, scarcely glancing at them. He sat on the edge of the chair, toes on the ground, legs jiggling to the throb of the music he'd been listening to and that was still thrumming in his head. That constantly thrummed in his head, never stopped. 'It's up to you,' he said. The conversation was over, the warning issued. He couldn't be bothered with Eileen.

Whenever Eileen spent an evening at home, she'd ask Rowan across the landing to drink wine, smoke a little, chat. Eileen would sit curled on her bed, leaning against the wall. Rowan would be on the floor cushion. Eileen would talk. She'd take off on verbal ramblings. She had too much to say. She'd start a sentence, stumble across a word in it that evoked a memory unrelated to what she was saying and embark on whatever story that memory started up in her. That would inevitably lead to another memory, another story. Every now and then, Eileen would stop, take a breath and say, 'Ooh, where was I? What was I saying again? I've lost me gist. Give's a sec till I remember what I was talking about.'

Sometimes it seemed Eileen had three or four conversations on the go at a time. All of them with herself. Rowan didn't mind. She thought Eileen had lived a movie trailer of a life – fantastic, amazing, wonderful, action-packed, thrilling, unmissable. Whereas nothing much had ever happened to her. She'd been born. Well, hadn't everybody when you thought about it? Except, of course, Eileen, who hadn't been born. More, she'd burst spectacularly into the world, three weeks early. And had made her first very public appearance in the back of a taxi on the way to hospital. 'Couldn't wait,' she'd say, 'to get started living. Partying.' At least, that was the way Eileen told it.

Rowan thought little of her past. She'd been brought up in a small town, with a mum and a dad – a couple of normal, everyday folk. She'd gone to school, left school. Gone to secretarial college, got a job in insurance, then another with a law firm. And now this one, with Mr Frobisher. Nothing much. A normal humdrum, tum-ti-tum sort of existence. She did not take proper stock of her achievements. She had left home, found a series of relatively well-paid jobs and kept herself clothed, fed with a roof over her head. She paid little heed to James Frobisher's promise when he took her on that if she shaped up she could move up, join the editorial staff. Unaware of her biscuit campaign, he thought she was shaping up very well indeed. Rowan did her job as best she could, mind fixed on the day she would leave. She did not even congratulate herself on having – through finding the cheapest housing possible, walking to work, eating little and buying clothes only at the sales – saved several thousand pounds. She had decided she was not a fabulous person. Maybe it was the strain of constant denial.

There was nothing humdrum about Eileen. Everything she did, she did in Glorious Technicolor. Shoving on the famous cony coat – 'I'm just nipping out for a pack of fags. Coming? No?' When Rowan shook her head: 'Oh well, don't blame me if you miss something.'

'What could I possibly miss nipping out for a pack of fags?'

'You never know.' Eileen's face melted with anticipation.

Rowan would inevitably heave herself up from her floor cushion, put on her coat and go with her. You just never did know. And she always paid for the cigarettes.

One Saturday afternoon, late February, smoking dope, Eileen looked at the sky, clouds scudding. 'I think these are spirits. They're not clouds at all. It's the dead visiting us. Sometimes I look up at them and I see the faces of people I've known. My Uncle George, I saw him once. And my Aunty Else.' She handed her spliff to Rowan. She refused it.

'You speak rubbish. What a lot of nonsense.' She stood up. Kicked the floor cushion. 'All sorts of interesting things are happening and I'm in here talking crap.'

It had taken Rowan all this time to realise that Eileen spoke a lot of nonsense. More and more, during the long Saturday-afternoon sessions with Eileen talking about Eileen, Rowan was bored. Eileen would watch Rowan's face, noting its lack of expression, and the way her eyes moved to the door, or watched the sky. It always happened, Eileen thought. Faces always fell that way. People switched her off. All she wanted was to be friends.

Eileen was not skilled in any neighbourly graces. It never crossed her mind that Rowan might want some peace. Or even that Rowan had work to go to in the morning and needed to sleep. Eileen would, any time of day or night, bang on Rowan's door demanding she come talk about her latest adventure. Rowan would raise her heavy head from her pillow, shards of her dreams lingering in her mind, and grunt, 'Go away.' She no longer had any wish to hear Eileen's stories with their inevitable ending, 'You should've been there.' Or, 'You missed yourself.'

She was beginning to wonder what it was she'd seen in Eileen in the first place. Her absurd spontaneity? Her overwhelming friendliness? No. Rowan knew what it was. Eileen touched her. That little thing. In the world Rowan came from, people did not touch. Birthdays, Christmases, New Year celebrations would pass year in year out and her family did not kiss, did not hug. A smile, a chink of sensibly-filled glasses was all you got. Partings merited a small sorry wave on the doorstep. At some time in her past, Rowan's mother Norma had tucked her feelings neatly away not to be used, certainly never to be revealed. Rowan did not know why. In fact, she'd only realised how afraid of emotions her mother was after she'd left home and looked back on her childhood.

Other girls had relationships with their mothers – friendships, even. Norma had always been withdrawn. Other girls' mothers had discussed sex, periods. Norma had more than shied away from life's messinesses. She had hurtled in the opposite direction. Knowing she ought to tell her daughter about sex, she had sat Rowan at the kitchen table, looked at her firmly and said, 'There's things you ought to know.'

'I know,' Rowan agreed.

'Yes.' Norma was relieved. 'I thought you knew. Most young girls do these days.'

And that had been that. Rowan did know the basic facts of life – she'd been told at school – but she felt a chat with her mother about it would have been intimate, interesting. Would have helped them open up to one another.

Rowan's first period had been a shock to her. She'd known that it was bound to happen to her one day. But knowing did not stop her thirteen-year-old fear when she discovered blood on her knickers in the school lavatory. 'I've started,' she told Norma when she got home.

Norma had been busy wiping the kitchen unit at the time. She did not look round, did not welcome this first step towards womanhood. 'I'll get you something from Jolly the chemist,' she replied. Continued wiping. And that was as far as intimacy went in the Campbell household. Whenever sweaty moments cropped up on the telly Norma would turn frosty. She never said anything. No need, she could speak volumes with an intake of breath, a stiffening of the shoulders.

Rowan's mother was good at silences – years of practice. She found she could convey more, get her way, by saying nothing than she could by voicing an opinion. Silences were wonderful. Nobody ever argued or reasoned with them, and she didn't have to think what to say. They were her ultimate weapon.

Rowan found her passion a few years later in the lane behind the village chip shop. It enthralled her. It scared her. Little wonder, then, she was a sucker for anyone who reached out and put a hand on hers. Eileen, for example.

One night, Eileen, thrilled at having spotted Mick Jagger across the room at a gallery opening, burst into Rowan's room; it was then she saw the maps. 'Wow,' she said, gazing round. 'Look at this.' The room was candlelit. Rowan never did like the dark. The maps . . . the colours were mellow, softly shining from the creases and shadows of the room. 'Wow,' Eileen said again. 'Your room.' Then she turned, pointed at Rowan, a gleam in her eyes. A glimpse of a different, harsher, jealous Eileen. 'You never told me about this.'

Rowan shrugged. 'You never asked.'

It seemed to Rowan that things were never the same after that. Her relationship with Eileen changed location. Eileen, like Elvis, kept coming to her room. Hardly a day passed when Eileen did not come to follow on one of the ageing maps, the route Rowan planned to take east across Europe.

Eileen knew a lot of people who had gone off, travelling east, to find their mystic selves. Sometimes she thought she might go, too.

But she was too engrossed making her way in the world she moved in. She wasn't quite sure if she wanted to explore her mystic depth. She didn't want to find what was lurking in her subconscious. She preferred to restrict her mysticism to reading Tarot cards for friends and studying her horoscope in the tabloids. Actually, horoscopes frustrated her. They were never precise enough, never immediate enough. She wanted to be told she was going to be rich and happy. She wanted to be told she was going to be rich and happy, very, very soon. In fact, her frustration with horoscopes went further than that. Sometimes being told what to look out for during next week or month was no use at all. Hell, her day-to-day dealings with the world were so immediate, sometimes she just wanted to know what was going to happen in the next twenty minutes.

Rowan's travel plans excited her. They had nothing to do with mysticism or self-analysis. Their sheer energy and optimism came from Rowan's view of the world which was gleaned from nature films, books, television documentaries. Rowan was not concerned with destinations. Voyages were her passion. She had mastered the language of travelogue. When she spoke about trekking across Africa, or visiting a Mexican lagoon to watch orgying grey whales, or catching the Trans-Siberian express, she spoke fluent holiday brochure. Eileen wanted to know all about Rowan's route across the globe. 'Tell me,' she'd say, hugging her knees, drawing thoughtfully on a cigarette, her face graced with a new earnestness. And Rowan, fool that she was, unfolded her dreams for her.

On the Friday night that Rowan came home from work and found Eileen in Lou Reed T-shirt and knickers in the kitchen eating chocolate cake straight from the box, she knew something was wrong. There was something desperate in the way she shoved a huge slab into her mouth and watched the ceiling as she chewed, shifting from foot to foot, eager to get this mouthful down so that she could bite into another. Eileen jumped when Rowan dropped her supermarket bag on the table. 'Christ,' she squealed, wheeling round. Then, relieved: 'It's only you. Thank God.' She slumped onto a chair. 'I was in bed and I just had to have some chocolate. Know what I mean? Everyone was out, so I thought I'd just nip down. Didn't bother to put anything on. Fright you gave me.'

The kitchen was worn, neglected, peeling yellow paint, tired yellow units, doors – handles hanging off – stained beyond redemption. Years before, some distant, long-gone tenants had shoved up a Neil Young poster. Now it was grease-splattered, but nobody thought to remove it. Nobody planned to stay long enough to put up another. And nobody lingered in the kitchen long enough to object to it. The surfaces were never free of crumbs, the sink always crammed with dishes. In the centre of the room was a wooden table, painted yellow, which Eileen, having finished a frantic mouthful, dramatically slumped across. She laid her head next to this morning's set of coffee cups and cereal bowls, and moaned. She had a thick crusting of icing round her mouth which she wiped with the back of her hand. 'Guess what.'

'What?' Rowan started to unpack her bag. Whilst she was no longer surprised at Eileen's semi-clothed body, Rowan couldn't understand how someone could feel relaxed in that state. She couldn't bear her body and knew she couldn't possibly walk around the house with it so uncovered. She'd feel too vulnerable – too, well, not exactly naked, but overly conscious of a certain unseemly dimpling of the thighs which she could not help but notice when glancing at Eileen. In fact, Eileen's whole body was beginning to succumb to her excesses. She always wanted too much.

'I'm pregnant,' Eileen told her.

'How do you know?' asked Rowan.

Eileen looked at her in derision. 'You're not that naive, surely. How do you think I know? I did a test. I reckon I'm six weeks. Baby'll be due in November. Except, I'm not having it.'

'No?' Rowan understood that. She thought having a baby the worst thing that could happen to a woman. It did horrible things to your body. Furthermore, babies were funny little things. Bald, gummy, incontinent. You never could tell what they were thinking. She was relieved Eileen wasn't going to have one.

'No.' Eileen was adamant. 'I'm having an abortion.' She hated that word. She was too aware of the indignities it involved. 'Next week. Tuesday.' The hideously bright fluorescent light overhead buzzed. Rowan picked a piece of icing from the cake and ate it.

'Come with me.' Eileen said. Her voice was frail, pleading.

'I can't. I have work.' Rowan opened a tin of cat food, clattered through the cutlery finding a fork to empty some into Elvis's dish. All this done more noisily than usual, as if that would hide her guilt.

'Work,' Eileen scoffed. 'Yes sir, no sir, three bags full sir when your best friend needs you. I only wanted you to be there. I need you. Sorry I asked.'

Rowan stroked the cat. Felt its skinny back arch against her hand. 'All right,' she sighed, 'I'll come.'

'Oh, don't come if you don't want to. I'll be fine.'

'Don't be like that. I said I'll come, so I'll come. I'll tell Mr Frobisher I have a tummy bug.'

'Diarrhoea and vomiting. Couldn't you think of a more glam excuse?'

'No, diarrhoea and vomiting will keep him at bay. He won't want any details.'

'Good thinking,' Eileen approved.

On Tuesday Eileen threw a small over-stuffed bag onto the back seat of her Beetle, and roared off. Rowan gripped the passenger handle with one hand, pressed the other against the dashboard and stared straight ahead. She knew her face was ashen.

Eileen was an exuberant driver. She hurtled the car onwards, top gear all the way. She took her hands off the steering wheel, gesticulating about some point she had to make, and if someone or something got in her way she knocked furiously on the windscreen shouting, 'Hoi you, get out of the road.' Cheery radio pop songs blared, but their vibrant jangle did not disrupt her constant banter. Was this woman really on her way to have an abortion?

'What's in the bag?' Rowan wanted to know.

'Something fabulous to wear afterwards. We could go on to a club, make a night of it.'

'I don't think so,' Rowan said. 'You'll be tired. You should expect to get depressed. I'll have to drive you home.'

'You think?' Eileen let this roll round her brain for a couple of minutes. 'Nah.' She shook her head. 'Not me. Life's too short.'

After they'd been driving for an hour, Rowan asked, 'Where is the clinic, anyway?'

Eileen waved her hand, indicating a vague direction somewhere to the left. 'Oh, over that way. Dunno really.'

'Aren't you going to miss your appointment? Didn't you have to be there by nine?' Rowan looked at her watch. It was now half-past.

'Yes. I've missed my appointment. Let's not go. Let's just drive. Have a nice time instead. Life's too short for appointments.'

She drove to Brighton. All the way there Rowan clenched her fists, despairing. She felt hi-jacked. Trapped in a car, speeding too fast to leap out, radio rock'n'roll blaring too loud to make her protests heard. She sulked instead. When they got there they walked on the pebbly beaches. Rowan, still not speaking, stuck her hands deep in her pockets and watched the imprints her feet left in the narrow strips of sand. Eileen danced. She took off her shoes and ran into the sea, leaping the waves as they diminished into ripples at the edge of the shore. 'C'mon, Rowan. You can't come to the seaside and not paddle.'

Rowan shook her head. 'It's freezing.'

'It's only freezing for a minute. Then you get used to it.' She spread her arms, embracing the day. 'It's great. It's so cool. I feel wonderful!' she shouted and took off, running, through the shallows, water sparking round her.

The mid-March chill was so deep it was visible. It lay, a bitter mist on the water, pushed against their faces. The beach was empty save for a man in a mac walking a small black dog. His pale whistle sounded along the sand. Both moved miserably. Rowan sank her hands deeper into her pockets, hauled her coat closer to her body, and watched, sourfaced. She kicked glumly at a small single shell. Her nose was running. Every now and then she looked furtively back over her shoulder lest someone from her office was there observing her having a fun time in working hours. She could get fired.

When Eileen was done frolicking they set off to find a pub and a sandwich. The bottoms of Eileen's jeans were sodden and encrusted with sand. She started to shiver, considered Rowan resentfully. 'It's all right for you. You're dry. This isn't doing the baby any good.'

'I thought you weren't going to have it.'

'I'm not. But as long as she's in here,' Eileen patted her tummy, 'I should look after her.'

'It's a girl, is it?'

'Definitely. I just feel it's a girl.'

In the pub Eileen refused alcohol, drank orange juice with her cheese sandwich saying she had to be careful on account of the baby. She could not meet Rowan's eye. She was confused. She did not want to have a baby. Then again, she did not want to have an abortion. Smitten with indecision and fear of the future, she hid from the new little fact growing in her life, whilst taking care of it.

Three weeks later Eileen had another termination date. This time she actually drove to the clinic. She and Rowan sat in the car outside (this time Rowan invented a sickly grandmother in Luton). Eileen drummed her fingers on the steering wheel humming snatches of some distant song that had snuck into her mind, chasing away her fear. 'I hate hospitals, don't you?'

'Yes,' Rowan agreed. 'It's the smell.'

Silence whilst they considered smells in their lives, moments of fear. Eileen switched off the radio. She always buried herself, her thoughts in noise. Quiet made her insecure. 'Tubes and funnels,' she agonised, crossing her arms over the wheel, laying her head on them. 'Oh God.'

'Do they give you an enema when you get an abortion?' Eileen asked.

'Dunno. Expect so. I've never, you know, had one. An abortion, that is. Actually I've never had an enema either.' Rowan had a horrible feeling that this termination trip was going to end as absurdly as the last.

'I had my tonsils out when I was eight. Got an enema then. Rubber tubes and funnels. Some people actually do that for fun. Ugh.' She shuddered. She started the car, that clumsy roar of air-cooled engine. 'Nope,' she said, waving her hands in horror. 'Not today. Today is not an enema day.' She reversed out of her parking place and took off.

'Funnel and tube, singular,' Rowan said. 'You only have one bum. When is an enema day, anyway?' she wondered. She was in her passenger position again – gripping the handle above the door whilst steadying herself against the dashboard. 'You're going to have to go through with it one day.'

'One day,' Eileen agreed, happy again now she was headed away from funnels and tubes and hospital smells. 'But not today.'

'One day soonish,' Rowan said. 'Or it'll be too late.'

This time they picnicked on oranges and chocolate in Hyde Park. Rowan felt even more shifty than at Brighton. She feared Mr Frobisher would at any moment appear from behind a bush, pointing and accusing, 'Taking a sickie, Miss Campbell? We shall have a chat about this in the morning. And, by the way, I know about the biscuits.' She pulled up her collar and now actually looked like the conniving sort of person she thought she was. Eileen turned the collar back down and patted Rowan's cheek. 'Don't be sad.' She felt Rowan's guilt was attracting attention.

Two weeks later Eileen had another appointment. Rowan refused to go. 'I can't. I can't take any more time off work.'

'I thought you were my friend.' Eileen looked disappointed. 'I thought you cared about me. I care about you.' She was sitting cross-legged at the foot of Rowan's bed, at seven o'clock in the morning.

'I do care about you. Of course I care about you. I just can't risk losing my job, that's all.'

Eileen didn't answer that. Instead, she climbed into Rowan's bed as Rowan vacated it. 'I hate you. You have my cat. Why does my cat always sleep with you?'

'I'm always here. And I feed him.'

Eileen paid no attention to this. 'Your bed's warmer than mine,' she said.

When Rowan got home that night Eileen was still in her room, still in her bed, sitting up thumbing through one of her travel books.

'You didn't go, then?' Rowan said.

'Nope. Couldn't face it.'

'Tubes and funnels?'

'The whole thing. Dr Henderson was cross with me,' she pouted. 'He said I have repeatedly wasted time. He won't give me another date. He wasn't very nice to me.'

'I don't blame him.'

'You're not being very nice to me, either.'

'Don't blame me.' Rowan left her to brood, went to the kitchen to feed Elvis, and herself.

After a while, Eileen came to sit at the table watching her eat.

'I'll just have to have it,' she said, reaching over to Rowan's plate, picking up a piece of cauliflower, dunking it in cheese sauce, eating it. 'That's quite good.' She took another piece. Then another.

Rowan pushed the plate in front of her. 'Here, have it why don't you. You need it more than me.' She leaned back. She did not know why, but the thought of Eileen having a baby filled her with foreboding. 'Who is the father, anyway? You've never said.'

'He's married. He's gone away, back to America.'

'Does he know about the baby?'

'Yes,' Eileen nodded. 'He gave me money. A thousand pounds.'

'A thousand pounds! What for?'

'The baby. The abortion. One of those.' Eileen stared at the wall. She didn't like to be questioned. She shrugged. 'I could always have it adopted. I mean, what sort of a life would I give a child? There are lots of women who'd be far better mothers than me. You, for example.'

'Me! Never. I never want to have children.'

'You'd be a wonderful mother. You're so quiet. So patient. Even my cat prefers you to me.'

'Cats always prefer people who feed them. They're opportunists,' Rowan said. Like you, the thought struck her as she spoke. But she kept it to herself, and headed into her dreams. Sometimes the great longing to escape was overwhelming. And sometimes, now for example, she wished she was back at home in the village where she was brought up.

She hadn't left that village, she'd fled from it as fast as she could go, as soon as she could go. Fretterton, gateway to the glens, population at the last count 6,000. Now, she was swamped with nostalgia for it. The tiny crumbling village with its little Square. Over the years, all the locals had moved to the new houses springing up on the village outskirts, leaving the Square to all sorts of newcomers who preferred the old buildings with their tiny windows and twisting staircases. Newcomers came from all over. Old Walter the birdwatcher from London, for instance, who moved in after he retired. Every weekend he'd drive up the glens to sit in some remote spot watching, waiting for whatever species might come his way, binoculars and notebook in the pockets of his anorak. Or Miss Porteous from Glasgow, who wrote horoscopes for the local newspaper. George O'Connell from Sydney, who ran the County Hotel. These people, so boring to her as a teenager, seemed fascinating now.

She remembered the narrow wynds and little twisting lanes she had walked as a child. Cootie's Lane, dripping dog roses in the summer, that led from the Square up to the library. My God, she thought, the library, where Janice Buchanan put all the dirty books on the bottom shelves so's the pensioners couldn't get them and be offended. Rosie Jamieson had done her back in reaching down for *Lady Chatterley's Lover* and had threatened to sue. 'Lawrence, D.H.,' she cried in The Squelch – the local pub – 'should be in the middle along with Levi, Primo and Llosa, Mario Vargas.' The village pensioners were not as daft as Janice Buchanan thought.

The surge of homesickness was so strong it shook Rowan. She had not, till this moment, known it was there within her. She almost cried remembering the kitchen she'd come home to every day after school. Her mother, small, smaller than Rowan (and she was only five feet three inches) with badly permed, greying hair would come through from the living room. 'Good day, today? Any homework?' she always asked.

'No,' Rowan always replied, tossing her bag into the corner beside the fridge, then slumping at the little Formica table. 'Anything to eat?'

'I'm sure you'll find something if you look.' Her mother would indicate the kitchen cupboard. It was always the same. They'd had that conversation almost every day from when Rowan started school at five, till she'd left at seventeen.

If she stepped outside the back door at six o'clock in the evening, the air she breathed would be heavy with the scent of frying. Someone, somewhere was always making chips. Every Sunday the church bell rang. 'Chips and religion.' The words whispered out of her. 'I came from the kingdom of the lard.'

Every Friday night she would gather with her friends outside Rossi's, the fish and chip parlour that sold sweets, tablet and ice cream. They would hang about, laughing, shouting – from the safety of their numbers and their lookalike fashions – rude remarks at any stray adults who wandered too far into their territory. They drank Coke-Cola laced, when someone could get hold of it, with vodka. They flirted, experimented with swearing, cigarettes, cider and sex. In the lane behind the shop Rowan had experienced her first drag on a fag, her first kiss, first grope. With Duncan Willis. To the sound of the nine o'clock country bus rumbling out of the Square, under a jagged sky full of torn clouds stealing past a glowing, lumpen moon, against a moss-encrusted wall, Rowan discovered her passion, the feel of it on her throat and tongue, the smell and surge of it, the wildness that came from the deep of her, that took hold of her and never ever lasted long enough. It was something she liked to keep to herself. She thought if she gave into it, her dreams would come to nothing. After all, look what had happened to Eileen.

Chapter Three

Eileen loved being pregnant. She was, effortlessly – no applying of make-up, no low-cut frocks, no wiggling of hips and irritating howl of *'Partee!'* – the centre of attention. In pubs friends insisted she take the best seat. Giggling fabulously, she'd squeeze into the tight space between fixed-to-the-floor table and bench. 'I don't think there's room enough for both of me.'

It renewed Rowan's interest in her. She allowed herself to forget what a bore Eileen was beginning to be. Now she thought her brave. A woman on her own bringing a child into the world. But then, she was prone to romanticising.

Every morning, before she left for work, Rowan would bring Eileen a cup of tea and toast in bed. Showered her with compliments. 'You look gorgeous. Glowing. You should have more babies. Pregnancy suits you.'

'I know. I'm good at it. Born to reproduce.' Eileen would grin and, without any embarrassment, lift her caftan to display her swelling stomach. 'Look, just like a Christmas pudding. All I need is a sprig of holly in my belly button.'

Rowan would stare in wonder at the bulge, watching it move as the infant within shifted and kicked. Rowan, who never intended to ever get pregnant, was secretly horrified at the details of Eileen's pregnancy – its swellings, bloatings, secretions and its heartburn. Eileen accepted them all blandly.

'You'd think you'd done it before, it comes so naturally,' Rowan said.

'I'm a woman,' Eileen told her. 'I just go with the flow.'

By the time she was seven months gone, Eileen was sick of the whole thing. 'Look at me,' she'd wail, standing in front of the mirror, sideways on to allow herself to view the full horror. 'I'll never get my body back. I hate having a body. It never does what I want it to.'

'It'll be over soon.' Rowan remained calm during Eileen's outbursts.

'It's all right for you.' Eileen turned on her. 'Your jeans zip up. Your fingers aren't swollen. All I do these days is sit here alone retaining water.'

'You could go out. There's no law against appearing pregnant in public. You could go to ante-natal classes.'

'Never!' Eileen screamed. 'Never! You have to lie on the floor and practise giving birth. Pushing and breathing. It's full of pregnant women.'

'It would be. You sound like you know all about it.'

'Seen it on telly,' Eileen said. She fished a bar of Milk Tray from her bedside drawer. Broke off several squares, ate them.

'You're stuffing yourself with rubbish. Won't do you or the baby any good.'

'It soothes me.' She started on another couple of squares. Chewed and looked out of the window. Conversation over.

During the months of pregnancy Eileen and Rowan followed Sadie's (for that was to be the baby's name) development in the womb. They brimmed with interest at what was developing and when: 'She'll have fingers and toes now.' They put on favourite records so that the baby could hear the music they were listening to and like it as much as they did. If Eileen cried, the baby would cry. If she laughed, the baby would laugh. When they read that Sadie might be sucking her thumb in there, they worried.

'Her front teeth could get pulled forward,' Rowan said.

'She won't have teeth yet,' said Eileen. 'I won't let her suck her thumb once she's past whatever age it is you don't let infants suck their thumbs. And I'm not going to dress her all girlie-girlie. And if she asks something, whatever it is, I'll tell her the truth.' She protectively patted her lump. She was still at it, still hiding from her truth. Making plans to bring up the baby she wasn't planning to keep.

Once Rowan asked Eileen about her parents. 'Won't they want to know that they are going to be grandparents?'

'No. They don't want to know about me. We never got along.'

'Maybe you would now. Surely they'll want to see the baby?'

'Doubt it.' Eileen sounded sour. Then she gave a small rendition of *She's Leaving Home*. 'Bye, bye,' she sang in a small, plaintive, sorry-for-herself voice.

Rowan couldn't understand how Eileen could so easily abandon her past. She had found her home, her village, claustrophobic and had fled as soon as she was old enough. Visions of herself running, top speed, down the garden path, carrying her grandmother's old suitcase the day after she finished school haunted her. This, she knew, was not true. After school she'd worked in Rossi's chip shop for two months before starting a year's secretarial course in Edinburgh. Then after two jobs in that city, she'd come to London.

She was proud of herself. She was making her plans work; every step in her life was taking her further from her small beginnings and nearer to her vast and fabulous future. Sometimes the joy of it overwhelmed her. She would stand in her room, alone, arms spread, fists clenched, triumph. Yes. This is me. *Me.* And I am going to see the world. All of it. She could hardly believe herself. But she knew what she was going to do. Still, she phoned home every week. She knew her mother would worry if she didn't. 'Why doesn't Eileen want to tell her folks about the baby?' she asked Danny from the ground floor one day. He had known Eileen a lot longer than she had.

'Dunno,' he shrugged.

'Where does she come from?'

He shrugged again. 'She told me Liverpool. Told someone else she'd been brought up in South Africa. She makes up a new life every few years.'

'Goodness me. Still, her mother and father might want to know that they are going to be grandparents. Do you know,' she sat down across the kitchen table from him, 'I don't really know anything about Eileen. She talks all the time, but she doesn't *say* anything. Have you noticed that?'

'That's Eileen. Ask her her life and she'll tell you a story. I expect she came from a very normal, basic, boring family. Obviously that's hardly Eileen. So she's upped her image a bit. Made herself more exciting. She's been here for yonks – since she was sixteen. Long before me. You used to see her in the tabloids clubbing, hanging onto some bloke's arm. I've never known her to be any different. It's hard for her now that she's older. Those blokes she hung out with don't want to be seen with an old bird.'

'She's hardly an old bird.' Rowan was shocked.

Danny drew on his cigarette. 'Oh, yes she is.' He waved his cigarette. 'Look where she's ended up. She used to share a place in Chelsea.'

'She's still good-looking,' Rowan protested.

'Not first thing in the morning, love.'

In the last month of her pregnancy Eileen wallowed in depression and chocolate. 'I'm going to be like this for ever,' she said, rolling over and clumsily pushing herself upright. 'In a few weeks it'll all be over. But I'll stay huge. That happens, you know. Some women in the maternity ward look like the baby's still in there.' She swigged from the small bottle of stuff she'd bought to cure her heartburn. She kept it by her always, unscrewing the top and tippling regularly like a wino. She burped.

'How do you know that?' Rowan wondered.

'I see things. I've been around.'

'Well, it won't happen to you.'

'It will, I know it. I hate this.' She punched her stomach. 'And I hate you. Look what you've done to me. My life's over.'

'Stop it.' Rowan was finding Eileen a bore again. 'You're feeling sorry for yourself.'

'Suppose. The baby will be born and I can drink and smoke again.' She did a small wiggle of the hips, a demonstration of the good times ahead. 'I can hardly wait.' Then, for the umpteenth time she lifted her top and looked down at the toll the past nine months had taken. 'Look at me. What am I like?' She turned to Rowan: 'Party, party.' She said it flatly now, no joy at all. She didn't think she would ever party, party again. 'Soon I'll be old.'

'Rubbish.' Rowan tried to sound cheery. 'You'll never be old. And you'll have a baby to look after. It'll be lovely.' She wished she sounded more convincing.

They both stared round at the mountains of baby things Eileen had accumulated: clothes, nappies, bottles, a steriliser, a crib, a changing mat. A second-hand buggy stood out on the landing. It seemed she hadn't got round to mentioning adoption to anyone at the ante-natal clinic. She had, instead, gone ahead with gathering all the things her baby would need.

'What a pile of stuff for a tiny infant,' Eileen said. 'I don't want these things. I'll tell you the truth, Rowan, I have no maternal feelings at all. Never have had.'

'They'll come with the baby. It says so in the book we got, remember? And you need all this stuff for the baby.' She looked wildly round the cluttered room as if there was some solution she was missing.

'What am I going to do?' Eileen wailed, tears in her eyes, face torn with despair.

Rowan hated conversations like this. 'What does anybody do? They get on with things. They deal with things. They cope.'

Eileen's hands dropped to her sides. She looked at Rowan with a new strange coldness. Get on with things – what did that mean? Deal with things – how did you do that? Cope – what a daft notion. She had never coped in her life, and had no intention of ever doing so.

On 28 November, Sadie was born – at seven in the morning Eileen shook Rowan awake. 'It's happening. The baby's coming. We must go.'

'How long have you been in labour?' Rowan sat up and looked about for some clothes.

'Hours and hours.'

'Why didn't you tell me? We should be there. They told you at the clinic not to leave it till the last minute.'

'Oh, I don't pay any attention to them. If you leave it late they don't have time to fuss over you. Besides, I don't want it,' said Eileen. 'I've changed my mind.'

'You can't change your mind. You have to have it now, for God's sake, Eileen. You have to grow up. Face the facts. You are going to have a baby.' Rowan threw back her covers, jumped from bed, pulled on her jeans and a jersey, ran from the room, down the stairs to the front door. Eileen stayed put.

'Eileen!' Rowan called up, her fears sounding louder than she intended. 'You have to come. I'm not delivering the baby here.'

She raced up the stairs again, took Eileen by the arm and started pulling her towards the door. Then she stumbled into Eileen's room, picked up her bag, and stumbled back to yank Eileen to the door and out into the car.

'You don't understand,' Eileen cried, hanging back like a spoilt child. 'I don't want this. I've made a mistake. I can't have a baby. It's all right for you to make plans. I've never thought about anything.'

'There's nothing you can do about that now.' Rowan opened the passenger door and shoved Eileen in.

'I can't have a baby. I'll be a mother. All mumsy and speaking about properly fitting shoes and vests. I don't like vests.'

'No, you won't.' Rowan slammed the car door shut and ran round to the driver's seat. Trembling as she put the key in the ignition. 'Think about Elizabeth Taylor. Marianne Faithfull. Doris Day. Marlene Dietrich. All mothers. Never mentioned vests, any of them.' She put the car into gear, roared off.

'She'll be a Sagittarian,' Eileen said, writhing in her seat. Heaving herself up, she cried out, 'Christ, here's another one! It's sore. Really, really sore. I should've had that enema. I should've had the abortion. This is awful.' Then, criticising Rowan's driving: 'Brake, will you – brake!' Stamping her foot on the floor of the car. 'You have no idea of the pain I'm in. And you can't fucking drive.'

'I can drive better than you.' Rowan was hurt. She did not realise the lunacy of women in labour. She thought she was dealing with a sane person. 'You take your hands off the wheel and talk all the time. You don't even look where you're going.'

'Rubbish. I just don't look like I'm looking. But I am. Jesus,' she complained as Rowan screeched the car round a corner, 'don't jolt me. I'm in fucking pain.' Then, after an anguished moan, she panicked. 'I've changed my mind. I mean it. I don't want it. I don't want this. I can't do it. *I can't*. Make it stop. Please, make it stop!'

Rowan had come out in a sweat; she felt it, a thick, clammy layer of damp, slide down her back, across her scalp, seep from her upper lip. Wet fear. She wanted to get Eileen out of the car. Her jersey was sticking to her, and to the driving seat. What if they didn't make it and the baby was born on the passenger seat and she had to deliver it. What if she dropped it. Oh God.

'Don't push. Don't you dare push till we get there. If you bloody push I'll never bloody speak to you again.' She hated this. She wanted to throw back her head and scream. Foot to the floor, ninety miles an hour, screaming.

They arrived at the hospital, parked at an angle and ran inside. Rowan carried Eileen's bag, which had been packed for the past three weeks, and contained – just in case – jeans, T-shirts, underwear, a red velvet frock – she stupidly thought the girls might have a bit of a get-together on the ward – an emergency supply of dope and a bottle of Bacardi.

They stormed up to the desk, looking, Rowan blushed to realise later, absurdly obvious. Eileen's waddle, hand gripping her lower back, their ashen, crazed expressions, the bulging bag said it all. Eileen was put into a wheelchair and whisked away. All the way down the corridor Rowan could hear her disappearing voice cry out, 'No. No. I don't want this. I've fucking changed my fucking mind.' She dropped the bag at her feet, and leaned on the desk.

'Name?' said the nurse, pulling out a form.

'Rowan,' said Rowan.

'Surname?'

'Campbell.'

'Age? Religion?'

Rowan realised. 'No,' she said. 'No. That's me. No.' Pointing up the corridor where Eileen had gone. 'It's her, Eileen's having the baby.'

The nurse sighed and pulled out another form. 'Name?'

'Eileen.'

'Surname?'

Rowan looked at her blankly. 'Gosh,' she said. 'Gosh. She never told me.' All those months she'd known Eileen. All the tales Eileen had told. All the confessions, confidences and dreams, fortunes, futures, shapes in clouds – and Rowan did not know her last name.

The effect a baby had on people surprised Rowan. Even on that first day when Sadie was born, when she asked to get away from work early.

'I hope you have a good reason for asking,' Mr Frobisher said.

'My friend's had a baby. I'd like to go and see her. She hasn't many other people in London. Well, nobody that's interested in babies anyway.'

'A baby? Which sort?'

Rowan stared at him blankly. She did not know any new baby parlance. 'Human' she wanted to say, but stopped herself.

'A boy or a girl?' Mr Frobisher asked.

'Oh, a girl.'

'Ah, yes.' Mr Frobisher approved, smiling. Almost gooey, Rowan thought. 'Best sort. I've got four daughters.'

'You have children?' Rowan found this hard to believe.

'Oh yes. They're up a bit now. Twenty, eighteen, seventeen and Emma's four. Quite a handful. A surprise to everybody, was Emma.' He looked away a moment, sighed. 'Everybody,' he repeated. 'Yes, by all means take time off. Go and see your friend.' He waved her from the office. He seemed almost good-natured. Babies, Rowan was to discover, did that to people.

Five days after the baby was born, Eileen brought her home. She arrived in her room, clutching the infant in her arms, and looked round. She seemed uneasy. Well, I've had it, she thought. Now what? Wrap it up and put it in the cupboard and get on with the rest of my life? She voiced her doubts to Rowan. 'Now what?'

'Now you get on with things, I suppose.' Rowan wasn't sure either.

'I don't want to get on with things. I've had the baby. Now I want to go back to how things were.' The words of protest she had yelled as she was trundled down the corridor to the delivery room echoed over and over in her brain. *I've changed my mind. I've changed my mind.*

'You were going to have her adopted,' Rowan said.

'I know. I know. I just never got round to arranging it. And now look,' Eileen held the baby out, 'here she is. All little and that. And how can I have her adopted? You don't know what sort of folk they'd put her with. Maybe someone who doesn't know all the words to *Leopardskin Pill-Box Hat*, who works in the Inland Revenue, a nine-to-fiver, a grey person, a Mr Jones. We can't have that for Sadie.'

The baby started to cry. Eileen handed her to Rowan. 'Here. I need to sit down.' She lowered herself stiffly on to the bed. 'Oooh. I am never, absolutely never, going to do that again. This time I really mean it.'

'This time?'

'Yeah. You know how you say you're never going to do something again. Then you go and do it again. Like getting drunk. You wake with fuzz on your tongue and your stomach heaving an' you say never again. Then you have another drink.'

'Right,' said Rowan. She looked down at the baby. 'She's perfect. Isn't it amazing.'

The child lay in her arms, quiet now, little lips moving slightly. She made tiny sounds. Rowan smiled. 'Sssh, sssh,' she whispered, putting her lips to the infant's forehead.

'You've got the hang of it,' Eileen said.

'So will you.'

'Not me. I'm not maternal – I told you.'

Rowan handed the baby back to Eileen. 'Cope,' she suggested for the second time. It was the only way to go. 'That's what people do. They cope.'

Cope? For the second time Eileen dismissed this idea. Cope – what did that mean? She had never coped in her life and had no intention of starting now. Coping was not the sort of thing a woman of her wit and seductive powers did. To be reduced to coping was to admit defeat.

Chapter Four

The screaming started that night. Rowan was woken at two in the morning by the baby's howls. She lay rigid in bed waiting for the noise to stop. Surely Eileen would do something. But no, the high-pitched spats of infant rage went on and on. Rowan got up, pulled on her robe and went through to see what was happening.

The infant was in her crib, swaddled and bawling. Her tiny face was red, little beads of sweat on her brow. The fury and insecurity came screaming out, then with shivering jaw she drew breath for the next outburst. Rowan had no idea such a huge din could emanate from someone so little.

Eileen was across the room, crouching in the corner, arms over her head. She wore a prim yellow nightie covered with pink rosebuds (her hospital outfit). It made her seem more vulnerable than she'd ever looked naked. 'Do something! Do something!' she cried. 'Make her stop.'

Rowan looked nervously down at the baby. 'What?'

'I don't know. Pick her up.'

'Shouldn't you?'

Eileen shook her head, a violent rolling movement. 'I can't. You do it.'

Rowan reached awkwardly down and lifted the howling infant. She held it stiffly at arm's length. 'Now what?'

Eileen watched carefully. 'Dunno.'

Rowan pulled the baby to her. Held her, patted her back, said, 'Sssh.' And, 'There, there.' And, 'That's a terrible noise to make.' The howling stopped. Oh, glorious silence.

'See?' said Eileen. 'You can do it. You're better at all that maternal stuff than me.'

Rowan put the silenced infant back in her crib. The noise started up again. Rowan picked her up again. This time with more confidence. 'Doesn't she want to be fed?' She'd read about middle-of-the-night feeds. 'Or.' Horror. 'Changed.'

'Probably,' said Eileen. 'In hospital they used to wake me at two in the morning to feed her and change her. I never got a night's sleep. It was awful.'

Rowan started to pace the room, the baby draped on her shoulder. It was a reaction to the noise that came naturally.

'Then,' Eileen continued her terrible tale, 'no sooner had I got to sleep than they'd wake me to do it all again.' She looked grim. 'You have no idea. I had some really nice clothes with me. I never got a chance to put them on. And nobody would have a drink with me. All the other mums were so boring.'

'Nine-to-fivers? Grey people?' Rowan said sardonically. 'Shouldn't you feed her now?' She longed to hand Eileen the baby and go back to bed.

Eileen shook her head, stiffly rose from her crouch, clutching her back and groaning. 'I can't. You do it. It's only a little feed. She only needs two ounces.'

'I have never fed a baby in my life,' Rowan protested. 'I don't know what to do.' She was terrified. 'What if I make a mistake? What if she dies?'

'Don't be silly.' Eileen was getting back into bed. 'She won't die. Babies are tough little things.'

'What do I do?'

'It's easy. Take a bottle from the steriliser. Put in two ounces of boiled water, add two scoops of milk powder from the tin. Shake it about a bit. When it's cool give it to her. She's no problem. She's a good little feeder. The nurses at hospital said so.'

The whole dire business – making up the bottle, juggling the baby as she did so, giving her the feed, changing her nappy – took Rowan over two hours. Fear that she was doing something wrong, that she might drop the baby head first onto the kitchen floor brought her out in a lather. She felt her hands huge against her tiny face and body. She fumbled. She whispered to her, 'There you go. That's good, isn't it?' She tasted the feed. It wasn't. 'You'll be keen to get onto egg and chips.' She confessed to her, 'I have never touched a baby before. I'm crap at this. Actually, if you want to know, I'm crap at everything.' Complained to her, 'I shouldn't be doing this. Eileen should. I've got work in the morning. Not that she cares. She's never done a day's work in her life.'

She'd put on the heater, and once she'd finished her terrifying chore she sat in front of it, baby sleeping in her arms. The persistent electric heat, the minute gurgles of dormant infant, the feel of Sadie in her arms, Rowan found pleasant and comforting. She did not want to move. So she sat, drinking coffee, dreaming. She'd been almost a year in London now. In a few months she reckoned she'd have enough saved to leave. Then, at last, her proper life would start.

She imagined herself setting off, rucksack on her back. She did not plan to say goodbye to anybody, except Eileen. And she would make one final phone call home. Would her mother give that same sad sorry little wave she'd waved when Rowan set off for college? After that, all she would be to anybody she knew was an occasional postcard from some rugged distant place. She ached for that moment when she would slip from this house and walk down the road. Going away. Away, she thought, what a lovely word. She sat till the heat prickled her front and her back was chilled.

Then she switched off the fire, went upstairs, put the sleeping baby back in her crib – Eileen, sleeping, hair spread over her pillow, did not stir – and went back to bed. Two hours later, the howling started up again. This time Rowan picked up a shoe, threw it at the wall and shouted to Eileen to get up and see to her child.

Chapter Five

Looking back, Rowan decided it was the rucksack that did it. It was March when she brought it and a pair of walking boots back to her room.

Eileen stared at them with horror. 'What are these for?'

'My trip. My travels. I'll get most of my stuff in here.' Patting the rucksack. 'And I'll wear the boots. Really tough. Boots like these can last a lifetime.'

'They're ghastly.'

'If you say so. I rather like them. I'll wear them to work for a couple of weeks to break them in.'

'They'll let you wear something like that in the office?'

'Probably not. I'll walk in, and take something more suitable, more ladylike with me.'

'Then you're going. You're just going?'

'Yes,' Rowan nodded blandly. 'I told you I was going.' She fiddled with the straps on the rucksack. Doing something helped her cope with Eileen's sneering, and the apprehension she felt at what she was about to undertake. Talking about going round the world was a lot easier on the nervous system than actually doing it. Since buying the rucksack and boots, definite signs of departure, Rowan's stomach had been fluttering fear.

'But what about me? What about Sadie?' Eileen demanded.

Rowan stopped playing with her new acquisition, turned to face Eileen. 'What about you? You have your life, your parties. And Sadie's just a baby. What about me? I'm going to do what I've always wanted to do.'

'But . . .' said Eileen, 'I never thought you'd actually *do* it. I thought it was all just talk.'

'Oh no.' Rowan shook her head. 'I'm doing it. I'm going.'

As time distanced Eileen from the shock of giving birth, and becoming a mother, as her body returned to normal, she tried as much as possible to return to her old life. Monday to Friday she looked after her baby: 'I'm becoming all mumsy.'

Mornings she bathed Sadie, washed her clothes, made up the day's feeds. She just about coped. If only she felt real, like other mothers, proper mothers, then she would have managed, she thought. Sometimes when Sadie cried, her persistent endless howl, Eileen would hold her at arm's length shouting, 'Stop it. Stop it. Shut up!' When the baby, confused and crying louder, didn't stop, Eileen would shove her roughly into her cot and leave the room. She would stand pressed against the landing wall, shaking her head. Her mouth open, cords twanging on her neck, she would silently scream – not a sound would come from those fraught lips. She did not dare let go and shout out loud – someone might hear. Then again, sometimes when the baby cried, Eileen would sit silently still on the bed, hands folded neatly on her lap, watching her, feeling nothing.

Sadie's birth was clear in her head. She could recall it all, every second of it. The faces round the bed. The heart monitor. The voices. As soon as she arrived at the hospital she'd been whisked to the delivery room, shaved and given an enema. 'God, you buggery people always get folk, one effing, bloody way or another. I could've had this done nine months ago and none of this would fucking have happened.'

'You're swearing well,' the midwife said.

'And it'll get better.' Eileen was wild-eyed and fervent about that.

Five hours later Sadie was born. For a few surprised moments Eileen held her. Bathed and fed on toast and tea Eileen was taken with Sadie to the maternity ward where she was greeted by all the other mums. 'What did you have? Boy or a girl?'

'Yes,' said Eileen. 'One of those.'

'What weight?'

'Quite light. No need to diet yet.'

'Did you have any stitches?'

'Well, I won't be doing any horse-jumping for a while.' Then she pulled her covers over her head and fell asleep. Next day, she was woken at six in the morning by a nurse.

'Time to feed baby. Breast or bottle?'

Eileen raised her head a fraction from the pillow.

'Breast or bottle?' the nurse repeated.

Eileen had been asked this several times during her pregnancy, but had so far avoided making any decision about what she regarded as a trifling technicality of motherhood. Now the moment was here. 'Breast or bottle?'

'I'm very much a bottle person myself,' she said. 'Though milk isn't my usual tipple.'

A bottle was placed on the bed trolley. The baby was in a crib at the end of the bed. Eileen stared down at her. She felt nothing.

'Time to feed baby, Mum,' the nurse bossed. Eileen hated her. 'Then you'll have to bath and change her.'

Eileen was horrified. She hated motherhood. A swift glance round the ward at the other mothers, all busy with their babies, feeding, cuddling, cooing, showed Eileen that there were no fellow rebels here. She wasn't going to wear her party frock; her bottle would stay untouched in her case. She smoked a little dope in her bath one morning, but it made her sweat. The paranoia she felt.

It didn't get any better. After she got home the numbness didn't ease. She sat alone in the house staring at little Sadie, her eyes blank, her face motionless. She wouldn't be thinking anything real, anything at all really. Her mind would be a swill of confusion, emotions – anger and dread. She hated this mum person she now was. She was angry at the baby for doing that to her.

Sometimes she found a way to ease her ache. She pretended she was looking after Sadie for another woman, her real mother. When she did this she firmed her lips, moved about with a new resolve. She was being very, very good. She wouldn't let this other woman down, she'd take great care of her child till she came to get her.

Afternoons Eileen took Sadie out in her buggy, swishing along streets in her cony coat, smiling. She strode, an upright walk, head up. She did not look about her, did not consider passers-by. Should anyone stop and admire Sadie, leaning into the pushchair, crooning, 'What a lovely baby,' Eileen would smile and deny motherhood. 'Isn't she gorgeous? I'm just looking after her for a friend.' Or, 'You wouldn't believe this, but she's my little sister. My mother surprised us all. Ha, ha. And herself. This was the last thing she thought would happen. Of course, she's delighted.' Eileen could see the mother she'd invented – a smiling, fading beauty, little lines round her eyes and mouth. A kindly woman, overwrought, of course, at her carelessness and the new arrival it had brought.

Eileen couldn't shake the feeling of unreality she'd had since Sadie was born. She felt she was living in a void. That all this feeding the baby, changing the baby, bathing the baby would stop soon. It really had nothing to do with her. She knew it was actually happening, but there was a darkness within her that she hadn't acknowledged. She didn't know what to do about it. Sometimes she thought that if she didn't keep a grip on herself, she might start crying and crying and be unable to stop herself. Alone in her room she could feel the despair building up inside her, and had to sit down, take huge gulping breaths, lest the huge weep started. When the baby's demands got too much for her, Eileen would sniff and ask herself, 'What would a real person do?'

Sometimes she would treat the baby roughly. She did not dip deeply into cruelty. She just wasn't gentle when she changed a nappy, or she rammed the feeding bottle harshly into Sadie's mouth. Sensing her mother's anger, insecure at the feel of unpredictable hands, Sadie would cry, little fists locked in fury and fear.

'I hate this,' Eileen would wail. 'I hate it.' She would curse her fortune. 'Hate everything. Everybody.' She would make a swift mental rundown of her friends and what they might be doing now. None of them, she knew for sure, would be doing what *she* was doing. They'd be working. They served in fashionable boutiques, or answered phones in record companies, or worked as personal assistants. Those rich enough not to have to work would probably still be in bed. Then there was Rowan. Eileen would toss the dirty nappy across the room, and start to wipe the baby's bottom, lifting her off the changing mat. It wasn't a savage action. There was, simply, no kindness in it. The baby screamed louder. Sometimes Eileen hated Rowan. She wasn't the sweetie she pretended to be. She kept on and on about travelling. 'Tramping the globe,' Eileen mimicked her. 'Stupid cow.'

Eileen considered she only had one escape route, her secret option – suicide. This was her only really private thought. She had it worked out. She would wait till the house was empty, and it was always empty during the day. She'd feed and change the baby. Then put her safely in her cot. After that she'd take enough pills to do the job, wash them down with a bottle of whisky and keep it all in place with a slice of bread. 'That'd do it,' she said. But whilst contemplating doing away with herself, she knew she'd never actually go through with it. She enjoyed life, when she could escape the baby and get a crack at it. Also, death terrified her. Still, the suicide option was there should she ever really, really need it.

Every weekend, Rowan baby-sat. She did it gladly. Anything, anything not to make excuses to avoid being dragged off to dreadful parties, to spend uncomfortable evenings sympathising with suicides and watching dramas. She'd take the baby into her room so that Eileen could come home as late as she liked without waking her.

Sunday mornings Rowan fed the baby and took her out. She didn't mind at all. In the four months since Sadie had come into her life, she'd grown to love the child; the older Sadie got, the more she responded to smiles and the sound of a friendly voice, and the more enthused Rowan felt about her. They played silly, tiny games. Peeking round the side of a newspaper, making gurgly noises with a straw, blowing bubbles in the bath. Rowan enjoyed any excuse to indulge in a spot of mindlessness.

She smiled at Eileen. 'Actually, when I think about it. I'm going to miss little Sadie. She's so sweet.'

'I don't think you're going to miss her at all,' Eileen snapped. 'Else you wouldn't go. You can't think much of Sadie and me, can you. Just going off.'

'I told you I wanted to travel.' Rowan spoke patiently. 'I'm not just going off. I'm doing what I want to do. Seems to me you do that all the time.'

'I don't know how you can just go. How can you turn your back on me? I'm your best friend.'

'I don't think I'm your best friend. I don't think you've got a best friend.' As soon as the words were out, she regretted them.

Eileen stormed from the room, leaving her baby on Rowan's bed. Across the landing in her own room, she started to frantically search through her pile of CDs. She found the one she was looking for, put it on. The noise wailed out, flooded the house. Sadie started to cry. Rowan picked her up, hushed her. Eileen stormed back in, waving a cigarette, holding a drink. 'After all I've done for you. All I've given you. This is what you do to me.'

'What?' said Rowan. 'What have you done for me?'

'Parties I've taken you to. People I've introduced you to.'

'I hated those parties.'

'Oh?' Eileen sneered. 'It didn't seem like that to me, the way you flashed yourself around.'

'What are you talking about? I never flashed myself around.'

Knowing Rowan's denial of any flashing herself around to be true, Eileen ignored it. 'All the things I've given you.'

'What things?' Rowan couldn't think of anything.

'Oooh,' Eileen growled. 'You ungrateful bitch. What about the Italian meal?'

'Right,' Rowan nodded. 'I forgot.'

Once, one of Eileen's fleeting boyfriends had given her a diamond solitaire ring that she had sold next day. She had blown some of the cash on an Italian meal for herself and Rowan.

'Three courses, with wine,' Eileen reminded her now. 'And Sambucco with the coffee. Then there was our picnics. You'll have forgotten them, too.'

'No,' Rowan shook her head. 'I won't ever forget them.'

Eileen had been given a walk-on part on a soap. Three weeks' work. They'd picnicked in her room. 'Proper picnics,' Eileen reminded her. It was true. Eileen had bought a wicker basket and a checked tablecloth that she'd spread out on the floor and covered with proper picnic food. 'A posh picnic, too, it was.'

'It was,' Rowan agreed.

Under the gaze of Eileen's heroes, Jimi Hendrix, Bob Dylan and the Beach Boys, they'd drunk champagne, eaten pâté and smoked ham, pecorino cheese and salamis and slabs of carrot cake. They'd got messy.

'Where do you come from, Eileen?' Rowan had asked. And Eileen had told her a story.

'Liverpool,' she said, broad Scouse accent.

'You don't sound as if you're from Liverpool.'

'You lose it, don't you?' Then, pointing at Rowan: 'You haven't. You still sound Scotch.'

'Scots,' Rowan corrected.

Eileen paid her no heed. 'I arrived here with nothing. No money. Nothing. I just had to get away. My father used to beat us. There were six of us and he'd beat us when he got drunk. One day I just got up and left. I took my clothes, put them in an old Asda bag and hitched to London. And here I am. Lived in a squat. Moved in with a bloke in Earls Court. Met people. Made my way. You can do it if you want. Of course, in those days a Liverpool accent was a ticket to anything you wanted. People all thought you knew the Beatles.'

'The Beatles! That was ages ago.'

'Yeah, but,' Eileen shrugged, 'they're a legend, aren't they?'

Rowan stared at Eileen. The Beatles, she thought now. Maybe Eileen really was a lot older than she looked. Maybe she really was old. Eileen stamped back to her room, took off the CD that was playing, put on another, reappeared, waving a new cigarette, drink topped up. 'Just go. Just go. Leave me. Leave the baby. You don't care, do you?'

'Yes, I care. But this is what I've been planning and saving for.'

'Oooh, Miss Prissy. Saving up.' Eileen sing-songed her mockery, jiggling her body with derision. She stubbed out her cigarette. Lit another. 'You just used me, didn't you? You just wanted someone to show you around till you were ready to move on.'

'What?'

'Well go,' said Eileen. 'Go. I hope you'll be happy. I really do.' She disappeared again. Then reappeared, drink topped up once more, music still blaring. Now she was wearing her coat. 'I'm going out – hope you don't mind. After all, once you're gone I won't be able to go anywhere, will I? I'll be stuck in all the time.' She drained her glass, slammed it down. Left.

Rowan shrugged. She let Eileen go. She thought it better to let Eileen work out her fury somewhere else, out of the way. She picked up the baby, bounced her. 'Better get you to bed.' She didn't mind; she was used to it. It seemed these days she spent all of her free time looking after Sadie.

Eileen came home smiling at two in the morning. Her mood was so sweet, Rowan could hardly believe the temper tantrum had happened. She could hear Eileen in her room, tucking up Sadie, singing her a little song. It sounded like Dylan's *Mr Jones*.

Rowan couldn't understand it; every day Eileen got sweeter and sweeter. She sang songs – *Leopardskin Pill-Box Hat* and *Most Likely You'll Go Your Way and I'll Go Mine*, patted Rowan's cheek should they meet on the stairs, gushed, 'Soon be gone. Ooh, bet you can't wait.' On Friday she said, 'You won't mind if I have one last fling before you disappear? One last wild night out?'

Rowan shook her head. 'I'll be home next weekend, too. I leave the Tuesday after.'

'Well,' Eileen spread her arms, 'goody. Two last wild weekends for me.' She did a little joyful twirl.

It had been a while since Eileen had come home with tales to tell, adventures she'd had. At four in the morning she arrived in Rowan's room reeking of alcohol, oozing good fortune, frothing rapture. She'd made a conquest. Rowan surfaced from sleep, snorted, heaved her head from the pillow and said, 'Huh?' Then: 'What?'

Eileen sat at the foot of the bed spilling out her story. Sadie slept across the room in her cot. She was always moved through to Rowan's room for Friday and Saturday nights. Four months old now, she slept through the night, hardly stirred. Sudden excitement, loud music, laughter and the chink of glasses were sounds she was used to. They rang with a certain normality for her. Rowan reckoned that had someone sung Sadie a lullaby and attempted to rock her to sleep, she would have screamed uncertainty. This soothing stuff wasn't right.

'I've met a man.' Eileen bounced on the bed. 'No,' she corrected herself, 'I've met *the* man. The man of my life. Mr Bloody Right.'

'Oh good.' Sleep made Rowan sound dull. But then in Eileen's company she always felt dull anyway.

'Maurice – he's French.' Eileen gripped Rowan's arm. The Rightness of this man. The Frenchness of him. He was all any woman

54

could want. 'You should see him. His hands.' She held up her own, stroking them. 'Oh, they're perfect – long and thin. And his hair – black and sort of sexy. You should see his suit. Oh God. He's wonderful. And he's nuts about me.' She waved a single red rose that Maurice had bought her. 'Isn't it gorgeous?' She sighed. 'He's a diplomat. Imagine it – a diplomat. Oh God.' She squealed. Couldn't believe her luck. 'A diplomat. And he wants to meet Sadie. He loves children.'

Suddenly serious, she gripped Rowan's arm. 'Isn't it always the way? Just when you think things are really, really bad, something wonderful happens. Thing is,' she looked at Rowan, a longing in her eyes, 'he wants to see me tomorrow night. You don't mind, do you?'

'Looking after Sadie? No. You go. Have a good time.'

Eileen's return on the following night was even more jubilant. 'Oh God.' She fell across the bed in a swoon. 'You should see his place. Oh God. I mean, you should see it. Pillars. There are pillars in the hall. Then this long flowing staircase to the upper floor. A balcony sort of thing. It's all mellow, soft honey colours. Then his living room is huge. There's one vast sofa and a tree. A tree in a huge blue pot right there in the room. He made us dinner. Chicken all stuffed with butter and herbs. And we had wine out of huge glasses.' Small silence, then with a grin, 'You should see his bedroom. He has a four-poster and carpet so thick your feet disappear. Oh Rowan,' she spread-eagled on the bed, 'I'm so happy. It's all worked out, hasn't it?' As she left to go to her own room: 'He's got a Siamese cat.'

Slumping back under the covers, numb with the need to get back to sleep, Rowan said, 'Humph.'

In the morning Eileen was still glowing good fortune. She sat Sadie on Rowan's knee, leaving herself free to waft and dance for joy. She opened her arms wide as if welcoming her luck, then, clutching it to her, keeping it safe, she hugged herself. 'One last favour,' still wafting, still dancing, she spoke to Rowan, but did not turn to look at her. 'He wants me to go to Paris with him for the weekend. Leave Friday, back Sunday night. Would you . . . ?'

'Look after Sadie?'

'Yeah. I know it's a huge favour, your last weekend and all. But would you? Would you? Would you?' She wheeled round, palms pressed in prayer. She was overplaying her plea, she knew. She never could resist a bit of drama.

Rowan shrugged. 'Why not?' She touched Sadie's head. Stroked her soft down of hair, then folded her arms round her, held her close. 'It'll be nice. Our last weekend, Sadie. We'll have fun, won't we?'

On Thursday Rowan withdrew most of her money from the bank and changed it into traveller's cheques. She bought a ticket that would take her to Paris. She decided against buying one that would take her on across Europe. She thought she might travel through France, into Italy then buy a ticket east in Rome or Milan. Or she might just hop across the Mediterranean to Africa. Then east. No hurry. She wanted to see the world.

That night, Eileen threw a small party at the house for her. Danny cooked lasagne. 'You going to Italy, Rowan?'

'Probably.' Rowan nodded. 'I'm starting in Paris. Then on to Italy then east.'

'She's off to tramp the world.' Eileen put her arm round her. 'She's going to walk the Mountains of the Moon, sail the White Nile, follow in Mungo Park's footsteps, kneel before fields of wild orchids in wildernesses we haven't even heard of.'

Rowan watched her face as she spoke; the blatant mockery on it shocked her. But no wonder it was there. She deserved it. Had she really said that stuff? How embarrassing. 'I just want to travel a bit before I settle down,' she said. 'That's all.'

'You should see the wad she's got upstairs. She's loaded.' Eileen gleamed her piece of information.

Rowan slowly ate a mouthful of meat sauce before apologising. 'Traveller's cheques. Not much of a wad, really. I've been saving. It isn't that much. I'm going to have to be careful.'

'You will have to be careful. You shouldn't be travelling alone. People aren't nice, you know,' Eileen warned.

'I'll be fine,' said Rowan. But she wondered about that. The nearer she got to that moment of leaving, the more scared she was. 'The highways out there are packed with people like me, tramping off to see the world. I'll soon hitch up with somebody,' she reassured herself.

''Course you will,' said Danny. 'You'll have made friends before you leave the station.'

'No, she won't,' Eileen said, draping a patronising arm over Rowan's shoulders. 'Not our little Row. She's shy.'

'No, I'm not,' said Rowan. 'And if I am, so what? I'll be fine. Lay off me.' It was bad enough worrying about going off across the world without Eileen mocking her. She couldn't cope. The kitchen walls were steam-stained. There were splatterings of jam, tomato sauce and who knew what else on the unit doors and round the cooker. The single, relentless fluorescent strip glared down. When the light was on the room was hideously bright. Mostly the residents chose to cook and eat by candlelight. It dawned on her how much she'd miss this house. This disgusting kitchen. She'd become ensconced. She liked it here. She took a deep drink of her Californian wine, and said, 'I'll miss you guys.' Then she put her hand to her face, covered her eyes. She feared she was going to cry.

Next day Rowan said goodbye to her fellow secretaries in the green room. They gave her a small travelling clock in a leather case. Once again, as she thanked them, Rowan feared she was going to cry. At a quarter to five Mr Frobisher asked her into his office. 'He'll be seeking revenge for all those coconut cookies,' Rowan said.

But no, Mr Frobisher had bought her a brass compass. 'There,' he said. 'You'll always be able to find north. And from there you can work out your way anywhere.'

She stared at it. A small perfect thing, needle quivering.

'The needle stays still,' Mr Frobisher told her. 'You turn the compass till the needle points north. I worry about you, Rowan.' He did not pause for breath as he changed the subject. 'Setting off alone. I don't know what I'd do if one of my daughters said she was going to do what you're going to do.'

'You'd let her.' Rowan was sure of this.

'I'd make her life hell. I'd do everything I could to dissuade her. Then I'd let her go.'

Rowan smiled.

'I have written my home number on this card,' Mr Frobisher told her. 'Should you ever get into trouble, should, God forbid, anything nasty happen to you, phone me. You'd be surprised at the people I know. Educational books, you see, they get every-where.'

'Thank you,' said Rowan. 'I'm sure I won't need it.'

'I have always had a bit of a soft spot for you, Rowan,' he told her. But Rowan was too taken up watching her first name form on his lips to hear what he said. It was only as she walked home that his words registered. She wondered if she'd got him wrong. She was beginning to think she got everybody wrong. Maybe Mr Frobisher wasn't the rude man she thought he was. 'I have always had a bit of a soft spot for you,' he'd said. She hadn't thought Mr Frobisher could possibly have a soft spot for anybody, anything. Now she felt guilty for disliking him.

She always enjoyed the walk home. It interested her how she'd become expert at metropolitan living and moving. She could swish through evening crowds, barely scraping a passing shoulder or arm. She could walk by a million faces and not notice any of them. She could waltz against red lights, dance through the rattle and rush of evening cars and touch the far kerb unscathed. Back home, living and moving was different, careless. A street could contain only two people and they'd bang into one another. 'Ooh, sorry. Didn't see you.' On empty pavements a little dreaming wasn't too dangerous to resist. In London, early spring, darkness was already here down amongst the people and the cars. Rowan stopped; she was swamped by a surge of nostalgia that was so bitter and so sweet she could feel it, smell it, taste it.

She touched Mr Frobisher's compass in her pocket. North. Back home, Fretterton, smack dab in the middle of Scotland – up a bit, right a bit – darkness would still be far overhead. The streets would be light and cold, with that turn-of-the-season chill that was raw and filled with hope. The air would smell of coal fires.

Already this year's crop of summer boys would be gathering outside the Rossis' chip shop. They'd hook their thumbs on the back pockets of their jeans, or suck on cigarettes, brows slightly knit against the smoke, discussing their evening ahead. There would be a couple of cars, windows open, thumping music. These boys would have the swagger and young strut of people who have not yet found their confidence. They were all Jimmy Dean.

When she got home Eileen had moved Sadie, her cot, nappies, toys and two days' supply of clothes into her room.

'Couldn't get everything in,' Eileen said, 'so I shoved that rucksack thing into my room. You don't mind, do you?'

'No.' Rowan shook her head. She minded. Having her room rearranged whilst she was out angered her. She thought that if she wasn't leaving she'd have a new lock put on.

'Right,' Eileen grinned. She tossed the keys to the Beetle onto the bed. 'You can have the car – I won't be needing it.' Then, in a sudden wild generous gesture, she went and got her coat. 'You can have that, too. You'll look glam. Everyone will think you're me.'

Rowan stared at the coat. She hated it. 'Won't you need it?'

'Nah. Not where I'm going. It'll just weigh me down.'

'I have to eat,' Rowan said through a sigh. She picked up Sadie and went downstairs. In the kitchen she sat Sadie in her high chair, fed Elvis, then heated a bottle and a little jar of puréed chicken and vegetables, and opened a carton of yoghurt for herself. She was sitting at the table spooning food into Sadie's eager mouth, catching the spillage that landed on her lips and chin, spooning that in too, occasionally feeding herself some yoghurt, feeling absurdly melancholy, when Eileen stuck her head round the door.

'I'll be off, then.'

'OK.' Rowan tried to smile. 'Have a good time.'

'Oh, I will. Can't wait.' She looked at Sadie and Rowan a moment. 'You two look good together.' Pointing at her daughter; 'She's like Elvis, she prefers you to me. You'll be fine. I know it.'

Rowan smiled.

Eileen came across the room, kissed her, then kissed Sadie, lips lingering on her head, her fingers softly moving over her little face, peachy skin. 'Be good,' she said. Then she walked out of the kitchen door.

Rowan turned to Sadie. 'What do you think of that? Ungrateful bitch didn't even say goodbye.'

Chapter Six

Rowan had a Hollywood childhood. It was filled with cowboys and Indians, gangsters, adventurers, dreamers, lovers and songs. Mamie Garland who owned the Rialto cinema in the High Street showed her favourite old movies whenever she could. At least three times a week Rowan sat in the stalls, alone in the soaring dark clutching a packet of Butterkist, high on anticipation, waiting for some magic to unfold. She adored all sorts of films for all sorts of reasons. *Gunfight at the OK Corral* for the props and ironing. (Burt Lancaster's shirts were starched and pristine.) She saw *Camille* on television one rainy Sunday afternoon and was moved to tears. She wanted to be like that – a tragic heroine, dressed in white. Furthermore, when she saw it she was young enough to think dying young an exquisite thing to do. When she was fourteen her English teacher read *Ode to a Nightingale* to her class. Rowan was deeply moved and planned to part from this world before she was thirty in some serene and painless way. She loved the old Katharine Hepburn, Spencer Tracy movies. There was a woman who spoke her mind. Did as she pleased. That was the way a person who was going to die tragically when she was twenty-nine-and-a-half should live.

There were other films, momentous dialogue, fabulous moments. Rowan's young mind gleamed with it all – there was little room for school, her mother and father and the three-bedroomed terraced house they all lived in.

Norma had little time for movies and her daughter's passion for them. Rowan remembered well the time she'd persuaded her mother to take her to see *Jaws*. She was seven at the time and had been scared out of her wits. That night she'd refused to go to bed

61

lest there was a shark lurking in the dark at the top of the stairs. Her mother had greeted the outburst of fear with a well-if-this-is-what-movies-do-to-you-we're-never-going-again silence. It did the trick. Fear of not going back to the Rialto was greater than any fear of any shark, even Great White man-eating ones.

After that, Norma had been dragged to the Rialto every week. She'd silenced her way through *Close Encounters of the Third Kind* – Rowan had watched the skies for weeks looking for signs from beyond; maybe they'd come for her, whisk her away to a new life in the stars; *Bugsy Malone* – she fancied herself as a gangster's moll; and *Flashdance* – she could go to work in a steel mill (well, since there was no steel mill in Fretterton the cannery would do), and she could learn to dance; *Fitzcarraldo* – she wanted to go to the Amazon to live amongst tribesmen listening to opera . . .

Eventually Norma refused to take her daughter to the cinema so Rowan went alone – even better than going with her mother. Her ambitions reflected week in week out what she saw at the Rialto. After *Breaking Glass* she wanted to be a misunderstood post-punk singer. After *The Blues Brothers* she bought the hat and glasses but wanted to run a diner in a sassy Aretha Franklin sort of way. Growing up hadn't changed her. Two years ago Rowan had seen *Fatal Attraction* and had fleetingly fancied herself as a high-powered, over-sexed, manipulative mistress who could bring men to their knees with a look – *that* look. By the time she'd caught the bus home, she thought perhaps not. She did not think she'd make it as a bunny boiler.

Norma blamed Hollywood for her daughter's serial ambitions. She did not see they were just a set of transient adolescent desires that Rowan herself did not take seriously. Recently she had blamed the whole media for her daughter's notions.

'It's all the fault of these films she saw. I should never have let her go. "No good will come of it," I said. "No good." That and the books she read. And all the rubbish she watched on telly. She could have taken up some sort of wholesome activity. Like Claudia Rossi – she played hockey. Rowan's too easily swayed. She has no notion of who she really is, what she is. People are drawn to her. She never notices her own worth. Always wanting to be someone else.'

George, her husband, sitting at the kitchen table, hadn't the heart to point out that Claudia Rossi had got herself pregnant at eighteen and now had three children. And was fat.

'You worry too much,' he said. 'She's got a good head on her. She'll do the right thing in the end.'

He often wondered why Norma didn't knit. It seemed the sort of thing women who ardently disapproved of things did. He imagined her sitting bolt upright, needles a blur. Then he thought not. It was best she didn't. If her output matched the vast amount of things she objected to, then he'd have drawers full of hideous jumpers upstairs. He'd refuse to wear them. She'd disapprove of that. More knitting. More jumpers.

Of course, Rowan went to the cinema in London, but it wasn't the same. You could hear what the actors were saying, the screen didn't flicker and jolt, and you couldn't shout up to the projectionist to speed onto – or replay – the good bits. All that, and there weren't the hens.

Mamie Garland kept prize Rhode Island Reds. Adored and pampered beasts, they wandered the yard between Mamie's kitchen door and the back door of the cinema, which was often kept open. And even when it was shut, it was two foot short of the ground, giving easy access to young folks like Rowan who didn't have the entrance money, howling draughts and hens who made their fussy way up and down the aisles, scratching and pecking at stray bits of popcorn.

The up side of this, of course, was that there were always speckled free-range eggs on sale at the kiosk, along with Mamie's home-made treacle toffee. Rowan found city cinema visits oddly silent, sterile almost, with only the odd rustle of sweets to drown the sounds coming from the screen. In the Rialto there had been the slow intake of sugary juices as chunks of toffee were shifted, mid-suck, from left cheek to right, the in-house discussions about Elizabeth Taylor's husbands, Paul Newman's eyes, Jimmy Dean's jeans, Kim Novak's sex-life, Robert Mitchum's drug bust. All that against the pleasant backdrop of hens, puck, puck, pucking. No, cinema in the city wasn't the same. And they didn't put on *Somebody Up There Likes Me* every Wednesday night because that was the owner's favourite. Rowan had seen it so often she could speak along with Paul Newman and Pier Angeli.

Though they hadn't seen each other for almost five years, Rowan always thought of Claudia Rossi, daughter of the chip-shop family, as her best friend. They had grown up together. Rowan had spent so much time at the Rossis' her mother had actually broken her silence and complained openly about it. 'You're there so much I don't know why you don't just move in. I think you prefer them to us.'

She was right. Rowan did. She wished she was a Rossi. She wanted to be part of a big family that argued, laughed, spoke constantly and touched each other. That most of all. The touching.

Whilst Rowan had escaped the small town, there had been no thought that Claudia would do the same. She had grown up knowing that as soon as she'd finished with school, she'd join the family business. Still, she often put her elbows on the chip-shop counter, stared out the window at the village goings on and wondered how her old friend Rowan was getting on. Rowan, she imagined, would wear exquisite clothes. Work in some sort of tower block office, gazing out at city skylines. She'd have a personal assistant. She would live in a beautiful flat, with polished floors, white sofas, glossy plants. Claudia would sigh with envy.

Rowan shoved a last spoonful of gooey chicken and veg into Sadie's mouth. 'Christ, you know nothing. Do you?' She removed the child's bib, wiped her fat cheeks with it. She picked up the dirty dishes and took them to the sink. She dumped the remains of a chicken tandoori (not hers) left solidifying on the kitchen unit into the bin. Removed the dripping cereal bowls and cups from the greasy water, emptied the sink, wiped it out, filled it with hot water, washed Sadie's dishes, put the greasy dishes back into the sink. 'What do you think of our cesspool?' she asked Sadie. 'Crap, isn't it? No place for a sweetie like you.'

Sadie smiled.

Rowan took her from her high chair. Held her close. 'So what now? What do you fancy for tonight? A trip to the pub, a few drinks, on to a club? See if we can find some good-looking six-month-old boy to show you a good time? No? What about a bath, then?' She considered the layer of spilled food encrusting Sadie's dungarees. 'You're going to have to do something about your eating habits.' The meal took its toll on Sadie's digestive

It Could Happen To You

system. The child slipped into a rapture of concentration, rolled her eyes upward, turned red with effort, shat copiously into her nappy. 'Then there's that,' said Rowan. 'You're never going to make it in any sort of society if you carry on like that.'

Sadie smiled. Reached out, grabbed Rowan's lower lip and pulled it out. *Should I Stay Or Should I Go* soared out of the radio. Rowan held Sadie, danced with her round the kitchen. Here at last in her life was someone she could wholeheartedly love. Someone she could take to her whenever she wanted, and hug. And who adored her back. 'Bath, I think,' Rowan said.

She filled the tub with foaming water, undressed Sadie, cleaned her. Pulled her own clothes off and climbed in. They played in the foam; Rowan dunked the baby, then lifted her high out of the water, dunked her again. Then she lay back, child on top of her, and stared up through the steam at the flaking damp ceiling.

'You only know London, and the folks here – Danny and that. They're all seriously working on their cool. The people I could tell you about. Back home in the village I come from, there were all sorts of folks coming and going. I never paid them any mind. They were part of my childhood backdrop.'

She told the baby about the little old lady who lived in the village square, across from the County Hotel. And swamped by nostalgia, her voice sang out like a lullaby. 'She's an astrologer. No kidding, she does horoscopes. Most folks have had their chart done. Every morning, seven o'clock, she goes to the SPAR to buy milk, newspapers and whatever. She flows along in this velvet cloak and luminescent floppy purple hat that droops over her eyes. Now, *she's* a real wafter, not like your mum. She's an amateur compared to Miss P. Christ, now I think about it, she's ancient. Seventy at least. And she skims the pavement as if she's on roller-skates. Anyone looking out of their ground-floor window as she passes gets a glimpse of flying purple hat. "Out the way," she cries, waving people aside. She's scared folks will ask her for a free prediction. People might stop her and demand facts. Is it a good time for Geminis to book a holiday? And where should they go? What do the stars say on the matter of Libras finding a funny lumpy thing under their left arm? She writes the horoscopes for the *Gazette*: *Porteous Predicts.* There you go, bet you didn't know about her.

'I never thought about her before. But how did she come to live in our village? Wasn't born there. Who is she really? Know what I mean? All my life she was always just there.'

Silence. Not a gurgle from Sadie.

'Am I boring you?' Rowan asked. She looked down. The child was lying on her, head against her breast, sound asleep. 'Guess I am.'

Rowan gently got up, wrapped them both in her bath towel and went upstairs to her room. She laid Sadie on the bed. Dried her carefully, slipped on a nappy and little red babygro. She rubbed herself with the towel, tossed it across the room and climbed into bed taking Sadie with her.

Rowan always enjoyed holding the baby. She loved the feel of her nestling in her arms, and the fearless way she slipped from consciousness. She wondered what babies dreamed about. Being carried down long corridors, arms stretched out for huge elusive feeding bottles that always slipped from reach? Huge faces looming and cooing? She would sit holding Sadie, watching her sleep long after it was time to lay her in her cot. She never could understand why Eileen would lay her down as swiftly as possible, raise her arms, do a small on-the-spot jig, jubilantly whisper, 'Free at last. Free at last.'

'I fear for you, little Sadie,' Rowan said. 'Your mother's such an arse. I don't trust her with you. What do you think she's up to now? Laughing and drinking and wafting, no doubt. And what do you make of this Maurice stuff? Do you believe any of it?'

The room was dark, shafts of light from the street outside spread a thin light across the end of the bed. Normally she would light a candle, but was afraid the room might go on fire in the middle of the night. She didn't bother to reach across and light her bedside lamp. Didn't want someone as little as Sadie to know she was, at her age, afraid of the dark.

'I had a love,' she said, her voice hollow against the still of the room. 'Nelson. He's still back there. He's editor of the *County Gazette*. He's about twenty years older than me. When I was thirteen he'd have been about thirty-three. Oh, I had such a crush. I was smitten. The full teenage horror. I'd blush and squirm if he passed me in the street. Or I'd rush past him giggling. God, I'm squirming now just remembering it. He wore fantastic suits. "Fab" is the word I used for him. He always wore rebel shirts.'

Sadie moved in her arms. Made sucking movements with her mouth.

'Oh, I know,' Rowan said. 'You're a London girl. You're used to brazen shirts and sod-you trousers that say their owners do not seek redemption, acceptance or understanding. That's the city. But back there a pink or a red shirt is worn only by anarchists, spendthrifts, lechers, louts, wastrels and generally untrustworthy fellows. That's the sort of place it is. Anyway, my Nelson wore rebel shirts and had gorgeous long lashes. When you're thirteen that's all you look for in a bloke.'

She moved down the bed, pulled her duvet cosily over them both. 'This is me. Friday night and in bed by eight.'

Chapter Seven

On Sunday Rowan put Sadie into the Beetle and drove out to Heathrow. Eileen had promised to be on the four o'clock flight. 'Back in time to put my baby to bed.' Rowan thought, when she was thinking magnanimously, that Eileen would like a little welcome home, a small, smiling show of two familiar faces. And, Eileen's new man, dizzy on Parisian wine, food and Eileen, would be in a mood to meet his new little friend. Then, when her thoughts were less kind she took some glee in imagining she'd catch Eileen out. Rowan wanted to be there when Eileen appeared at the arrivals gate with a fat old Frenchman, triple layers of tummy hanging over his belt, bald head glistening under the airport lights. He'd reek of Gauloises and garlic. As Eileen came across to greet them, he'd slap her bum, making incomprehensibly French sort of noises. And when he caught sight of Sadie that would be that. Of course he didn't really know that Eileen had a child; that was just one of her lies. And no way would he want the pair of them to move in with him!

'Here's your daughter, Eileen,' Rowan planned to say.

Eileen would flush. Flap her hand guiltily. Try to explain. 'Ha, ha. Yes, Maurice. Er . . . this is Sadie.'

'Merde!' her Frenchman would exclaim. *'Merde et adieu.'*

Rowan grinned, thinking about it. Of course it wasn't malice. It was a spot of innocent wickedness. And why not. Eileen often advocated a spot of wickedness.

'Have you ever been wicked, Rowan? Really, really wicked just for the hell of it?'

Rowan didn't have to think about this. 'No.'

'Have you ever slept with your best friend's bloke just so you'd know what he was like? Then when she said what fantastic sex she had, you'd know the truth?'

'No.'

'Not even a quick blow job at a dinner party when your best friend was at the table boring folks about her holidays in Acapulco?'

'No!' Rowan made a mental note never to introduce Eileen to any boyfriends she might have.

'Haven't you ever stolen something from a pal, knowing she'd be looking everywhere for it? Nothing serious. Her diary.'

'Never! Eileen, how could you? A diary's serious.'

'Yeah. But you can read it and know all about her.'

'That's wicked.'

'I know. Great.'

'You can't have had any best friends if you did that. Not real ones.'

'I've had lots. You're my best friend.'

Rowan's heart chilled. What might Eileen do?

'Didn't you even steal money from your mother's purse when she wasn't looking?'

'Absolutely no. She would've known. She always knew exactly how much she had.'

'Oh.' Eileen sounded bored.

Rowan started that conversation feeling virtuous. Ended it feeling dull. Now she was redressing the balance. Getting her own back for being made to feel such a dowdy little soul. *She* was doing something wicked. She drove out to Heathrow, smirking all the way. This was delicious. She should've taken up being wicked ages ago.

She stood, holding Sadie facing out towards the oncoming faces, little hand in her hand, poised ready to wave to Mummy. But Mummy didn't come. They waited till the last person had emerged from the arrivals gate staring in disbelief. Then Rowan thought, What did I expect? Reliability – from Eileen? She'll be on the next flight. But she wasn't.

By that time Sadie was squirming with hunger, and being embarrassing with her screaming demand to be fed. So Rowan took her home. Fed her and put her to bed. All evening she listened for Eileen's arrival home. Every time a car door slammed, every voice outside, every rattle or squeak at the front door, Rowan rose and went to the window to peer out at the street, a pale and apprehensive face, anxiously steaming the glass. The comings and goings of strangers out there prattling, slamming car doors, seemed mindless, relaxed. Doubt and worry wormed into her, shuddered nervously in her stomach.

Next day Rowan phoned the airport to find out if an Eileen Johnson was booked on a flight from Paris. She wasn't. But then, she thought, she might be travelling under Maurice's name. She phoned the French Embassy and was told that there was no Maurice employed there.

'No,' she argued. 'Maurice,' she said again, slightly louder. As if that would make whoever she was talking to understand. 'He's not there now. He's gone to Paris with my friend Eileen. They were meant to come home yesterday and didn't turn up. I wondered if anything was wrong. If you could give me his address in Paris. Only Eileen's left me looking after her baby and I have to know when they're getting back. I'm going away myself tomorrow. I have to get in touch.' She was talking too much; her throat was tight, her voice getting higher and higher. Tears were on the way. Furthermore, she could tell from the bristling silence breathing down the telephone line that the person she was talking to did not want to hear what she was saying. No comfort there.

She didn't know what to do. So she fretted and paced a pathetic route from kitchen table to window. Every time she stared out she was surprised that she did not see Eileen jazzing up the street, waving and smiling. When she wasn't fretting or pacing she sat on the stairs watching, ashen-faced, the front door, willing Eileen to come through it. She ran her fingers through her hair. She smoked. When Sadie, sensing her agitation, howled, Rowan irritably shushed her. She could not bear this noise, the guilt it invoked in her, to distract her from her dismay. Furthermore, she cursed herself that this was her comeuppance for wanting to be wicked.

The house was empty. Without the constant hum and bass of music the other residents played, it felt hollow and just as awful as it looked. Wasn't it strange how the jangle and beat of music could mellow the ratty appearance of a place?

She wished someone else was home, then she'd be able to discuss her dilemma. When eventually she did put on some music to ease the silence, she used the length of the tracks she played to measure her hope. Eileen will come by the time this one's finished. No. Well, this one takes five minutes and forty seconds, she'll be back by then. At last Danny came home. As soon as he opened the door he knew from the rush of tension that greeted him that something was wrong.

'What's up?' he asked Rowan, who had abandoned pacing to take up her place at the foot of the stairs watching the front door once again. She dangled Sadie on her knee.

'It's Eileen.' She did not look at him. If she looked at him she might see concern. And that would crack her resolve; she would cry. 'She hasn't come home. I've been here all day with the baby. I've phoned everybody I can think of. Now I don't know what to do. Do you think she's had an accident?'

'Nah, not Eileen. She'll be back. You know what she's like. She'll be having too good a time to come home. She's got to come back, hasn't she? Bring you your rucksack. You'll be needing it.'

'Rucksack?'

'Yeah. You lent it to her.'

'No, I didn't.'

'Well, she was carrying it when she left. I saw her. I thought you'd let her have it.'

'Rucksack?'

'Yeah.'

Rowan handed Sadie to him. 'Rucksack,' she said. She turned and thundered upstairs. 'Rucksack.' She burst into Eileen's room, stared round. The rucksack was not there. She ran into her own room, checking that Eileen really had removed it when she brought the cot through. No rucksack. Back into Eileen's room. Rowan threw open the wardrobe. All of Eileen's clothes were gone. Rowan opened her chest of drawers. They were empty. 'Jesus,' she said. A harsh panic in her throat. 'Jesus. Jesus. Jesus.' She stood still a moment, trying not to allow the dire thought that had just occurred to her into her mind. 'Oh, Jesus Christ Almighty. No.'

She ran back into her room. Fumbled wildly through her books but she could not find *Travels With Myself and Another*. She had placed all her money, tickets and travel plans between its pages. One by one she opened all her other books – perhaps she'd made a mistake, perhaps she'd put all those precious things in another book – fanned their pages, held them from her, shaking them. But nothing happened. Her traveller's cheques did not spill out onto the carpet. They were not there. Her money was gone, traveller's cheques gone, route maps gone. Her beloved book was gone. Eileen had cleaned her out.

Chapter Eight

On the night of her betrayal, when she discovered Eileen had taken her rucksack, her money, her beloved book, her dreams, Rowan's headache started. Now, two weeks later, it still had not eased. It was a constant ache behind her eyes, a river of pain that ran over her scalp to her neck. The relentlessness of it made her puffy-eyed and nauseous. She felt she was burrowing through a nightmare. Every so often, twenty minutes or so, she'd lift her head trying to shake herself from the hideous unreality she was living through. Then she'd go to the window and stare out, believing every time she did so that Eileen would be there, laughing and waving. Shouting, 'Ha. Ha. You'll never guess where I've been. You really missed yourself.'

When, after a solid five minutes' staring and hoping, Eileen did not appear, Rowan would go out the front door and stare some more up and down the street. The headache deepened. It was fear. It was stress. It was eyestrain.

Her moods flew in wild swings. Sometimes rage – a rage so hard her lips shivered and she shook all over, had to sit down breathing slowly, fearing she might implode with fury. That bitch had stolen all her stuff. *How dare she?* And sometimes she felt a fool. She should have seen it coming. She was a victim, doltishly gullible and absurdly naive.

Once she even felt saintly. It was a noble thing to take in and care for an orphaned infant. To let her friend roam the world, experience life whilst she stayed home, scrubbed the floors, stewed cabbage, carried bundles of laundry, wept and sighed. Thinking of this, feeling holy, Rowan lifted her head high, sucked in her cheeks and clutched Sadie to her and let out a raw laugh. When had she ever stewed cabbage or scrubbed a floor? Still, it was a fine moment imagining St Rowan sacrificing herself for her wildly nonsensical pal. Nonetheless, decisions had to be made.

Through it all, the moods, the staring, the praying for Eileen's return, Rowan's life became a matter of minutiae – small moments. She looked after Sadie, dealing with details of routines that, if forgotten – no clean nappies, no feeds made up – caused havoc.

At the end of a fretful fortnight, Tracy arrived. Eileen had passed on her room to her. She was younger than Rowan, was starting work in advertising and she was full of assumptions. 'I hope you don't mind my saying so, but I found your cat in my room lying on my bed. I know he's probably perfectly clean and all. But you never know where he's been. Would you please keep an eye on him?' She jiggled with self-confidence as she spoke. 'Also, I've moved your baby's things to one shelf in the fridge so I have room for my yoghurt and vegetables. Do you think this place is really right for a baby? I mean a garden would be good . . .'

Rowan stared at her. She was tired; too many emotions crammed into too short a time, too much hoping, despairing and worrying. She could hardly be bothered explaining. 'It's not my cat,' she said.

'Whose is it?'

'Eileen's.'

'She just left it? I suppose she had too much to think about, going off on a world trip like that. What a marvellous adventure.' Tracy was rapt with admiration and envy for Eileen, this wild and valiant soul. She turned on sad, fraught Rowan with pity. 'Eileen had such imagination.'

'She told you about it, did she? What did she say?' Rowan was feeling low enough to go further, to want more and more pain. The full crucifixion.

'Oh yes,' Tracy patronised. 'She wanted to wander, to find herself in South Asia. And to follow in other travellers' footsteps. Martha Gellhorn. And, of course, Mungo Park. She is off to walk the route he took up the Niger. Don't you just love it?'

'Yeah,' Rowan said. No tone in her voice. No expression on her face.

'If you're too busy, I'll take the cat to the pound tomorrow. Have it re-homed or put down. Whatever.'

Shocked by this threat to Elvis, Rowan pointed a furious finger at Tracy. 'Don't you dare,' she said. 'Don't you fucking dare.' She shook as she spoke. That did it. Letting go of some of her venom, dumping her bile on another person instead of absorbing it all herself forced the absurd reality of her situation on Rowan.

'Jesus,' she said. 'Jesus. Jesus. I have nothing.' She sank onto the stairs. She had no money, couldn't pay the rent. Couldn't feed herself. Or Sadie. She looked up at Tracy who was fiddling with her shirt-sleeve, tugging at it, desperate to get away, to flee this moment but too polite to let it show.

'I have,' Rowan raised her hand, fingers spread to count the things she didn't have, 'no money. No job. Can't pay the rent. My share of the bills. Can't buy food for myself. Or Sadie.' She'd run out of fingers. Sat clutching her bunch of woes. 'What am I going to do?'

Tracy shrugged. She wanted to say that Rowan should have thought of all that before she got pregnant. But, considering the reaction she'd got at the suggested assassination of Elvis, held her tongue.

'Sadie's Eileen's baby,' Rowan told her. 'I was going to travel the world. Eileen stole all my money, buggered off and left her with me.' Rowan got up and walked through to the kitchen where Sadie was sleeping in her carrycot. 'She said she was my best friend. She's stolen my life.'

'My God,' said Tracy. This was a fabulous predicament. This would make a good discussion in the pub later with her pals. She followed Rowan into the kitchen, eager for more details. 'Surely no mother would leave her baby.'

Rowan nodded. 'Oh yes. Eileen did. Not all women take to mothering.'

'But you're so good with the baby! I just assumed she was yours.'

Rowan shrugged. 'It's all pretty basic. You just do what you have to. Feed one end, wipe the other.'

'Why don't you *do* something? Tell the police. Hand Sadie over to some social workers. They'd put her with foster parents till Eileen comes back.'

'I couldn't do that to her.' She looked down at the infant. 'She's my friend.'

Tracy peered into the carrycot. 'She's a baby. Tiny. You can't go out for a drink together. You can't borrow any of her clothes. And she's hardly going to discuss the latest Bertolucci or anything like that, is she? Give her up to foster parents. She won't remember a thing. It's for the best.'

'I like her,' Rowan defended her friend. 'She smiles when she sees me. Nobody else does that.' Oh God, she thought, how pathetic can you get? She rummaged in the pockets of her jeans for a tissue, she thought she ought to be wiping her eyes. Except there were no tears. She'd noticed that recently. She was drained as though she'd been crying her eyes out. But her eyes were dry. She sniffed, dabbed at her nose with a hardened, screwed-up tissue. A good bawl would sort me out, she thought. Clear my head. But it wasn't to be.

She shoved her hands into her pockets, sadly considered the ghastly kitchen and sighed. 'As far as I can see, I've got two options. Stay here in London. Find another job. I could temp if I can't get anything permanent. Fix up some sort of nanny or nursery to look after Sadie whilst I'm out. Or, I could go home. Sort myself out. Get a job up there for a while. Save some more cash. Come back to London and wait for Eileen to turn up.'

Tracy sat at the table, waiting for a decision. Watching other people's traumas was always interesting. It added to her experience of life, without the pain of actually experiencing them herself.

Rowan thought about home. About her mother. She could do with a mother right now. She chose her old friend Claudia's; didn't think her own would have much sympathy. She imagined what her mother would say. 'For heaven's sake, Rowan. Hand the child over. She's not yours. No need to take responsibility . . .'

Deciding that what she needed more than anything was a friendly voice, Rowan went upstairs, fished in her coat pocket, found the note Mr Frobisher had given her. She went downstairs to the phone, dialled his number.

'Hello, Mr Frobisher. It's Rowan Campbell. Remember?'

'Rowan.' The man sounded enthused. 'Of course I remember. Where are you? Somewhere exotic, I hope.'

'I'm here in London.'

'You haven't set off then?'

'No. Something's happened. My friend stole all my money. And she left me with her baby.'

There was a long silence. Then: 'Where exactly are you?'

It took James Frobisher an hour to get to her. He was wearing jeans and a huge woolly jumper. Rowan never knew he wore jeans. Had to stop herself remarking on them. But when she saw him, she threw herself at him. It was so lovely to press herself against someone. She needed the contact. But after she had been ensconced in his embrace for a couple of minutes she felt embarrassed. This man used to be her boss. 'I'm sorry,' she said. 'I've thrown myself into your arms. I didn't mean . . .'

'I love it,' he interrupted her. 'These old arms like young women to throw themselves into them.' He smiled at her. 'Doesn't happen very often. Actually, ever.'

She led him into the kitchen. Shrugged an apology when she saw his face. 'Sorry.' Experienced that moment of realising how truly awful a place is when showing it to someone you don't want to see it. 'It's a bit of a mess.'

'The place I lived in when I first came to London was worse. Off the Cromwell Road. This is a palace compared.'

Still, he refused a cup of tea. Rowan didn't blame him. Didn't think she would accept anything made in this kitchen if she didn't live here. He looked round. 'Where's the baby?'

'Sleeping. Upstairs.' She pointed at the ceiling. Heard a small cry. 'Stirrings.' She moaned. 'I'll get her. She's unsettled these days. She knows something's going on.'

'They do.'

When she brought Sadie to the kitchen, James took her. Held her comfortably. Here was someone very used to babies. 'So,' he said. 'What about you? How do you feel?'

'Confused.' She made an apologetic face. 'There you go. It isn't Sadie – I've got used to having her around. More than used. I don't want to hand her over. I couldn't function for wondering about her.

And she's good to talk to. She doesn't answer back. It's having all my stuff stolen. I feel a fool.'

'These things happen. It's not your fault.'

'I don't know – I should've seen it coming. Eileen was so over the top. At first I thought she was magic, couldn't get enough of her. Then she got too much; I tired of her. Now I think I was stupid. I was warned. Not just by Danny, who lives here, but Eileen herself told me she was wicked. Stole from people. I just didn't think she'd steal from me.'

He held the baby whilst she told him about Eileen. 'She always gave the impression something fantastic was just about to happen. It never did. Do you know, I think she did things so she could tell people about them afterwards. You could see her reinventing parties and other things, small moments as she lived through them. Everything was a fiction. I'm so angry at her. And there's not a lot I can do.'

'Report her to the police?'

'I don't want them involved.'

He looked at her. 'It's a simple should I stay or should I go decision, is it?'

Rowan nodded.

'Make a list,' James told her. 'Get paper and pencil. Write down all the pros and all the cons of staying in London and going home.'

Rowan fetched a notepad and biro. Whilst Sadie slept in James's arms she wrote down *Reasons for Staying In London*:

1. Better pay. 2. I like it here. 3. More opportunities for me to move to better jobs. 4. My hairdresser is here – she thought this trivial, but terribly important, somehow. *5. More things going on*. But then, if she had Sadie, would she ever get out nights? Still, there were weekends. She imagined taking Sadie to the British Museum. *6. My mother isn't here* – she thought this a bit unfair. Her mother wasn't that bad.

When she'd sixteen reasons for staying she listed her reasons for not going home. *1. Crap pay. 2. I can't remember if I liked it there, I was too young. 3. Few jobs. No jobs? 4. Crap hairdressers. 5. Nothing to do nights. 6. My mother's there. And I don't want to face her*. That was as far as she got.

'From these lists so far, I can see no reason for going home,' she told James.

'OK,' he said. Reached across, took the list. Tore it up. 'Now, you know what your head says. But what does your gut tell you? What do you *want* to do?'

She looked at him. She knew, and she didn't want to admit it. She stared at the floor.

'Well?' said James.

'I want to go home. I don't really, but I feel safe there. I want to feel safe. Having missed out on the lure of the unknown, I'm drawn to the opposite – the lure of the known.' Silence. 'For a while at least.' Longer silence. 'I feel a bit defeated.' Even longer silence. 'Going home with my tail between my legs.' She scratched her head. 'I'm such a fool.'

'You're not a fool, Rowan. In fact, I think you're very brave.'

She smiled at him. A compliment, right now, was what she needed.

'Um,' she said. 'You know when you come to the office all dressed up? Where are you going?'

'I take my wife out to lunch,' he told her.

Of course, thought Rowan. He would. Nice people do nice things, and Mr Frobisher was totally, almost unforgivably nice.

Rowan stood up. 'I should go. Now. Before I change my mind. I have to do it.'

'How are you going to get there?'

'Drive. Eileen left me her baby, her horrible coat and her car.'

'Drive then?'

'Yes. It'll be best while Sadie sleeps. Instant decision.' She clapped her hands.

'Have you any money for petrol?'

Rowan slumped back into her chair. 'There's that. I closed my bank account, can't use my credit card.'

James took out his wallet. Removed fifty pounds, handed it to her.

'I can't.' Rowan refused the offer. Waving her hands. 'Really no.'

'Take it.'

'No.'

'Take it. How are you going to get home?'

'I'll send for cash.'

'By that time you'll have changed your mind. Do it. Listen to your gut. Do it now.'

She took the money. 'I'll pay you back.'

'It's a gift. For Sadie.'

'Thank you.' Rowan held her cash. 'You're a nice man, Mr Frobisher.'

'James.'

'James.' She hung her head. 'I'm sorry about the biscuits.'

'The biscuits?'

'Yes. It was me always bought the biscuits you hated. I did it to annoy you. I'm sorry.'

'Perhaps I was a bit of an arse to complain.' He put his arm round her. 'You'll do, Rowan Campbell. You'll do.'

By the time Rowan had packed all her own and Sadie's belongings there was no room for her maps and books. She left them in the cupboard vowing to return for them. She never did. As she started the car, Danny rushed from the house waving Elvis above his head. The cat hung, a limp lump of fur, solemnly gazing round. Being waved in the air was no more than he expected from humans.

'I can't take him.' Rowan watched in horror as he opened the car door and tossed Elvis in.

'You have to. Nobody here will care for him. He'll end up starved and misunderstood. Eventually he'll join other great rockers in the sky.'

Rowan heard the cat's claws scrape against the back seat and the indignant rasp of his tongue busily settling the ruffled fur on his back. A few seconds' peace before Elvis took stock of his situation and started to protest about it.

Rowan rolled down the window, leaned out. 'I'll send you the money for the phone bill I ran up,' she offered. In the past fortnight she had phoned every Johnson she could find in the Liverpool phone book she'd stolen from the library. Nobody knew Eileen. Or nobody was owning up to knowing Eileen.

'Forget it,' he said. 'We'll all chip in.' He reached over and opened the glove box and put in a small Nat West money bag filled with dope. 'Here,' he said. 'For when being at home gets to you. When you can't think straight and the muscles in your neck are twisted and your face aches with tension. Get happy.'

'I think I need some now,' she smiled. 'You have my number.'

'Yes,' said with a sigh. She'd pressed her home number on him a dozen times. Had left it with everyone she could think of. It was on the noticeboard, beside the phone and stuck on the front of the fridge. It was written on the bathroom wall and on the note that was lying in the cupboard under the stairs with the rolled-up maps. *Eileen, you shit. Come and get your child.*

'I'll go then,' she said. She started the car and moved off. Elvis's plaintive howls turned to a deep angrily fearful yowl. Sadie joined in. It was not going to be a jolly journey.

By the time she left London behind Sadie had silenced, but Elvis wasn't taking a trip north lightly. His yowling became incessant. He climbed into the well behind the back seat and bawled from there.

Whilst they were rattling up the motorway, the wind howling round the Beetle, that feeling of travelling at great speed when the car was struggling to get past fifty miles an hour, Elvis moved into Sadie's carrycot. In a panic that he would lie on the child's face and suffocate her, Rowan turned, flapped her hand at him. 'Get out! Get out!' The car veered into the fast lane in front of a Jaguar travelling at a ludicrously illicit speed. The driver slammed his hand on his horn, his foot on the brakes. As Rowan slipped, shamefaced, back into the inside lane the Jaguar screamed past her, lights flashing. It disappeared into the distance. Until he disappeared over the horizon, the driver made gestures at her indicating how insane he thought she was. She agreed with him. 'This is the stupidest thing I've ever done. Driving hundreds of miles with infant and cat.'

The Jaguar confrontation – the roar of aggressive car screaming past, the furious flash of belligerent lights, the driver's tantrums belting out on the horn – still upset her. Her nerves still jangled. 'See the trouble you cause,' she said to Elvis. 'Damn cat.' Tight-lipped she drove on. 'You're just a cat. You should remember that. People throw animals like you out onto roads like this to meet their fate. Don't get above yourself.'

She shoved Toots and the Maytals into the tape deck. *Pressure Drop* sang exuberantly out. She drove on. Decided this jubilant music did not suit her mood. Snapped it out of the machine, rummaged about amongst the tapes littering the shelf under the steering wheel till she found some Schubert. 'Something soothing,' she told Elvis. Put it on.

The cat, sensing a certain mellowing in her attitude towards him, crawled into the front of the car and onto her knee. Sat in a heap for the next fifty miles. She could feel him trembling. The incessant yowling calmed. Now, he only started up every ten minutes or so. He did not like change.

'What do you suppose that means?' Rowan asked Elvis. 'Getting above yourself? My mother used to say that. When I won the hurdles on school sports day, she said, "Don't go getting above yourself. It's only a race." D'you think she thought I'd become over-confident and therefore a problem child? Or did she think if I got above myself I'd only fall in some dire social tumble till I was way below myself? Or maybe,' warming to her theme, 'they think you'll get so above yourself, hit some dizzying heights, and won't want to speak to them. Still, you'd think parents would want their children to get above themselves. I can understand why people wouldn't want their cats to get above themselves. Well, if you don't mind me saying so, cats can be a trial. Overly pushy if you let them be. But people are different. I think I shall make that my new ambition. I shall strive to get above myself from now on.'

The night and the road wore on. Sadie slept. Elvis complained and shivered. At times she had the motorway to herself. She could just about hear her loneliness. It was a roar in her ears, the constant batter of wind against the windscreen. The headlights flooded the way ahead, illuminating vast signs to places she'd never heard of. She thought she might be the last person alive.

At two in the morning, as she was approaching the border, Rowan saw an old man in a long flowing coat, carrying a spade walking along the hard shoulder. But as she approached, the vision disappeared. A few miles further on, she saw two huge black dogs running ahead of her. She was hallucinating. She saw a woman on an old creaky bike who turned to laugh at her, but did not realise what was happening to her till a child poised to dash in front of her, appeared. She jammed on the brakes, Elvis slid from her knee, dug his claws into her leg, yowled, but not as loudly as she screamed.

'I'm seeing things. I'm having small nightmares and I'm not even asleep. The only decent thing about nightmares is you wake to realise it was only a dream. I'm not going to wake. This is hell,' she said, horrified. To Elvis's consternation she opened the window and took deep gulps of air, keeping herself awake and sane. She had been up since six o'clock in the morning. Twenty hours. She was gripping the wheel, staring ahead, driving on auto-pilot. Wide awake and sleeping, she rattled north.

Just after three in the morning she crossed the border. Felt a stab of joy at having travelled so far unscathed. She was almost home. Driving, exhausted, off the motorway was a worse hell than driving on it. Every turn, every dip, she bit her lip and negotiated it with trembling caution. The road became a phantasm. It arched, curved and spread before her, upwards, into the sky. She had to stop. Think. This isn't happening. Every time she stopped, Sadie cried out. When the car started again, Sadie slept again. Seven hours' driving, and Sadie, apart from small outbursts when Rowan stopped and worked out her hallucinations, had hardly stirred. She breathed baby sighs, and tiny snores. She cried out, dreaming baby dreams. But she did not wake.

Rowan celebrated this minor triumph by buying a sandwich and can of Coke at an all-night garage that was overly-lit, and filled with the ghetto-blasted blare of Marvin Gaye. The boy behind the counter, whey-faced and even twitchier than she was, told her the Detroit sound was brilliant, and Marvin had been misunderstood, and the sandwiches were all crap so it didn't matter which kind she chose. She had taken prawn and mayo over cheese and chutney in a feeble start to her new ambition to get above herself.

''S'at a cat?' the boy asked, peering out at Elvis who was sitting like a constipated hen on the driving seat headrest.

'Yes.'

'Against the law to drive with a cat loose in the car.'

'Is it?'

'Do you always take it with you?'

'No. I'm never going to take him anywhere again. He's got delusions of grandeur. He has protested all the way from London.'

'Come from London, then?'

'Yes.'

'Where are you taking the cat, then?'

'Home to my folks.'

'Do they like cats?'

'In a few hours we shall find out.'

A small, mildly absurd middle-of-the-night exchange, but it reminded her of home. Folks there were just like that, slightly sanctimonious, mindlessly nosy. They didn't really mind who you were and what you did, as long as they knew all about it.

It was almost five when she arrived. No longer dark, a slow light creeping in. She stopped on the hill above the village, saw it glisten below her. Street lights. 'Edelweiss, Edelweiss,' she sang. A wan little impromptu performance that took her by surprise. She banged her head on the steering wheel. 'I hate that song. I hate that song. Bloody Julie Andrews.'

She started down the hill into the village. 'In about ten minutes all hell will break loose.' She turned to Elvis. 'It's going to be bad enough when my folks see Sadie, but when they see you . . . Christ, they wouldn't even let me have a goldfish.' She shrugged. 'They're not animal people.' Then: 'There's been a smell in here since the garage. You've peed, haven't you? That's not very nice.'

The Beetle rustled into the village square. Rowan leaned over the steering wheel and looked round. The place hadn't changed. It was more neglected than she remembered. People had moved into the new houses on the edge of the village, leaving the old buildings, red and yellow, small windows, to crumble. Which made the black BMW gleaming outside the chip shop seem even gleamier.

'That'll be Paolo Rossi's,' sighed Rowan. 'Beemers will be this year's babe-mobile.'

The air was scented morning. Drifts of smoke, hill air that was not yet laden with the heavy grease and vinegar blasting from the Rossis'. She could hardly breathe – the joy, nostalgia, affection and horror she felt. Joy, nostalgia and affection that nothing had changed. Horror that nothing had changed. She felt safe here. That had been what she wanted. Yet, feeling safe was scary.

Sadie stirred on the back seat. 'Here we are,' Rowan told her. 'Bet you didn't think you'd wind up here. Christ, it's a surprise to me.' Her folks didn't know she was coming. Didn't know about Sadie. As she drove north Rowan had rehearsed her reaction to their surprise. Cool: 'Yeah, well. There you go, a baby. It happens.' Passionate: 'Eileen was my friend. I cannot leave her child with strangers.' Rattling across the border, having switched from Schubert back to rock'n'roll, humming nervously along with *Papa Was a Rolling Stone*, Rowan acted out the scene taking every part.

Rowan: I couldn't leave Sadie with folks she didn't know! What sort of person would that make me?

Her mother: Sensible?

Her father: Honest. Normal. Where are we going to put a baby?

Still debating how to explain Sadie to her parents, she revved the car and turned out of the square. Sadie started to cry.

Rowan drove up the hill and home. She parked outside her parents' house, sat staring at the front door. Should she wake them? Perhaps it would be best to wait till seven when they always got up. Her mother first, moving through the house in her pale blue velour housecoat and fluffy mules. First to put on the kettle. Then to the loo. By which time the kettle would have boiled. Radio on whilst she made tea. Then George would appear in the kitchen in his maroon dressing gown. He'd fetch the papers, mail and milk. He'd stand a moment on the front doorstep considering the day, sniffing the weather. Was this a day for the garden? Or a day for strolling down into the village? The man loved life since he'd stopped work. Rowan thought he'd been born to retire. He'd given up work when he was fifty-eight, two years ago. Norma was forty-five at the time. She was thirteen years younger than him. She hadn't kept him young. She'd adjusted to the gap – aged up.

Sadie's crying deepened into distress. Rowan got out of the car, leaned into the back and picked her up. The child was upset. Tears streaming down her pale and perfect cheeks. Her jaw shivered with each inhaled breath. Rowan held her close, pulled her little duvet round her, kicked the car door shut and walked up the path. It hadn't changed. Same rose bushes, pruned now, waiting to bloom into huge vibrant flowers later in the year. Same glossy black front door. Same ping-pong bell.

Her father answered it. Maroon dressing gown tightly belted, hair askew. 'Rowan! What are you doing here?'

Rowan could hear her mother calling from the bedroom: 'Who is it? Has something happened? It's the middle of the night.'

'It's Rowan,' her father shouted upstairs, ushering Rowan and Sadie into the living room.

'Rowan?' Rowan could hear her mother bustling in her bedroom, putting on her dressing gown and fluffy mules. 'What's she doing here?'

Rowan looked round the room. It had hardly changed. But it was so small. Had it been this small when she was a child? She didn't think so. New lamp beside the sofa. Same sofa, same matching green chairs. Same brown patterned carpet. New telly and a video.

'You've got a video,' she told her father.

'You've got a baby,' her father told her. 'It's not . . . ?'

'No,' said Rowan. 'It's Eileen's. She had the room opposite me in London.'

Sadie still howled. Norma appeared. She took a moment to take in the scene. Her daughter, who should have been travelling the world, was standing in her living room nursing a child.

'It's me,' Rowan told her. 'I'm back.'

'You've got a baby,' Norma accused. 'It's not . . . ?'

'We've been through that,' Rowan said. 'This is Sadie. And no, she's not mine. She's Eileen's. The woman I lived with.'

Norma melted. She almost dashed across the room, arms outstretched. 'Oh, poor little thing.' She scooped Sadie into her arms and cooed, 'Now, now. That's an awful noise to make. Poor little thing.'

Sadie quietened.

'Yes,' crooned Norma, 'that's better. You've come a long way, haven't you? We'll have to get you fed. Dear, dear.'

Rowan turned to her father, arms spread. This was not what she had rehearsed. Norma, still shushing Sadie, turned to Rowan. 'What have you done with your hair?'

Rowan grinned and sheepishly put her hand to her head. 'It's bleached.'

'So I see.' Norma was non-committal. She envied Rowan. She wished she had the nerve to do drastic things with her hair, but didn't say so.

'I like it,' Rowan said defensively. This was more like it. Criticism. This was what she expected from her mother. This she could cope with. 'I had it cropped and bleached.'

They stared at each other a moment. Rowan did not say she was glad to be home. Norma did not say how overjoyed she felt to see her daughter. Did not say how much she liked the new hairdo. They never did communicate well. Then Norma noticed Rowan's ears. Pointed at them and cried, 'You've had your ears pierced!'

'Yes.' Rowan was unrepentant about the silver earrings dangling from her lobes.

'Oh my.' Norma sank into a chair. 'My daughter appears in the middle of the night. Unannounced. With a baby. And her ears pierced. What next?'

Cue Elvis, Rowan thought. But then again, perhaps not. Better ease them into the idea of Elvis.

'I'll make tea,' said George. It seemed the thing to do. Get out of the room.

'I'll fetch Sadie's stuff from the car,' said Rowan. Getting out of the room appealed to her, too.

She shut the front door behind her. Sucked in some fresh air and thought to herself that, all in all, things hadn't gone as badly as she'd thought they would. There had been no hysterics.

Half an hour later, tea drunk, Sadie fed and changed, Rowan told her story.

'She what?' her mother said. 'She just took your money and left you with the baby? I don't believe it.'

Rowan shrugged. 'That's what happened.' The corners of her mouth twisted as she spoke in a kind of resignation. Them's the breaks.

'But . . .' was all her mother could say. That little protest, however, seemed to cover everything anyone could say about the situation.

'But,' Rowan's father repeated, '*a baby*. You can't take someone's baby.'

'What else can I do?'

'Hand it over to the authorities.'

'What if Eileen comes back? She's bound to come back. She won't abandon her daughter. When she does, she'll expect me to have looked after Sadie for her. Anyway, I've become sort of attached to the baby.'

'So you just came here.'

'I thought . . .' Rowan ran out of words. 'I thought you'd help.'

Norma looked at Sadie. She wanted to say something about Rowan not coming home to say goodbye properly. About her going off across the world. Maybe being away for years and years. Then just turning up home when something went wrong. But then there was this baby. And she loved babies. Always wanted another after Rowan was born. But, somehow, not for want of trying, it hadn't happened. And she'd long given up hope of ever becoming a grandmother. Now this. A lovely little girl with peachy cheeks, blue eyes and soft white hair. Who could resist her? Already she was praying that Eileen stayed away for a long, long time. So, she said nothing.

'But,' George was still protesting, 'why didn't you get in touch with your friend's family? They could take in their granddaughter. That'd be the thing to do.'

'I couldn't trace them.' Rowan shrugged. She was ashamed to admit that she'd become so friendly – exchanging secrets and confessions – with someone she knew so little about. It seemed, in the face of her parents' scrutiny, an incredibly young thing to do.

'But . . .' Her mother's 'but' this time. She'd thought of a problem. Her forte, coming up with snags. Rowan could tell she was getting agitated. Her voice was sliding up an octave, getting squeakier and squeakier. The more perturbed Norma became, the higher her voice. There was something horribly disturbing about the pitch her anxiety could take her to. At full stretch her distress could empty rooms. People would rush to the kitchen to make tea, or into the garden to gulp fresh air and ease raw nerves.

'But,' her mother squeaked again, 'how are we going to tell people? What will the neighbours think? They'll think you've gone and got yourself into trouble, that's what they'll think. Or they'll think you've lifted it from outside some supermarket or something. You hear things like that on the news.' She panicked. What if Rowan *had* stolen the baby? What if her story wasn't true? There would be a national outcry. Tabloid press at the door. The police. Scandal.

'Let them.' Rowan didn't care about the neighbours.

'I can't let them.' The voice was reaching room-emptying point.

'I'm not going to let them think the worst of you. I'm not letting them think you've gone and disgraced yourself. How dare they?'

'They haven't thought anything yet,' Rowan said quietly, reaching down to pick up the baby, who had cracked. Too young to cope with a strange room, strange new people talking in strange anxious voices, Sadie started to howl. Rowan started to pace the room with her, patting her. Soothing herself. 'The neighbours don't know anything yet. Just tell them the truth. It's my friend's baby; we're looking after her for a while. Eileen'll turn up. I've told everybody I can think of where I am. In a couple of days she'll walk up the path, knock on the door and demand to get her baby back. You'll see.' Her pacing was as frantic and despairing as her mother's voice. Still patting the baby she crossed the room, moved aside the curtain and peered out into the dawn. Eileen would come. She was sure Eileen would come.

'There's more,' she suddenly confessed. 'I haven't told you about Elvis.'

'Elvis?' said Norma. 'Who's Elvis?'

'I'll get him.' Rowan handed Sadie to Norma, left the room, returned a couple of minutes later clutching Elvis.

'He's a cat,' Norma told her. 'Poor wee thing. He's shivering.'

Rowan put him down. He scuttled under a chair, took up his constipated hen position and glared round the room.

George and Norma, cuddling Sadie, gathered to watch him.

'Oh, he's lovely.' Norma was overjoyed. 'I always wanted a cat. Especially a black one.'

'You wouldn't let me have as much as a goldfish when I was little. I wanted one too.'

'Too much of a tie,' said Norma.

'You never went anywhere.'

Norma looked at her, said nothing. She would save this argument till later.

'So lucky,' she enthused instead. Norma's superstition was legendary. It went way beyond not walking under ladders. 'You do not wash your windows on a Friday,' she'd declare. 'Very unlucky.' She'd regularly come home with one glove, having dropped the other and been unable to pick it up. Picking up your own dropped glove was to invite misfortune. She'd stand in the street looking helpless, not understanding how passers-by couldn't see the predicament she was in and retrieve her fallen glove. Inevitably she would abandon the wayward thing, leaving it on the pavement. Over the years she'd amassed a small collection of single gloves that she would not throw away. Presumably, that was unlucky too. If Norma put something on outside in, she would not take it off, turn it the right way round, put it on again. That was unlucky. As was putting new shoes on the kitchen table. As was sneezing three times in a row. As was seeing a single magpie. She seemed to have a superstition for all sorts of ordinary events. What Rowan objected to was that it had rubbed off on her. Even though she didn't believe any of it, really. When Eileen had put her new walking boots on the table, Rowan panicked. 'Don't do that. It's unlucky.'

'Don't be daft,' Eileen had said. She'd stared at the boots, wondering. 'Is it?' Snatched them up, threw them on the floor. Superstition was infectious.

Suddenly, Rowan's overnight drive caught up with her. A wave of exhaustion swept through her. 'I have to sleep,' she said. 'I have been driving since eight o'clock last night. I must lie down.'

'Of course, of course.' Norma waved her from the room. 'Sleep.' She was longing to be left alone with Sadie, to fuss and coo unobserved. 'Your bed's made up.'

'Is it?' Rowan was surprised.

'Always has been ready for you,' George told her. 'Ever since you left.'

Rowan went upstairs to the room she'd had as a child. It was as if she hadn't been away. But, if the living room seemed small, this one was tiny. School books that should have been returned on the shelf alongside her copies of *The Hobbit*, *Breakfast at Tiffany's* and *Lace*. Her Wet Wet Wet tapes beside her old cassette-player. A picture of a horse galloping through waves, Culture Club and Duran Duran posters on the wall. In the bedside cabinet she found a tidy pile of her old school jotters. All her essays, carefully preserved. Her cocker-spaniel pyjama case lay on the bed. In the cupboard she found her entire childhood. All her favourite toys were there – the little pull-along telephone she'd had when she was eighteen months, a couple of little cars, her Rubik cube, her Barbie doll, a luminous yo-yo, a skipping rope that jingled, her beloved stuffed elephant, Rodney. Why Rodney? She couldn't think. This room was a shrine to her.

She peeled off her clothes, climbed under her old pink and white striped duvet. Wished she could light a cigarette. Knew she couldn't. The Rowan that slept in this room was forever ten years old. She didn't smoke or she'd get a serious talking-to. She lay staring at the ceiling. So tired. She wondered if she'd ever sleep.

Six hours later she woke. That moment of wondering what the hell she was doing in this room, mixed with thinking this was where she should've been all along. Her clothes, washed, ironed and neatly folded were on the chair beside the bed. Her cigarettes lay on the cabinet. Now her mother knew all about her. Well, almost all. She got up. Went through to the bathroom, ran a bath. And fifteen minutes later went downstairs.

Sadie was being proudly carried round the garden by her father. As she bounced in his arms, he was giving her a plant-by-plant tour of his alpines. All her little clothes flapped on the line.

Elvis was curled up in front of the fire. He looked up sleepily when Rowan came in. She went through into the kitchen where her mother was puréeing carrot soup for Sadie's supper. On the unit was a pile of new bibs, a rattle, nappies and other baby stuff.

'You've been busy,' said Rowan.

'We've been to the shops,' her mother beamed.

'Who's been to the shops?'

'Sadie and me. We went to buy her formula, a new little cup for her.' She showed off a new yellow plastic baby cup. 'Oh, and loads of things. I had a lovely time. And she's such a dear little thing. A smile for everybody.'

'You took her down into the village?'

'Yes. She met such a lot of people.'

'You told everybody about her.'

'Oh yes. People were so shocked to hear she'd been abandoned. I don't know. What's the world coming to?'

'Everybody knows about me and Sadie?' Rowan was upset.

'Well, they'd have to find out sometime.'

'I know. But it's so soon. Couldn't you wait? People gossip.'

'Well, this'll be good gossip.'

Rowan felt her life was rushing forward too fast, too soon. She wanted to make a slow comeback. Elvis came into the room. He rubbed against Norma's legs.

'Hello, puss,' Norma gushed. 'We didn't forget you. Tuna and salmon for you tonight.' She bent down and stroked the cat. 'And he's a lovely animal. Such a sweet nature. I think he likes it here.'

'You'd never let me have a pet.' Rowan sounded peeved. She lifted Elvis, rubbed his head, claiming him as her own.

'Well, you were always talking of going away. We'd have been left with it.'

'I might have wanted to stay if I'd had a cat.' This was nonsense.

'You'd think you'd want to stay because of your mother and father, not some silly cat.'

Rowan said nothing. Fiddled with the new bibs. Her mother stiffened, did not look at her. Busied herself with the puréeing and the lamb chops she was making for supper.

'You're not going to have one of your silences?' Rowan accused.

'No,' said Norma. Voice clipped. Hurt.

'Good,' said Rowan. She went out into the garden to speak to George and Sadie.

'Well, congratulate me. I've just had words with Mum. Didn't take long.'

'What about?' George dangled Sadie on the lawn. 'You'll be walking soon, won't you?' Then to Rowan, 'She's a bright little thing.'

'About cats. And me travelling the world. And not staying here with you.' Rowan looked round. 'The garden's nice.' Then the outburst came. 'How come she wouldn't let me have a cat? She said it was because I was always on about going away. But you're here. She never seemed to want to go anywhere.'

'For heaven's sake, Rowan, don't be a baby.' George was irritated with her. 'Your mother's a homebody. Never had a mind to see the world.'

'Well, I did,' said Rowan. 'It's all out there, and I wanted to see it. Still do. And I will. Before I die, I will.'

George stared at his forsythia, thinking about this. See the world before you die. He hadn't until this moment bothered about doing things before he died. But he was past sixty. Thirteen years older than Norma. If death was coming, it was him would be getting a visit. 'You don't see it, do you?' He spoke calmly.

'See what?'

'*You* were her world. You were all she wanted.'

Rowan looked back at the house. In the kitchen her mother was standing at the sink peeling potatoes, chatting to Elvis.

'I didn't know,' Rowan said. 'She never told me.'

Chapter Nine

Two days after arriving home, Rowan braved the village square. She pushed Sadie in her buggy down the hill, dreading whom she might meet, but knowing she couldn't stay in Fretterton without encountering all her old friends.

She knew the score. She'd be an A-list village celebrity and talking point for a few weeks. Then interest would wane. This business of her turning up with a child in tow, a child that was not hers, would be judged and decided upon. Some folks in some bars and shops would declare her a saint, others would say she was a fool. That decided, talk would move on. Gossip stopped for no man. It was a ceaseless river of trivia, sometimes a torrent, always lots of trickles. Facts and speculation. Rowan decided she'd be a swift-flowing burn for a couple of days. Soon some other poor soul would be in the spotlight and she would be accepted for whatever gossipers had decided she was.

Sadie's buggy rattled over the pavement, and Rowan turned into the square. She looked round. Nobody. Relief. She walked down the street, stopped to stare with feigned interest at the display of TCP and Optrex in Jolly the chemist's window. Moved on to look at the jumble of faded Mars Bar boxes and pencil cases in Dunbar the newsagent's. Next stop, Rossi's. She looked fondly at the giant plastic ice-cream cone that had been in the chip-shop window for the past twenty years. How awful if the hideous thing had been replaced! The place would not be the same without it. She read the menu. Fish and chips, sausage and chips, scampi and chips. Chicken tandoori and chips. That was new. Ah well, life goes on.

Claudia Rossi saw Rowan standing outside, contemplating plastic ice-cream cones, menus and the meaning of life, and rapped

97

frantically on the window, waved and came out. She was fat. When she and Rowan had been best friends, Claudia had been thin, gorgeous and the queen of the sixth year. A different date, a different drama every Friday night.

'Hey.' Claudia spread her arms, scooped Rowan into them and kissed her cheek. 'I wondered how long it was going to take you to come and see me.'

'I was settling in,' Rowan apologised.

'I know. I know. It takes some getting used to. Being back here.'

Rowan nodded. They stood considering one another. She's got fat, thought Rowan. She's too old for that haircut and those jeans are too tight, thought Claudia.

'Well, look at you.' Claudia stepped back. 'You're so . . . you're so . . .' She plainly didn't like the new-look Rowan. Bleached hair, pierced ears, those jeans and black jacket.

'Sophisticated?' suggested Rowan. 'Urbane? Cosmopolitan? Gorgeous?'

'Yes.' Claudia sounded unsure.

'Slutty?' Rowan added an alternative suggestion.

'We-ll,' said Claudia. 'No. I wouldn't go that far.'

'And look at you,' said Rowan.

'Don't talk about it.' Claudia felt apologetic. 'I got three children and a husband who likes to eat.' She looked at Sadie. 'And this is the baby.' She knew all about Sadie. 'Poor little thing.'

Sadie, who had been getting shown about the village since she'd arrived, gave Claudia her best smile.

'She's a sweetie,' Claudia crooned. 'I love babies. I want six – at least. So what does she do?'

'Do?' asked Rowan. 'She eats. She sleeps. She shits in her nappy. She's a baby. What do you think she should do?'

'Is she reaching out for things? How's her spatial development? I've been reading all the books. My little Joey's so advanced.'

'Ha!' Rowan rose to the challenge. Child-upmanship, was it? Sadie would not be outdone. 'Ah, but can he ride a bike?'

Claudia stared at her. Ride a bike? At six months? It was a joke, surely. God, she hadn't done that in years. She'd taken motherhood so seriously. 'Only with no hands,' she boasted.

'Sadie can play the violin.' Sadie sucked her knuckles, demonstrating her genius.

'Joey is working on his Third Symphony.'

They smiled at each other.

'So how are you?' said Claudia. 'Come in. Have an espresso. What are you doing these days?'

'Eating. Sleeping. Now I come to think of it, shitting.'

'Like Sadie.'

'We're soulmates.'

Claudia made a mental note to lighten up with her children.

Inside the shop Rowan was welcomed like the prodigal daughter. The whole Rossi family came to her, embraced her. 'Ah, Rowan.' Claudia Senior came beetling across to her, smiling her face off, arms reaching for her. 'Rowan. It's so good to have you back.' She held her close. Then took her face in her hands. Alarming, and perfect, red fingernails. 'You're not planning on leaving us again?'

'No,' said Rowan. She didn't dare admit she had been.

'And this is your little girl.' Claudia Senior looked at Sadie, looked back at Rowan in delight. 'She's beautiful. Beautiful! Just like you.'

'She's not mine,' Rowan said.

'I know. Everybody knows. But you've rubbed off on her. She's got your expressions.'

'I don't suck my knuckles.'

'Wait till she gets to teenage. You'll start.'

Claudia Junior watched. Her mother never joked like that with her. Perhaps she should go away and come home again, then her family would fuss over her. All her mother did, she thought, was criticise. 'You're too fat, Claudia.' 'You fuss your children too much, Claudia. Leave them be.' 'Do you think you can get away with wearing that, Claudia?' 'You should do something about yourself, Claudia. Get your hair done. Look at your nails. Join a gym. Why don't you use lipstick, Claudia?' Here was Rowan looking young, younger than she did, anyway, cool and dammit, Claudia thought, *thin*. Thin was easy when you hadn't actually carried and given birth to your child. She was jealous.

Customers were ignored, left standing holding their bars of

chocolate and pints of milk whilst Paolo came to Rowan. He stood back from her admiring her. He could make love to a woman at fifty yards. Rowan remembered him ten years ago.

Afternoons, all that time ago, Paolo would sit at the open window, one floor up, looking at his Alfa Romeo (the babe-mobile before the Beemer) parked by the kerb below. Music, Gerry Mulligan or Stan Getz, always played – a stream of smokey saxophone that brushed past him and out into the air, to mix with the sounds of cars and country buses and people talking small talk. He'd speak Italian to someone behind him, scarcely glancing over his shoulder. He wore a sky-blue crew-neck cashmere sweater, sleeves pushed up, hairy arms. He was gorgeous, he knew that. Sometimes he would watch women below and speak to them softly, a flowing, lilting drift of words, incomprehensible to the one he was speaking to, but such a croon that they'd squirm and redden and look to their feet for reassurance. Looking up at him made them doubt themselves and husbands, lovers, their whole lives and the ham or kippers they were taking home for supper. Paolo did that to people.

He did that to Rowan now. 'Rowan. You look gorgeous. You've grown up.'

'People do that,' she said crisply. Aware of the effect he was having on her. The pangs inside her knickers. She wasn't going to give him the slightest inkling of what he was doing to her secret places.

'I'll take you to dinner,' he offered. Right there in front of everybody. Not that his family noticed. They were used to his flirting.

'I've got a baby now,' said Rowan. 'I won't be going out nights for the next fifteen years.'

'That's right,' Claudia Senior agreed. 'You tell him. He's too old to behave like this. Time he settled down, had children of his own. You tell him.'

'Time you settled down, had children of your own,' Rowan told him.

'I will with you.'

Rowan grinned. Reddened. Paolo had won. He always did with women.

They brought Rowan a cup of espresso from the back shop. A tiny gold cup with a couple of mouthfuls of intense sweet brew that they drank themselves throughout the day. Whenever Rowan was with the Rossis she felt they did not need a house or a shop. All they needed was the constant smell of Lavazza and the proximity of each other. This was a family.

Claudia Senior took Sadie behind the counter, fed her a tiny spoonful of vanilla ice cream. The child took it suspiciously into her mouth, tasted it, sucked it down, tongue moving against the roof of her mouth, then she opened her mouth wide. More.

'You've corrupted her,' said Rowan. 'Next thing she'll be round at the Squelch drinking Guinness with Jude and the regulars.' Thinking about this: 'Is Jude still here? Does she still live in the square?'

'Yes, above the newsagent's. Mamie still lives above the Rialto. Miss Porteous across from her. Everything's just as you left it,' young Claudia told her. 'Except old Walter. Remember him?'

'The birdwatcher.'

'That's him. He died last month.'

'Really?'

'Yes. His flat's empty.' Claudia pointed to the building across the square. 'Nobody wants it. People want the new houses on the hill.'

'Right,' said Rowan. She looked across at Walter's old flat. First floor in the red building across the way. Six-paned windows, and wilting winter-flowering pansies in the box on the outside sill. 'That's interesting.'

She refused the offers of lunch, saying that her mother would already be mushing vegetables for Sadie. Claudia Junior sighed. All the years when she and Rowan had gone to school together, been best friends, she had envied Rowan her mother. Norma was so quiet, so devoted. She never took tantrums. She didn't make a fuss when Rowan hadn't wanted to eat with her family. 'There's a sandwich in the fridge if you want it.' Claudia's mother created hell if someone missed the family meal. 'Mealtimes are for us. Family is the most important thing in the world. What is it you have to do that you turn your back on your family?'

'I just wanted to go to a club with my friends. Maybe have a Chinese first,' Claudia remembered saying weakly.

'Chinese? Chinese!' Claudia senior threw her arms in the air. 'What sort of food is that?'

Rowan's mother had quietly stood back and let Rowan go off to college. Then to London. No nagging. No hysterics. Claudia had grown up knowing she would end up working in her parents' shop. No way out for her. Rowan was so lucky.

Rowan walked home up the hill, spirits raised. She wished she belonged in a huge Italian family. She had notions of bustling mealtimes, plates overflowing with pasta, people waving their arms, talking, arguing. If she ever married, and she doubted she would, she wanted a wedding like the one in *The Godfather* – music, wine, people dancing in a huge garden, people putting their arms round each other. She sighed. Claudia had got happy and fat. She did not know how lucky she was.

No 4, The Square had been empty for a month, ever since Walter Dean died. A retired postman, he had come to the village twenty years ago seeking the peaceful life. He wanted to walk and to birdwatch. A quiet man, he'd come and gone in his green waxed coat, walking boots and corduroy trousers. He made a few friends, went to the pub evenings, left after a couple of pints. He said little. His arrival all that time ago had caused few ripples. He was shy, nobody knew much about him. They'd assumed there was nothing much to know. He'd only been a B-list village celebrity, and at that only for a fortnight after he'd first appeared.

His daughter lived in Australia, had not come back for the funeral. His ex-wife expressed no interest in his death. So, after arranging Walter's cremation, Rodger Snype, the village solicitor who'd leased Walter the flat, let Oxfam have what they wanted and had left it at that.

Viewing the flat a couple of weeks after the Rossis had told her it was empty, Rowan found Walter's cracked leather walking boots sitting next to the hallstand, an umbrella propped neatly against the wall beside them. The house had three rooms; its cavernous living room, with Art Deco fireplace and high corniced ceiling, contained two red tublike chairs on either side of the fireplace, and a grey sofa with wooden arms against the wall. In the window

alcove was a small desk and chair and a filing cabinet with W.D.
(War Department) stamped on the side. The carpet was a deep
bluey-grey. She liked it. The kitchen was sparse – with a fridge
that had seen better days and a gas cooker that was immaculately
clean; Walter kept it scrubbed. The units were painted blue. There
were two small bedrooms, one with an ancient wooden double
bed, one with an ancient wooden single bed, looking out over the
back yard. Not so much a garden as a narrow walled stretch of
tangled overgrown lawn, lupins, nettles and foxgloves. A yellow
bird clung, chittering wildly, to a withering stem.

Rowan watched it, then went back into the living room. She
sat at the leather-topped desk by the window swinging in the
seat, looking out at the Square. A good view; she could spot
all the goings-on. Then she rose, idly opened each of the five
drawers, peered inside. She found a couple of hard-backed note-
books and some old photographs. A fifties' family by the sea. A
man with trousers rolled up, paddling, holding squealing children
by the hand. The same family in a summer garden, sitting on
a daisied lawn waving old-fashioned, rather flaccid, sandwiches
at the camera. Fish-paste, Rowan decided, peering closely at the
group. Spread before them on a white cloth was a teapot and cups,
fruit cake, bags of crisps and a bottle of lemonade. An ample
woman, a comfortable broad-faced person in a vast floral frock
that was never going to be part of any style revival, grinning so
hugely her face almost disappeared, a shiny little girl with hair
swept firmly from her forehead, tied with a bow at the side,
front teeth missing. Beside her was a small man – Walter Dean,
Rowan presumed – tanned, bald, button-nosed. He looked like
Santa after a close shave. He wore an open-necked checked shirt
and wide trousers. It was such a cosily familiar scene, Rowan
could have wept to be part of it. It reminded her of her own
childhood.

She liked Walter Dean. Here was a man she could have talked
to. She propped his photographs on the mantelpiece and turned to
the books. They were not, as she dreaded, meticulous notes of a
humdrum life. She did not want to read the worries and confessions
of the man she had so recently come to admire. He might let her
down. He might not turn out to be the quiet, strong, humorous

person she'd decided he was. No, they were observations of a dedicated birdwatcher.

4 April, 1989. 4.40 p.m. Westhills Farm, on the Loch Gill road, three miles from main turn-off, five Northern Wheatears, three female (grey-brown sight face mask), two male (grey crown, black face mask), flying south. Possibly passing through, unlikely to take up residence in these parts.

10 April, 1989. 6.10 a.m. Gowan Wood, south edge, Green Woodpecker (male) foraging on ground for ants. Very exciting. Will return next week, check if it is nesting.

12 April, 1989. 3.20 p.m. Two Collared Doves on main road past Gowan Wood, tasteful buggers, pale buff with pinky colour underneath and of course, neat little black collar. You'd think they were upmarket undertakers. Didn't think they were going to move for the car. But at last minute they flew off. I like Collared Doves. They seem to be on the increase.

As Walter had become more comfortable with his notes, his written conversation with himself became more and more relaxed.

10 May, 1990. Magpies in Gowan Wood. I have been watching them for a while. Amazing antics. The other week there was a gathering of them, forty, more. Couldn't count. They were chattering, jumping up and down on the branches, chasing each other. They were just like the kids in the Square. I think it's a meeting where the young bloods show off to the girls.

20 May, 1990. Touch of flu, could not get to my Magpie watch for a week. Returned today. Only two now. The party's over. All the young dudes have gone off. They'll be mating, looking after kids, grubbing for food. That's where lust gets you. The two make mating look lovely. I could do with some of that. The male hovers about a foot above his lady. It's exquisite. What's he doing? Showing off? Telling her he'll protect her? I don't know. It reminds me of me. When me and Jean first got together, married, I was going to protect her. I was going to keep her and make enough money to give her anything she wanted. And I couldn't wait to get home to her. I started work early, finished early. We'd spend whole afternoons in bed. I loved to see her come to me. And I'd watch her move about the room. Her hair hung right down her back. We'd play Sinatra and Ella Fitzgerald. The joy of it. I could make her come and come and come. I could do that then.

Rowan snapped the book shut. She felt like a voyeur. She looked round the room, fearing Walter was not dead, but about to burst in on her and find her poking about his private property. She stood a moment, ashamed of herself. Then could not resist a further peek.

25 May. Marie and the kids coming to lunch Sunday. I'll do a nice roast and get in an apple pie. Then must see about pension on Thursday, and stock up at supermarket. Doubt if I'll get back up to the Magpies till the 25th. I expect they'll manage without me. In fact, the way they're behaving they'll be wanting a bit of privacy.

Rowan turned to a later entry.

1 September. 3.30 p.m. High-pitched call, an abrupt little song. Tiny bird, constantly moving amongst the conifers. Goldcrest, I thought. But no, got a good look. A green back, white supercilium and black eye-stripe. My heart stopped. At last, a Firecrest. Well, well, well – the years I've wanted to spot one. Cheeky little blighter. Marie called by this evening. Haven't seen her since she brought the kids to lunch last May. She phones, though. She is moving to Australia. God, she's turned into a beauty. I watched her drive away in her little red car and I thought, That's the last I'll see of you, lass. It was raining, chucking it down. I thought about my Firecrest in the trees. I wondered if the little thing was warm enough or if this weather would take it. Hearts are always getting broken.

Rowan did not want to read any more. She did not feel she was up to any more sadness. She found Walter's pen in the desk drawer. A fine, sturdy pen, thick and black with a gold nib. The sort of pen the doctor had used to write indecipherable prescriptions for foul-tasting brown medicines when she was little. She unscrewed the top, opened Walter's last book and wrote.

22 April, 1992. 6.45 p.m. A yellow bird in the back garden. Jiggling and singing a constant song.

She did not know what the bird was, so she opened one of the reference bird books from the filing cabinet and thumbed through it. *Yellowhammer*, she found. *Resident. 17cms. Yellow bunting, usually seen perched on top of bush. Bright yellow head with black underparts. Female less yellow.* Rowan went back to the notebook.

Yellowhammer, she wrote. Male probably, judging by the cheek of him. Too cocky by far. I like it here. I have been looking it over with a view to moving in. Think I will. This will be my home till Eileen appears. It has a good feeling. I could be happy here – well, happyish here. Sadie and I will have the bigger bedroom till she needs a room to herself. One day soon I will go to Loch Gill Forest to check up on Walter's Firecrest. Did it fare better this winter than me? Hearts are always getting broken.

She crossed the room and sat on the bashed dark red tublike armchair by the fire. She was beginning to feel settled. Which unsettled her. She worried about becoming too comfortable and losing the urge to wander. She lit a cigarette.

The town was not the same. The cinema had been de-henned. Rowan put her hand to her mouth. *De-henned.* The cinema had had hens running around in it. Until now it hadn't struck her how odd this was. It had been part of her youth; she'd accepted it. Still, she didn't think the cinema would be the same without them.

Last week she had run into Mamie Garland who owned the Rialto. Rowan had steeled herself for the usual comments on how thin she'd become and what had she done to her hair. But Mamie said a casual hello, as if the last time she saw Rowan was yesterday and not umpteen years ago. It was a sign of acceptance. She was slipping off the gossip A-list. Mamie knew all about her. No need to discuss it further.

'So,' said Rowan. 'No more hens in the Rialto.'

'I know,' said Mamie. 'Had to do it. Had to move with the times. It may be all right for a hen to cluck through a Doris Day, Rock Hudson film. But your Coppolas and your Scorseses, you can't have hens with them.' Then she dug her hands into the pants of her pin-striped suit. 'Besides, the health folk said they were a hazard. Not that it matters, as nobody comes to see films these days.' She looked mournful. 'There's all sorts of new folk moved in to this village. The world has caught up with us.' Then she leaned over, touched Rowan's arm, lowered her voice. 'We are no longer alone.'

Rowan knew what she meant. The new folk weren't local. She, however, was. No matter how far she travelled, she'd always be local. It was comforting to belong.

The room grew dark; from across the Square came the rollicking *yee-hah*! of the Country night at The Squelch. Slow cars rattled past, lights momentarily grazing the ceiling as they squeezed up the narrow street below. It was noisy here, busy here. There was a thick grey-blue carpet to lie on, an elaborate ceiling to gaze at. She thought, This'll do whilst I'm waiting for Eileen. Right now, for Rowan, 'This'll do' was as good as it got. She stood up. Tomorrow she'd take the key back to Snype the solicitor and tell him she wanted to move in. Meantime she had to break the news to her mother.

'I have grown up,' Rowan said to Norma.

'That's just a technicality,' her mother countered. Growing up was something that had happened to her daughter whilst nobody was looking. It had taken her by surprise. 'You've only just got here and now you want to go.'

'Only down the road. Five minutes away – less. Like I said, I can't stay here for ever.'

'But you could move into your new place and a couple of days later that woman' (she never referred to Eileen by name, as if that small denial might keep her away – she had given her heart to Sadie) 'could turn up, take Sadie and then you'd be away again.'

'Look' Rowan said, 'I need space to be on my own. I'll soon start getting in your way. We'll argue – you know we will. I'm messy, and you hate that. You'll still see Sadie. Every day if you want.'

'It's not the same,' Norma complained. 'What'll everyone think? They'll think we don't get along, that's what.'

Rowan didn't know what to say. She didn't want to insult her mother. She just wanted a cigarette. Norma Campbell refused to allow the filthy reek of tobacco in her home. So, whenever Rowan wanted to smoke she hung out of her bedroom window like a naughty teenager, blowing the evidence of her addiction away into the wind.

'How are you going to pay the rent?' George asked.

'I'll have to get a job,' Rowan said. Turning to her mother: 'You can have Sadie all day whilst I earn some cash. You can't keep me.'

'What about the deposit?' George was always practical.

Rowan shrugged. George sighed. Went to the chest of drawers in the living room, brought out his cheque book. 'How much?'

'George!' Norma protested. 'You're encouraging her. If she has a place of her own she'll smoke herself to death. I know all about it,' she said to Rowan, 'how you hang out the window. You've been seen. The neighbours,' she said before Rowan could ask.

'Let her go,' said George. 'It's only down the hill. Not as far as she was originally planning to go.'

Next week, she and Sadie moved into Walter Dean's old flat. She had the tub chairs, the old desk and the filing cabinet. She put Sadie's cot in the big bedroom. Inevitably, as she went to bed Rowan would pick up Sadie and take her with her. It was good to have such a confident little sleeper to hang onto in the dark.

Nights she lay in bed listening to the laughter of late-night drinkers leaving the lock-in at The Squelch. Night after night the same old faces would gather round the bar eyeing everybody that entered, expounding the same old gripes, laughing at the same old jokes. Wasters and dreamers, Rowan thought. Then sat up. That was why people like her parents scoffed at her dreams: they thought drinking after hours at lock-ins was the inevitable fate of dreamers. They were convinced she'd end up with the losers at The Squelch, locked in, drinking gin, overtired and telling weary jokes.

There were four jobs available in the village. One as receptionist in the doctor's surgery, one serving behind the bar at The Squelch, one in the canning factory and one at the *Gazette* – setting up the small ads, fetching tea, taking messages. She applied for them all. She wasn't suitable for the surgery because she wasn't a comfy sort of person. Nobody would want to confess to her unsuitable or embarrassing conditions over the phone. The Squelch thought her too sophisticated. 'We want someone jolly,' they told her. 'Someone to keep folks drinking.' She admitted she wasn't good at jolly. Sadie was sick on her jacket the day of her interview for the canning factory. She was late turning up and missed the job. 'We want punctual,' they told her.

She got the job at the *Gazette* because Nelson, the editor, liked her CV, her haircut, and her. She was unnerved to be alone with him in his office. This man had been the love of her young life. Whilst her classmates in the second year went stupidly giggly over Paolo Rossi, Rowan to her immediate horror remembered having wet dreams about Nelson Hayes. She crossed her legs and stared out the window, trying not to blush. They had been steamy young dreams. He was older now. The mop of curling hair was greying. She loved that. He wore jeans and a grey jacket. Drummed his fingers as he spoke. It wasn't rude. He just thought more quickly than he spoke. He was impatient with himself. He still wore rebel shirts. Today's was black, open at the neck. She loved it. Bit her lip lest she found herself telling him.

'What were your duties in your last job?' Nelson asked.

'I did Mr Frobisher's letters, his memos. Filing. Hated that. He had writers and illustrators he wrote to. Monthly reports. Stuff. I fended off folk he didn't want to talk to. You know the sort of thing.'

Nelson nodded.

'Then I brought him coffee. Mopped up when he spilt it. And every four weeks it was my turn to go for the biscuits.' She looked at him. 'I always bought ones he hated. Terrible, that. I'm ashamed. He was so nice to me in the end.'

'Did he ever find out?'

'I told him,' Rowan said. 'I apologised for the coconut cookies.'

'Well,' said Nelson. 'You seem to be bolshie enough in a small-time way to fit in here. Start a week Monday. Nine o'clock.'

He loved the way her attention wandered from him to whatever she was watching out of the window. She bit her lower lip. She shifted in her seat. She smiled sheepishly when she confessed about the biscuits. She was different. He liked different.

'I hate ginger snaps,' he told her. 'I'll be looking out for them.'

'Ginger snaps,' said Rowan. 'Nobody hates ginger snaps.' If this was a double bluff, she was impressed.

It was the best job with the best pay, but she couldn't help being disappointed. The cheery mindlessness of the canning factory appealed to her. She had no real idea of what went on there. Every summer, lorryloads of raspberries arrived one end, left the other in lorryloads of tins. The place reeked constantly, overwhelmingly, of cheap sugar. She imagined long conveyor belts of gleaming cans shuffling ceaselessly along, stopping to get filled with fruit gloop, shuffling along again to be sealed, labelled, packed and sent off into the world. She thought watching it day after day would be therapeutic. She fancied herself in green overalls and hairnet, spending her days watching peas or whatever it was being canned that day splash into cans, singing songs from the hit parade and yelling bawdy remarks at the top of her voice over the conveyor-belt clatter and bustle.

She spent the week from moving into her new house and starting work making and breaking decisions. Every day she vowed to clean up, paint the walls – anything, anything to keep herself busy. 'What I do not need to do,' she told Sadie, 'is think.' But that is exactly what she did every day. 'It isn't you,' she lifted Sadie, danced her little feet on the floor. 'Love you. It's me.' She had thought she was going to travel the world, see all sorts of exciting things and places. But here she was, back where she'd started from, once again about to embark on what Eileen called 'the boring nine to five'. She was angry at herself for not spotting Eileen's intentions. Whilst she wasn't looking where she was going, Rowan felt she'd got on the fast track to innocence.

She loved her new flat. She could show Sadie the goings-on in the Square. Feel the child's breath on her cheek, watch her earnest huge-eyed stare. Mornings, carrying Sadie, she'd walk over to the chip shop, buy milk and a packet of cigarettes. She could exchange baby chat with Claudia Junior, flirt with Paolo. There was always someone to say hello to. She was beginning to enjoy herself. She just wasn't ready to admit it yet.

Elvis, the opportunist, quickly took to his new life. It did not take him long to find his way to Rossi's. He settled comfortably on the window ledge outside, perfected his hungry look. Titbits aplenty were offered. He got fatter. Soon the local joke was that Elvis was alive and had been spotted outside the chip shop. As time passed he no longer fitted snugly on his ledge. Overfed and deliriously happy he'd settle, one paw hanging over the edge. In time the chip shop became known as Elvis's. The name remained long after he was gone, long after he was forgotten and nobody could remember why the place had such a strange nickname.

On the Sunday before Rowan started work she realised it would be five days before she had a day off and that she had wasted a whole ten days prevaricating, when she should have been doing something constructive. Or at least enjoying herself. She stared ahead blankly, considering the business of enjoyment. When had she last done that? Had she *ever* enjoyed herself? How did you do that anyway? What exactly *was* fun? Fun for Eileen had been jazzing around at parties. Smiling too much. Drinking too much. Making major dramas out of minor emotional hiccoughs. She lay on the sofa, Sadie on her stomach. 'What's fun, Sadie? You should know, you're nearly six months old. So what is it? Blowing party tooters? Wearing silly hats? Making whooping noises? Boogying on down? Saying, "We're mad, us"? Tell me.' She danced Sadie's hands in time to a Madonna track on the radio. 'Let's have some fun, whatever it is. We'll go look for old Walter's Firecrest. See if we can spot his capering Magpies. Have a picnic. We'll tell stories. Or I'll tell stories, and you listen. That'd be more interesting for both of us.'

She put Sadie in her seat in the front of the car and took the Glen road out of town. Humming along to an old Motown on the tape, tapping her fingers on the steering wheel she felt slight pangs of happiness. Every few miles she stopped the car, pointed out to Sadie the site of one of her youthful memories. The picnic spot her family drove to on hot summer days, just by the bend in the river easily reached from the road. Her father hated leaving the car out of sight. He'd fuss about turning so he didn't have to reverse out. And when that fuss was over he'd fuss over his primus stove. He'd insist on, 'A proper brew-up. Nothing tastes right out of a Thermos.' They'd spread a tartan travelling rug on the grass, and always ate tinned salmon and cucumber sandwiches – always soggy – that her mother brought in a plastic box. After the fuss and the food and when everything was cleared away, her mother and father would split the paper. Read. Then pretend to read whilst they slept. Then they'd just sleep.

Rowan and Claudia Rossi would go looking for caterpillars which they'd collect in a jar. 'We had this dream of collecting a thousand caterpillars that would turn into a thousand butterflies, and we would set them free. Watch them fill the air.' She grinned. It had seemed so simple then. 'Maybe we could catch a million caterpillars, and a whole cloud of a million butterflies would scatter up over the village. They'd cover the sky,' Claudia enthused, her black eyes shining. She was enthused then, in those fleeting years before she gave herself over to chocolate bars, fish and chips, Stu MacGregor and Stu MacGregor's appetite for Italian food. 'Of course if it was Sunday, Claudia wasn't allowed to come,' Rowan said. 'Sundays are a big day at the Rossis'. Mama Claudia cooks.' She turned to Sadie, explaining, 'You know, seriously cooks. Much waving of the arms and tasting of sauces. She gets up at five in the morning to start. In fact, she starts the night before. They are big-time family folks. Not like us.' Sadie looked at her mildly. Blew little saliva bubbles.

She drove on a few miles, stopped again by a track that led into a dense conifered forest. 'See that track? It leads to a grassy sort of clearing bit. That's where all the parking goes on. You know – sex. Half the village was conceived there. That's where me and Duncan Willis used to come. It's called "going down the track". If anyone says you've gone down the track with a bloke, everyone'll know what you've been up to.'

Teenage nights she would rumble up that track with this week's love. Trailing larch would brush the top of the car. They'd park between the trees where it was dank, dank and sweet. It smelled of moss and cigarettes and cider. The ground was littered with cans tossed from steamed-up car windows, cigarette butts, condoms and Snickers' wrappers; the quiet air broken by Bono's incandescent howl on tapes, *With Or Without You oooh-ooh*, and the groans and mumbles of young lust from jiggling cars.

She put the car into gear, revved the engine. Laughed out loud. What seemed so urgent and sweaty then, seemed wonderfully innocent now. 'Eileen would have been a big hit down the track. She always went all the way.' Pulling back into the road she warned Sadie, 'Don't let me catch you going down the track. What am I talking about? You won't go down the track. You won't be here – neither will I. Eileen'll come fetch you, take you away, and I'll be off, too, round the world. There'll be none of this small-town hanky panky for you. For either of us, in fact.'

Then a feeling of sadness surged through her. She didn't want Eileen to come back. She didn't want to part from Sadie. She leaned over the steering wheel, peering into the trees. Was anybody there? Was any naughtiness going on? 'Too early in the day,' she said. Then, 'I won't let her take you away. I will fight her for you.'

She drove to the top of the glen and, leaving the Beetle in the car park of the Drover's Inn, she took the path up to the fishing pool, Sadie a sleeping dead-weight in her backpack. It was one of those balmy spring days when all sorts of tiny creatures took, in frenzy, to the air celebrating the warmth. 'They are fools,' Rowan said, panting, for the climb was harder than she remembered. 'They've come out to play too soon. They do not know the dangers of spring frosts. A couple of chilly nights will see them off before they have a chance of any naughty moments down the track.'

The fishing pool was three miles from the car park. The path, tree-lined on one side, exposed to the open valley on the other, was at first rubbled, much trodden by guests at the Drover's working off their set three-course lunches, and steep. Half a mile up, the path levelled off and the grass became lush because most lunchers would climb no higher. 'Grand view,' they'd wheeze, patting their chests, gazing back longingly at the Drover's, a tiny red-roofed speck far beneath them. Then they'd consider with wilting interest the path ahead. After a level hundred yards or so it sloped cruelly up. 'But enough's enough.' Only an intrepid few tackled the sheer climb up past the Scots pines, then down the half-mile into the valley, to the fishing pool.

Rowan did so today, hands against her thighs, easing the ache of rudely awakened muscles. Her throat burned from too many cigarettes, and bitter, nicotined saliva moved against the back of her tongue. 'Got to give up,' she coughed and vowed. Her heart thumped. Sweat lay in beads across her forehead, across her upper lip. She listened to the child's soft breathing against her neck and to the thud of her feet on the track. The air was scented spring, a soft wind blew down from the hills. Every few yards she turned and walked backwards, relieving one set of leg muscles, awakening another. But at least walking this way round, she had the view. At last, she reached the top. She stood a moment breathing, triumphant that she'd made it. Below her she could see the pool, a small lochan. The river stretched beyond it, sometimes deep, sometimes flowing in turbulent torrents over stone and rock, from the loch several miles up the glen.

She'd thought the downhill part of the walk would be easy. It wasn't. Her ankles ached. She thought that at any moment she would slide onto her bum and descend violently, clumsily straight into the water. Small stones scattered and tumbled ahead of her down the track. She looked at her feet, clumping through the heather. Her precious boots, her dreaming boots, were scratched.

Eileen, Rowan remembered, had considered them with disdain. 'They make you look frumpy.'

'I don't care. I don't want to look desirable in any way. Frumpy's good. Frumpy's safe.'

'You want kick-ass stilettos. They'd keep you safe.'

'Walk the world in stilettos? I don't think so.'

Eileen shrugged. 'Whatever. It's your dream – wear what you want. But I wouldn't be seen dead in them.' Pointing at the boots.

Rowan wondered if Eileen was teetering, right now, down long dusty roads. No, not her. She'd have hitched a lift. She'd be sitting in the passenger seat of some expensive car, giving the driver glimpses of a leg he would never touch, pouting at him with lips he'd never kiss, talking to him about his car, the journey, an undertow of juicy things, promises she'd never keep. She'd be tempting her way round the world. Actually, when she thought about it, Rowan couldn't imagine Eileen tramping remote places. She was a city girl. Maybe she was doing a tour of cities like Amsterdam, Rio, Tokyo. Where the hell was she?

Still, and rumoured to be fifteen feet deep towards the middle, the fishing pool was where Rowan and her schoolfriends used to come swimming in her long teenage summers. In those fondly-remembered times, the nights stayed light till dawn and the days were always hot. Logic told her that this could not have been true. But she took comfort in this small nostalgic rewriting of the days of her youth.

But when she reached it, the fishing pool surpassed her memories. It had fallen out of fashion. New generations of young dudes did their showing off and displaying in clubs and pubs. She remembered how she and her girlfriends would thrill and simper when Duncan Willis and his cohorts ran along the rocks and threw themselves into the air, smashed into the water, giant waves foaming round them. The bigger the splash, the bigger the man.

The girls would sit on towels on the bank drinking Coke, smoking, talking about true love and real relationships. The boys would strut and shout, discuss football and music and move their shoulders in a manly fashion. Then the boys and girls would pair off, swim to the far bank to lie on the soft lush grass that grew under the willows to make love, or at least, do some seriously heavy petting. Undisturbed by any adolescent swaggering, the lilies round the edge of the pool had grown dense, and the willows on the far side trailed the surface of the water. The trees behind the water were deciduous, at this time of year, tenderly leafy.

The air was soothingly cool. Shaking from the effort of her climb, Rowan stood staring across the water. Recovering. After a few minutes looking into the distance, absently watching some small birds move in undulating flights around the willows, she slipped the backpack to the ground and propped it against a rock. Sadie did not wake. Rowan took off her frumpy boots and thick woollen socks, rolled up her jeans and walked slowly up and down the edge of the water, easing her feet. She pulled off her jersey and threw it to the bank. Then her T-shirt. 'What the hell,' she said. Her jeans and knickers joined the bundle of clothes. A swift glance checking Sadie was still asleep, then Rowan waded into the pool and swam to the other side. She slid in and out of the lilies, staring back across the water. Sadie seemed far away and worryingly tiny. She should go back to her. But this was wonderful. Moving through the water, swimming along the sunshine track. She did a slow crawl back, but stopped midway to tread water and consider her surroundings. She had forgotten how small and vulnerable swimming in the fishing pool always made her feel; the surrounding landscape – mountains with vast waves of conifers sweeping across them – was so immense. She ducked under the water. Turned on her back, floated a foot or so below the surface, staring up at the sky, letting her breath bubble out of her till her lungs were empty. Still she floated, lips stubbornly pressed shut. She started to ache to rise back into the fresh air, but stayed under. Her lungs hurt. She forced herself further under. The need to resurface pushed through her. She stayed down, strumming her arms by her sides till her body could no longer defy its need. Then she burst through the surface, scattering showers of sparkling water around her, mouth wide, gasping. The world was still there, still quiet. Only the chirping of Willow Warblers and Long-tailed Tits that dashed like flying commas amongst the far trees. She somersaulted and plunged back under, pushing herself deep. Too late she remembered the secret of swimming in the fishing pool. Do not disturb the sludge at the bottom. Tumbling down, too fast, she stuck her arms out into the mire. Clouds of ancient silt spread up round her, filth. She twisted into it, panicked. Then rose spluttering and wheezing out the murky water she'd swallowed.

Wailing caterwauled over the pool. Emerging from the deep it seemed to Rowan that noise was all there was. Sadie, finding herself abandoned in this strange wide, empty place was screaming her rage and fear, face red, little fists flailing. A man was standing over her. Rowan started for the bank as he put down his fishing rod and leaned towards the child. By the time she emerged, streaked with gunge from the bottom of the pool, the man had picked Sadie up and was jiggling her, an awkward comfort. Sadie was silenced. The man turned to watch Rowan's frantic scramble ashore. It was Nelson, editor of the *Gazette*, and her new boss person.

'It's you,' Rowan told him.

He held Sadie out to her. 'Your baby was making a bit of a fuss.'

Rowan did not take her. 'I'm wet.' She looked around for something to dry herself on. Picked up her discarded T-shirt and ineffectually rubbed her body with it.

'The secret of swimming in the pool,' Nelson did not bother to hide his amusement at the state she was in, 'is not to touch the bottom.'

She scrubbed herself with the damp T-shirt. He watched as she desperately tried to pull on her jeans, jumping up and down to force them over her wet legs. 'I know that.' Jump. Jump. 'I forgot.' Jump. She put on her sweater and reached out for Sadie. 'Thank you.'

'No problem.'

'I'll have disturbed the fish. You won't catch much now.'

'Wasn't going to fish here.' He gathered his rod. 'Going upstream. Too early in the day, anyway.' He walked slowly off. All she could do to regain some dignity was to make a face behind his back. 'If that had happened when I was thirteen,' Rowan told Sadie, 'I'd have been a mess. But as it is, I thought I coped rather well. I'm cool. I didn't mind him seeing me naked and filthy. Oh God.' She pulled on her socks and boots. Put Sadie into the backpack and started home.

The bird that flew out of the farm woods was yellow. Vivid yellow, with black wings. It floated from the trees, a slow careless, fuck-you flight along the road in front of the car. It perched on a fence-post and, she was convinced, stared at her. Marvin Gaye sang *Let's Get It On*. She stopped the car to stare back. It did not move. She thought this staring thing would go on for hours; she would not be the one to give in, move. Sadie broke the spell. The sudden stillness had broken the lulled dreaming into which the car's movement sent her. She cried out to be picked up, and the bird flew away. Drifted back into the trees. Disappeared. The road, the farmlands still brown, the grass roadside grey, the trees, starkly budding – everything seemed drab without it.

Rowan intended to look up the bird in Walter's book as soon as she got home, but as she was taking Sadie from the back of the car, she met Mamie Garland clinking back from the SPAR.

'Italian Chardonnay,' she said, lifting the bag. 'Thing about having actual Italians living nearby, the local shops have actual Italian food and wine. Come and celebrate your homecoming tonight.'

'I'd love to, but I can't.' Rowan smiled her apology.

'Why not?' Mamie didn't take refusals kindly.

'I have this one.' Raising Sadie towards her. 'I have to stay in nights these days.'

'Bring her. It's just round the corner. We'll watch a movie, drink wine – eat nibbley things. It'll be grand. We won't have to chat. No regrets. No recriminations.'

'I can't bring Sadie. She goes to bed at six.'

'Bring her. I love babies. They're little and cuddly. And they fart without shame. You can put her carrycot thing on one of the golden divans. You can't start her too young. We have to think about her film career.'

'She wants to be a lawyer. She told me. Lots of money.'

'Nonsense.' Mamie put her face close to the child's. Won a smile. 'See? She's a star. You'll come. Screening starts at seven, after Sadie's settled.'

Mamie had arrived in town forty years ago with her friend. For several years they ran The Squelch – the Jubilee Arms back then. 'In them days,' Mamie would stuff her hands into her pockets, and rock on her heels, establishing her authority. She was an expert on them days. 'In them days the beer was warm and everyone enjoyed a cheese sandwich and a singsong.'

Mamie's cheese sandwiches were a legend amongst the town's older drinkers. 'There was nothing like them. Cheese, just cheese. Sometimes onion. But cheese,' was the most accurate description of them available. People pleaded with Mamie to produce the famous sandwiches at pub dart nights, but Mamie always refused. She knew the truth. The sandwiches were the stuff of golden memories, nostalgia. And nostalgia was best left back where it belonged, revisited only in memory, never to be recreated. In secret, dark moments she'd allow a small truth. 'They were crap. Absolute stale rubbish. Tired bread, curling at the edges, sweaty yellow cheese.'

She'd look in the mirror doing a stale cheese sandwich imitation. This admission was only made to herself. Most of the time she embellished the myth. 'None of your cellophane rubbish for us. We kept our sandwiches under a pure white Irish linen teacloth on the bar. Let the air at them. A good cheese sandwich has to breathe.' Those in the know doubted this, but didn't like to say. Mamie in authoritarian mood was awesome. And, hell, why deny someone a bit of cheese sandwich glory?

'In them days my friend and me used to entertain the lads with our act.' They'd relived their showbiz days putting on the show they'd done for the troops in Gibraltar and North Africa – a mix of Noël Coward songs and quickfire naughty jokes. More innuendo than lewd. Mamie's friend, Lavinia Hattersley, played the piano; Mamie leaned on it.

One raucous evening, someone poured the remains of their beer into the piano. After that the beering of the piano became a ceremonial occasion. Anyone who won at darts or sang a song all the way through remembering the lyrics was given the glorious honour of buying a round for the piano. The instrument became squelchier and squelchier till at last only two or three notes sounded true.

'One for me, one for you and one for the piano,' privileged drunks would cry. And everyone would gather round cheering. Soon the Jubilee Arms became known as the Squelchy Piano. Then, affectionately, as The Squelch.

'Them were the days,' Mamie said, looking beatifically sad. Then, leaning into whoever she was telling her tale to, and she told it often: 'My happiness went the way all happiness goes. *Phfft.*' She threw her fingers into the air. 'It blew away.' Lavinia took off with Rosie Carstairs, who was younger, handsomer than Mamie, and was killed in a car crash on her way south to London. *Where folks like me are more the mode,* she wrote in her goodbye note.

'She was always a city girl,' Mamie said, no bitterness at all. 'And that's the story of me. And of how the Jubilee Arms became known as The Squelch.'

'How did you come here in the first place?' Rowan asked, when it was her turn to hear Mamie's tale. She'd been sixteen at the time.

'Well,' Mamie smiled. The question pleased her. 'It was the

smell.' She shoved her nose up, sniffing. Searching for that old aroma that made her put her roots down. 'Oranges. I was passing the fruit shop up Robertson's Wynd and there was a huge display of them outside on a big tray. The air was full of them.' She drew a fulsome amount of air into her lungs. Grinning and rolling her head, enjoying her memories, as if they were around her, in the ether. 'And there was the smell of someone making soup. Ham bone. And washing on the line. You could hear the crack of sheets flapping in the wind. Voices from windows. Lives being led. But mostly it was the oranges. Reminded me of Christmas. "Vin," I said. "Vinnie, this is where I want to be." And she said, "OK, Maim. If it's what you want, it's what I want." But she didn't. She was city-minded. She only said it to please me. Still, ten good years we had.'

'Weren't you angry at her, running away like that?' Rowan asked.

'I forgave her that long ago. But I was so angry at her for dying. I'd wake in the night and cry into the dark, "Why did you go and do that?" I was *so* angry! But you've got to forgive. It's good for you, forgiveness. She's up in the cemetery now. We buried her in her Rita Hayworth dress – a Gilda number – though I always thought she was more of an Ava Gardner. She preferred Rita, though.'

Lavinia's headstone was pink marble. *Here Lies Lavinia Hattersley (1910–1956). She died in pursuit of pleasure. Another glorious scandal. Go for it, Vin.*

'I hope she's shocking them all up there.' Mamie pointed to the heavens.

The Rialto, when Rowan entered it that night, had not changed at all. The walls of the foyer were still lined with the huge framed pictures of stars. 'Proper film stars,' Mamie said, welcoming her, taking the bottle of Australian white Rowan offered her. 'Proper charisma.'

There was James Stewart, Robert Mitchum, Kirk Douglas, Rita Hayworth, Kim Novak, Elizabeth Taylor, Lavinia, Sean Connery and Burt (after Lancaster), Mamie's prizewinning cockerel. There were more stars lining the stairs to the balcony – Jerry Lewis, Elke Sommer, Jayne Mansfield, Bing Crosby, Gene Kelly and another picture of Burt. This time with his preferred hen Ingrid (after Bergman).

For the first time Rowan realised that the beautiful bare-shouldered woman between Clark Gable and Dean Martin was not an actual Hollywood star. 'Is that her?' Rowan breathed admiration. 'Your Lavinia. She's gorgeous.'

'I told you she was. Yes, that's her.'

'My God,' said Rowan. 'Didn't people mind? This being such a wee place. And you and Lavinia – well, you know. Two women.'

'Couple of dykes.' Mamie was proud. 'Scandal, did you say? Oh, such a beautiful scandal. It was lovely. Vin loved it – but she would. She loved being in a scandal. Revelled in it. Put on special scandal-raising frocks. But, it passed. Folk got used to us. There were a few wouldn't look my way. Still are. But for the most part people got bored by our scandal and moved on to talk shock about other things. There's always some doings to discuss. Fourteen-year-olds getting in the family way. People running off with other people. Husbands beating wives. Wives beating husbands. Incest. Deaths. But they're not beautiful scandals, these things. Murky. You'd know all about that.'

'*Me?*' said Rowan.

'You've caused quite a scandal, turning up in the middle of the night with a baby that isn't yours. A beautiful scandal, I'd say. You are a courageous person, Rowan Campbell.'

'I don't feel courageous. I think I'm a bit foolish, if you must know.'

'Nonsense. You've turned up. Dropped like a new and shiny stone into our little pond here. You will make a difference. Things will happen. Ripples. You'll see.'

They drank wine from long glasses. Ate Napoli salami and pecorino. Sadie slept on her special bed on the double seat between them. The cinema was empty. Flecks of dust danced in the light filtering from the projection room. They watched Mamie's favourite film, *Somebody Up There Likes Me*. 'Hey,' said Paul Newman, bruised and battered, 'sumbody up der likes me.' And Rowan burst out crying.

'There,' said Mamie. 'A good film should do that.'

Rowan cried harder.

'For goodness sake,' Mamie said. 'What's wrong?'

'It's the film,' blubbed Rowan. 'It's everything. Nelson saw me naked this afternoon. He didn't even react.'

'Nonplussed, was he? Nelson always is. It's an act. He'd have been plussed all right, believe me.'

'He didn't even seem to look. I was plussed. I was plussed as hell.' She sniffed, continued her reasons-for-crying list. 'It's having all my money stolen. Coming home. I wanted to be off seeing the world. I had dreams.'

'Don't you like it here?'

'Yes. But I don't want to.'

Mamie snorted. 'You young ones make life so complicated. Sometimes I'm glad I'm a wrinkled old dyke.'

Chapter Ten

Life became routine. Rowan rose, fed Sadie and Elvis, took Sadie to spend the day with her mother and father. Trundling the child in her pushchair, she walked up Robertson's Wynd past the fruit and veg shop and Pamela's Pantry with its wrought-iron TEAS sign squeaking in the breeze, and the smell of fried bacon belting from the ventilator in the wall. Then up the long brae to the terrace of Victorian houses where her parents had lived since they were married over thirty years ago. A neat house, perfectly carpeted, sprayed three times a day with Gardenia air-freshener.

George and Norma were always waiting at the breakfast table, George ensconced behind his *Telegraph*, Norma drinking tea, listening to the radio and making comments about the news and weather. 'It says rain. We won't be able to take Sadie to the park if it rains.' Whatever she said George would always answer, 'Uh-huh. Suppose.' He could not bear any conversation before ten in the morning.

Unless, of course, it was his one-way dialogue with Sadie. He'd developed a special bond with the baby. To begin with, Norma had found caring for the child exhausting. On their first day Rowan had phoned them several times, checking that everything was all right. 'Put her down on her back.' 'She'll need her coat on. It's cold.' Now Sadie was part of Norma and George's life. Norma loved it sometimes. Resented it sometimes. Why should she be tied by a baby that was not actually her daughter's? Why should her life be so disrupted by some distant woman's selfishness? Rowan shouldn't just assume they'd always be available to care for the child. Then again it was nice, yes, just plain nice, to have a young one about the house again.

As soon as the child arrived the two would jump from the table, hurry through the living room and down the hall, arms outstretched. 'Here she is, little darling.' George would always win the welcome run down the brown and gold patterned carpet. He'd sweep Sadie from her pushchair and, folding her into him, putting his face close to hers, he'd coo, 'And how are you today? Did you sleep all night?' Muttering endearments, 'Snookums. My favourite little dumpling,' he'd carry Sadie back to the breakfast table to tuck her in behind his paper and chat about the shares on the Financial Index. Rowan could never quite hide her jealousy. As far as she could remember, her father had never allowed her into his inner sanctum behind the *Telegraph*, far less called her his favourite little dumpling. Until Sadie came into his life Rowan would never have guessed her father included the word 'snookums' in his vocabulary. Several times, her mother, noting how miffed Rowan looked, would grip her arm, confiding, 'He never ever called me snookums, either.'

After leaving Sadie with her folks, Rowan would take an absurd and devious route back to the Square to the *Gazette* office, avoiding her old childhood haunts. She figured she was too young for nostalgia – besides, revisiting the mischief scenes of her early years embarrassed her; she did not remember them kindly. She knew her childhood hadn't been unhappy, she just couldn't bring to mind anything about it that pleased her. She also dreaded meeting any of the people she had gone to school with. She didn't want to have any conversations about what she'd been doing. The myth was that she'd been living the high life in London, clubbing, going to parties, mixing with celebrities. She wasn't ready to confess she'd stayed in most nights listening to her radio and reading travel books. She rather liked her new image as city sophisticate.

At work, Rowan sat behind the front desk at the *Gazette*; she answered the phone, took in small ads, the church news, compiled the *Country Roundup* from the bits and pieces various organisations sent in. The Women's Institute's monthly meeting had taken place on 30 April. Erica Nisbit had won the W.I. bakery competition with her Raspberry Pavlova, Sonia Hetherington had come top of the chutney section with her walnut pickle, and Jean Watson was awarded first prize (again) in the floral section with her arrangement of dried flowers and early-flowering pansies entitled *Prayer for Bosnia*. Rowan enjoyed taking in the small ads, noting that in the county there was a neverending supply of guitars, ice skates, moquette sofas, dance shoes, budgie cages and fish tanks for sale. She found it all absurdly fascinating.

On Monday afternoons she went round to collect the horoscopes from Miss Porteous. They were always left, sealed in a manila envelope, on the hallstand just inside the front porch. Miss Porteous hated to be disturbed. Rowan would take the long route back to the office, down the hill and round the green, then back up to the Square through the back lanes. Ambling mildly in her high-heel boots, staring at walls and into gardens, thumbs hooked on the back pockets of her jeans. Once she caught a glimpse of herself reflected in the window of the empty shop in Robertson's Wynd that had once been the shoemaker's. She looked gaunt. Hair bleached, roots showing, ears pierced, silver earrings dangling. She wore a white shirt, jeans and a pink linen jacket Eileen had picked out for her.

Three weeks after Rowan's arrival in London, Eileen had decided she needed a revamp. 'I'll reinvent you. Make you interesting.'

'Don't want reinventing,' Rowan sulked.

''Course you do. We all do. A little reinventing makes life worth living. Who am I going to be next?'

At the end of a gruelling Saturday, Rowan came home reinvented. Her hair was bleached and cropped even shorter than it had been when she arrived, and it was short then. She'd had her ears pierced and sat all night in the kitchen twisting the studs as the jeweller recommended.

'Leave your ears alone,' Eileen scolded. 'It isn't cool to fiddle with them.'

'I want to fiddle,' Rowan said. 'They feel weird.'

She was wearing her high-heel boots, jeans tighter than she'd ever dared before, a plain white shirt that cost more than she thought any plain white shirt had a right to cost. In her wardrobe hung the pink linen jacket, reduced, left over from the autumn sales, and her black leather jacket.

'I've spent too much. That was my travelling money.'

'You can never spend too much,' Eileen insisted. 'Besides, all that stuff will see you on your way. Leather jacket? Can't go wrong with that. Linen jacket? A summer perennial. I know, I used to be in the fashion trade.'

'Did you? What did you do?'

'I covered Paris and London for an American magazine. Bedlam. Absolute bedlam. Couldn't get into Vivienne Westwood. Had to stamp and cry. Made such a fuss they didn't dare leave me outside.'

'What magazine? I didn't know you wrote for magazines.'

'Oh, I didn't do it for long. I can't remember the name of the magazine I worked for.' She looked into the air, thinking. Pretending to think? Then waved this tiresome remembering business away. 'Doesn't matter.'

Rowan was unaware of the stir she'd caused, reappearing in the village in a Beetle, defiant hairstyle, child in tow. Now, tapping Miss Porteous's manila envelope against her leg, making her way back to the Square, she met herself. Coming towards her was a girl, younger than she, wearing tight jeans, white shirt and linen jacket. Her hair was bleached and cropped, silver, Inca-style earrings dangling. Rowan watched her pass. Then walked several yards backwards, watching her go. That's me, she thought. Hope she's making a better job of being me than I am.

She always stopped off at the chip shop for an espresso and a gossip before returning to the office. Only family, and one or two privileged friends, would get that tiny gold cup of dark sweet brew brought out to them from the back shop. Rowan would clasp the cup in her hand, sip and watch the Square, people passing. Claudia would prattle small tales, tittle tattle that she had the knack of turning into epic stories of love and death, hate and betrayal. 'Mary Reynolds tripped on the pavement outside yesterday. Ripped her tights. She could sue the Council, get thousands of pounds. Thousands and thousands. She'd be able to leave her husband and go live in Monte Carlo.' And she could take fascinating stories and turn them into tittle tattle. 'See that Jean Gibbs that died last week? Well, when her family went through her things they found twenty-five thousand pounds stuffed into three chocolate boxes. You know, the big fancy ones with the pictures of flowers or *The Haywain* on the front.' The *Nuns' Chorus* hummed somewhere behind them.

'What about you,' Rowan asked, still staring out at the Square, 'how are you?'

'It was Cadbury's Milk Tray,' Claudia informed her. Details. It was all in the details. Her stories, her view of life. 'What do you mean how am I?'

'I dunno,' said Rowan. 'It's a remark. Something you say. "How're things? Has this been a good day for you so far? Are you happy?"'

'I'm fine. What do you mean, am I happy? What sort of question is that?'

'An ordinary, everyday sort of one.' Rowan put down her cup.

'Are *you* happy?' Claudia countered.

'When Sadie's about. Then when she goes to bed and I'm alone I can get quite wretched thinking about having all my money stolen. I kick the chair and stamp about.'

Last night, after an evening thinking about Eileen and what Eileen might be doing with her money, Rowan had got ready for bed. When she was cleaning her teeth, a bland activity, visions of Eileen came to her. This time she did not come, however, as a goodtime girl advocating mischief. She came with that throbbing boredom she always turned into malice.

'Let's do something naughty. Just for the hell of it.'

'Can't be bothered,' Rowan had replied.

'Oh come on. Don't be a bore.'

'I'm not a bore,' Rowan defended herself. 'I'm naughty more often than you think. And you are naughty less often than you make out.'

'Oh you,' Eileen said. 'You've got it all planned, haven't you? Your whole life is laid out neatly before you,' she accused. 'Well, take care, young Rowan. The best laid plans . . . blah, blah, blah. Know what I mean?' Two weeks later she'd disappeared.

Rowan spat toothpaste into the sink and stared hard at her foamed reflection in the mirror. For the first time she realised how desperately unhappy Eileen must have been. 'She screws up all the time,' she told her reflection, waving her toothbrush. 'Poor soul.' It dawned on Rowan at last that if Eileen really *was* travelling round the world, she'd be making a mess of it. 'Poor soul.' Rowan decided she was finished with Eileen. Pity did that every time.

Now she asked Claudia, 'Doesn't anything make you kick the sofa and stamp about?'

'No,' Claudia said.

'You should. It's cathartic.'

Claudia didn't answer. Rowan shrugged, told Claudia she was sorry – she hadn't meant to upset her, and left.

Paolo ran after her. 'Don't be wretched in the evenings. Come out with me.'

'No.' Rowan did not hesitate in refusing.

'Why not?'

'You know.'

'No, I don't.'

'You've slept with every woman in town.'

'Not true. There's Mamie Garland and Miss Porteous.'

'Oh piss off. You know what I mean.'

They watched as a beat-up, rust-encrusted, mud-splattered Mini-van took the Square by storm, tooting. It shuddered to a halt outside the *Gazette* office; two heavy, mild-mannered black Labradors on the back seat missiled forward, crunched their snouts on the front seats, then glumly climbed back into position, yawned. They were used to this. Lord Dorran got out, flapping some sheets of A4 paper – his *Country Crack* column. Leaving the van door wide open, keys in ignition, engine chuntering, he strode into the middle of the road where he stood, arms on hips, legs apart, glaring across at the chip shop. A small fury of a man, thinning grey hair, ageing twills stuffed into green wellingtons, check shirt, two generations old, flapping in the gusts trapped and eddying round the cluster of buildings.

Paolo laughed, stuck a sneering thumbnail under his front teeth and snapped it out, upper lip leering, curled. 'Old man.' There were a million insults to choose from, but Paolo with his perfect bum and costly hairstyle reckoned old was as vile as any insult could get.

Lord Dorran reddened, stiffened and stood his ground. 'Filthy foreigners.' His dogs bent their heads, watched the stand-off mildly, yawned again.

'Uncle Bruno?' Rowan asked.

'Uncle Bruno,' Paolo nodded.

Years ago, Paolo's Uncle Bruno, on a visit from Sicily, had been caught on Lord Dorran's land carrying a gun. His bag had been stuffed with a grouse, a pheasant, three lapwings and a kestrel. Uncle Bruno had been fined heavily and now refused to come back to see his family. Not that the Rossis minded. Uncle Bruno always overstayed his welcome for at least a month, eating too much and drinking too much. Then there were the dead birds in the freezer. But the family honour had been undermined. Paolo felt duty bound to return the glare and the aggressive stance.

At last, Lord Dorran moved. Making expansive, I-am-important arm gestures, sweeping aside any underlings who might get in his way, though there was nobody about, he strode into the *Gazette* office. 'Your damn receptionist is over there with those chip-shop louts,' he yelled as he burst into Nelson's office, slapping his copy down on the desk. 'My monthly piece. See the cheque is in the post.'

'Righto,' sighed Nelson. He longed to get rid of the monthly *Country Crack* column and replace it with something more up-to-date, but how could he? Lord Dorran was his father-in-law.

When Rowan got back into the office, Nelson called her in to see him. 'How come it takes you three-quarters of an hour to go round the corner to collect the horoscopes?'

'I walked slowly?'

'You went to the chip shop.'

'Who told you that?'

'Lord Dorran.'

'Old telltale.'

'You're talking about my father-in-law.'

'Sorry.'

'And while we're at it, stop smoking in the office. I hate it.'

'Sorry.' She turned to go. At the door, waved her arms in some sort of defiance. 'Sorry. Sorry. Sorry.'

'If that's going to be your attitude, I'll be watching out.'

'What for?' asked Rowan.

'Ginger snaps,' he said.

'Well, you're certainly headed that way.'

Nelson grunted.

Rowan went back to her desk. The man, she decided, was master of the grunt. But then, she knew why. Everyone knew why. Nelson's story was more than first-class gossip. It was a legend, told and re-told in pubs and bars across the County. A story too good to be embellished.

Twelve years ago, before Rowan left Fretterton, Nelson married Lord Dorran's daughter, Justine. They had seemed a fairytale couple. 'A match made in heaven,' Rowan's mother said. Him so handsome, so talented. Editor of the local newspaper and not long past his thirty-second birthday. 'The sky's the limit for that young man,' Norma enthused. And her so rich, so beautiful. Rowan didn't think so. Thirteen years old, wildly in love with Nelson, she thought Justine would break Nelson's heart. Other girls in her class copied Justine's hairstyle and clothes, walked about the Square in junior Justine outfits. Not Rowan. To her, Justine was one of those human beings who seem as if they are fraying round the edges. Always on the verge of tears.

Exquisite, dark-haired, pale, Justine gave the impression of never stopping moving. Once when Rowan was going home after her school play, ten o'clock at night, December and freezing, a frost forming on the cars in the Square, she saw Justine dancing alone outside the County Hotel, wearing only a thin silky frock that folded round her body. She seemed to float across the cobbles, arms spread, and she sang a frail song. *La-la-la.* Rowan stood shivering in the doorway of the newsagent's shop, watching. She was so engrossed in Justine's dance, it was a few minutes before she saw Nelson at the entrance of the County Hotel, also watching. He seemed to be in despair. I knew it, Rowan thought. She's breaking his heart.

It was well-known in the village that Nelson would wake in an empty bed. Mornings, Justine had been seen by the postman and the milkman on the lawns in her front garden waltzing alone. Her cream nightdress clinging to her, she'd sing that same flimsy song, *La-la-la*, never any lyrics, music for her dance. Even in February, drifting across a sugar-coating of snow, she never seemed to feel the cold. In bars and restaurants she fidgeted in her chair, fiddled with her cuffs, stared hungrily round at other people.

'Do I bore you?' Nelson asked.

'No.' She didn't look at him whilst answering.

He thought he bored her. He wanted children. He told the

people he worked with. They told the regulars in The Squelch. Word spread. It was not a happy marriage.

Nelson and Justine moved into a house on the outskirts of the village. Nelson dreamed of taking his longed for children to Dorran Castle, walking the long lawns on summer evenings down to the river to watch the fish, to talk about the movement of water, to consider the light. Justine wanted none of it. Sometimes driving home she would stop the car in the middle of the road, and swoon with teary delight at an old Echo and the Bunnymen track. *'The Killing Moon*, listen to that. Doesn't it make you cry?'

'No,' he'd say. Voice flat with disinterest. He was a Mozart person.

At dinner parties Justine would shove aside her food, light a cigarette and sing the fragile tunes that hummed endlessly in her head. *La-la-la.* 'I'm not wearing any knickers,' she might tell the table. Some would look embarrassed, some would laugh and others – women, mostly – would retaliate. 'Why is that, darling? Can't you afford any? Or haven't you got a clean pair?'

Justine would smile. 'I just don't like wearing them. So restricting.'

Nelson always waited till they got home before he started the argument. 'Do you have to behave like that? Do you have to say these things?'

'Yes.' Then the songs would start. *La-la-la.* Dismissing him. He wondered why he hadn't noticed his wife's strange behaviour before they married. Was love really blind? He went to work in the morning not knowing, worrying what he'd find when he came home at night. Once she'd painted the bedroom red. At least, she'd started, finished a wall and a half, given up and left the rest of the room as it was, white. Then started on the furniture. She gave his shirts away to Oxfam. He had to go and buy them back.

The village knew, of course, that Justine had been a wilful child. Such things were hard to hide in a small, meddlesome society. Justine had been expelled from four schools. Had given up on education at sixteen. Had moved from job to job. A salesgirl in a boutique. Something in advertising. Her father put up the money to start a design studio. It didn't last. Nothing did. When she was twenty-two, she lay in the bath of her flat, turned on the tap and slashed her wrists – ineffectually. Lord Dorran brought her home. The simple country life, with plenty of fresh air, would sort her out, he thought. He had faith in such things as a cure for conditions as diverse as flu and schizophrenia.

When his daughter took up with Nelson, Lord Dorran thought his troubles were over. He forgave Nelson his hideously humble background because they got along. Nelson was his sort of chap. Fished. Didn't say much. In fact, they could communicate a lot by curt nods, pouring drinks or standing backs to the fire, side by side, bums getting overheated. Had anyone asked what the hell it was they were communicating to each other, neither could have put it into words.

Of course, everyone knew why Justine was so, so . . . nobody knew how to put it. 'Loopy?' suggested Mamie Garland. 'Slightly deranged,' said George O'Connell at the County Hotel. Nobody liked to say it was madness. It was such a fragile and beautiful madness.

Justine's mother killed herself twenty years before Justine married Nelson. She drove the Land Rover up the track through the estate forest, parked, put one end of a hose to the exhaust, the other through the passenger window, sealed the car with yards and yards of sticky tape, switched on the engine. She had always been prone to sudden disappearances and unannounced reappearances. It was August, the estate was humming. The shooting lodge full. Jim, the gamekeeper, and estate workers were busy with the grouse shoot on the hill. Nobody worried excessively about her absence. 'She'll be back,' Lord Dorran growled. 'Wagging her tail behind her.' She'd been dead three days at the time. When they found her, they found her note. *It's all so unbearable*, it said.

'What's unbearable?' Lord Dorran asked the gamekeeper, who shrugged. Looked away. He did not know.

Demented with grief, Lord Dorran considered his castle, his estate – his walled gardens, lawns, forest, grouse moors and farmland that had been in his family for over a century, and could not understand how anything could be unbearable. He loved every inch of it. So, he drank. And, at last, decided he must do what he could to make unbearable things bearable.

Every spring he pressed seeds into fist-size bombs of earth bound with yoghurt. He drove about the countryside tossing them into the wayside. In time, there were vibrant clusters of wild flowers – poppies, campion – on all the roads leading from the estate. He called them his Lisa spots. That done, he spread his area wider. There were Lisa spots at crossroads and junctions, round blind bends on roads for miles and miles. Now his bombing raids took him on hundred-mile journeys to motorways and tiny, rutted backroads. Tossing his floral grenades from the sunroof of his Jaguar – his good car – he'd cry: 'Bearable! I'll make it bearable!'

Justine got worse. She'd smear her face with lipstick and run in bra and cami-knickers through the streets. Billy Watson the police sergeant insisted whatever the time, on duty or not, he would be the one to drive her home. By now, Nelson knew his wife was ill. The sort of illness neither he, or Justine's father, knew how to discuss. Far less deal with. Side by side in front of the fire, bums roasting, 'Well,' they'd say. 'What do you do?' Or, 'There you go.'

Once, when she was in the car with Nelson driving down the motorway, Justine opened the door. When Nelson slowed to shout at her to shut it, she jumped out and ran, peeling off her clothes into the oncoming cars. She spent two months in hospital after that. Came out calm – the Justine Nelson had married. It lasted three weeks. Justine stormed that she hated this peace. She missed the ecstasy of her madness. 'I want to go back there. I want my poetry back.' She thought every word she spoke when she wasn't taking her tablets was exquisite. Sanity was dreary. Her voice sounded dull.

One day she disappeared. Came back a week later with a blues band who wandered the long castle corridors saying, 'Get this place. This is great.' They drank Lord Dorran's fifty-year-old port and his Islay single malts. It was Justine's idea that they hold a concert in the grounds. They put up posters in The Squelch and the County Hotel, and all the kids from the village came. The noise boomed for miles, sent Lord Dorran, ears plugged with cotton wool, mind plugged with half a bottle of Bowmore to his bed at half past eight. When he woke at four in the morning he went outside. It was a soft July dawn. The lawns were covered with cans and bottles, crisp bags and 'God knows what else,' he raged. His greenhouses were broken and stripped of peppers and tomatoes. His vegetables had been uprooted and thrown aside. The gates to his field had been left open and his prize Highland herd was halfway to the village. 'If you want unbearable,' he cried, 'this is unbearable!' He drove his Mini-van into the village and stormed through the streets blasting his horn, round and round, waking everybody up. He wanted culprits. Didn't get them. Justine smiled mildly at his fury. Nothing could touch her now. She'd fallen in love.

Mark Harrison was fifteen. Tall, blond, floppy-haired. He wanted to be a rock star and wrote his own lyrics that he'd read to Justine. She was bedazzled. Why did nobody but her see the genius he was? Every morning she was there at Mark's gate to follow him to school. At four she'd follow him home again. She sent him notes, phoned him all hours of the day or night. She thought he looked like Byron, though she had no real idea what Byron had looked like. Mark was simply Justine's private notion of the poet. The boy was flattered. His mother was furious. She accused Justine of harassing her son.

'Nonsense,' Justine said. 'I understand him. I want to encourage him. I have connections in the music business.' She seemed reasonable till she decided the conversation was over. She stared blankly ahead and started her tiresome song, *La-la-la.*

Nelson thought it wouldn't have been so bad if it had been him who discovered Justine and Mark together. But it was the cleaner. Four o'clock in the afternoon, she thought Justine was in the village tailing her love. But she had at last won the boy. He was in bed with her, busy in bed with her. By six o'clock everybody in The Squelch and the County Hotel knew all about it. It was a scandal. Not a very beautiful scandal, Mamie Garland thought. But not altogether nasty, considering the gorgeousness of the people involved. She imagined them lying sleeping, perfect faces, no marks, no stress lines, becalmed on a silken, peach-coloured pillow.

Sergeant Watson drummed his fingers on his desk. The boy was a minor. The woman, however, was Lord Dorran's daughter. He didn't like to tangle with the gentry. Nelson drove home early, but by the time he got there, Justine and Mark had run off together. Nelson never saw her again. They'd been married three years.

Justine sent him a postcard from Amsterdam, then a few weeks later another from Milan saying she was going to India. She told him she was all right. *There are angels lining my path, nobody can hurt me.* Postcards came once a week at first; they always had Justine's poems scrawled on them. *Welcome to my gloom cold mama says/warm your hands at my despair/she wants the world to find her lying there/it's cold, it's cold in there. Don't worry, Nelson. The angels are still here with me.* Nelson worried. Another week, another postcard, more nonsense. *There were cherubs and unicorns leading me through the streets of Delhi. La-la-la.* The woman wasn't safe. Nelson didn't know what to do. He raged. He'd been cuckolded by a schoolboy. He felt a fool. And through all that he fretted that his wife might meet a dreadful end alone out there skipping half-naked through the dangerous backstreets of some city. Amsterdam? Milan? Delhi? Where was she? He wanted to go to her.

Mark came home, head down. After a few days' disgrace staying in, hiding, he went back to school. In time his misdeeds were forgotten, though some schoolfriends considered him a hero. Mamie thought the scandal sumptuous. 'Bittersweet,' she said. 'What have we done to deserve such a juicy gossip. Somebody up there,' pointing upwards. 'Likes us,' the bar of The Squelch chanted.

Nelson came and went, to work and home again. He did not drink at the County Hotel for six months. He thought the whole village was laughing at him. He wanted to rip Justine's postcards up and throw them on the fire, but there was something so frail about them. He could almost hear her fragile voice singing her mad poems, *La-la-la.* After two months the postcards petered out. One came four months later. Then another after a year. Then nothing. He put them in a box and never, ever looked at them. They were unbearable. He loved Justine, he knew that. Now he asked himself why. She was beautiful; he felt proud to be seen with her. But she had always been emotionally fragile. He'd flattered himself he could save her from that fragility. He'd seen himself as her rescuer, a knight in blue jeans. His love had been some kind of arrogance. And that he found unbearable too.

He moved out of the house he and Justine had shared to a cottage up the glen. He fished. He stood with his back to the fire drinking whisky. He survived. He grunted.

Claudia pondered on Rowan's words. They spun round and

round in her head. 'How are you?' Rowan had said. What exactly did that mean? Did it mean are you well? Are you happy? Did she mean how can you be well, or happy when you've stayed in a village all your life, working for your family, working in a chip shop – *and* have got fat? Rowan was so sophisticated now. She'd been away – that great big place, Away – she'd done lots of things.

That night, when Stu came home he found Claudia sulking.

'What's up?' he said, picking up his paper. 'Where's supper?'

'It's not ready yet.'

'Why not?'

'I've been thinking. I'm not happy.' Claudia kicked at a toy car, sent it skimming across the quarry tiles.

'Of course you are. Don't be stupid.'

'No, I'm not. It's that Rowan. Do you know what she said to me? She said, "How are you?"'

'So,' said Stu, 'what's wrong with that?'

'She didn't mean how am I? She meant, "You're fat, Claudia." And she's right. I'm fat. I hate it. I hate me.'

'No, you don't.'

'Yes, I do. I'm going on a diet.'

'Don't do that.' Stu worried that if Claudia went on a diet, he'd have to go on one too. Goodbye, wonderful food. 'I love you. You look beautiful to me.' He came to her. Put his arms round her. 'Please don't diet.'

'I will. I work in a chip shop. Look at Rowan. She's been in London. Done goodness knows what. She's thin. She's got fancy hair. She walks about with that little girl and everyone says, "Hello, Rowan," and, "Hello, Sadie." Nobody says that to me. I've stayed here. I did what was expected of me. I have lovely children. Nobody notices me.' She was jealous.

Stu worried. He watched Claudia put a small heap of flour on her cooking board, make a well in the centre, break an egg into it, pour in some water, some olive oil, and knead the mixture into a perfect glistening ball. He marvelled. How many men did he know who came home to fresh pasta? None. Claudia rolled out the mixture into thin squares. Held them as she fed them into one end of her pasta-maker, scooped out the shredded tagliatelle at the other. It was a miracle, Stu thought.

'I'm not happy,' Claudia complained.

'Well, get happy,' said Stu. 'What will make you happy?'

'That's it,' wailed Claudia. 'I don't know.'

Chapter Eleven

Rowan sighed.

'Sighing, Rowan?' said Nelson. 'It's only twenty past nine.'

'I know, I know. I'm fed up is all.'

'Why are you fed up?'

'I'm fed up being a woman.'

'I won't pursue that line of conversation.' Nelson backed away from her.

'Well, you shouldn't ask,' said Rowan. 'In my next life I'm coming back as something else.'

'A man?'

'No, not that. Too competitive. Too logical. And I don't really like beer. No, I'll be a sloth. Hanging upside down all day in some warm South American jungle. Not moving. Reaching out for a handy leaf to chew whenever I want something to eat. Seems like the perfect life. No washing up. No having to buy a disc for the car. No bills. No crap quiz shows on telly.'

'When you put it like that,' said Nelson, 'I think I'll join you.'

'You're not getting on my branch if you're grumpy and grunt.'

'You're not getting on my branch if you smoke and go off to the chip shop when you should be putting in a hard day's hanging upside down.'

'Ooh,' she said. 'Narky.'

'I'm a narky boss,' he said. 'Been working at it for years.'

'Ginger snaps for you,' said Rowan. 'Or is it no ginger snaps? I suspect you of double bluffing me on the ginger snaps issue.'

Nelson smiled. He liked Rowan. She offered him a new kind of dialogue.

It was an average day at the *Gazette*. Billy Gibbs got quite excited when he heard on the grapevine at The Squelch that a group of sixteen young mothers had gone to the headmaster of the local infants' school protesting that a child with AIDS would be joining Class One next year. 'Quite a nice little story,' he told Nelson. 'We could do a sort of humane thing about AIDS, and then take the mothers' point of view, and the headmaster's, and get the official view from . . . whoever it is you get an official view from.'

The story came to nothing, as did the mothers' protest group. The child was partially deaf, did not have AIDS, just a hearing aid.

Rowan read letters to the *Gazette* about the bus timetable, the monstrous decision to remove the cobbles from Robertson's Wynd and the disgusting state of the American soldiers' feet in the Second World War. *Our boys knew the importance of clean socks.* Billy Gibbs and Freddy MacKenzie decided to fax a radio network with their list of workforce requests. Billy wanted Bruce Springsteen's *Dancing in the Dark*. Freddy argued for U2's *Desire*. 'That's rubbish,' scorned Billy. 'They'll never choose that.' 'It's a bit more modern than Bruce Springsteen. He's past it,' Freddy countered. They got quite heated. Nelson told them to shut up. Rowan wanted The Pretenders' *Brass in Pocket*. They both turned on her for that. 'We're getting bloody nowhere with this list,' said Billy.

Someone handed in the results of the darts competition at The Squelch. The Women's Institute phoned in a piece about a talk they'd had on cooking with a wok. Dr Barnes came by with his weekly health column: *The Perils of Insomnia*. Rowan had a dark phone call from someone in the village who wanted to sell bondage equipment in the small ads. 'I don't think so,' she said. 'You'd be better with a specialist magazine.'

Billy and Freddy argued about who the bondage person might be. Then Freddy suggested to Nelson that they start a dating column. Come five o'clock Billy Gibbs still didn't have a story for the front page. Freddy was in a huff about the list of songs for the radio. And Rowan had decided that in her next life she'd not be a sloth after all. 'A hippo's better,' she said. 'Lying all day in warm mud. And I don't think anything actually eats hippos.'

Nelson grunted that perhaps lions, and he still wanted to be a sloth and why didn't they just fax a list of all sorts of songs and let the radio station pick which one, and they'd all better do more work tomorrow or there would be no paper. Then he went off to the County Hotel for a pint. He sipped it slowly thinking how fine it would be to be a sloth, hanging upside down all day, listening to the sounds of the jungle, reaching out for the odd leaf whenever he fancied a bite to eat. Really, Rowan had something when she said that.

Rowan picked up Sadie from her folks, then walked back down the hill. It was May now and swallows had arrived in force, swooping and squealing. She tilted the buggy back into her, leaned over it. Sadie beamed up at her. 'So how're you? Has it been a good day for you? I've been fine. One whole day and I haven't thought about Eileen once.'

She trundled on into the Square, the evening scent of fish and chips spread on the air. She met Miss Porteous in her black Laura Ashley velvet dress and bright red shoes skimming across the square, top speed, on her way home from the SPAR. Miss Porteous stopped, looked piercingly at Rowan. A look so penetrating, Rowan apologised, though she hadn't done anything wrong. 'Sorry.'

'Don't apologise. It's unbecoming in a young and independent person,' Miss Porteous scolded.

'Sorry,' said Rowan again.

Miss Porteous leaned towards Rowan, looking her legendary mystic self – soothsayer and teller of fortunes. 'You will have a wish come true,' she said.

'Will I?' said Rowan. 'When?'

'Ah,' said Miss Porteous, 'I cannot predict exactly when. I do not ever give precise times, the when and where of things. I do not foretell the future. I only analyse the present, what is happening in the now. And for you, Rowan, Mars and Venus are very optimistically aligned. So I can confidently tell you that you will have a wish come true.' Miss Porteous nodded, affirming her prediction. Then moved on, shimmying through the small gatherings in the Square, and was gone.

Rowan smiled. Smiled and smiled after her. A wish come true. On a soft spring evening, with swallows crying overhead and the allure of the chip shop across the way, what more could a person ask for? She clenched her fists by her side, shut her eyes and wondered what to wish for. Money? A perfect life? Love?

141

Nelson? World peace? No, not that. She did not want to waste her wish on something unattainable. No, she wanted something for herself. Then she thought, maybe she couldn't make a wish. Maybe the wish was already happening. The planets were aligning to make her dreams come true. Maybe Eileen was coming back, bringing with her the stolen money. Maybe then she could take off and travel the world. But then there was Sadie. Rowan did not want to go off across the world leaving Sadie behind. Sadie was a problem. Loving Sadie was a problem.

Rowan stood wondering, then shook her head. This was all nonsense, wasn't it. She was indulging in a rush of speculation about a wish. A wish, she thought. What is a wish? It's nothing. Forget it. Have a fish supper.

'Can't be bothered cooking,' she told Sadie. 'You can have your first chip. Seven months, it says in the books – at seven months a child should be eating chips and drinking lager. I'm sure it said that.' She lifted Sadie from her buggy. 'You're a lucky bum, do you know that? Everything is a first for you. First summer coming up. First chip.'

A bee swam past, floating heavily through the evening. Sadie watched it, face earnest. 'First bee,' said Rowan. 'Then there's all the other things. Loads of stuff. First dance. First wish. First fag. Oh, you'll do it. And hate it. Everybody does.' Listing firsts Rowan went into the chip shop. 'First time you hear the blues, Howlin' Wolf hollering out. Your heart stills. First pair of decent jeans that don't make your bum look fat. First taste of chocolate.' She warmed to her theme. 'You haven't read any Auden, have you? There you go. First poem.' To Jim Rossi, she said, 'A fish supper, please.'

'Salt?' he said. 'Vinegar? You want a pickled onion?'

'Everything,' she said. Then, to Sadie: 'There's a word to get you into trouble. Everything. I want everything.' Then, returning to her original dialogue: 'First chocolate. First sunrise. My God, Sadie, I'm jealous. You've got it all going for you.'

'What're you telling her?' asked Jim.

'I'm listing all the things she's got to come. She just saw her first bee. Think about that. All the things she hasn't seen yet. We take it all for granted.'

'Yeah,' said Jim. 'Suppose we do.'

Claudia Senior came out from the back shop. She wore a black scooped-neck silk top, tight black skirt. A necklace of amber stones. Hair swept fiercely off her face, tied at the back. A tight bun. Nails and lips were bright red. 'Thought I heard your voice. What are you doing buying fish and chips? That's not good for you.'

'It is,' argued Rowan. 'Iron. Vitamin C. All sorts of good things.'

'You should eat fresh,' said Claudia. 'Fresh vegetables. Working, looking after a baby, broken nights . . . You need good food.'

Rowan felt her fish supper slipping away from her. 'Fish and chips *is* good food. *Are* good food.'

'You come upstairs eat with us,' Claudia instructed. 'Spaghetti with mussels.'

Claudia Senior, Mama Claudia, was an irresistible force. She never quietly told people what to do; she issued orders. She shooed Rowan, carrying Sadie, into the back shop. Into the courtyard outside, clay pots filled with lavender, geraniums. Scented air. 'Sadie's buggy is still on the pavement outside,' protested Rowan.

'Jim,' called Mama Claudia. 'Bring in the buggy.' She would be obeyed.

Rowan was one of the few local people who had ever been upstairs into the Rossis' home – the inner sanctum. Giorgio, Claudia's husband, had no intention of letting actual people come upstairs from the chip shop into his home. He did not want anyone to know the opulence in which the family lived. The furniture, wall hangings, original paintings, antiques. He figured if people knew he had all this, they'd know how rich he'd become from selling them fish and chips. They'd decide he'd made too much money and stop coming in to buy them.

'Rowan,' he said, coming across the room to greet her. A kiss on each cheek.

Paolo smiled from across the room. A small smile; he had not forgiven her for refusing to go out with him. From her place by the fire, Claudia Junior said hello. She had sat down on the armchair when Rowan entered the room. She had the notion she was thinner sitting down – less of her to look at. She watched Rowan with envy; thin body, no tits. She wished she could cross a room with the confidence Rowan exuded. Smiling. Hand outstretched. Claudia knew she slunk into rooms hoping not to be noticed. Every time she went out to dinner, to a parents' meeting at the school, she hoped there would be another fat person there. Preferably a fatter person than she was.

'Good to see you,' said Giorgio.

'I've been ordered upstairs to eat with you. Your wife is formidable.'

'I know,' said Giorgio. 'She's been bossing me for thirty years.'

'You need it,' said Claudia. 'Sit, sit.'

Everybody sat round the table. Didn't dare do anything else. Young Claudia sat as far from Rowan as she could. She kept her youngest child on her knee. The other two sat one on either side of her.

'Where's Stu?' asked Rowan.

'Working late. When he does that I eat here.'

Rowan had seen Stu getting out of his car a couple of days ago. He'd gone soft around the middle and was going bald. Once she'd got over the shock, she thought he rather suited it. Stu had grown a thick moustache, a deal of facial hair to compensate for the dearth up top. Claudia and Stu had been the darling couple of the school. A perfect match, people thought, both so young and good-looking. Rowan remembered how the boys in her class had sat staring at Claudia Junior. Her presence in the same room as them emptied their minds of whatever it was they were meant to be doing. She had been exquisite – long dark hair, brown eyes, olive skin. Young men sighed for her. At school dances they thundered across the room to ask her up. Rowan had always felt like the plain, reliable best friend. The one who got the bloke with spots and a passion for heavy metal music on double dates. Now look at her. Her whole body, every movement, every tiny twitch, leaning over the table for a piece of bread, twirling her glass round and round, said unhappy. Rowan thought her old best friend was more than unhappy; she was completely and utterly miserable.

Claudia Senior brought bowls of pasta with glistening opened mussels. Filled glasses with chilled wine. Silence as they ate.

'You eat like this every night?' Rowan asked.

'Of course,' said Paolo. 'Doesn't everybody?'

'You know they don't,' said Rowan.

'You got a boyfriend, Rowan, in London?' Claudia Senior asked. Mouth full of pasta, Rowan shook her head.

'Why not?'

'I never met anybody. Maybe nobody fancied me.'

''Course they would,' said Claudia Senior.

'She,' Paolo pointed at her, 'is a tough woman. She wouldn't go out with me.'

'Why not?' Claudia was shocked. Somebody had refused her boy.

'Well, you know.' Rowan squirmed in her seat. She couldn't say she didn't want to go out with the man who had bedded every young woman for miles and miles. 'I just, well . . . I needed to settle in.'

'Of course.' Claudia understood. 'But you're settled in now. Now you can go out with him.'

Paolo grinned. He knew nobody argued with his mother.

'There's Sadie,' Rowan pointed. 'I can't leave her.'

'You can – you should,' Claudia ordered. 'You have your own life. Let your mother baby-sit. Let *me* baby-sit. Let young Claudia baby-sit. No excuses. You go out with Paolo.'

'He can't go out Saturday,' Claudia Junior protested. 'He has to work.'

'You can fill in,' her mother said.

'I can't do that. I might be doing something Saturday.'

'What?' her mother wanted to know.

'Nothing.' Claudia Junior backed off.

'There you go. All fixed. Paolo, you take the evening off. Claudia, you fill in. Paolo, you work an extra day next week. Let Claudia off.'

Rowan nodded. 'OK.' A wan smile at Paolo.

'Paolo,' Claudia commanded, 'you take Rowan somewhere nice, special. The Greenlands Hotel. Fabulous place. And no nonsense.' To Rowan, patting her hand. 'If my boy isn't good to you, you tell me. If he's a bad boy, know what I mean, you come see me.' She glared across at Paolo. 'Saturday night. You'll take Rowan out. It's fixed.'

Paolo reddened. It was his turn to squirm. His mother had just fixed him up with a date. Oh, the humiliation.

When her mother wasn't looking, young Claudia glared at her. A look of silky hatred. This wasn't fair.

Time to change the subject, Rowan thought. 'This food is amazing,' she told Claudia Senior. 'You're so clever. Why don't you cook like this for everybody?' Expansive wave of her arms. 'You could serve this down in the restaurant where folk sit in. Nobody knows how good you are.' She thought she was being lavish with her compliments. 'You're hiding your light under a bushel.'

At nine o'clock she walked back across the Square to her flat. A huge moon glimmered summer yellow in an indigo sky. Promises of hot days coming. Rowan looked up at it, showed it to Sadie. 'You should be sleeping, Sadie. Late nights will give you bags under your eyes. But look at the moon. There you go, first moon.'

Elvis jumped from his perch on the chip-shop window and followed them home. Late swallows soared in the night sky. From the County Hotel came the drum and murmur of incessant chat. Rumours being brewed.

Rowan got Sadie into her night clothes and gave her a bottle. The child cried, overtired. Rowan held her till she slept, then gently put her into her cot. 'It's been a big day for you. First moon. First dinner party. First bee.'

Rowan bathed, then put on the oversized T-shirt she used as a nightdress. She lifted Sadie from her cot, someone to cuddle in the dark. Climbed into the ancient double bed and slept, Elvis curled up on her duvet.

The fat moon drifted above the village. Paolo lay in his bed, squirming still; Rowan would think he was a mama's boy. Perhaps he was a mama's boy. Twenty-nine years old and still living at home.

Claudia Senior in the room next door, watched the shafts of moonlight spread across the carpet, shine on her Irish linen sheets. Rowan was right – she *was* hiding her light under a bushel. Everybody thought all she could cook was fish and chips, or sausage and chips or plain old spaghetti bolognese. Not even proper spaghetti bolognese. She should let people know. She should cook for everybody.

Claudia Junior couldn't sleep. It was such a night. Such a moon. The sort of moon that unsettled you. Everybody thinks I'm fat, she thought. Fat and boring. Rowan thinks I'm fat. She's come home and she thinks I've let myself go. I have to get thin. I have to do things, like she has.

Lying next to Norma, listening to her soft snores, watching the moon through the chink in the curtains, George thought, Rowan's right. She wanted to see the world. What if I die? I haven't been to Venice. I haven't drunk wine in a Paris café. I haven't been for a ride in a yellow cab in New York. I should do these things. I should take Norma. We should live a little.

Nelson sat in bed drinking whisky. This moon was disturbing. It was the sort of moon that made you shiver. Made you doubt yourself. He shouldn't drink whisky in bed; he'd wake with a headache. He heard an owl outside, that eerie night call. A sloth, Rowan said. Just hanging there, upside down in some humid Amazonian jungle. Chilling out, she'd say. That was her sort of language. Look at the girl. Three weeks she'd worked for him, already she was bantering with Billy and Freddy. Laughing. He never did that. He should relax. Let go. Stop being grumpy. Old before his time. A sloth. Think sloth, he told himself.

Rowan had arrived in the village. She made what she imagined to be mindless, simple remarks. But people didn't think she was their old Rowan. She was a new woman, bringing some sort of city wisdom. She dropped into their little pool. Made ripples.

The fat moon moved towards morning. Rowan slept, innocent, like the baby in her arms.

Chapter Twelve

Judybonk liked bonking. Real name was Hanson, she'd been nicknamed after her favourite activity after she became pregnant for the first time at fourteen. The father of her child was Paolo Rossi, but Judy had chosen to keep his identity a secret. Whenever she was asked she'd recite a raw and famous poem.

> '*Mary, the maid of the mountain glen*
> *Shagged herself with a fountain pen.*
> *They called the bastard Steven*
> *Because that was the name of the ink.*'

Actually in the verse it had been Stephen, but she changed it to match the name she'd chosen for her unborn child. She had, after all, been fourteen and in deep disgrace at the time. She was a rebel. Her defiant attitude, her refusal to act shamed, shocked people. Judy discovered something about herself: she liked shocking people. It gave her some power when she was secretly feeling bad about herself. These days she cringed when she thought of herself reciting that vile verse in the school playground, fourteen years old, hair dyed bright red, cropped, a fake tattoo on her cheek, eyes plastered with make-up.

Girls in her class whispered about her. 'Jude's done it.' At the time she discovered that she really did not care what people thought of her. Besides, she had not known until her son was born how much she would love him. Now she cared, and cared deeply what her children thought of her. And what her children's friends thought of her. Steven had the sort of friends a child with a mother like she was reputed to be, had. Delia, her daughter, a year younger than Steven, rarely brought anyone home. Rarely even spoke of having a special pal at school. Jude had earned herself a reputation that stuck. She was a slut. It was one of Fretterton's longest-running rumours.

The names were run together – *Judybonk*. She'd been known as Judybonk for so long she almost said it herself when someone new in her life asked her name; had to stop herself writing it when signing credit card receipts. Judith Hanson just didn't seem to fit her any more.

She lived in the flat above Dunbar the newsagent's. Had four children, and was aiming for seven. She thought it a lucky number. 'I just love being pregnant,' she told anyone who might raise their eyebrows at either her present achievement or her ambition. 'I'm good at it.'

Paolo Rossi was the father of that first child, Steven. He was born exactly nine months and ten days after a night of passion on the Hansons' grey velvet sofa when Judy's mother and father, Ella and Bruce, were at Country 'n' Western night at The Squelch. Ella on accordion, Bruce on guitar, wearing identical checked shirts, jeans, cowboy boots and hats. They sang Jim Reeves – *put yore sweet lips a little closer to the phone* – and Patsy Cline, unaware of the naughty antics of their little Judith back home.

Up until child number four, Sonia, was born, Judy lived with her parents in the High Street. But then it became obvious she would have to find a place of her own.

On the day that Ella decided Judy and her brood had to go, she had lain back on the sofa in a swoon. Hand on forehead, she announced that the menopause was bad enough, but hot flushes with all these young ones running around was too much to bear.

At the time, little Sonia was asleep in the bottom drawer of the chest in the bedroom, Charmaine was riding her trike up and down the hall, Delia was experimenting with pinking shears on the living-room curtains, and Steven was sitting on the roof with his grandfather Bruce's cigars and a Zippo lighter. Ella stormed from the house. Stood a few minutes by the front door, flapping the Iron Maiden T-shirt she'd acquired after Judy had stopped listening to heavy metal, letting fresh air at her heated body, saying, 'Too much. Too much.' Then she went to ask Jolly the chemist if he had anything for, you know, a sheepish nod, the change. Reeling at the price of Evening Primrose Oil, Ella had gone for a bar of chocolate at the chip shop instead. There, she had sounded off to Claudia Senior on the trials of being a grandmother with hundreds of infants running round her ankles.

A couple of weeks later Judy moved into No 2, The Square. The flat above Dunbar the newsagent's she lived in now. 'Handy for fags,' she said.

The flat was rented through Mason & Snype the solicitors, acting for the Rossis. Over the years the Rossis had quietly acquired every building in the Square. On hearing Ella's distress, fearing Judy might move out of the village, Mama Claudia insisted the flat be given to Judy. 'The boy,' she said at Sunday lunch. 'The boy.' Looking at Paolo, who suddenly found the wallpaper fascinating.

Through Judy's pregnancy and for the first year of Steven's life the Rossis had claimed that the boy had nothing to do with their son – though Paolo himself was strangely quiet on the subject. But the older Steven got, the more obvious it was that Judy had been wronged. By the time the boy was two, his parentage was plain for everyone to see. With his olive skin, long nose, little dimple on the chin, dark and brooding eyes, and tumbling curls of black hair, the boy was a clone of his father. So to make amends, while still not publicly admitting Paolo's guilt, they made sure Judy got the flat for a nominal rent.

'Ten pounds a week?' Judy couldn't believe her luck.

'It's fixed,' Rodger Snype lied. 'The landlord can't put it up.'

'I'll take it.' Judy thought her life had just been saved.

Mama Claudia could now keep an eye on her grandchild. He was fifteen, growing taller and wilder daily, it seemed. By the time he moved into the flat three doors along from the chip shop, he'd already been arrested for possessing cannabis and speed. He smoked. He drank cider Friday and Saturday nights sitting on the pavement leaning on the telephone box – the town's only bright light after eleven. He'd broken into the County Hotel, stolen cigarettes and twenty pounds. He'd broken the windows of his school and driven the teacher's car round the playground at break-time.

Mama Claudia, however, watched him with his sisters. How he

carried them indoors when they fell. Herded them inside mornings when they escaped screaming and hallooing at commuters in their cars, shining from Sunday's polishing. How he brought them across to her shop for fish and chips or ice cream, holding them by the hand. He was, she declared, a good boy.

The children – all girls except Steven – spilled out into the Square every morning. Still wearing their Spiderman pyjamas, they'd take over the pavement on trikes and roller-skates, squealing and shouting abuse at motorists. 'Hey mister,' wild shrill cries, 'yer car's rubbish.' Judybonk would emerge wearing a grubby, pink quilted dressing gown, fluffy mules hanging from her skinny feet, the first fag of the day dangling from her lips. The voice that rattled from her abused throat was harsh. 'Get inside. What huv I told yez!' She'd swipe the air, aiming blows that her children were well used to avoiding. When she failed to shoo them indoors, Steven would emerge, pick up the smallest ones, and usher the bigger ones back through the front door.

Children rounded up, Judy would acknowledge Rowan standing at her window, watching, with a full-bodied wave. 'Hiya, Rowan.' Rowan couldn't tell if this was a hugely friendly gesture, or a bit of morning mockery because Judy thought she was being spied on. Whatever it was, the whole scenario would happen again tomorrow.

Whenever Judy met Rowan and Sadie, she would scrutinise Sadie closely. 'Like her father, is she?' Rowan would grunt a kind of yuhuh agreement. She didn't like conversations about who Sadie looked like. She did not want to talk about Eileen. And she did not want to admit she had no idea what Sadie's father looked like. Or indeed, who he was.

'You've missed the best bit,' Judy told her. 'Expecting is fine. It's the babies get on my nerves.' She waved a cigarette-ed hand towards the sleeping Sadie; smoke wound over her. 'They're fine that age. They don't move and they don't answer back. It's later on gets you.' Puffing deeply, frowning, brow heavy with thought: 'If they could invent a baby that didn't grow up, that'd be the thing.'

After the special showing of *Somebody Up There Likes Me* Rowan would meet Mamie in The Squelch at least once a week for lunch.

Usually when Norma and George drove to Tesco in Perth for their weekly shop, taking Sadie with them.

Mamie was a privileged patron of The Squelch. The landlord always brought her a pot of tea, she rarely drank alcohol. She'd sit in her favourite corner seat, near the fire, aluminium pot and pink-flowered china cup in front of her, knitting. Speaking movies. And, feeling she had showbiz connections, rarely showed up till after midday. She never rose before eleven. Film stars did that. 'I love it here. Love it,' she told Rowan, needles flying. 'You can still walk up Robertson's Wynd and smell people's lives. There is something homey about knowing what people are doing. Not judging. Just knowing. Aroma. That's my favourite word. What's yours?'

Rowan thought about this. 'It used to be "away". That was where I wanted to be. Now it could be "rusk". Or "nappy". I say them a lot. Or "someday". That has a ring to it. An optimism.'

Rowan sipped her Guinness, Mamie dropped a couple of sugar lumps into her tea. 'Guess what,' said Rowan. 'I've got a date with Paolo Rossi on Saturday.'

'Really? Odd choice for you. He's a bit flashy, don't you think?'

'Perhaps. Anyway, it was his mother coerced me into it. There's something about her that you can't say no to.'

'You and Paolo Rossi,' said Mamie. 'Interesting. Ripples are starting sooner than I expected. Are the two of you going to provide us with a little scandal? Something quietly juicy?'

'No,' said Rowan. 'Absolutely. Definitely. No.'

'Still,' said Mamie, 'it might be fun.'

'Yeah,' said Rowan. 'Fun – whatever that is. I could do with a bit of it.'

That night, when Rowan went to pick up Sadie, she asked her mother if she would mind baby-sitting Saturday night. 'I have a date with Paolo Rossi,' she explained.

'Paolo Rossi!' Norma said. 'What are you doing going out with him? He's a womaniser.'

'I know,' said Rowan. 'Great, isn't it? I feel like being womanised. It'd cheer me up.'

Rowan left. Norma stood looking after her. What did she mean, 'I feel like being womanised'? That wasn't right. Norma went through to the kitchen, started to make supper. She fetched an onion from the vegetable basket in the cupboard, set it on her chopping board, sliced the top off. Stared out of the window, knife poised mid-chop.

'What are you doing?' George came up behind her.

'Cooking supper,' Norma said. She did not move.

'Good. What are we having?'

'I don't know,' Norma. 'An onion.'

'What's up with you? You've gone all funny.'

'There's nothing up with me. I haven't gone all funny.'

'Yes, you have.'

'No, I haven't. What's up with *you*, I could ask. You've been playing your old Frank Sinatra records all day.'

'I like Frank Sinatra. I was just lying in bed last night looking at the moon, and I thought it'd been a long time since I did things I like doing just because I like doing them.'

'So you play *Come Fly With Me* all day and drive me mad.'

'Is that what's bothering you?'

'No. It's Rowan. Do you know what she said? She said could we baby-sit because she's going out Saturday night. And then she said she was going out with Paolo Rossi. So I said that he was a womaniser. And she said, "Great. I could do with a bit of womanising." Really. It stopped me in my tracks, that's all.'

'Why?'

'Because so could I. I never thought about being womanised when I was young. I wish I'd had a bit of that before I married and settled down. It just isn't fair.' She aimed a savage blow at the onion. 'I've missed out.'

George stuck his hands in his pockets, stared out of the window. 'Did you see the moon last night?'

Norma continued her attack on the onion. 'No, I didn't.'

'It was,' said George, 'a moon to set you dreaming, fill you with regrets. It made me wish I'd done more living too.'

Back at her flat, Rowan fed Sadie and herself. She slipped into her evening routine. Bathing Sadie. Playing with Sadie. Telling Sadie about her day, how many old mountain bikes and guitars were for sale in this week's small ads, what Billy had said in the office today, the latest update on Nelson's rebel shirts. Dancing round the room with Sadie to tunes on the radio. Putting off the business of laying Sadie down to sleep. Putting off the moment she'd be alone. She hated her evenings alone. She'd pick up the toys, toss them into the wooden chest in the living room. Put the encrusted bibs and dirty clothes into the wash. Clean up the supper dishes. That would take her to eight o'clock. Then she would listen to the radio, sitting in the red tub chair. Reconsider her decision not to get a television. Rearrange herself on the red tub chair sitting sideways, leg dangling over the arm. She'd sigh. Read. Get fed up with reading. Sigh some more. She'd try not to think about smoking. She had given up. Cigarettes plagued her. She longed to light one up. She fretted. She lit imaginary fags, the muscles round her neck ached, she wanted to scream at people. She scratched her thighs. Chewed her nails. Nights, she had cigarette dreams.

At last, when there was nothing else to distract her from her nicotine yearnings she turned to Walter Dean's diaries.

20 June. Keeping my eye on a couple of swans on Loch Gill. Cob and pen and two young cygnets. Nice couple. Homey. One cygnet is a rebel, always going off on its own, just like my Marie. I have cancer. Doctors want to operate – I won't let them. What good would it do? I'm a goner. Saw a couple of buzzards on the way back down the hill. Hate buzzards – belligerent bastards. I have to tell Marie about the cancer. Can't face it.

Rowan looked up. Eyes misted with tears. God, she needed a fag. This was too sad.

29 June. Great sadness: the rebel cygnet is dead. A fox must have got him. Life is cruel, unfair. A vixen – I heard her bark. Is that a bark? More of a howl, or a shriek. Those swans are keeping to the middle of the loch, little cygnet swims between them. Dun-coloured thing. Plenty of fish jumping. I am coughing blood. I watch my body for signs.

A small wind curdled the water. The loch is two miles long, conifers – larch, pine, Scots Pine – right up the far bank and stretching up the mountain so it hazes into one greenness.

When the wind sweeps over the forest it moves, not single trees, but the whole moving as one. Little birds, Goldfinches, take to the air, complaining, and settle again, only to rise and complain at the next gust. They keep themselves busy.

Walked by the shore, the damp sucking my boots, a healthy squelch. Saw frogs. Sat on a big rock. Listened to the loch and the ducks up the near side, rising up flapping, splashing, droplets of water in a drizzle all about them. Drank tea, ate fruit bread and tried not to think. Trick is to become part of the landscape, one with the rocks, trees, damp grass and water. I would like to know the things only swans know. The wind, the depths of water. There are Buntings in the reeds. Chaffinches.

Never felt so sad in years. I was just about to get up and go when I heard this cry, like, '*He-ha-heeya.*' And there high above me, cruising the thermals, circling in that slow way of his – a Kite. Definitely a Red Kite, nothing else like it. That forked tail, that lazy way of his, bowed wings. Oh my. Looked up at it. Sun hurt my eyes, and I was crying. I haven't done that since I was eight. My father hit me for it.

Rowan snapped the book shut. Threw it on the floor. She did not want to read any more. The sigh that she let out emptied her lungs. Oh God. She put out the light and went to bed. Dreamed cigarette dreams.

Chapter Thirteen

Next day, Saturday, the day of Rowan's date with Paolo, Rowan took Sadie to spend the night with Norma and George. On her way home she met Miss Porteous, today in green Laura Ashley frock and blue shoes.

'You said I would have a wish come true,' said Rowan. Miffed at being deprived of wishes.

'And didn't you?'

'No,' said Rowan.

'There was nothing you desired. That you got. Nothing has happened that you wanted to happen.'

'No,' said Rowan. 'Nothing. I have had nothing, not even a cigarette for the last few days.'

'You haven't had a cigarette? You've given up smoking. And did you wish to give up smoking?' Miss Porteous sounded imperious.

'Yes.' Rowan was cautious about the way this conversation was going.

'There you go – a wish come true.'

'But that's not a proper wish. It's not like getting something in my hands.' She made a grabbing gesture. 'A thing. A present. Something unexpected.'

'You young ones are so materialistic. You wished to give up smoking, and you have. I was right. A wish come true.'

Rowan shrugged. She could not argue with this. As she moved away, Miss Porteous caught her arm. 'There will be unexpected developments in your love-life.'

'Oh, come on,' said Rowan. 'I don't have a love-life.'

'You will,' said Miss P. 'Wait and see.'

Rowan didn't believe her. Kept her lips under control, lest they curl into cynicism. Miss Porteous hurtled off. Rowan turned, made her way through the crowd of young boys gathered outside the chip shop. They stopped their chat to watch her. Right now, she was the only thing happening.

'Hey, Rowan!'

She turned. Judybonk was hanging out of her window above the newsagent's, beckoning her. The full-arm wave. Fearing she might tumble headfirst to the pavement, Rowan went over to chat.

'You've hardly spoken to me since you got back,' Judy complained.

'Sorry,' said Rowan. 'I haven't seen you much. Hello Jude, I'm back.'

'Hello, Rowan. Nice to see you back. Is that her,' nodding after Miss Porteous, 'making predictions for you?'

'She said I'd have a wish come true.'

'And have you?'

'I stopped smoking.'

'That's amazing.' By the time the day was out, it would be the talk of The Squelch that Miss Porteous had helped Rowan to stop smoking. 'What else did she say?'

'She told me there'd be unexpected developments in my love-life.'

'That'll be your date with Paolo Rossi.' The full name. No indications of the intimacy Jude had once shared with him. She hadn't forgiven him for abandoning her to bring up Steven on her own.

'You know about that?' asked Rowan.

'It's a small place. Everyone knows about it.'

'Of course,' Rowan shrugged. 'I forgot. Are you going to tell me to watch myself with him? Him being such a womaniser?'

'Oh no,' said Jude. 'There'd be no point in going out with him if you were going to watch yourself. He's only good at one thing.'

'You'd know,' said Rowan.

'I do.'

'Do you ever see him these days?'

'Nah, not since Steven, and he'll be sixteen soon. Paolo hardly speaks to me now. I'm a fallen woman.'

'It's him made you fall. That's terrible.'

'No, it's not. I love being a fallen woman. I can do whatever

I like.' There were screams from behind her. 'I have to go,' Judy said. 'Sounds like someone's getting murdered. See ya.' She shut the window.

Paolo came for Rowan at eight o'clock.

'You look gorgeous.' Rowan couldn't help enthusing. 'Is that Armani?'

'Yes.' Paolo spread his arms, displaying the suit. Did a twirl.

'That's fantastic.' Wasn't he meant to say flattering things to her? Wasn't that the way it was meant to be? She was wearing her frock. *The* frock. Her only posh frock. A plain black shift, short, no sleeves. Nothing to it.

He smiled at her. 'You look nice.'

Yes, Rowan thought, she did look nice. But it was Paolo who would be turning heads tonight.

The dining room of the Greenlands Hotel was full of Saturday-night people in their Saturday-night clothes. She could hear the prattle of their Saturday-night conversations all round her. Holidays, new cars and what Alice said to Dee-Dee in the gym. It didn't make four-star eavesdropping. The room was plush, pink tablecloths, Burgundy place-mats. The waitresses who seemed to Rowan to be either sixteen or ninety hovered politely. 'Enjoy your meal, sir.' Their faces all seemed familiar. Locals. The young girls nudged each other when Paolo came in.

'You've probably slept with them all. Or their mothers,' Rowan accused.

Paolo smiled. 'I doubt it.'

She ate asparagus soup with a heavy spoon, wondered what Eileen would do. She would, Rowan decided, instigate some sort of conversation laden with naughty innuendo. Or she'd be downright dirty. Grinning. Rowan understood the mischief. Places like this invited it. She imagined Eileen slipping her foot from her shoe, sliding it between Paolo's legs, stroking his crotch with her toes. Painted nails. Eileen would pride herself on getting Paolo in a state that rendered him immobile. He'd have to stay hidden behind the table thinking sensible thoughts – income tax, his mother – till his ardour wilted. Or would she have kept stroking him till excitement took its natural course, then leaned forward saying sweetly, 'Now, *that* is premature ejaculation' Rowan smiled.

'Why are you smiling?' Paolo asked.

'Oh, nothing,' she told him. Changing the subject. 'Is it true your father puts his profits in cash in a secret compartment in his Rolls-Royce and drives it to Italy every year?'

This was Rowan's favourite Fretterton rumour. Paolo's father had in his courtyard a 1967 Rolls-Royce – his pride and joy. Every October he drove it out of the village, to Dover, on the ferry then across France to Italy, to Sicily where he had family. Gossip had it he stuffed hundreds of thousands of grease-stained pounds undeclared to the taxman into a hidey-hole under the rear seat.

'Who told you that?'

'Don't know, can't remember. It's a local myth – a legend. That's like asking who told me not to stand on cracks on the pavement.'

'It's a good rumour,' said Paolo. 'I like it.' It was true. But he'd never tell.

Rowan wondered if she'd allow herself to become a fallen woman tonight. The way Jude described it, it sounded a fine thing to be.

At quarter to eleven they were back in the Square. Paolo manoeuvred his car through the milling young throng, baggy outfits, baseball caps and huge shoes, laces undone.

'You gonna invite me in?' asked Paolo. He put his arm across the back of her seat. Face close to hers. The baggy people stared in at them.

'Do you want me to invite you in?'

'Of course.'

'Are you coming in? I'm inviting you.'

'Thank you. I'd love to.'

'Do you find it a curse, being so good-looking?' She wished she hadn't said that. Hadn't meant to. It was just his face was so close to hers. And it was such a face she reached out, touched his cheek.

'Do you mean that I'm so pretty people will think I'm thick? A bimbo? No, I don't find that. Do you find that?'

'I'm not pretty.'

'Who told you that?'

'Me. I told me that.'

'Well, you should give yourself a telling-off. You're wrong.'

'You won't like my coffee if you come upstairs with me. It's instant.' Rowan was beginning to feel womanised. She liked it. Didn't like herself for liking it. This man was far better at flirting than she was.

'I don't want coffee,' Paolo said.

'Neither do I. I've got some whisky. My father brought half a bottle of Glenfiddich to celebrate my new flat.'

'Whisky's good.'

They went upstairs. He sat in the red tub chair whilst she poured them both a drink.

'Your place is nice,' he said, looking round.

'It isn't really. Not compared to your place.'

'Well,' he smiled. 'Still, it's yours.' He put his glass down. 'Are you going to sit over there all night?'

'Are you going to sit over there all night?'

He crossed the room to her. Kissed her. Outside, the Square thrummed Saturday night. The thud of drum 'n' bass from souped-up sound systems in souped-up cars. Yells and cries. The smash of tossed bottles landing on tarmac. Rebels without a clue. Hungry for life. And life in Fretterton had nothing to offer them but a chip shop and a lamppost to gather under. So, they shouted each other's names in wild voices, they gathered under the lamppost getting ready to attack the night as if it was a tangible thing. Rowan kissed Paolo back. She closed herself into him. Let go. The air was soft, the windows open. It was a night for frenzy.

'Listen to them out there. What are they on?'

'LSD. Ecstasy. Dunno.'

'Where do they get that sort of thing round here?'

'They put their money together and somebody goes to Perth to buy supplies.'

'Goodness.'

'There's nothing for them to do round here.'

The baggy throng outside their window seemed to be doing nothing with passion.

'Don't mind them,' said Paolo.

Rowan thought about Jude. She didn't want to, but there was Jude in her head. 'Why do you never speak to Jude?'

'She never speaks to me.' He started to take her dress off.

She unbuttoned his shirt. Kissed each bit of him she revealed.

He tasted of soap and Hugo Boss. She thought she'd taste of baby feeds, sweat and Sadie's shampoo which she'd used before going out.

'Yes, but you're Steven's father – everybody knows that. God, you just have to look at him.'

'She doesn't want me.' He pushed her away. 'Why now? Why suddenly do you want to speak about her?'

'It just came into my head.'

'I don't want to talk about it.'

'Sorry.'

'It was a long time ago.'

'But don't you give her money? She has to struggle.'

He turned on her. 'You think I didn't offer? You think I didn't try? Her parents forbade me to talk to her.' He started to button his shirt.

'I thought it was your parents didn't want her to talk to you.'

'Yes,' he said. 'That too. We were kids.' He put on his jacket. 'I don't want this. Not now. Not now you're talking about Jude. You put me off.'

'She's not that bad. In fact, she's pretty good-looking. I think so.'

'So do I.' He left.

Rowan went to bed. Squirming. Said, 'Oh God,' several times. 'Why did I say that?'

The thumping on the door woke her. She peered through the dark at the luminous dial on the clock. Quarter to two.

'C'mon, Rowan. Open the door.' It was Paolo.

'No. Go away.'

'I want to come in. I want to see you. I want to explain about Jude. I want to tell you. It wasn't what you think. I'm not so bad.'

'I never thought you were.' She went to the door. Didn't open it.

'There's more than you think. I'm not the bastard everyone thinks I am.'

'I don't think you're a bastard, Paolo. Just a flirt. A womaniser, my mother said.'

'I'm not that,' he said. 'You don't understand.'

'No,' said Rowan. She was very tired. 'Go to bed, Paolo. I need to sleep. Leave me alone.'

He heard him flounce down the stairs. Got out of bed to watch him cross the Square. He turned, saw her. Stood glaring up at her. The feeling of being observed crept over them both at the same time. He turned slowly back. They both saw Claudia Senior at the window above the chip shop at the same time. They both waved to her. Then, under the scrutiny, waved to each other. What was it about the woman? One look from her and they both behaved like good little children.

At ten o'clock next morning Norma and George brought Sadie home. Their insistent rapping on the door woke Rowan. She pulled on her jeans and irritably let them in. Sadie was howling. Norma handed her over as soon as she stepped inside.

'Has she been good?' asked Rowan.

'No,' said Norma. 'She cried all night. I think she's teething.'

'Your mother's exhausted,' George said. He went through to the living room, flopped onto a chair. 'So am I. We're too old for this staying up all night stuff.'

'Sorry,' said Rowan.

'When you were gadding about having fun, doing all sorts.'

Rowan said nothing.

'When you were doing all sorts, goodness knows what, we were pacing the floor with your child. It was four in the morning when I finally got my head down. I'm not up to it, Rowan. Just not up to it.'

'Sorry,' said Rowan again. She went through to the kitchen to put on the kettle.

'Yes,' said George. 'We really need our holiday.'

'Holiday?' said Rowan. She looked at Sadie. 'Hey,' she asked her, 'have they mentioned a holiday to you?'

Sadie smacked her cheek, little open palm and bounced in her arms.

'Yes,' said George. 'We're going on a cruise.'

Rowan came to the kitchen door.

'He just sprung it on me last night. He's booked us on a cruise of the Mediterranean: Spain, France, Italy, North Africa. Just us,' said Norma.

'You two?' said Rowan. 'A cruise?' But she wanted to cry, *What about me? What about Sadie?* 'That's wonderful,' she said weakly.

'Yes,' said George. 'I cashed in some savings. "What's that for?" I asked myself. "My old age? I may not be around to see it." So I took some of it and booked us a holiday.'

He'd come home on Saturday night waving the tickets.

'What's that?' Norma asked.

'A cruise. We're off to see the world.'

'I don't want to see the world,' Norma protested. 'I'm happy here.'

'Of course you're happy here. Here will be waiting for you when you get back and you'll love it all the more for having been away. Think about it. Just us sitting on the deck of a luxury liner sipping cocktails. Stopping off to see the sights.' He slipped his arms round her. 'I'll womanise you.'

'I'll make the tea,' Norma said. 'Pork chops.'

George followed her into the kitchen. 'It was something Rowan said about seeing the world. I thought, Damn, I want to do a bit of living. I want to see the world before I snuff it. And I want you to be there with me. Wouldn't be the same without you.'

'What about Rowan?' said Norma. 'What about Sadie?'

'They'll manage. People do. We did. You complain often enough that she shouldn't just assume we'll always be around.'

'Complaining's different,' Norma said. 'It's not the same as actually doing something, going off somewhere. Besides, that's just to you. I wouldn't dream of saying anything to Rowan.'

The kettle boiled. Rowan went to take it off the heat.

'Don't bother making us anything,' said Norma now. 'We're off to Edinburgh. The shops are open on Sunday. I want to get some new clothes for the trip.'

George got up from the red tub chair. Went off down the hall, shouting goodbye. Norma hung back. 'He just sprung it on me,' she whispered. 'He says he wants to see the world, do some living before he dies.' She clutched Rowan's arm. 'He says he wants to womanise me.' She flushed excitement. Then followed George, almost running down the hall.

Rowan made coffee; slumped in the chair, Sadie on her knee. Her mother was off to see the world, and be womanised. That was what *she* wanted. Bloody hell, that wasn't right.

Chapter Fourteen

'Good weekend?' asked Nelson, Monday morning. 'Enjoy your date?'

Rowan hung her jacket on the hook by the door. 'You know about that?'

'Small place. Everybody knows everything. Where did you go?'

'The Greenlands,' she told him.

'Nice place.'

'It's OK,' she shrugged. 'Not my scene. I got the impression that Paolo had slept with every woman there. Or if they were too young, their mothers. Or if they were too old, their daughters.'

'I didn't think anybody was too young or too old for Paolo.' He looked at her.

She looked back. 'No, I didn't,' she said.

'Didn't what?'

'You know – sleep with him. That's what you were thinking.'

'No, it wasn't.' He went into his office.

'Yes, it was,' she called after him.

'Wasn't,' he said. Though it was.

'Was!' she shouted.

Across the Square, in the chip shop, Claudia Junior was arguing with her mother. 'It's not fair. I had to work Saturday night to let Paolo have the night off.'

'He needs a night off now and then.'

'He gets Mondays and Wednesdays. That's always been the way.'

'Well, he got Saturday this time.'

'He got Saturday to take Rowan out. It's not fair. It's Rowan,

165

Rowan, Rowan – you're always talking about her. I think you prefer her to me.'

'How could you say that? That's a terrible thing to say to your mother. Rowan's on her own, with a baby. We should help. Look at you. You got beautiful children, a nice house, a good husband. What more could you want?'

'A life,' Claudia mumbled.

'What did you say?' her mother said, in that penetrating voice that nobody could defy.

'Nothing,' said Claudia. She went to the back shop to bring through a new box of barbecue-flavour crisps. She ached all over, every muscle.

'Hi,' Cher had said to Claudia Junior, half-past five in the morning when the house was sleeping. 'Have I got a gift for you,' Cher smiled. The video hummed. The room was lit by the beam from the television.

Curtains drawn, Claudia in a pair of knickers, training shoes and one of Stu's vast vests had started to exercise. Cher was all in black. Claudia did not have a step, so she heaped six large glossy cookbooks on top of each other, pushed aside the coffee table and started. Steppenwolf howled *Born to be Wild*; young Claudia stepped on and off the books. She jerked her elbows, she lifted her arms up, fingers spread. She kicked her legs out, hoisted up her knees. She puffed. She wheezed. Halfway through, Cher thought it time to stop and measure her pulse-rate. Claudia's heart pounded, sweat rolled in lavish drops down her neck. Her hair was soaked. Robert Palmer sang *Addicted to Love*. 'Like you mean it,' shouted the trainer. 'I do. I do,' Claudia gasped. Cher complained mildly about all this jumping about. Claudia thought she was going to die.

In her flat above the Rialto, Mamie sat in bed, multi-coloured cardigan draped round her shoulders. She drank tea and considered her bank statement. 'Not good,' she said. Looking up at the ceiling, and beyond. 'Things are bad, Lavinia. Ten grand in the red. Something has to be done.'

Jude lay back on her sofa. She lifted her foot and considered it. Life was a bitch. Her head hurt. Too much of whatever it was she was drinking last night. Vodka? Definitely. Lager? Definitely.

Whisky? Gin? She couldn't remember. 'This has got to stop,' she said. 'Whisky's a killer.' She leaned over, lifted the phone and dialled the cannery's number. 'I'm not well,' she told her boss.

'This is the fourth Monday in a row.' The voice at the other end could be heard across the room. Steven and Delia turned down the morning show on television to listen.

'I've got flu.' Jude improvised a fluey voice.

'You had flu last week.'

'It's come back. I came to work too soon. I should've stayed off longer last week.'

'Bring a medical certificate or you're through, Jude.' The voice was adamant.

'I can't get to the surgery. I'm not well.' Jude exaggerated her fluey act.

'A medical certificate, Jude.'

'Christ.' She put down the receiver.

Steven and Delia looked at her. 'You fucked up this time,' said Delia.

'Take Charmaine to school, Delia. And Steven, you drop off Sonia at the nursery.'

'No,' said Steven. 'I'll be late.'

'I can't do it. What if I'm seen? They'll know I'm not ill and I'll lose my job.'

'You've lost it anyway.' Steven put on his anorak and left.

Jude lit a cigarette, said, 'Shite. Shouldn't've done that.'

Rowan took in small ads. Kittens to good homes. Mrs Winton won the Women's Institute bakery competition with her toffee cheesecake. The Operatic Society were putting on *Oklahoma* at the Town Hall. The County Hotel was having a grand opening night: *The New Raffles. The bar has been refurbished in the style of the famous Singapore watering-hole. Happy Hour 8 till 9.*

Miss Porteous, sitting at her kitchen table, rolled a sheet of paper into her ancient Olivetti portable. With two deft forefingers she typed: *Aries (Mar 21 – Apr 20) The full-moon phases could make you restless. You may well feel like getting out and about, meeting people. Do not make any moves you may regret later. Thursday sees a breakdown in some electrical or mechanical equipment. Make contingencies. The weekend has you on top form. You will meet someone who excites you.*

Rowan put a cup of coffee, two ginger snaps balanced in the saucer on Nelson's desk. 'Was, too.'

Nelson took a ginger snap. Dunked it. Ate it.

'I knew that was a double bluff when you said you didn't like them.' Rowan was miffed.

'So, I lied. I'm not going to be at the whim of a biscuit blackmailer. Was not.'

Mama Claudia looked scathingly at the day's batter. 'Too thick.'

'People like it thick,' said Claudia Junior.

'I don't like it thick,' her mother said, 'and it's my batter. Anyway, Rowan's got problems. Her mother and father are going off on a six-week cruise. Who's going to take Sadie when she's at work?'

'How do you know this?' Claudia looked up. Her first smile of the morning.

Mama Claudia made a face. 'How do I know this. In this place everybody knows everything. There are no secrets.' She put her face close to her daughter's. 'Are you gloating? You're gloating. It doesn't suit you.'

'I'm not gloating. I'll water the batter.'

Mamie Garland got out of bed. Walked carefully across the room. 'Creaky. Creaky. I'm getting old. I'm up, but my body's still sleeping.'

Five years ago a speculator had offered her a deal of money for the Rialto. He wanted to convert it into a block of luxury flats. She turned him down flat. 'Foolish move,' she said now. 'People are going to the cinema, but not mine. They want comfy seats. Popcorn. Explosions. Wide screens. Coke Cola. What do people do when they're up shit creek? Top themselves? Disappear to Rio? I'll have a pee and a think.'

Taurus (Apr 21 – May 21) Miss Porteous typed. *Oops. Mars clashes with Neptune in your seventh house.* She looked at the wall. What did this mean, exactly? She didn't want to give precise details. *Things could get tricky. Do not make any rash decisions. Watch your cash. And try to hold your tongue; you could say things you will regret. Things look better on Sunday. A good time for relaxing.*

Every week she liked to give one sign a hard time. This time it was Taurus's turn.

The day wore on. Every time Rowan saw Nelson she mouthed, 'Was too.' She hated people to make assumptions about her. Especially when they were not true. At last Nelson leaned over the desk and said emphatically that he had not been wondering if she had slept with Paolo. He was not interested in her sex-life. He hated it when people made assumptions about him. Especially when they were right.

Mama Claudia ticked her daughter off for gloating.

Mamie worried. She was getting old. 'Getting,' she called out loud. 'Forget getting. I *am* old. Old is not good.' She had no pension. No savings. Face frozen in horror, she stared blankly ahead. She imagined she would end up in an old folk's home, sitting in the corner of a cavernous room called the lounge. She'd be on a green plastic chair, wooden arms, joining in painful singalongs led by hearty do-goody people in dungarees, reluctantly mouthing *Yellow Submarine*, a slow drool spilling unchecked from the corner of her mouth. 'Jesus Christ,' she hissed. 'I hate old.' Old was scary. Very old was terrifying.

And Miss Porteous got the horoscopes ready for Rowan to pick up. Next week she'd give Virgo a tough week. Logical, prissy folks, Virgos.

Rowan sat at her desk staring ahead. For the first time in weeks she thought about Eileen. She wondered what Eileen was doing. Was she watching sunsets over strange landscapes? Or drinking some exotic drink in a tiny café with people all around talking in a language she did not understand? Or walking through a market-place where the air was scented with spices?

Jude put on her jeans and Steven's Adidas sweatshirt – £1.25 for forty-five weeks. 'Thing'll be done in before it's paid for.' She dressed Sonia then took her to the nursery. 'We're late,' she said, putting Sonia's coat on the lion hook at the door.

'When are you not?' said Mrs Ashton.

'Mummy's got a hangover,' said Sonia. 'We've not to speak loud.'

'Right,' said Mrs Ashton.

'I'll get you for that.' Jude pointed at her child. 'Wait till you're sixteen, you little bugger, I'll make you wear heavy shoes and go to Sunday school.'

Sonia and Mrs Ashton stared at her with disapproval so heavy it was crazed.

At lunchtime Rowan found Eileen's birth certificate in the pile of papers she'd brought with her from London and took it round to Miss Porteous.

The old lady opened her front door. Peered round. 'Hello, Rowan.'

'I want a chart done,' Rowan said.

'You'd better come in.' She let Rowan in, led the way to the kitchen. A small, neat room, painted pale blue, it was pristine, well wiped, if not quite shiny enough to mask Miss Porteous's poverty. A tiny pot sat on the Formica unit beside a small tin of Heinz vegetable soup and some cold rice pudding in a blue and white bowl – Miss Porteous's lunch. Rowan longed to eat it. There was something alluring about this tidiness. She imagined Miss Porteous sitting at this little table, eating in a neat, birdlike way, spilling not a drop, listening to one of the Bach organ music tapes in the neat pile on the dresser next to her radio-cassette player. She would wipe her mouth, gather, then wash her dishes before putting them back in their appointed places. A disciplined life.

'Let me see.' Miss Porteous took the chart. Looked at it. 'This isn't you. This is someone else.'

'Yes. It's Eileen.'

'Eileen Johnson. Who's this – little Sadie's mother?'

'Yes.' Rowan felt guilty. 'How did you know?'

'Who else would it be? Born 23 August, 1960.'

'I know. She never told me she was that old. Thirty-eight,' Rowan said. 'Pretty old.'

'That all depends on how far from thirty-eight you are, and on which side of it you are. It seems pretty young to me.' Miss Porteous gave the birth certificate back to Rowan with her long thin hand, pale translucent skin. 'I don't do people I don't know,' she said.

'Why not?'

'No good will come of it. You want to find out about somebody. It's like spying. No, I won't do it.'

'Please,' said Rowan.

'Absolutely no.'

'This woman,' Rowan flapped the birth certificate, 'stole my money. I just wanted to find out what she's doing with it.'

'I can't tell you that.'

Rowan noticed on the table in front of her a copy of *The Times*, neatly folded at the crossword which was half complete. Beside it lay a Parker ballpoint pen, packet of Benson & Hedges and a small jewelled lighter.

'You smoke?' She couldn't imagine Miss Porteous indulging in any sort of vice.

'I allow myself two a day. One with the crossword in the morning at eleven. The other at nine, before bed. Breaks up the evening.'

'You must have discipline.'

'Oh yes. A disciplined life, that's the thing.'

A small crucifix hung on the wall above the table.

'You're religious?' asked Rowan.

'I believe in a higher power.'

'But you're an astrologist.'

'What difference does that make? The universe, the movements of the planets are all in the great scheme of things. Astrologers visited the infant Jesus. They had seen the star.' Miss Porteous ushered Rowan to the door.

'I didn't know that,' said Rowan.

'Astrologers can have religion; it isn't denied them. You wouldn't find them seeking solace in a small weekly paragraph printed in the paper.'

Rowan supposed not. But she, like half the village, was addicted to Miss Porteous's weekly horoscopes. There was something soothingly familiar and accurate about them.

'What sign are you?' Miss Porteous asked as she opened the front door.

'Cancer,' said Rowan.

'Ah,' Miss Porteous nodded. As if that explained everything.

When Rowan was gone she went to her typewriter. *Cancer (June 22 – July 22) You may well find that the disappointment of last week was for the good. Do not seek knowledge that may only bring pain. Leave your past where it belongs. Behind you. There is happiness to be found nearby. Just look for it. Treasure the now.*

Mamie made a decision. 'Drastic action,' she said to her kitchen.

'We need to take steps. A little drama. No, with my overdraft, I need a big drama. A great big drama. Something huge.'

Jude picked up Sonia from the nursery. Turning into the Square she met her supervisor at the cannery. 'Thought you had the flu.'

'I do,' said Jude. 'I'm feeling a lot better. Fresh air.' She spread her arms, soaking it up.

'Come in tomorrow and collect your cards. You're through.'

'You can't fire me. I've got kids.'

'You weren't thinking about them all the times you've phoned in sick.'

'Oh, fuck you. It's a crap job anyway.'

Miss Porteous, on her way home with her fortnightly pack of Benson & Hedges, stopped to watch the day. Swallows overhead. She breathed in the summer. Scents of honeysuckle drifting from back courtyards. Schoolchildren coming from the chip shop with crisps and tins of Pepsi. What sort of a lunch was that for growing people? She heard Jude's cry, *It's a crap job anyway*. Oh dear, Judy. What are you saying? Rowan making her way to The Squelch for a drink. Nelson standing at his car watching her. What was he? Capricorn. *Capricorn (Dec 22 – Jan 20) If you don't reach out and grab what you really want, you'll never get it*. Mamie Garland sneaking into the County Hotel. Now why would a long-time Squelch faithful go in there? Claudia Rossi sniffing and sighing. Mama Rossi with her perfect fingernails and painted lips leaning out of the upstairs window looking even more terrifying than usual. Librans, both of them. *Libra (Sep 24 – Oct 23) Stop dreaming. Get doing.* Who needed to study the planets? It was all going on down here. What was Jude, anyway? Scorpio.

Scorpio (Oct 24 – Nov 22) You really have only yourself to blame for recent dramatic events. Take time now to reconsider your life. Can you avert a cash crisis? It is possible to turn disasters into blessings. Look to your future.

Claudia leaned on the counter of the chip shop watching the one o'clock bus leave the Square. She sighed. She wanted to go further than the bus would take her. She wanted to get away. To go as far as she could. She wanted to wear smart suits, carry a filofax and a mobile phone. Make big decisions. She wanted to be important. Like Rowan.

Mama Claudia shut the window. 'I want people to know,' she told her husband.

He did not look up. 'Know what?'

'About me. *Me*. What I can do. Who I am. I see them out there. They think I'm an old Italian dragon. I work all day downstairs. Nights I feel like a knackered old bag.'

'You're not a knackered old bag. You're beautiful.' Giorgio turned on the lunchtime news. He kept his back turned, didn't want her to see his irritation. Thirty years they'd been married. They could have whole conversations without uttering a word.

'I want everybody to know how I can cook. *Everybody*.' Mama Claudia spread her arms for the world to rush into her embrace.

'Who is everybody?'

'Everybody is everybody – people we have known all our lives. I want to say, "This is who I really am. This is me." It'll be good.'

'How do you mean, good? Good for business?' As far as he was concerned, good for business was the only good there was.

Mama Claudia shrugged. 'Maybe. But good to be nice. Good to be remembered well.'

He shrugged. 'You're not planning to die, are you?' His cigar had gone out. He reached into the pocket of his ample cord trousers to find his lighter. He didn't like this. Still, if they quarrelled, good would come of it. Mama dealt with all situations in the same way. Births, deaths, anniversaries, arguments, making up after arguments – she cooked. Still, he asked, 'How cook?'

'A feast. *Spagnolismo* – entertain friends lavishly. Let people see what I can do. I am not just fish and chip and sweets.' *Spagnolismo* – she was small, too muscular to be fat. She moved at speed. When she cooked, she turned the kitchen into frenzy. People kept clear. Her hair was dark, drawn severely off her face. Her lips were painted, morning till night, bright red. Nails too, always brightly polished. She was a woman on fire. People thought, Papa thought, she'd burn herself out before fifty. But no. As she got older the flame burned harder. She spread her passion wider, from husband to business to children to grandchildren. Nobody, nothing was spared.

'Not *spagnolismo*.' Extravagance. Feasting to keep up appearances. Showing off. Papa was tall, lean, calm. He wore a collarless

173

white shirt under a grey cashmere V-neck sweater. Balding. Stroking his gleaming head, he claimed this was what such a woman as he had married did to men. 'No showing off.'

'A huge meal. A whole table laid out, *bellissima*. People laughing, drinking wine.' Mama Claudia had made up her mind.

'We do that Sundays.'

'That's just family. I want people to come too.'

'No.' He had no intention of letting actual people come upstairs from the chip shop into his home. 'No,' he repeated, lighting his cigar. 'No. No. No.'

'*Carciofi alle mandorle. Caponata*,' said Mama. Artichoke leaves in almond sauce!

'No,' said Papa.

'*Spagnolismo*,' Mama beamed. Stood up, imagining the glory of it. The food. The laughter. The wine. '*Focaccia*. Fish soup. *Pecorino. Calamari imbottiti*. Stuffed squid. *Scaloppini cu la marsala*. Veal escalopes with marsala. *Conigilio all'agrodolce*. Sweet and sour rabbit, raisins, pine nuts, olive.'

'No.' Papa put his hands on his head. This was awful. He did not want these fish and chip people up here knowing about this food.

'Mussels with lemon.' Mama was truly, truly happy. *Cozze al limone*. '*Cassata*,' she cried. Rum and ricotta cake with marzipan – and fruits. 'Almond ice cream.' She was off in her own wonderful world bringing heaped plates to the table hearing the cries of wonder at each new dish.

Papa walked to the door shouting, 'No! This is not good.' He turned, pulled the cigar from his mouth and the two stared at each other, saying nothing. Mama walked past him. She was on fire. And when she was on fire the very air parted before her, let her through.

Giorgio had lost. Mama smiled and smiled. She stood outside the living room.

'There you go. You were right, Rowan. People *should* know. No lights under no bushels,' she said. '*Spagnolismo*. They shall know what real food is like. They shall know what I can do. One evening in their lives they'll say, "So this is how heaven tastes".' She clapped her hands with glee.

Miss Porteous sat at her typewriter. She broke her cigarette rules, lit up her third of the day. Why would Mamie Garland go into the County Hotel? A small event; folks might think nothing of it. But she knew different. What had happened at the County Hotel other than it had burnt down last year and was re-opening as the new Raffles of the North? Pah, what rubbish. She sucked on her cigarette. *My God, that was it!* Everybody knew the Rialto didn't make money. Folks went to Perth to the multiplex. So Mamie was going to burn it down – an insurance job just like at the County Hotel! My God – a fire, and she lived just two doors down.

Pisces (Jan 21 – Feb 19) Sometimes we feel like a leaf. Out of control, at the whim of all seasons, tossed about, open to the condemnation of others. Madness takes hold of us. If you are planning drastic things please let others know. They might not agree with your folly.

There, she was done. She folded her hands on the table and looked up at her crucifix. 'That's it for another week. I think I've covered everyone.' She did not consider she wrote horoscopes. She was sending messages to people she'd known all her life. It was easier than actual face-to-face confrontations.

At five o'clock Rowan collected Sadie from Norma and George. A new set of suitcases were standing in the hall. They were real leather, with *Atlas* stamped on the side. George's Frank Sinatra records were playing, *Fly Me to the Moon*. What had got into the pair of them, Rowan wondered. They were ebullient. Singing along with Sinatra. 'Let me play among the stars,' Norma trilled. Badly, Rowan thought. There was a bottle of Chianti on the table. 'Getting in the mood,' George said. He was wearing Norma's flowery apron, helping with the salad. It was never like this when she lived there, Rowan remembered. Norma made tea, George read the paper or caught up with the sports news on Teletext. They were so happy. Bloody hell.

When Sadie was in bed, Rowan took Walter Dean's diary from the desk drawer. She felt glum enough to read it. There was nothing like feeling glum and reading something that would make you even glummer. Why, it could almost cheer you up. She put Nirvana Unplugged on the CD, fetched the Glenfiddich, and settled in the red tub chair. Kurt Cobain sang desolation songs – *All Apologies* – Rowan drank her whisky and Walter Dean reached the loch and broke his heart. Outside it started to rain.

July 19. It is almost a month since I visited the loch. Prayed as I climbed that the swans and family would be well. The climb near about killed me. All that wishing and walking too quick did my heart in. It was fairly battering against my chest. Had to stop several times to gather my breath. I could hear it wheeze and rattle in my lungs. I hate that, the sound of being old. My throat was tight, I couldn't get any air down me. I was sitting on a rock, mouth open, bent over, rasping, and Jesus have mercy, I thought, this is it. Stonechat on a gorsebush had a good look at me. Nice little thing, orangy breast, black head. My death moment passed. The heart calmed and I carried on up the track. I used to be scared of dying. Now it's something I must go through – pretty soon at that. Every time I hear about the death of someone I know, I think, Well, if he can bloody do it, *I* can bloody do it. I remember that's what I used to think about getting through my driving test.

The room filled with a burst of whistles and applause – Nirvana's audience. Rowan had forgotten what was playing. She looked up, startled, then poured herself the last of the whisky – a huge glass. Then went back to the diary.

July 20. The little cygnet has gone. No sign of it anywhere. The swans are moving about the loch, necks dipped. Couldn't write about it yesterday. They looked so forlorn.

Rowan put the book down. 'Bloody hell.' Then, turning to the empty pages at the end of the book, she wrote:

16 June. Eileen is in Africa. Miss Porteous would not do her chart, but I feel it in my waters: that's where she is. Eileen will be making her way south, through a landscape of dry, burnt colours, under skies – I have read – that are always pale indigo. The air that she breathes now is a living force, burning, moving. Shining in the distance like a lake. The trees loom up like ships fully rigged and the grasses are scented, spiced so strong they'll sting the insides of her nose. She might see a herd of eland moving slow along some headland. Graceful, gentle beasts out walking. Or elephants shoving through forests so deep, so thick the sun only streams down in small patches. Saw a strange yellow bird the other day. Bright, and shy and lazy. Nelson thinks I slept with Paolo. I wish he didn't. I really, really wish he didn't.

Rain splattered on the window. Rowan watched it. The CD had stopped long ago; she hadn't noticed. She had been engrossed writing in Walter Dean's diary, her prose pure holiday brochure. Rowan's Africa was the Africa of Mungo Park, and BBC wildlife documentaries. It was a romance.

'Ya bastards!' A single howl from the street. Rowan went to the window. The rain turned to downpour, stotting off the pavement with venom, mini-torrents in the gutters. Steven was standing soaked and alone in the Square. Hair plastered to his head, T-shirt translucently drenched, in the absence of a moon he was baying at the streetlamps.

Across the Square Mama Claudia stood at her bedroom window watching. Giorgio lay in bed feigning a snore. He wanted none of this.

'The boy,' said Mama. 'The boy. Who does he remind you of?'
Papa snored.

'And who does the person he reminds you of, remind you of?'
Knowing Mama Claudia was at the window, her hair, loosened from its oppressively tight bun, tumbling round her breasts, waving her arms, making her point not just to him, but to the room and the world beyond it, Papa deemed it safe to open his eyes slightly.

'The boy's another Paolo who is another you. Drinking and yelling at the moon, or at streetlamps when the moon is hiding. We have let him down.'

Papa resumed his fake snore, said nothing. Though he knew this to be true.

Rowan went to bed. Lay listening to the last bus lumber out of the Square, and drinkers leaving The Squelch. She did not want to sleep. On a night like this when she was indulging herself in sorrows, she worried what dreams might bring.

She drifted off. Dreamed she was smoking a thick black cigarette;

when she lit it her hair went on fire. She inhaled deeply, too deeply. A huge lump of ash dropped from the end, fell on her skirt, burned a hole through which it fell to the carpet, which it burned. Then it burned the floorboards, fell through to the room below, where her mother was standing, looking up through the huge charred gap. 'Are you smoking?' Norma called. And Rowan, hair ablaze, smoke gushing from both nostrils, huge black fag dangling from her lips, squeaked, 'No.'

Chapter Fifteen

Rowan greeted the morning vomiting. Wearing only the dubious bright red Acid Jazz T-shirt she slept in, that didn't quite cover her bum, she shuffled from the bathroom clutching her head, cursing whisky and all who drank it. She picked up Sadie, who was vibrantly complaining at being left in her cot when the sun was slanting in through the chink in the curtains and she could be up, sitting in the high chair George and Norma had bought her last week, getting her face in a mess with her morning egg.

Rowan held her hands up as if holding back the racket Sadie was making. 'Ssh. Oh please. No noise.' She carried Sadie through to the kitchen and, holding her on her hip, boiled an egg, mashed it in a yellow plastic cup and made herself a cup of tea.

Groaning she fed Sadie her egg, sipped her tea. She was a fool. She'd drunk too much last night, got herself in a silly depression. Things weren't that bad. She fell into the small rhythm of blowing on the surface of her tea, swigging at it, loading the spoon and shoving it towards Sadie's gaping mouth. She sang mournfully to herself, a song that was still humming through her head from the night before. 'Come as you are,' she sang. 'Come as you are . . .' She didn't know any more.

Sadie's little face puckered. This unseemly noise from the one she adored, the source of food and comfort, was too much for her. She wept. She opened her egg-filled mouth and howled.

Rowan stopped singing. 'Sorry. Gosh. Sorry.' She knew she hadn't the voice for the blues. The only thing her voice could carry with any conviction was *Away In a Manger*. She swept Sadie up. Cuddled her. 'I'll never sing again. Or never when you're around anyway. I'll wait till you've left home.'

179

The words were out. The thought she'd been cradling. That this looking after Sadie situation would go on for as long as Sadie needed it. Rowan held the child from her. 'Then I'll sing. Then I'll travel.'

She went through to the bathroom, started to run her bath. The room was chilled, so she climbed onto the lavatory seat to reach the window. 'Bit nippy in here,' she told Sadie. The little bathroom window, high on the wall above the lavatory, was the only one she hadn't peered out of. The bathroom was the room with the view. The tiny window looked over the rooftops to the hills beyond. Sloping roofs, red and brown and grey, small spirals of morning smoke and looming faraway hills, peaking blue into the sky. Rowan lifted Sadie to show her. She felt the child's tiny face against hers. Peachy skin, soft tiny breathing in her ears, huge eyes looking eagerly and uncomprehendingly out. 'We have a view, Sadie. We can see the hills from here. What is it about hills? Looking at them just fills you with longing.' She decided that this Saturday she and Sadie would go climbing. They would get to the top of a mountain, or a hill, not too high a hill, they would breathe the air and jump about. The joy of getting high.

'What are you doing at the weekend?' Nelson asked at work.

'I'm going to climb a mountain. A smallish mountain, and jump about.'

'Can I come?'

'If you want. I thought you always went fishing.'

'I do. I will. I'll fish. You climb.'

'I thought men didn't like women coming along when they went fishing.'

'They don't,' he said. 'See you Saturday.'

At five, just before she left to go and pick up Sadie, Rowan went through to Nelson's office. 'What do you mean, men don't like women coming fishing with them, but you want me to come along Saturday? Does that mean you don't think of me as a woman?'

He looked at her. Why did women always twist things round? 'No, it doesn't mean that. It means I'd like your company.'

'Woman or not?'

'Well, you can be an honorary man for the day.'

'Does that mean I have to batter the catch, shouting, "Die, trout, die"?'

'That's why men don't like women going fishing with them,' said Nelson.

When Rowan was alone that night she put on *Carmen*. It didn't sound satisfying with the volume down at her usual don't-disturb-Sadie level, so she put on her earphones and let it roar. She waved her arms about. She was Carmen. She was going to lure men to tragedy and doom with her exotic beauty and lustrous voice. *L'amour est un oiseau rebelle*, sang Carmen. She did not hear someone knocking on the door. She was too busy trying to get Don José to succumb to her charms, taking an exquisite flower from her bodice, tossing it in his face, to hear the front door open. *L'amour, l'amour*, she sang. Did not hear someone coming down the hall calling her name. She was leading the chorus when she turned and saw Nelson standing across the room staring at her, amused, embarrassed. He was holding a bottle of wine in one hand, a huge bunch of wild flowers in the other.

'My God!' she jumped. 'What are you doing here?' Shouting because of the noise in her head, not realising she was the only person who could hear it. She took off her earphones.

'Sorry,' said Nelson. 'I knocked and knocked, but you were obviously lost in your own world.'

'I was being Carmen.' The opera still hummed in the earphones. 'You can be Don José if you like.'

Nelson shook his head. 'I've given up being a tormented lover.'

'OK, you can be Escamillo. But remember, she rebuffs him. You won't mind that though, what with me being an honorary bloke.'

'Ah well,' he offered her the flowers. 'I thought I'd bring you these. Help you get in touch with your feminine side.'

'Thank you. They're lovely. What are they?'

'Wild flowers. I saw them by the roadside.'

'You picked them? For me?'

'Looks like it. Don't let my father-in-law know. He planted them. He throws them down in seed bombs in memory of his wife.'

'That's beautiful. He's obviously in touch with *his* feminine side.'

'Don't ever let him hear you say that.'

Rowan put them into a straight-sided pint glass. She had no vases. 'I love them.'

He opened the wine. Poured them both a glass. 'I hope I'm not disrupting your fantasy.'

'No, I can get back to it anytime. It's always there, the allure of being a temptress.'

'You want to be a temptress?'

'Of course, but I'm no good at it. A failed temptress. What's your fantasy?'

'Nothing as exotic as yours. I'd like to play football for Italy in the World Cup. Or maybe fish for marlin like Hemingway.'

'That's quite exotic. I could go for that. Hey, you never bring fish into the office. Big shiny trout for us to take home for tea.'

'I let them go – big shiny trout.' He indicated the hugeness of the trout. Fisherman's gesture.

'A likely tale,' she teased.

'No, really. It's sport. Me and the fish and the water. I stand there and think till I get to a place inside me where I'm not thinking. That's the moment.'

'Like Walter Dean. He used to want a oneness with rocks and water so he'd know what the swans know.'

'You met old Walter?'

'I found his diaries.'

'You read them.'

'Shameful,' she admitted, 'but I couldn't resist. They're sad. Was he sad?'

'Not face to face. Are you sad? Do you like it here?'

'No, I'm not sad. I was angry at first. I was furious at Eileen, you know, Sadie's mother. But I seem to be getting over it. I worry about her coming back and claiming Sadie. Are you sad?'

'I was. I was very unhappy when Justine ran off. I think I went mad with unhappiness.'

'Aren't you scared of being unhappy again? I am.'

'Oh, you shouldn't be. What is it Dostoevsky said? "Happy people have no history".'

'You have a history.'

'Yes, but it's fading.'

They poured another glass. And, heady on *Carmen* and wine,

Rowan confessed, 'I used to fancy you something rotten when I was thirteen.' Her hand flew to her face. She shouldn't have said that; had to stop herself saying, 'Still do.' Instead she apologised. 'I'm sorry – ignore me. I shouldn't have said that.'

He stood up. 'Work tomorrow. I must go.'

'You can stay a while. The wine's not finished.'

'No. I'll go before I take advantage of your thirteen-year-old crush.'

'Oh please. Take advantage.'

But he didn't. He took his jacket and left. Rowan sat turning her glass in her hand. She felt a fool.

Next morning, Rowan could not face going to work. She dawdled down the hill to the Square after leaving Sadie with her folks.

Nelson was alone in the office. Freddy had called in sick. Billy was out interviewing a man who was trying to get into the *Guinness Book of Records* for eating the most beans picked up with a toothpick in a minute. Rowan quietly shut the door and sat at her desk. Nelson came out. She did not look at him. At last she apologised. 'Sorry. I made a fool of myself last night.'

'You?' he said. 'I was the fool. I refused your offer.'

'You're being a gent.'

'No, I'm not. I was the fool.'

Well, she wanted to cry out: *The offer's still open. Take me. Take me now, on this desk* but kept her mouth shut. A woman should only make an arse of herself once. Well, once a week anyway.

On Saturday they drove up the glen, Sadie on Rowan's knee.

'That's not legal,' said Nelson.

'I know. I hope we don't get done by the police.'

'Could spoil our day.'

'More than that. I don't want to be arrested for something tiny like having a child on my knee. When I go off the rails I want to be captured by the police for something big. The full bank raid and car chase. Sirens wailing.'

'Let us know in advance. We could do with a big story at the *Gazette*.'

'I'll oust the Council meetings from the front page.'

They took the glen road past Gowan Woods.

'I saw a yellow bird here,' said Rowan, 'the day before I started work. Big, lazy thing. Could hardly be bothered flying away.'

'A Golden Oriole,' he told her. 'I saw it, too.'

'It was an omen.'

'You believe in omens? Good luck? Horoscopes?'

'Oh yes. You don't?'

'No.'

'Not even *Porteous Predicts*? Good heavens, you have to believe that. Everybody believes that.'

'There is something worryingly accurate about it.'

'Yep,' said Rowan. 'Don't know how she does it.'

'I think it's the only thing anybody reads. Actually, I think that's why a lot of folk buy the paper.'

'She's amazing,' said Rowan.

They passed the track where lovers went on Saturday nights. A lark flew up singing.

'An exultation of larks,' said Rowan. 'Don't you just love that. Have you ever seen an exultation of larks? I only ever see them one at a time.'

'No. It's a great thought. An unkindness of ravens. A quarrel of sparrows.'

'There should be new collective nouns. A nerd of computer operators. A distraught of teachers. A flamboyance of television chefs. A frown of bank managers.'

'Do you always talk this much?'

'Only when I'm with someone who talks back. Sadie doesn't speak, which is fine. She agrees with everything I say. But after she goes to bed at night it gets sort of quiet.'

'Lonely?' he asked.

'Suppose. I don't mind lonely now and then, but every night is too often. Do you get lonely?'

'No. I worry that I've lost the knack of chatting.'

'Maybe you're lonely and don't notice it.'

They parked the car and took the path Rowan had taken weeks before, up to the fishing pool, then beyond to the loch. It took two hours. Nelson carried Sadie. The child was getting heavy, did not sit still. Squirmed in her carrier, bobbed up and down pointing. Her legs moved, little eager kicks, in readiness for the great mobility ahead. 'She'll be walking soon,' he said.

'She's already bumming her way about the living room. Then she'll talk. Wonder what she'll say.'

'She'll probably ask why you've done nothing about the décor in the house.'

'Is it that bad?'

'Well, I don't think you'll ever be pestered by style magazines.'

'I don't like to change things. It's Walter's wallpaper; I don't want to offend him.'

'He's dead.'

'I know, but I've been reading his diary. He doesn't seem dead to me.'

The march took up their energies. They stopped speaking. Breathed companionably, listened to the stamp of their feet on the path. Soft brackened slopes on either side of them, stretching into hills, distant mountains, grey, purple. Rowan turned to look down the path she'd just climbed. 'You come here nearly every week, and you never told me.'

'What?'

'What it's like. It's amazing! No wonder Walter came here.'

'It's the availability of mountains. They're there for the gazing at, if you're not up to climbing them.'

'It's a trudge though, getting to this loch. How did he manage it? He was so ill. He could have dropped down any moment. Death makes you fearless.'

Nelson looked at her.

'I mean, if you know you're going to die, what have you got to fear? Except death.'

Nelson stopped. 'Just getting my breath.' He punched his chest.

'It's your age,' Rowan joked. 'It's getting too much for you.'

'I'm forty-four. It doesn't seem old to me. How old are you?'

'Twenty-six.'

'I'm almost twenty years older than you. Twenty years wiser.'

'Or twenty years more stupid.'

'That's what it feels like.'

They walked round the edge of a small copse, Scots pines and larch. Climbed an incline and the loch spread before them.

A sudden expanse of water, shining grey, glassy, still. The air changed, scented damp. Four swans were out swimming. Two adults, shimmering white shifting across the surface. Two young – dun-coloured. They swam in a slow line away from them.

'The fox didn't get them.'

'Mum and Dad are older and wiser,' said Nelson, setting Sadie down. 'Unlike me.'

She gave him a reluctant smile. 'Who'd have thought it? I'd pictured myself tramping across Africa, following Mungo's path up the Niger, and here I am. With you. With a child. And I don't mind, not at all. Life happens. It sneaks up and smacks you on the face. Don't think it won't. It could happen to you. It *will* happen to you.'

They sat on the grass by the shore, ate soggy tuna sandwiches, drank sludgy coffee. Spooned puréed chicken and vegetables and yoghurt into Sadie's eager, gaping mouth. 'First picnic, Sadie.'

Rowan and Sadie sat by a rock watching Nelson fish. He waded into the water, cast out, line drifting into the air, landing feather-soft on the surface. Rowan observed him for a while, then put Sadie on her shoulders and walked along the bank. It was a narrow, rutted path, overgrown with pinkweed higher than she was. Lilies in flower, vibrant yellow, grew by the water. June was a yellow month. Gorse on the hills. Fields heady with rape, a sea of yellow, shimmering into the air. She preferred August, a deeper bluer month with whiffs of change in the air. June was settled, as if summer would never end. Purple on the hills.

She watched the swans, smelled the damp and wondered if Walter was part of it all. Did he reach that state of oneness, knowing what the swans knew? The ways of the water. The fox trails. Right now, for her, Sadie banging the top of her head, kicking her shoulders, babbling, bouncing, this was not possible.

She walked on till the path became impenetrable and Sadie fell asleep slumped over her head. So she turned back and stood watching Nelson. She could hear the whir of his reel. Was he thinking till he'd reached the point of not thinking? What was that like? Just wind on water and the sounds of waterfowl and fish leaping?

She laid Sadie, wrapped in a blanket, on the bank in the shade.

The sun had stung her perfect skin. Sat beside her listening to the day, wishing she was not wishing for a cigarette. She thought she'd be a smoker all her life. Even now, weeks after she'd given up, the longing gripped her. A tension in the back of her neck, across her shoulders, a lust in the pit of her stomach, a biting tetchiness that was hard to fight.

'D'you want to try?' Nelson called.

'I don't think I could do it.'

''Course you can. Nothing to it. Come on.'

She took off her boots and socks, rolled up her jeans and joined him in the water. 'Keep an eye on Sadie. I don't want her to wake and find nobody there.'

'I'm watching.'

'What do I do?'

He showed her. She fed out some line, then let it fly from the rod, whipping it in the air. Flicking it up. The line reeled, sailed silver through the air, a gleaming arc. The fly danced above the water, landed and swam on the surface. She let it lie. Then tried again. The line tightened. Suddenly heavy. She panicked. 'I've got something. Oh God. There's a fish.'

'Reel it in,' said Nelson. 'Gently.'

She wound the line the wrong way. The fish headed off away from them. Nelson stood behind her, fixed the reel, arms round her. Tugged the rod, bringing the fish round. Then let her reel it in. It was a trout. Shimmying in the water. Gleaming, purples, greens, brown.

Rowan watched it. 'I don't want to catch anything. Let it go.'

Nelson gently lifted it out, took the hook from its mouth. Held it up. 'It's a beauty. Look at it.' The fish squirmed, swimming in his hands. 'Look at the colours.' Then stilled.

Rowan walked up the bank, picked up Sadie. 'Look, Sadie, a fish.'

Still sleepy, Sadie considered it. Then reached out to grab it.

'I'm counting her firsts,' Rowan told Nelson. 'She saw her first bee the other day. And her first moon. This is her first fish.'

'What do you think she makes of it?'

'God knows. What must it be like to be carried everywhere, shown strange things? Do you suppose her life is full of wonder?'

'Hope so. Isn't yours? Listening to you it seems you haven't lost your wonder. I ask myself, "How does she do that?"' He waded into the water, put the fish carefully under the surface, let it go. A small tumble of crested water and the fish was gone. It went deep.

'Will it be all right, my fish?' Rowan said.

'Of course. It'll have a tale to tell when it gets home. About this huge person.' He spread his arms, that fisherman's gesture again. 'Have you got a thing about being free? Is that why you wanted to go away? Just travel, no actual destination in mind.'

'No. It was control. I felt my life had always been controlled. Mealtimes. Schooltimes. Coming and going, back and forth. That's what my father did. He left the house at ten past eight – not quarter past or five past – every morning. He wore the same clothes, his suit and white shirt, black and blue striped tie, brown shoes that he polished every night. My mother cooked and cleaned and waited for him. It scared me. I was scared of that happening to me.'

He held her.

'They seem so different now, especially recently. They're happy – or maybe they were always happy. Now they're letting it show. I don't know,' she said.

'You don't think that's got something to do with you?'

'Me? Why?'

'Well, you came back. Then there's the things you say. Seeing the world before you die. Doing things.'

'Did I say that?'

'Yes. The day you came back, you said that to your father. Shook him to his boots.' He ran his hands across her back.

'He told you this?'

'No. He told Mamie, who told young Claudia, who told Jude, who told me.'

'I should keep my mouth shut.'

He kissed her. The water shimmered round their ankles. Swans called, honking. Far away on the hill, a curlew took to the air, wailing. A complaint of curlews.

'I could take advantage of you now,' he told her.

But Sadie woke. Complained, small cries. Then discovering she was alone, bawled for company.

'Later,' said Rowan. 'Right now I have to get back. I have to do Sadie things – bath her, feed her, get her to bed. All the usual stuff.'

They got back to Rowan's flat after six. She handed Sadie to Nelson. 'Here, hold her. My jeans are all damp and clingy round the bottoms.' She returned a few minutes later in a long cotton shift. 'Look, I'm in touch with my feminine side.'

'And it goes so well with the footwear,' he noted, looking at the huge bright red woollen socks flapping on her feet.

'My feet are cold. It happens to us feminine people.'

Nelson went across the road to the chip shop whilst Rowan prepared Sadie's supper. They ate fish and chips, drank wine Nelson had bought at the County Hotel, Rowan sitting on the red tub chair, Sadie on her knee. 'She's not going to sleep tonight, she's too excited. I don't often have visitors.'

But after her bath her day caught up with Sadie and she slept. Rowan put her in her cot and tiptoed back to the living room. Nelson had fetched a bucket of coal from the shed at the back door and was lighting a fire.

'That's Walter's coal.' Rowan didn't like using other people's things.

'He won't need it. Besides, I knew him – he wouldn't mind. He'd want you to be warm. He was like that.'

Rowan watched him screw up newspapers into tight rolls, put them in the grate, then place coal carefully on top of them. He lit a match, set the paper alight and leaned back. The flames crept round the coal, licked up the chimney.

Rowan sighed. 'It's a good thing I wasn't around in ancient times. *Homo Erectus* is a cheat of a name. It's not nearly as exciting as it sounds.' Behind his back she did a lumpen, hunched walk.

'Please don't tell me you are doing an imitation of *Homo Erectus*. Not in those socks,' Nelson said, still tending the fire.

Rowan straightened. 'No.'

He turned.

She shot him a liar's grin. 'Anyway, if I'd been Neanderthal Woman I'd never have thought of fire. It's so clever. It would never have occurred to me to rub two sticks together. Or the wheel – I'd never have thought of that. We wouldn't have advanced. I'd never have met you.'

'You'd still be back there. Fossilised bones.'

'Maybe I was back there. Maybe I've died and been reborn a thousand times. Sometimes it feels like it. This is me reincarnate. I've been through all the stages – worm, beetle, ant, bee, bird and on. And on. And here I am. Me again. It's a lot warmer this time round.'

'I thought you were going to stick at the sloth stage.'

'That was before you kissed me.'

He came to her. Kissed her again. Arms outstretched behind her, his hands were filthy. 'I have to wash,' he said, 'which is more than *Homo Erectus* would have done.'

They sat on heaped cushions in front of the fire. Drank the wine.

'Is this what you do nights? Read this diary?' Nelson reached over and picked up Walter's diary.

'Sometimes I look out the lavatory window at the hills. If I stand on the loo I can reach it. Pathetic, isn't it?'

He shook his head. 'Not really.'

'I think I must be boring.'

'My wife made me feel boring.'

'She went mad, didn't she?'

'I think there was too much going on in her head for her to cope with.'

'Where is she now? Do you know?'

'California. She found herself an understanding American. Her last postcard was over six years ago. She's fine. Might've known.' He poured some more wine. Took a drink. Gave his glass a disapproving look. George O'Connell served a dubious vintage. 'Why do you spend so much time looking out at the hills?'

'I like to think of them out there. All that life. All that space. They are constant; it's comforting. Do you think about fish when you're not trying to catch them? Do you think they are up there in the loch leaping about, frolicking behind your back?'

'Not really. I think about them in their secret places, where they idle beside the rocks. There's something cool about it. They're sane.'

'Ah,' she said. They sat whilst the darkness in the room closed about them. She did not put on a lamp. 'Do you like it here?' she asked.

'In this room? Yes. In this town? It has its moments. It's used to me. Knows about me and Justine. Once the gossiping's done, it makes no more judgements. I come and I go and everybody knows my name. This place has become a habit of mine. Do you like it here?'

'In this room? I'm addicted to this room. In this town? Dunno. I think it might become a habit of mine, too. I feel safe here. That scares me. Safety scares me.'

He said, 'Ah.'

The darkness was dense now. She asked Nelson, 'Did you cry when Justine left? Did you cry when she went wild like that?'

He shook his head. 'No, I don't cry. Can't. Did you cry?'

'Oh yes. I always cry at things. In times of despair crying's better than not crying.'

'Yes,' he said. 'It is. If you can manage it.'

They watched the fire. Rowan lay with her head on his knee till the day caught up with her and she slept. When she woke the fire had died and he was sitting, one hand on her head, Walter's diary in the other.

'You shouldn't read other people's diaries.'

'I know, but I couldn't resist it. It's more than sad, it's haunting. He came and went in that huge black coat of his. I never knew this was what he was thinking.' He put the book down. 'It's time for bed.'

'I'm not sleepy now.'

'Good. Sleeping was not what I had in mind.'

They made love. Whisperings. Verbal intimacies. Sometimes he would stop, lean away from her, stroke her hair from her forehead and gaze at her intently.

'Are you happy?' she asked him.

'I have no history.'

Afterwards he slept, his head against her shoulder. He held onto her. She looked at him, resting on her. It was what she'd wished for. Years ago.

Chapter Sixteen

The New Raffles bar was no surprise. Halfway through the refurbishments George O'Connell had run out of patience, time and money. New wicker chairs were grouped round the old chipped tables. The floor was sanded and polished. Placed, decoratively (George thought) round the room were several palms. They seemed surprised to be there. Overhead a huge fan, suspended from the ceiling, squeaked slowly round and round.

'It should swish,' George complained, giving the fan a vicious nod, 'but we can't make it go faster. It causes a draught – well, a gale more like. Blows things around. Ash,' he pointed to an overflowing ashtray. 'Destroys hairdos. Had complaints.' He wiped a bit of over-wiped bar, 'Last time I buy secondhand.'

Jude and Rowan sat in a corner, behind a palm. They'd met in the Square. Rowan was on her way home with Sadie; Jude was standing at her front door. 'Hi, Rowan. Just standing here to preserve my sanity. Had to get out. Steven and Delia are at each other's throats.'

'So I hear,' said Rowan.

From the upstairs window came the sounds of teenagers murdering each other for possession of the television remote.

'I needed peace; I couldn't hear myself worry,' said Jude. 'Do you fancy a drink? We could go to the New Raffles. Have you been yet?'

'No,' said Rowan. 'I have to feed Sadie.'

'She can wait ten minutes. C'mon, it'll do you good.'

'OK,' said Rowan. 'It'd be some light relief from my own worrying.'

They crossed the Square. Went into the bar.

'What do you think of it?' Rowan asked, looking round.

'It's Raffles – the B & Q version,' said Jude going to the bar, buying them both a half pint without asking Rowan what she wanted. They sat near to the door.

'There's something wrong. Maybe it's the old dartsboard,' Jude went on. 'No, it's us – the customers. We don't look glamorous enough.' The bar was filled with people in old suits, dungarees, jeans, women in second-rate cheap-shouldered business suits. The laughter was loud, coarse. The fug – cheap cigarettes. 'We've no glitter about us. No posh frocks. Nobody's sipping a cocktail. The jokes are all blatantly dirty – nothing left to the imagination. We've let George down. He had grand notions, and we are all amateur dreamers. Anyway, if Singapore was to relocate I don't think it'd choose to come here.'

'Well,' said Rowan. 'That's the bar discussed. And dismissed. Actually, I prefer The Squelch. It's jaded and stained, like me. Like how I feel anyway. I've never been so stained. Babies are messy.' She shifted Sadie, fearing the child was going to damage her neck from leaning back to watch the fan.

'Sorry,' said Jude. 'I'm a bit low at the moment. I've joined the great unemployed.'

'What are you going to do?' asked Rowan. Sadie reached out for the fan. Kicking and crying out.

'Go back to university. Only thing for it. There's no work round here.'

'Back?'

'Yes. I was a student for a year. A whole year. But I dropped out.'

'Why?' Rowan wanted to know. Sadie arched her back and waved her arms.

'I couldn't understand what people were talking about. The lectures were OK, but afterwards in the pub – you know. It was all blah, blah, blah. Books. Films. Music. Always but. They'd say something was great. Then but. But the ending let it down. But So-and-so wasn't convincing in her part. But. But. *But!* Drove me daft.' Jude lit a cigarette, looked away across the room. Rowan realised for the first time how beautiful she was. Long dark hair. A narrow face, heavy-lidded eyes, full lips. Jude looked deep, poetic.

Jude sighed. 'These folks, the way they speak. "Um. Ah. I think . . . Well, it depends . . . on the whole . . . quite simply . . ."' She ran her fingers through her hair. 'Why can't they just say what they mean? I'm getting all agitated now, thinking about it. Why couldn't they just talk about what was on telly last night, crack a couple of jokes and go home for their tea. Like ordinary people. Like me.'

'If you don't mind my saying so,' said Rowan, 'don't you think that's what you were doing just now? Going on a bit, whilst you were saying what you thought of the bar?'

'Christ,' said Jude. 'That's right – so I was. My God! Maybe being verbose is infectious.' She turned to Rowan, a new fierce look in her eyes. 'D'you know what happened to me?'

Rowan shook her head.

'I was at my mother's and she was doing a crossword. She couldn't get a clue, so I told her the answer. It was one of those facts you have lying about your head that you don't know is there till someone asks you. That sort of thing.'

Rowan nodded.

'So my mother suddenly says, "Old Mrs Lucas, your primary schoolteacher, said you were one of the brightest children she ever taught." Me. Miss Lucas said I was naturally intuitive and logical. A gifted mathematician.' Jude stubbed out her cigarette, lit another. 'Why didn't anyone tell me? It would have saved me going through my life thinking I was stupid.'

'They didn't want you to get above yourself,' said Rowan, 'lest you left them behind or something. I don't know. I've made it my ambition to get above myself.'

'That's it,' said Jude. 'They thought I was trouble enough without me going about thinking I was intelligent. But I was miffed. It was my brain they were keeping me from, after all.'

At the time Jude was living with Frank Ross, the plumber. He'd fallen into her arms when his wife ran off with Duncan Willis.

'Hey,' she said to him that night, putting a plate of micro-waved pizza in front of him, 'did you know I was intelligent? My old teacher told my mum I was one of the brightest children she'd ever taught. Good at sums.'

'Not surprised.' Frank picked off his anchovies, laid them along

195

the side of his plate. 'Look at when you go to the supermarket –
you always know what you've spent, the exact amount. You can
add it up as you go whilst speaking to me about what your pals at
work said, and swearing at your kids at the same time. Not many
people can do that. In fact, nobody can do that.'

'Can't they?' Picking up the anchovies, eating them. She couldn't
be bothered cooking for herself.

'No.'

They said no more about it, but Jude enrolled in night classes.
Every Tuesday evening she'd leave her children with Frank and
go to the High School to her maths class. After four weeks she was
moved to the high-grade group. Five months later she was doing
calculus whilst humming selections from her favourite Police CD:
'Every breath you take . . . tum . . . tum . . . tum.' She was aware
she irritated people around her, but singing mindlessly helped her
cope with the hatred. She stopped going to class, but was off work
with a cold at exam time, so she dropped by the school to see if
they'd allow her to sit it. She got an A. The teacher came to her
house and persuaded Jude to give up the cannery and go to college
to get the qualifications necessary for university entrance. She had
a gift, he almost wept with admiration and jealousy. She should not
ignore it. In fact, it was her *duty* to nurture it. Jude shrugged, said
she'd give it a go.

'I don't mind it,' she told Frank. 'The work's fine, and I can go
the computers. But the folk – they talk rubbish. Blah. Blah. Blah.'

Frank shrugged. He didn't like this new arrangement. Jude left
the house at half past six in the morning to catch the bus to college
and didn't get back till seven at night. He missed her. And he had
to make all the meals. This wasn't what he'd planned. He put up
with it till Jude finished college. She had a long summer holiday
till her university course started. Frank sighed with relief. Things
were back to normal. Jude cooked and cleaned. He came home, ate,
went to the pub, came home again, screwed Jude, slept. The perfect
life. Then the gruelling routine came round again. Frank got angry.
As the months passed he grew angrier and angrier.

At the end of the academic year, Jude's tutor took her out for a
drink. They sat in a pub exchanging childhoods. 'My mother used
to make me wear heavy black lacing-up shoes to school,' he told

her. 'All the others wore Hush Puppies, but I was never allowed a pair.'

'Yeah, me too,' she said. 'Big shoes gave you a red mark on the top of your foot.'

'Yes,' he agreed, nodding vigorously. 'I was left out of games after school. They laughed at me in the playground 'cause I couldn't play football. I always think that's why I never got into sport. My friends all talk football and snooker but I can't ever join in. It's the shoes, I swear it is. Don't you feel something like that?'

Jude lit up. 'Nah,' through a cloud of exhaled smoke. 'I left my shoes behind when I left school, kicked them off at the gate. You've still got yours on.' She took a huge swig of her beer.

Her tutor stared at her, aghast. He paled. Hit by a squall of revelation, he lifted his hands to protect himself from this blast of truth. 'My God.' He leaned towards her, voice hushed. 'That's Zen, pure Zen. You are a genius.'

Jude stubbed out her cigarette. 'I don't think so. I think I'm normal and you're all daft.'

She told Frank about it when she got home. He picked up his bomber jacket from where he'd left it draped over the top of the kitchen door. 'I don't care about your effing tutor. I don't want to hear what he said. All I know is you are never fucking here, and I have to sort out these kids every night. And they're not even mine.'

'Two of them are,' Jude told him, looking round to see if she could spot the relevant infants. 'Could you not even wash up? I have to come in and do the dishes and pick stuff up and iron and I'm knackered.'

To which Frank said, 'Fuck off.' And left, slamming the door.

Jude slumped down at the kitchen table. Life these days was far from rosy. She thought longingly of her days back at the cannery – the songs, the jokes, the friends. Now look what was happening. She was constantly arguing with Frank; she hardly ever saw her children. Steven was up to all sorts of nonsense, stealing cars, creating havoc at school, arriving late, mooning at the girls' gym class, stealing, smoking dope in the lavatories. Charmaine had twice this week gone to school with no packed lunch. Sonia had been left at her mother's house because Frank had forgotten to pick her up. And Delia had been caught stealing a Mars Bar and a pack of multi-coloured ballpoint pens from Dunbar the newsagent's. This bettering yourself business was not what it was cracked up to be. So, at the end of her first year Jude gave up bettering herself. It made no difference to her relationship with Frank. He moved out. Education had changed Jude. He noticed that despite her objections to the habit in the people she'd mixed with, Jude had started to um and ah herself. *But* she'd say after an episode of *EastEnders*. 'But, would that really be her reaction when she found out her man was a wrong 'un?'

'Christ,' said Jude now, 'if I'd known what life was going to be like, I'd never have bothered. I'd've been a nun. So, what are you worrying about?'

'My folks are going on a cruise. I've nobody to look after Sadie.'

'Is that all?'

'Well, it's a big deal to me.'

'I'll do it – I'll take her. Give me something to do.' Jude reached over and took Sadie. Stood her on her knee. 'We'll get along fine, won't we, Sadie? I can get a bit of reading in when she has a sleep.'

'She goes down for an hour or so in the afternoon. You can take her over the road to my place.'

'Even better. Escape from my family. Steven can take Sonia. He's good with little ones. Sonia'll keep him in check.' She smiled. 'I'll set about teaching you to be above yourself, Sadie.'

Sadie reached for the locket round Jude's neck. Turned it over in her tiny fat hand.

'They're good when they're this age,' said Jude. 'You don't have the same worries. Just teething, and when they get sick. But you can cope – not like when they get up a bit. My Delia's gone all funny. She's quiet, doesn't speak to me.' She finished her drink. 'Well, she never did speak to me, but she was noisy and didn't speak. Quiet and *not* speaking – that's a worry. She's up to something.' Jude remembered well being pregnant at fourteen. She'd been the same. Silent and sulky. Often she ran through the list of awful things that could be bothering Delia. 'You're not pregnant, are you?' she had demanded last week.

'No,' Delia snapped.

'You on drugs?' Jude asked a few days later.

'Mum,' said in a sing-song. 'Get lost. Of course not.'

'Well, what's up with you?'

'Nothing,' Delia said. And left the room.

Jude shifted in her seat with worry and irritation. Why didn't the girl just say what was bothering her! She mooned about the house not saying a word to anyone. Then there was the shoes. For months Delia had nagged Jude to buy her a pair of Caterpillar boots. Once, she'd worn them. Once only – then Jude hadn't seen them again. 'What's wrong with your boots?' she'd asked. 'You nagged me for ages to get them.'

'Dunno. I'll wear them. They nip my toes.'

Above them the secondhand fan went squeak, squeak, squeak. Sadie abandoned the locket, stared up at the fan, and finally, frustrated at not being able to reach it, started to howl.

Rowan scooped her up. 'Time to go.' She started towards the door. Turned back to Jude. 'Um . . . I can't pay you – I've no money. I can just about keep myself and Sadie.'

'So what's new,' said Jude.

That evening, Rowan and Sadie, faces pressed together, looked out of the tiny lavatory window at the hills disappearing into darkness. Wasn't it strange? Rowan thought. She'd moved from London, thinking she was leaving all the fabulous people she'd ever know behind. Yet here she was living in a crumbling square in the middle of nowhere, surrounded by misfits. She supposed none of them knew they were misfits. Or maybe they weren't misfits here. They came and they went every day till, at last, they fitted in. Belonged.

She put Sadie to bed. When the child was asleep, she wandered the flat. Late June, the windows were wide open. She could hear the sounds of the Square. Car doors slamming. People coming out of the chip shop. She stood at the window, watching. Young Claudia, in her new navy tracksuit, jogged slowly past. Rowan could hear her puff and pant and the buzz of David Bowie tapes from the Walkman plugged into her ears. Rowan knew it'd be David Bowie. He'd been the love of Claudia's young life. When she was thirteen her walls had been covered with his posters. The only rebellious thing Claudia had ever done was disappear to one of his gigs in Glasgow. Her father had got out the Rolls-Royce and driven down to fetch her back. Claudia Senior told him to do it. It had been a small scandal at the time.

Looking at Claudia now, trotting past, disappearing up the Wynd, Rowan thought she was getting thinner. She thought Claudia was thinner every time she saw her. Thinner, but no happier. But then, Claudia rarely spoke to her these days. Whenever Rowan went into the chip shop Claudia would serve her then make excuses about being busy and disappear into the back shop. Rowan missed her old best friend. She wondered what she'd done. She sighed and went across to the red tub chair, to slump and catch up on Walter's doings.

21 July. Young Steven from across the Square came by. He brought me some marijuana. Said it'd be the thing for me. Cures everything, he said. He rolled me a couple of joints. Spliffs, he called them. Reefers, I used to call them. He's a good lad, really.

24 July. That marijuana stuff is a treat. Got to the Loch in record time. Wish I'd been more reckless in my youth – would have discovered it sooner. A new pen on the water; she swims along behind the others. She's got her eye on the cob. I have seen enough of that sort of woman not to know what she's up to. I fear the old pen hasn't got the strength to see her rival off.

I remember watching jackdaws. Young pair nesting. New young female turns up. Next thing, the new bit of stuff is on the nest and the other female is out, sitting on a perch gaping at her old nest. That was not long after my Jean had left me for Bill Whyte. She took over his house and two kids while I stayed back at our flat, taking comfort in the antics of a floosie jackdaw. Stupid bugger, me.

25 July. Used to walk the house holding my sides lest I fall apart. Don't blame her. Never made money. Couldn't afford holidays abroad. Only had a small secondhand car. The silence got me. Even worse, the sound of my own voice alone in the silence. It was flat – lifeless. Listening to me, I bored myself.

Soon that poor cob will be the rejected one. A poor cuckold swan alone in the reeds, neck dipped, wings up. On the way down the hill a whole cluster of partridges ran ahead of me down the path. Funny fat things. Speed they go. Why don't they fly away? God, if I could fly I'd get up there and never come down.

Rowan shut the diary. 'Time for bed,' she said. She wondered if her voice sounded flat in the silence. Or like Zebedee in *The Magic Roundabout*.

Chapter Seventeen

Rowan wondered if summer drove people crazy. The hot days, endless nights. The languid moon. It was hot. People complained about it. But then they would complain if it wasn't hot. Complaining was what they did best.

Norma, trying to hide her fear of going to new, strange places, encountering new, strange people, hid behind a new pink cotton suit and a big smile, and George, looking dashing in pale blue jacket with white shirt and maroon bow tie, left for their cruise. Norma fussed. Did they have the passports? George patted his pocket. Money? More pocket patting. Camera? *Oh, c'mon Norma. Get in the car.* Rowan, surprised at their sudden new look, waved them goodbye. Then she drove up the glen to spend the day and night, that she hoped would be the best bit, with Nelson.

His cottage, tucked down a tiny side road, was surprising. 'Minimalist,' he told her. He'd knocked the ground floor into one big room. Polished floors, a wood-burning stove, with an arty pile of logs behind it. White walls. One white sofa. A white vase on a wide window sill with a carefully arranged set of what Rowan thoughtlessly called twigs in it. Upstairs a bedroom and a study. The hall between the rooms was lined with books. The whole place was spotless.

'Goodness,' said Rowan. 'Are you sure you want us in here? We're both messy, Sadie and me.'

'You especially,' said Nelson. 'I noticed.'

Rowan put down her bag and the collection of Sadie's favourite toys she'd brought with her. They stuck out garishly in this stylish setting. 'Perhaps I could arrange them artily,' she suggested.

'Forget it,' said Nelson. 'Fussy minimalist people need untidy scruffs like you as much as messy scruffs need fussy minimalists. We keep one another from going too far.'

They idled the day in the garden, drinking wine, making small talk, playing silly Sadie games. When Sadie slept that night, spread out in Nelson's bed, they made love on the sofa, talking softly. Making a point of making no plans. Though they both had the feeling that soon, or sometime, plans would have to be made. Don't rush it, Nelson thought. A day at a time, or better still, a night at a time, Rowan thought.

She left late on Sunday afternoon; Nelson saw her off. Leaning into the car, he said, 'Take care. Don't go hurtling down the road in your usual messy scruff's manner.'

'I don't drive like a messy scruff.'

'Yes, you do – I've seen you. One-speed Rowan. Parking squint. Kicking the door shut.'

'You've been watching me.'

'Only when there's no football results to read, or scrunged-up bits of paper to aim at the waste-bin. What are you doing Wednesday night?'

'Oh, probably staying in. Slobbing about, being messy. I'm planning a night of it.'

'I'll come by, then. I'll bring food.'

'You don't need to do that.'

'Yes, I do. I've seen your cupboards.'

'Oh well. See you Wednesday. Well, I'll see you tomorrow. But I'll see more interesting bits of you on Wednesday.' Rowan drove off. Sedately till she was out of sight, then she pressed the accelerator up to the full Messy Scruff hurtle.

She got back to her flat just after four. Sadie was bouncy after her sleep in the car, so Rowan put her into her buggy and went to the park. There she met young Claudia cautiously shoving her youngest child, Joey, on the swings. Rowan put Sadie on her infant's swing next to Joey, and pushed her – too high in Claudia's opinion. 'She could fall out. She's only little.' Sadie was squealing with joy. 'You'll get her overexcited. She'll end up crying.'

'Oh come on, Claudia. A few thrills are good for you.'

Claudia said, 'Hmm.'

'I think you're avoiding me these days,' said Rowan, lifting Sadie from the infant's swing and sitting on an ordinary one, the baby on her knee, so they could go higher.

'I'm not avoiding you,' Claudia said. She shifted slightly, looking away. 'I'm avoiding you,' her body said. She was tired. Had spent the day serving ice cream. 'A single cone, or a double? What flavour? Chocolate topping?' She ached. Her body was protesting about its daily pre-dawn encounters with Cher. 'Hi,' said Cher. 'Hi,' said Claudia, setting up her pile of books. 'Always do the warm-up,' said Cher. 'I do. I do,' said Claudia.

She groaned as she picked up Joey and sat with him on the swing next to Rowan, though she worried about this. What if her bum didn't fit?

'What's happened to you?' asked Rowan. 'You don't seem happy.'

'I'm happy. What's happy, anyway?'

Today she'd leaned on the counter watching people walk round the Square. Strangers on Sunday outings. Families licking ice-cream cones, pointing and staring. Older children two paces behind their parents, looking bored. She remembered that. Then there were groups of friends. Friends, she thought it an alluring word. She didn't have any. Oh, she had chums. Other women who shared the school run, or who turned up at parents' day at school. Then there was the dinner-party group. First Saturday of every month they met at a different house to eat, drink wine. The chat was about holidays, home extensions, cars. It bored her. Besides, she knew she was the least popular woman. Other husbands didn't flirt with her. Wives all knew she was a better cook than they were, and didn't hate her for it. Just resented her for it, which was worse. It was such a mild resentment, nothing serious. The groups of friends she watched today, fat arm resting on the counter, milled about each other, laughing. She imagined their conversations to be fabulous. Surely nobody could have such fun talking about holidays, home extensions or cars. That would be the sort of relationship Rowan would have with her London friends. All that talking, laughing, arms round each other. Claudia felt a knot tighten in her stomach. Jealousy.

'It must be dull for you back here,' she said to Rowan now.

'Not really. Not at all. It's fine.' Remembering last night with

Nelson. 'More than fine.' She swung back and forward. 'I wish you'd speak to me when I come into the shop,' Rowan said. 'You're my best friend. I've always thought of you as my best friend. Even in London if anyone asked, I always said you.'

Claudia didn't believe this. 'But we hadn't seen each other for years.' Actually until recently she'd felt the same. These days she sort of thought of Cher as her friend, though she knew this to be nonsense. Cher shared her pain every morning. Cher understood.

'I know, but that's what I thought. Now I'm home I get the feeling you run away every time you see me.'

'I'm busy,' Claudia shrugged.

'Still,' said Rowan, 'I feel there's something wrong. I never see you smile. You used to be so up, so full of life. All the boys fancied you.'

'Now it's you have men running after you. Paolo, Nelson.' It had not escaped Claudia's notice that Nelson's car had been parked outside Rowan's flat all night last week.

'Oh rubbish.' Then, cheekily, 'Maybe it's my turn. I used to think you had all the fun, and I was just your dowdy little friend. Remember the time you ran away to a Bowie gig and your dad drove to Glasgow to find you?'

'Oh, that.' Claudia dismissed the memory, though she recalled the occasion well. She'd had fun. Made friends. She didn't know who they were, just a bunch of people she'd got chatting to. They'd given her a spliff. They'd bought her a drink. It had been wonderful. They'd invited her back to their flat. They thought she was a lot older than she was. Then when she was coming out with them, that heady whiff of fresh air after the steam and smoke inside made her almost scream when it hit her lungs. But her world crumbled. Her father had been parked outside, leaning on the Rolls-Royce. Glowering.

'It that your dad?' someone said. 'Is that your car?'

'Yes,' she replied before she meekly crossed the road and climbed into the front passenger seat. She remembered turning round and watching her fleeting new friends drift away as she was whisked home to her raging mother. She'd been grounded for six weeks, and that had been that. Her teenage rebellion had been one night, one gig, one spliff, a few noisy hours with friends. She thought of it often. She wanted some more of it. She still hated her father for being there, embarrassing her in front of all her chums, whoever they were.

'I'd forgotten about that,' she lied to Rowan.

'I was always jealous of that,' Rowan confessed. 'I never did anything naughty in my teenage. We-ell. A bit of mischief with Duncan Willis.'

'I'll bet,' Claudia said. A brittle little smile flitted slightly on her lips. Claudia imagined that Rowan would have had hundreds of men. Hundreds. She'd only had one – Stu MacGregor, her husband. And the sex was boring. She knew how thrilling it ought to be; she'd read about it in *Cosmopolitan*. Stu did the business, rolled over and fell asleep. Claudia thought Rowan would know all sorts of things about sex – positions, stuff like that. It wasn't that Stu hadn't been willing to experiment. Early in their marriage he'd wanted to do all sorts of things – dress up, exotic positions. He'd a thing about nurses. But at that time Claudia had been unable to do anything. Every time she embarked on some sort of sexual adventure with Stu she had to stop. She had a vision of her mother bursting into the room, standing arms akimbo, shouting, 'What are you up to, Claudia?'

Claudia sighed. She turned to Rowan. 'Your roots are showing.'

'I know, I know. Where should I go to get my hair fixed?'

'Marla.'

'Who is Marla?' Rowan wanted to know.

'The hairdresser. She doesn't have a posh salon or anything. Folk go to her house. She converted her garage. Everyone goes to her.'

'Is she good?'

'Of course she is. She goes to demonstrations in London – Vidal Sassoon at the Hilton and that. Does all the latest styles.'

Rowan thought back to the list she'd made – the pros and cons of coming home. She hadn't wanted to come back because her mother was here. Now Norma seemed somehow smaller, less fussy. A human being, almost. Then there had been the hairdresser thing – pretty high on the list for pro staying in London. Now there was Marla in the garage. Sometimes, Rowan thought she got just about everything wrong.

They stopped swinging. Put their infants into their buggies and headed slowly back towards the Square. On their left, sloping up to a new scheme of houses, was a long grassy hill.

'Remember we used to roll down that when we were little?'

'Yes,' said Claudia mildly.

'Let's do it again. Let's do it now. C'mon.' Rowan was game.

Claudia stared up at the hill. She remembered afternoons after school when she and Rowan tumbled roley-poley down it. Soft grass on her face. Wildly out of control and giggling. 'Yes, let's,' she said. 'Race you to the top.'

They abandoned their snoozing infants and ran, puffing up the hill. Then lay at the top a moment before letting go and rolling screaming, over and over to the bottom.

They lay panting.

'Want to do it again?' asked Rowan. 'That was great.'

'Yes,' said Claudia, 'but I have to get back. Why do we grow up? Why do we have to stop rolling down hills?'

Rowan stood up and dusted herself off. 'Dunno. Seems a dumb thing to do.'

Claudia and Rowan walked together out of the park, up the hill to the Square.

'I always envied you your family,' Rowan confessed. 'All that speaking and bickering at the table. The movement. The life. My folks seemed so dull.'

'I always envied *you*. Your mother is so placid. She let you do what you wanted, never nagged. My God, my mother. The human volcano.'

'Remember Parents' Day?' asked Rowan.

Claudia raised her eyebrows. 'Wish I couldn't.'

On Parents' Day Rowan's mother would meekly take on board that Rowan wasn't trying. Could do better. Seemed distracted. Claudia's mother would not hear her children criticised. 'How dare you speak about my Claudia like that!' On hearing that young Claudia preferred flirting to schoolwork, hung about with the boys, giggled in class and had been caught in the cloakroom with Kenny Watson from sixth year, her tongue down his throat, when she should have been in French class. 'Take that back! I will not hear my daughter badmouthed by the likes of you.' To Claudia's guidance teacher: 'Nobody who wears a tie like that speaks ill of a Rossi.'

Young Claudia still blushed to remember.

Miss Porteous, at her living-room window, watched them go. *Cancer: Do not expect old friends to accept the new you. Be patient. Try to see yourself as they see you. Libra: Could it be you are letting personal insecurities interfere in your relationships? Perhaps you should relax and enjoy any friendship that's on offer rather than feeling you are the brunt of some sort of criticism. Do not doubt yourself.*

On Tuesday Rowan left Sadie with Jude whilst she went to Marla's garage to have her hair cropped and roots done. Jude took Sadie home, put her on the sofa in front of the fake coal fire and played with her. She loved babies, especially other people's babies. Besides, Sadie in her little denim dungarees and striped jersey was special. Sadie was an abandoned child. Sadie was still a local celebrity. Jude thought she was the only VIP who would ever enter her home.

When Delia came into the room and asked if she could go to a party at her friend Kathryn's house, Jude said, 'Of course. Didn't think you needed to ask.' She was delighted to hear Delia actually had a friend.

'Only,' said Delia, 'I'll be late.'

'So what's new about that?' Jude said. She hardly looked at the girl.

'Nothing,' said Delia. 'Just letting you know.'

Jude looked up. Delia was wearing jeans and an old, favourite T-shirt. 'You're not going like that, are you? Thought it was a party.'

'It is. This is how people go to parties these days.'

'Don't you want to get all done up? What about your purple frock? You look great in that.'

'I want to wear this.'

'Whatever,' Jude shrugged. Turned back to Sadie. 'We prefer her purple frock, don't we?'

Delia left the room. 'I'll be off, then.'

'You're going now? It's only six o'clock.'

'I want to be there early. Help get things set up.'

'Put out the crisps and that,' said Jude. Helpfully, she thought.

'Crisps.' Delia's face creased with derision.

Jude said, 'Sorry.' And, 'You be back here by midnight.'

'Fine,' said Delia.

Jude looked at her suspiciously. This wasn't right, Delia agreeing a curfew without a fight. 'You're only fourteen. You're not disappearing into the night at your age.'

Delia crossed the room and to Jude's astonishment kissed her. 'Goodbye, Mum.'

Jude lifted Sadie's hand and waved it. 'Say goodbye to Delia.'

Delia waved back. A sad little flap of her hand.

Rowan turned up half an hour later and, after the fussing and celebrations over her restored hairdo, took Sadie home. Jude fed her family, and settled on her sofa. At her feet, Sonia scribbled on a sheet of paper she'd found in Delia's room. It was half past seven. Jude had a whole four and a half hours before she had to start worrying about Delia.

Delia took the glen bus to the Drover's Inn. School rucksack on her back, she walked up the track to the fishing pool. Then took off through the heather till she was high above the water. She crested a small hill and saw the glen spread before her. The narrow road winding back to Fretterton. A car threading its way down the glen, tiny in the distance. Far away the rooftops and first evening lights of the village. Her mother would be down there watching a soap, smoking. Steven would be standing outside the chip shop bantering with his mates. Her sisters would be in her bedroom playing with her make-up. Her grandma and granda would be listening to their Jim Reeves records. She could imagine it all. She liked it here. This was a fine place to die.

She'd brought with her a bottle of paracetamol, whisky that Steven had bought for her when she told him she was going to a party, and some cigarettes pinched from her mother's packet. She lit one up, contemplated what she was about to do. It seemed the only thing. She wasn't afraid. She took the whisky and a glass from her rucksack and poured a drink. Took a slug. It rasped against the back of her throat. She coughed. Held her hand over her mouth, tears in her eyes. It was horrible. She wished she'd brought a bottle of vodka and some Coke. But she didn't think that would do the trick. Didn't her mother always say, 'Whisky's a killer.'

At school she'd been studying *Ode to a Nightingale*. Drowsy numbness, it said. She liked that. 'Drowsy numbness,' she whispered. It would be like that. She'd drift off. No more worries. No more pain. She took her first paracetamol. Broke it in two. Washed it down a half at a time with her whisky. She was not used to whisky. It swam through her. She would not, she realised, ever know what happened to the people in *Neighbours*. Or drive a car. Or make love. Or eat another Snickers bar. Or . . . or . . . The ors were endless. The evening was clear, hot. Tiny moths fluttered above the heather. A bee hummed nearby. Delia lay back. She wondered what Jude would say about her death. Would she miss her? She took another paracetamol. She could hardly see the bottle for tears.

One o'clock in the morning, Jude started to worry. *The Carpetbaggers* was on the telly, but she didn't feel up to watching something she might enjoy. It might distract her from her uneasiness.

She remembered her own teenage. The nights. Parties. Not wanting to leave because it was all happening. What was happening? She considered this. Absolutely nothing really. But it had seemed like a lot at the time. She remembered feeling she was the only one who had to leave to go home. She decided to send Steven round to bring Delia home. Mothers turning up, she remembered vividly, were humiliating.

Half an hour later Steven came back. 'She's not there.'

'Well, where is she?' Jude demanded. She was smoking furiously. Her mild stomach churns were turning to frenzy. Something was wrong. She was thinking rape and murder. This time of year there were all sorts of strangers about. Delia had been attacked on the way home. Delia was in bed with one of the village boys and about to fall like her mother had fallen all those years before. Delia had been run over. Delia had taken E and was crazed out of her mind wandering the streets. Delia was being gang-banged by a bunch of wild village boys.

'Where is she?' she asked again.

'Dunno,' shrugged Steven. 'She'll turn up.'

'Who could she be with? What other friends has she?'

'Dunno,' said Steven. 'When I bought her the whisky she told me she was going to Kathryn's. Weird, that. I usually get her vodka.'

'Wait.' Jude put her hands on Steven's shoulders. 'Rewind a couple of sentences. You bought her *what*?'

'Whisky.'

'Whisky! You bought her whisky! She's a child, Steven. What are you doing, buying her that? How come you bought her that? You're underage. What the hell is going on?'

'Dunno.'

'Don't dunno me.'

'She said she was going to a party and wanted whisky. So I got her some. Well, I didn't. Got a mate to get it. He's nineteen.'

'So you got her whisky and now she has disappeared.'

'Yeah.'

'What else does she do that I don't know about?'

'Nothing,' Steven shrugged. 'She doesn't do drugs. Offered her some. Nope, she didn't want them.'

'Well, that's a relief.' Jude spat out the sarcasm. 'Is she seeing somebody? You know, sleeping with some bloke.'

Steven shook his head.

'Well what?' Jude shouted. 'Tell me. Don't give me any of your nothing crap.'

Steven sighed. 'There's a gang of girls bullying her at school.'

'What do you mean, bullying?'

'They knock her about. Happens all the time. They steal her stuff. They wanted money.'

'Who? Who did this to my Delia?'

'Just some girls.'

'Just some girls. I'll kill them. Why didn't you tell me?'

'You don't tell your mother these things. You just don't.'

'Why not?'

'It's the rules.'

'Rules?'

'Yeah. You don't tell. That's the rules.'

'You are about to break the rules. Tell me. What did they steal?'

'Her lunch-money. Her calligraphy pen. Her shoes.'

'Her shoes?'

'Yeah. Her Cats.'

'What! The boots I bought her? I'm still paying them off and some bitch is walking around in them. Why didn't you tell me?'

'You'd interfere.'

'Too right I would. I am interfering. The interfering starts here.'

'She gets bullied because she's a swot. She's clever – she always does her homework. That's something else they steal. And there's you.' Steven sighed out his list.

'Me? What have I got to do with it? Oh, don't tell me. I'm a slag.'

'She doesn't know who her father is.'

Jude covered her face. 'Oh God.'

'Neither do I. Officially,' said Steven. 'Except it's Rossi. Everyone knows that.'

'Why didn't you help Delia?'

'I tried – I made it worse. They just knocked Delia about more. And took her shoes.'

'You broke the rules. You interfered. Were you ever bullied?'

'Yeah. Some boys said things about you. I kicked them in. Wasn't having it. You're a cool mother. You let us do what we like.'

Jude looked at him. 'Well, thanks for that.' She got up to go to the kitchen, slipped on the paper Sonia had been colouring earlier. 'Damn child,' she cursed, picking it up. It was scrawled with bright colours, but beneath the scribbles was a note.

Dear Mum, Steven, Charmaine and Sonia,
Sorry.
Love, Delia.

Jude handed it to Steven. 'What does that mean? Has she run away?'

They went to Delia's room. Sonia and Charmaine were sleeping on the bunk beds at one side. At the other, was Delia's empty bed.

Jude opened her wardrobe. It was full. 'She hasn't taken anything.'

'Harvey's missing,' said Steven.

Delia's toy rabbit. Her sleeping companion since she was four was not in his position, tucked under the covers, his furry head on her pillow. Jude turned cold with dread. She did not want to voice her fear, as if saying it out loud might make the dire thing she was

213

thinking actually happen. But at last she said, 'Do you think she's going to kill herself?'

'Don't say that,' said Steven.

Jude phoned the police. A soothing, slightly patronising voice at the other end of the line told her not to worry. Kids did this sort of thing. Her daughter would be with a friend. 'She'll turn up in the morning looking sorry for herself.'

'I don't think so,' said Jude.

The voice said, 'You'll see. We'll take details. And if she hasn't turned up, let us know.'

Jude put down the phone. Started pacing. 'I can't just stay here. I can't do nothing.' She took Steven's old torch and left. 'You stay here. I have to look for her.'

Two hours later, she returned. 'Can't find her. Searched the school playground. The sports field. The park. The old railway line. She's gone.'

'If I was going to top myself I'd go where nobody would find me. Up the glen.'

'You're such a comfort,' said Jude. 'I'll get Rowan. She's got a car.'

Four-thirty in the morning Jude ran across the Square. Mama Claudia, an insomniac since her menopause, was looking out of her window, watched her go. She saw Rowan's bedroom light go on. Then her living-room light. The curtains were not drawn. She could see Jude and Rowan speaking. Jude was waving her arms about; Rowan was trying to calm her down. Something was happening. The boy, she thought. She got dressed. Ran down the stairs, out through her courtyard. First blackbirds singing. A thin film of morning damp on the precious Rolls-Royce. And over to Rowan's flat.

The door was not locked. Mama Claudia knocked; when nobody came, she went in. Jude was sitting on the red tub chair, sobbing. Rowan was wearing her Acid Jazz T-shirt and knickers, holding two mugs of coffee. They both looked at her. It was the first time Rowan had seen her flustered. Claudia slunk through the door. Normally she took rooms by storm.

'Sorry,' she looked embarrassed. 'I saw Jude come here. Something's happened, hasn't it?'

'Delia's missing,' Rowan told her. 'She's been getting bullied at school. Jude thinks she's gone up the glen with some paracetamol and a bottle of whisky to . . .' it seemed too awful to say '. . . to do away with herself.'

'You know this?' said Claudia.

'Steven got her a bottle of whisky, I know that. I had some paracetamol – it's missing, I know that,' wept Jude. 'I want to go and look for her. I can't just sit and wait.'

'Well, go.' Claudia waved her arms at the door. 'Now.'

'I can't drive,' said Jude.

'I can't leave Sadie,' said Rowan.

'Go. I'll stay. If Sadie wakes I'll look after her.'

Rowan thought that with the number of people passing through Sadie's life, looking after her, the child was bound to develop a complex, but she didn't like to mention it, not now. 'I'll get dressed,' she said. She went to her bedroom, pulled on jeans and a jersey, shoved her feet into her walking boots, picked up the car keys, and told Jude she was ready.

'Where would she go?' Rowan asked as they drove out along the glen road. 'Up the track?'

'God forbid she knows about that place. She's only fourteen.' Jude was ashen with worry. She ran one hand through her hair. Used the other to hold her cigarette.

Rowan said nothing.

'I know, I know. I went up the track at fourteen. But Delia's different. There's brains in there under the constant baseball hat. *The fishing pool!*' Jude almost shouted it. 'We used to go for picnics there when she was little. She loved that spot.'

They drove on. Jude lit another cigarette. 'It's all my fault. Everything. It was all going on and I didn't know. What sort of mother am I?'

'You're fine. You're fine,' Rowan assured her.

'She was always asking who her father was. And I wouldn't tell her.'

'Um . . .' said Rowan. Was this the right moment? 'Who *is* her father?'

'Who do you think? Paolo Rossi. I'm not the slut everyone thinks I am. I just put on a tarty face, enjoying a bad reputation. It was a show. You know, everyone thought me a slut so I flounced about. It was either that or hang my head.'

It had been a lovely time in her life, Jude remembered. Exquisite. After Steven was born Jude had been forbidden to see Paolo. And Paolo forbidden to see Jude. The more they weren't allowed contact, the more they sought it. Nights, Paolo would climb the drainpipe outside Jude's window and enter her room. They spent illicit hours together swearing eternal love in whispers. They were misunderstood and miserable. They loved it.

They met at their secret rendezvous – the bandstand in the park. There they'd dance, humming favourite songs. They drank wine that Paolo stole from his father's cellar in long-stemmed glasses that he stole from his mother's glass cabinet. 'How could two glasses go missing?' The family had shrugged in unison. They all felt guilty; Claudia Senior did that to them. He brought her an equally long-stemmed rose. White, for he knew she didn't like red. She still had it, pressed inside the sleeve of her old Paul Simon album. They were in love, vowed to run away together as soon as Paolo finished school. They'd open a small restaurant someplace far away where nobody knew their names. They would be in love for ever. Under starry skies, one perfect summer, just like this one, Jude thought, they'd pledged themselves to each other. Then Jude got pregnant again.

She could not bring herself to tell her parents about her secret affair. Thinking she was protecting her love, she'd refused to say who was the father of her new baby. Paolo, unable to face his mother's wrath at being disobeyed, had let her. He hated himself for that. For years, whenever he saw Jude across the Square, he'd gaze at her. 'Sorry,' he said. She ignored him.

Several times he had tried to press money into her hands, but she wouldn't take it. When he refused to accept it back from her, she'd let it drop, sometimes hundreds of pounds, to the pavement at his feet. Why did she do that, she wondered. Pride, romantic pride. She'd been so very young. She had some absurd notion of being a wronged woman. Now she and Paolo could hardly look at each other. If they met in the street they'd both look away, pretend it all hadn't happened. God, Jude thought, if he handed me a wad of notes now, I'd grab it. 'I've only had two men,' she told Rowan.

'Paolo and Frank. Not like you going off to London, with all those wild parties. Lots of men. You've lived a little.'

'Hardly,' said Rowan.

Jude ignored her. She didn't believe her.

Delia woke. She emerged from a blackness. It was dawn. The peaks were rimmed red. A pale moon dying. Curlews called. Two deer were moving swiftly across the heather below her. Her head hurt. She threw up. Then threw up again. Groaning. Her guts jerked and she threw up till there was nothing left to throw up. But that didn't stop her retching. Her sides ached.

'Oh, not again.' Her stomach heaved, she put her face down, mouth agape, heather scratched her cheeks, and she watched a thin stream of green bile pour from her lips. She shook with cold; lay back shivering. Her hand fell against the whisky bottle. It was almost empty. The heather was flattened where she'd passed out, clutching Harvey to her. She shut her eyes against the light. She'd never known such a headache in her life. She was sore all over, shaking with cold. Right now, she really, really wanted to die.

When at last she sat up again she found the paracetamol. She rattled the bottle. How many had she taken? Six – seven? 'Not enough,' she said and threw the bottle half-heartedly away. The whisky had got to her before she could take more. She'd blacked out, filthy drunk. Trembling, she got to her feet, packed the whisky in her rucksack, picked up Harvey and started down the hill towards the fishing pool. In the distance she saw a car's headlights travelling up the glen. 'People,' she whispered.

Rowan parked the car in the Drover's Inn car park. She and Jude started up towards the fishing pool. Panting, dread coursing through them, they began to climb. Jude, despite her thirty-a-day habit, strode ahead. Rowan found it hard to keep up with her. They kept stopping, clutching their chests. Coughing. Rowan looked about her, fearing what she might see. A body, lying, lumpen and dead. It was a perfect morning. A slow mist rising, the day that was rolling in behind it was going to be another scorcher. Rowan and Jude did not speak till halfway up, when they saw Delia lurching towards them holding Harvey to her.

They got back at seven o'clock. The village was waking. Rowan stopped the car at Jude's door. They all sat in silence a small moment, too relieved, too exhausted to speak.

'Thanks,' Jude said, at last. 'Are you coming up?'

Rowan shook her head. 'I should get back.'

'I'll get your jumper back to you later today,' Jude promised. When they'd met Delia stumbling down the track, Rowan had taken off her jersey and given it to the girl. 'She's freezing.'

'Freezing with the worst hangover in the world,' Jude said, putting her arms round her daughter, rubbing some warmth into her. 'Christ, Delia. Don't you ever do that again.'

Rowan went home to tell Claudia the news. 'She's been getting bullied at school,' Rowan said. 'They even stole her shoes – her Caterpillar boots.'

'Shoes?' Claudia was amazed. 'How did she get home?'

Rowan shrugged. 'Barefoot.'

Claudia shook her head. She was feeding Sadie a mashed-up boiled egg. Even that looked delicious. 'She's a good baby,' said Claudia. 'A charmer.'

'I know.' Rowan stroked Sadie's cheek. 'I don't want any of this sort of nonsense when you grow up. How was she when she woke?'

'Surprised to see me, but she only had a bit of a cry. She's a friendly little thing.'

Rowan nodded. 'Do you want some coffee?'

'Oh yes.' She didn't, but felt it uncivil to refuse the offer.

Rowan made two steaming mugs. Handed one to Claudia. She sipped it, but couldn't quite mask her distaste.

'A perfectionist even in a crisis,' Rowan said. 'Is it that bad?'

'I like espresso first thing.' Claudia looked into her mug. 'It's my habit.' She took another sip. Made a face, and smiled. 'I'll take Sadie today. Jude won't be up to it.' She paused. 'So who is Delia's father, anyway?'

Rowan looked away. Couldn't answer.

'I knew it,' said Claudia. 'The way Jude and Paolo won't look at each other. I knew it. What a mess.'

Across the Square Jude ran Delia a bath. 'Get warmed up,' she said. 'Then sleep. We'll talk later.' She shook her head. 'You daft bugger. If you try that again, I'll kill you.'

'I know.' Delia was quiet. 'They kept shouting at me, shoving me. They'd follow me about shouting things. They wanted me to fail all my exams, but I couldn't. I'd have nothing. I'd—'

'End up like me,' said Jude. 'You won't. I won't let you.'

When Delia was in bed, Jude sat at the kitchen table with Steven. 'We nearly lost her.'

Steven nodded.

'Tell me.' Jude gave him one of her don't-dare-lie looks. 'You said these bully girls wanted money.'

'A hundred pounds,' said Steven. 'She gave it to them.'

'Where the hell did she get that kind of money?'

'From the bank.'

'She doesn't have that in the bank.'

'My mate does. He got a bank loan – said he wanted to buy a car.'

'My God,' said Jude. 'Your friend got a bank loan, and gave it to Delia?'

'Sort of.' Steven looked shifty.

Jude grabbed his arm, leaned towards him. 'Tell me.'

'We used it to buy stuff. Drugs.' He mumbled this last word. 'And we sold them. She got some of the profit.'

Jude jumped to her feet. 'Jesus Christ. My son's a pusher. My daughter's a suicide. I didn't know. What sort of mother am I?' She put her face in her hands. 'I'm a terrible, terrible person.'

Steven came round the kitchen table to her. Put his arms round her. 'You're not. Really you're not.'

Jude buried her face against his shoulder and wept. Steven patted her mildly and stared out of the window. Sometimes being the only bloke in a house full of women was too much.

Next morning when Jude opened her door there was a box on the landing. She opened it. Inside was a pair of Caterpillar boots. No note. The morning after, someone else left a second pair. When, on the third morning, Jude found another pair, she wondered if she ought to put a notice in the *Gazette* saying: *Thank you, but no more.*

Chapter Eighteen

Rowan didn't know exactly when the dread started. She knew it had been lurking within her for some days before she acknowledged it. Seven o'clock one evening, early July, she was walking past the Town Hall, where the Operatic Society were rehearsing *Oklahoma*, their big autumn production. '*O-O-O-O-klahoma . . .*' The song rolled out, vast waving plains of wheat. '*O-O-O-Oklahoma . . .*' Rowan stopped to listen. The people in there were singing their hearts out, playing at being stars, happy as anything. She hated musicals, but her heart momentarily lifted before the dread set in again. It was a small biting worry that would not go away.

'I have this feeling of dread all the time. It's there, gnawing away at my insides,' she told Mamie one lunchtime.

'You must be feeling all right,' Mamie said, pouring her tea. 'It's the price of happiness. You always think it's going to end. And end horribly.'

'You think?' Rowan asked.

'I know,' Mamie nodded.

'But I'm not happy,' Rowan argued.

'You must be. You just don't know it.'

Rowan's days were drifting past. She'd had three postcards from Norma and George. *Having a lovely time. Glad you're not here. Ha-ha, just kidding.* She left Sadie with Jude. She worked. Several times a week Nelson would come by. He always brought food.

'This is what shelves are for,' he said, filling her cupboard with tins of tuna, mayonnaise, hot chocolate. 'Food. It's a new concept for you, but you'll soon grasp it.'

'I used to buy food in London. I just don't have money for me and Sadie. She's expensive.'

Weekends she stayed at Nelson's cottage. Lay on the floor with a heap of plastic toys, and Sadie.

Saturday mornings, before she drove up to see Nelson, Rowan would take Sadie to the swimming baths. She'd lift the child high out of the water. 'Big jump, Sadie.' Or hold her, skimming her over the surface. 'You're swimming, Sadie.' Evenings they would press their faces together staring out of the little lavatory window at the hills. 'Do they fill you with longing, Sadie?' The child grew. Every time Rowan came into the room her face would crease into smiles. 'Who's your best friend then, Sadie?'

Rowan would leave work and rush to Jude's flat to get Sadie. 'Time to go home. Fish for tea. You should see the price of haddock.' She was turning into her mother. Mornings she would lie Sadie in her arms, listening to her breathing, waiting for her to wake and start a new day, smiling. Lips to her moist young forehead. 'You are mine.'

'I should take you to dinner,' Nelson said. It was Thursday morning. He was wearing his striped robe, boxers and a pair of socks with a hole in the toe. He'd moved some of his clothes and his shaving gear into Rowan's house. Last night she had cooked for him.

'Wouldn't you rather fish? It rained last night. Trout will be up there in the Loch leaping about, ripe for the catching.'

'I'd rather take you out. I've never taken you out.'

'You've bought me fish and chips.'

'Not the same. We'll go to the Italian place in Perth. Will Jude take Sadie?'

'Probably. Or Delia will sit in.'

'How is she?'

'She's all right.'

'How's Delia?' Rowan asked yesterday when she picked up Sadie.

'Still quiet. Doesn't go out much. When she does she can't decide which boots to wear. She got one pair from the school. They had a whip round. Claudia sent a pair, and Paolo. I don't know,' Jude sighed. 'Nothing for years. Then a pair of boots when his daughter tries to top herself.'

'Guilt,' said Rowan.

'I'm thinking it's a bit late to feel guilty. Anyway, I'm guilty enough for all of us.'

'Are you happy, Jude?' Rowan asked. She knew she shouldn't.

'Christ, Rowan. My daughter's just tried to do herself in. My son's been selling drugs to God knows who. My bloke's left me. I've lost my job. What do you think? Am I happy? Guess. No prizes for the right answer.'

'Sorry,' said Rowan. 'If you were Julie Andrews you'd find a reason to sing, despite all that.'

'Well, thanks. I'll just burst into *A Spoonful of Sugar* and dance round the Square. That'll do the trick. That'll fix everything.' Jude folded her arms, and considered Rowan.

Rowan said, 'Sorry,' again. Then, 'But do you trust happiness? I should be happy. Happiness is just a jump away. All I have to do is take the leap. But I'm scared.'

'Ah well,' said Jude, 'if there's one thing scarier than being unhappy, it's being happy. You know no good will come of it. It'll end in tears.'

Rowan nodded.

'When I first went to university, I thought: This is it. This is me, now. I'll get educated, get a job. Everything'll be roses. But I didn't think I fitted in. Know how I felt?'

Rowan shook her head.

'I feel like that guy, you know? I have been to the mountain-top and I have seen the other side. And know what I saw?'

'Another bloody mountain?' suggested Rowan.

'Too right. More effing obstacles.'

They sighed. Life was a bitch.

The Italian Place was humming with Saturday-night fervour. Hurtling waiters, drunken diners, atmosphere heavy with booze and fags. Thrumming kitchen at the end, clattering crockery and the occasional pizza being tossed into the air. Culinary juggling. A small guy in an overwrought tuxedo drifted from table to table serenading anybody who caught his eye. He sang *When Swallows Come Back to Capistano* and *I Left My Heart in San Francisco*. He'd hand his mike over to people eager to have a go. Saturday night, after the pub, it seemed to Nelson and Rowan that everyone wanted

223

to have a go. Except them. They kept the singer at bay with swift, fierce, keep-off looks.

Nelson ate *carbonara* and Rowan *pasta arabica* with olives. They spoke about fishing. Favourite flies – Greenwell Glory, Bloody Butcher, Spider. Work and Sadie. It wasn't what they wanted to talk about, but it staved off the silence they both hit whenever they considered how to broach the subject of themselves, their affair.

'How long do you think you'll stay up here?' Nelson asked.

She shrugged. 'Till Eileen comes back. Till Sadie grows up. Whichever comes first.' Then, twirling her wine glass. 'I don't want Eileen to come back.'

'No. You like it here, then?'

'I've got used to it. There're things about it I like.' She did not look at him.

Across the room a woman reeling with Chianti took the mike and launched into *Angie*. 'Angie, oh Angie,' she sang. Stopped. Took a breath. 'Angie, oh Angie,' she sang again. 'An-g-ie-eee, oh, Angie. That's all the words I know. But it's my favourite.'

The waiter minced top speed across to their table, refilled their glasses. They stopped speaking whilst he hovered, waiting for them to finish and order pudding. Not to be outdone, the singer, demonstrating his hipness, launched into *Wild Horses* – the cabaret version. It required a lot of shoulder work.

Rowan ate an olive, placed the stone on the side of her plate. Fished in amongst her pasta, found another, ate it and laid the stone beside the first stone. She found another, then another. She did not speak. Started instead to count the stones. 'Tinker, tailor, soldier, spy,' she muttered. He watched. She counted the stones again. A childish game. 'He loves me. He loves me not. He loves me. Loves me not.' Lips moving. Nelson found another olive in the salad. Ate it, though he hated olives. And placed the fifth stone alongside the others. 'There,' he said. 'Even though you are messy and drive like a deranged boy racer.'

Rowan looked at him. They didn't bother with pudding, raced home instead. Later, considering her dread and her decision to abandon it for a little happiness, she thought that it must have happened then, at that olive moment.

Four o'clock in the morning she lay awake staring into the

gloom. The room was lit by the thin film of streetlight rimming the curtains. New dawn light came into the room – a strange light, like an aquarium. She thought it a moving thing, shifting shades of blue-grey, black. She put her hands behind her head, listened to Nelson's rhythmic breathing. Unable to sleep she got up and made a cup of tea which she drank staring mindlessly out of the window at the empty Square.

She saw the window of Jude's flat open. Young Steven climbed out, slid down the drainpipe, jumped onto the pavement. He turned. Saw her watching, and waved. A rebel's gesture. Then he ran off, without a backward glance.

When, eventually, she went back to bed, she sat up, duvet pulled over her, sighing.

Nelson woke. 'What are you doing?'

'Thinking,' she told him.

'What about?' he yawned.

'Dunno. I've been thinking so long, I've forgotten. Should I paint this place up? If so, what colour? White? Blue-grey? A bright colour? About me. You. Sadie. About us. Life, love and the pursuit of happiness. Do I prefer Cheesy Wotsits to Kettles' New York Cheddar crisps? Important stuff.'

'So I see.'

'Blue-grey would be nice. I'd think New York Cheddars.'

'I don't know – Cheesy Wotsits just melt away. A bit like life. It's gone before you thought to enjoy it.'

'Is that your philosophy?'

'Yep.'

'A bit flimsy, isn't it?'

'So who do you think you're sleeping with – Nietzsche?'

'What did you come up with on the subject of you, me, Sadie, life love and all the rest?'

'I got muddled. I'm better with Cheesy Wotsits.'

'Are you happy?' he asked tenderly.

'Ah, that's the question. I think I am – and I don't like it. Are you?'

'Yes. And I don't like it either.'

'It's scary. It could just go, then you'd be really miserable because you'd have known what happiness is like.'

'It's a bummer. Lie down, will you. Go to sleep.'

She lay down, cuddled into him. 'Of course, you'd be secretly happy once you were miserable again, because that's your natural state.'

'That's true. Will we go for that? Never see each other again?'

'No. I don't want that.'

'Neither do I. We'll just have to risk it. We'll be dubiously happy together. Holding hands waiting for glorious misery to strike.'

'I'm up for that,' she said.

Chapter Nineteen

Mama Claudia planned her big dinner party. She would have it in the chip shop. Put out a long table up the centre of the restaurant, with a white tablecloth, candles, wine. She would bring dish after dish to the table. Set her guests reeling with the splendour of it all. They'd not know what to say. 'Such food. They will never before have eaten such food.' She would serve rice balls. Crushed olives seasoned with mint. Fresh *ricotta* cheese, shouldn't be more than twenty minutes old. People here bought it in tubs in the supermarket. 'No idea what it tastes like,' she cried out loud. Egg *tagliatelle*, hand-made. Fish, definitely. Fresh sardines were out of the question, but the cod was good. She could fry it, marinade it in wine and olive oil. Serve it cold. Or she could make a fish stew. Chunks of monkfish, bass, squid, plaice, mullet browned in olive oil cooked inside a casserole with onions, carrot, celery, tomatoes, anchovies, pine kernels and *porcini* mushrooms. Spot of wine. Served on thick slices of garlicky bread. Pork. She would do it in milk – *maiale al latte*. Golden, crusty meat, moist inside, seasoned with coriander, marjoram covered in an almost sticky sauce, lots of grainy bits of onion and ham. Vegetables. Roast aubergines, peppers and artichokes with olive oil, garlic and parsley. Or a *caponata*, sweet and sour aubergine, that was good. Carrots with marsala? *Zucchini fritti*. Or maybe make a *peperonata*, sweet peppers and tomatoes stewed, kept in the fridge a few days, topped with olive oil. Almond pastries. Almond ice cream. A fruit tart, fresh raspberries, strawberries and figs piled on top of a vanilla custard in an almond pastry. Crystallised fruit. 'Could be good,' she pursed her lips, wagged her head. 'OK.'

She would invite Rowan, Jude, Miss Porteous, Mamie Garland.

She wondered about her daughter. Time was when young Claudia would have helped, but these days she was so distant. And she seemed thinner every day. Thinner and thinner. Rumour was her marriage wasn't going too well. Rumour was young Claudia and Stu weren't speaking now Claudia had stopped cooking. Constant salads and grilled chicken had hardened Stu's heart. Then there was Paolo. Father to two children he had hardly ever spoken to. 'A mess,' she said. And somehow she felt it was all her fault.

It had been another failed trip to the supermarket for Rowan. The shopping had gone as expected – boring. But once again she had not made contact with the parking gods. Every time she went to Tesco she sent her songs and prayers ahead of her hoping there would be a place by the door. There never was. She decided that dreaming songs must have more to them than her simple chant: Let there be a space. Let there be a space.

A Jaguar came up behind her flashing its lights. It pulled past her, slowed. Let her overtake. Came up behind her again, lights flashing. Overtook again. Waited again. Let her go past. And repeated the whole process. The third time it overtook her it shot off, flashing its lights. She could see the driver waving goodbye to her. 'What was all that about?'

When she arrived back in the Square, Steven was waiting at her door.

'You didn't give me a race. I flashed you.'

'Was that you? In the Jaguar?'

'Yes. Nice car.'

'Whose is it? And do they know you took it?'

'Snype's. 'Course he doesn't know. He's on his hols – Tenerife. Crap tapes. Phil Collins, Dire Straits. Old man's music.'

'Oh right. You'll have to let him know what you'd prefer he kept in his car.'

Rowan balanced Sadie in her arm as she opened the front of the Beetle. Steven reached over and took her. 'C'mon then.' He stroked her chin.

'You must like babies,' Rowan told him. 'She certainly likes you.' Sadie was beaming at him.

'I'm used to them. Wouldn't say I liked them. This one's quite nice.' He jiggled her critically.

Rowan carried her shopping inside. Steven followed with Sadie. Looked round.

'This isn't bad.' Considering Rowan's pictures and the Indian rug she'd put down in the living room. 'Better than the old man had it. He was like you, came back.'

'What do you mean?'

'He was brought up here. Came back. Like a salmon, he said. To die.'

'I have no intention of doing that.'

'So why did you come back?'

'Nowhere else to go.'

'Everybody was talking about you, but now they're talking about Mrs Jolly, the chemist's wife. She's got breast cancer.'

'How do you know that?'

'Everybody knows. Doctor's receptionist told them.'

'Remind me not to get sick.'

He wandered about the room. Flicked through her CDs. Picked up the book she was reading. Weighing her up. 'Are you going to go away again? I'm getting out of here. First chance I get, I'm leaving.'

'I was going to travel the world,' Rowan told him. She put on the kettle. 'Coffee? But this happened. Sadie.'

'Yeah,' he said. 'Every time I take a car I go further and further away. One day I'll go so far I won't come back.'

'On your great not-coming-back day, you'd best not set off in someone else's car. That way the police won't bring you back. Was that you having a practice going-away moment when you climbed out of the window the other night?'

'I took Snype's car round the glen. Does it good. He doesn't drive it right.'

'Why?'

He shrugged. 'I'm bored.' Then he smiled, handed Sadie back to her. Took the mug of coffee she'd made for him. 'I go to school during the day, that gives me something to do. But between teatime and when I'm sleeping there's nothing to do. Unless there's football on. At least I'm not like old Snypey, knocking his wife around 'cos he owes the bank thousands. Thousands and thousands.'

'How do you know that? Oh, I know – somebody at the bank

mouthing off at the pub. Remind me not to get sick and not to get overdrawn.'

'There's no secrets,' Steven said. 'So when are you going away again?'

'Whenever,' she said. She surprised herself. The longing hadn't diminished; it just didn't feel so urgent any more. 'The world won't go away. It'll be there, waiting for me, when I get around to going to it.'

He walked round the room, read the titles on her books. 'Are these yours? Or his – your old man. Nelson.'

'A mix.'

'Why do you fancy him? He's ancient.'

'Forty-four isn't ancient.'

'You could have me.' He raised his arms. Showing himself off. Young body.

'You're all sweaty,' Rowan mocked him. 'You're only a kid of what – sixteen?'

Unashamedly he sniffed his armpits. Too young, too urgent for life's refinements. 'Yeah, but I smell twenty-two.'

Rowan threw a tea towel at him. 'Get out of here.'

'I'm out there,' Steven grinned. 'Any time, baby. Jude reckons you must be a bit of a soft touch, just taking someone's baby like that. And she says you're quietly fearless the way you just got a job and settled in and got on with stuff.'

'I don't feel fearless, Steven. I feel shit-scared. I was shit-scared of taking Sadie. Now I'm shit-scared of losing her.'

'I like being scared,' he said. 'I drive Snype's Jag, then when I get past seventy, I switch off the lights, put my foot to the floor and I yell and yell. Into the dark, can't see where I'm going.'

'Why do you do that? You could get killed.'

'I just want something to happen. I get bored.' He looked at his watch. 'I have to go. I said I'd play football in the park with Sonia and Charmaine.'

'I think you're a soft touch, too. Somewhere in there beneath the baggy clothes a nice person is waiting to leap out.'

'Yeah. But I'm better than you at not letting it show.'

In that hideous yellow kitchen, over a year ago Eileen was standing drinking tea. Three o'clock in the afternoon, she'd just come home from last night's party. 'Hi, Rowan. Great night last night.'

'I know. Guess what happened to me on the way home with your car? I saw a fox. It was in the middle of the road. Houses all round and there it was. Wild, and looking at me. I got out the car and walked up to it. But it ran away. It was wounded. I don't know, I thought I could help. Take it to a vet. Get it fixed.'

'It'd have bitten you. You can't go up to wild animals.'

'I just felt I could. I wanted to see it back to health then set it free again. Somewhere nice.' She shrugged. Felt foolish.

'Shit, Rowan.' Eileen was laughing at her. 'You're such a sucker. A soft touch even for foxes. It's you should be having a baby.'

Had that been the moment Eileen decided to dump her child? Rowan stared out at the tangled garden. That evening, when Sadie was in bed, Rowan found a rusting scythe in the coalshed and set about clearing the undergrowth.

For three hours Rowan hacked. Stiff at first, she found a rhythm, the swish of the blade as grasses, nettles and tangled weeds fell before her. Then she dug, yanking things from the ground with her bare hands. She sweated and cursed. Blisters on her fingers. Muck up her nose, in her eyes. Her T-shirt clung to her. She uncovered a small rockery at the back, found a broken garden frame, the decayed remains of strawberry plants. Towards the back door was a path, worn paving slabs. She uncovered old toys, two blackened tennis balls, a wooden train. There were matching cast-iron hooks on the side of the house, one on the far wall where a washing-line had once hung. When her scythe hit something hard, the clang of metal against stone, she pulled at the mass of entwined weeds and revealed an old birdbath, green with neglect.

When Nelson came, Rowan was still outside, digging, leaning into the overturned earth, watching the little underworld she'd uncovered – worms, centipedes scuttling as she shook weeds free, tossed them onto her new compost heap. She loved the smell of earth, the moistness of it, loved to watch it crumble through her fingers. She was filthy. The beloved walking boots caked with muck, her fingers engrained, streaks on her face.

Nelson stood, watching her. 'What are you doing?'

'What do you think?' She stopped, leaned on the spade. 'Gardening.'

He crossed to her. Took her to him. 'You smell of earth and sweat.'

'I'll have a bath.'

'No. I want you like this.' He kissed her again. Slipped his hands up her T-shirt.

'Stop it. The neighbours will see.'

'Who?' He looked round. 'You're not overlooked. Besides, let them see.'

'You want me here? On this pile of weeds?'

'Why not?'

'Are you going underneath? There's nettles.'

'When you put it that way, let's go inside.'

Too urgent to make it to the bedroom. They made love on the stairs. Afterwards, she ran a bath. Lay soaking. Nelson brought her a glass of wine. Then soaped her back.

'Was it cathartic?'

'Oh yes. Though my back hurts. Next time I'm going on top.'

'I meant hacking down the weeds.'

'A bit.' She stared at him. 'Shuttup your silence. Do you think I could adopt Sadie? Or become her legal guardian?'

Nelson said they could find out, but he thought they'd need Eileen's signature.

They, Rowan thought, he said they. 'I don't think I ever want to see Eileen again. All that scheming. I don't want to have to deal with that.'

'I have a feeling she'll turn up.'

'So do I,' said Rowan.

Chapter Twenty

It was not Eileen who turned up. It was Ronnie Barr. He arrived on Rowan's doorstep one Saturday morning. He was tall, awkward, bony-faced. Huge hands dangling from the sleeves of his suit – obviously *the* suit, taken out of the wardrobe on special occasions, pressed shiny, and twenty years out of date.

As he introduced himself, worried fingers ran round the inside of his shirt collar. This neck, this throat with its huge bobbing Adam's apple was not comfortable with being buttoned in. He did not have to explain who he was; the girl at his side was a replica Eileen. Same tumble of hair, brown eyes, same smile. She looked twenty, must have been sixteen. 'Rowan?' the man said, lips damp with awkwardness. 'Campbell?'

'That's me,' although Rowan was tempted to deny it with a: 'Sorry, pal. Don't know who you're talking about.'

'Got your address from Danny. You know, in London.'

'Ah,' said Rowan. She should have phoned, told Danny to remove all her notes, made him promise not to tell anybody where she was.

'Only I wanted to see you. Mostly I wanted to see the little girl. I'm Ronnie Barr, Eileen's husband. And this is Kelly, her daughter.'

Rowan stared at them. 'Now why doesn't that surprise me?' She opened the door wider. 'You'd better come in.'

They took a red tub chair each. Sat uncomfortably looking round, taking in the room: Rowan's rugs, her arrangements of things on the mantelpiece – a couple of tiny coffee cups with a pattern of cockerels strutting round the outside rim, an old porcelain ink bottle, a ram's horn discovered on a hillside, postcards. The house since Rowan moved in had become cluttered with baby toys – a large fluffy polar bear, assorted plastic toys that rattled, lit up or tinkled little tunes, a baby chair. Kelly cast a slow critical eye over the CD collection. Ronnie watched Sadie. 'She's a beauty.' No embarrassment at the tenderness he felt. Crossing to pick her up. 'Nothing like Eileen at all. She takes after her father, does she?'

Rowan shrugged. 'If I'd ever met him, I'd tell you.'

'Right.' He smiled to Sadie, let her gum the bony joint of his finger. 'Everything goes in the mouth. Funny how you forget about babies then remember all about them soon as you see one again. Sorry about just turning up like this. I thought it might be good for Kelly to see a relative. A sister.'

Rowan went into the kitchen to put on the kettle. She wasn't sure what to say. Ronnie followed her. 'She never met her father, either.'

'You're not . . .' Rowan collected cups, laid them out.

'No, not me. Eileen was four months gone when I met her. We only knew each other six weeks before we married. She was like that. Swept you along.'

'Tell me about it. Tea? Coffee?'

'Tea for me. Kelly'll have coffee. She thinks I'm old-fashioned.' He jingled his car keys for Sadie. 'What do you think of them? Grand for chewing. No, I knew nothing about Kelly's father. Or at least, I knew *all* about him. Except every time Eileen told me about him, she told me a new story. But by the time I realised that, it was too late. I was hooked.' He looked round. 'You live alone?'

'Alone-ish. My boyfriend stays sometimes – a couple of nights usually. He's smitten.'

'It's love, is it?'

'Well, with Sadie it is. He's crazy about her.'

'Jealous, are you?'

'Yes, sometimes.'

'Then it is love.' Grinning. Blushing at this intimacy with a stranger. A female stranger. He took the mug of tea Rowan handed him. 'Thanks. Where is he now, your young man?'

'He'd be flattered you thought he was young. He left early this morning, gone fishing. I'll be going up to his cottage in a while.'

'There hasn't been anybody for me, not since Eileen. Smitten, did you say? I was sick with it. Thought about nothing else night and day. Even after she left, I found myself trailing back and forward to the window looking out for her.'

'Sounds familiar.' Rowan leaned against the kitchen unit. 'I did the same. I couldn't believe she'd just gone and left me with Sadie. Even when I got back here I kept looking out for her.' She picked up Kelly's coffee and took it through to the living room. The girl was thumbing through Rowan's books.

'She's the brainy one,' Ronnie explained. 'Me, I don't pick up a book from one month till the next. She'll be off to university next year.'

'What are you going to do?'

'Law,' Kelly said.

'She's going to be a lawyer,' Ronnie glowed. 'You should see her school reports. A's all the way. Don't know where she got the brains.' Realising the significance of this remark, he cleared his throat. Feigned a deep interest in the carpet.

'I never knew my real father.' Kelly was not bothered where her brains came from. 'My mother left when I was six months old. I don't remember her.'

'She was something,' Rowan sighed. Turning to Ronnie: 'Did you meet Eileen in Liverpool?'

'Liverpool? Goodness no. I met her in a pub in Brixton. She was living in a squat with about six other people. Moved in with me almost immediately. Far as I know, she's never been near Liverpool. She's still at it, then. Making up her life story.'

'Seems like it.' Rowan glumly remembered phoning every Johnson in the Liverpool phone book. No wonder nobody had heard of her. She'd never ever been there.

'My mother,' said Kelly, her voice flat with disapproval, 'was born on a council estate in Coventry. Her mother worked in a shoe shop. Her father was a milkman. She had three brothers and two sisters. Big family. Small house.'

'Coventry? She never mentioned Coventry to me.'

'She wouldn't.' Kelly sighed. 'It was the truth.'

'You've been there?'

'Holidays and sometimes for Christmas. Huge gathering round the kitchen table. Turkey, roast potatoes, sprouts, crackers, Asti

Spumante, fake tree. Queen on the telly. Very jolly. Nothing to run away from. When she was seventeen she got pregnant by somebody round about. Her dad thinks it was the vicar – Eileen went through a religious phase about then. Her mum thinks it was the bloke across the road when she was baby-sitting. Whatever, whoever – she ran away.'

'Goodness.'

'She went to London – lived in a squat. Filthy, Ronnie says, but then she was used to that. She got chatting to him. Knew a sucker when she met one.'

'Ain't that the truth,' said Rowan.

'She moved in with him.' Kelly recited the story as if she had told it many times. 'Had me. Left looking for the bright lights. Dad was too smalltime for her.'

'Boring,' Ronnie nodded, enthused, it would seem, about how boring he was.

'What do you do?' Rowan asked Ronnie.

'Fix cars. Small business. Sell a few, but mostly I fix them. I see you've got Bessie.'

'Bessie?'

'The Beetle. I gave it to her. Still going, is she?'

Rowan nodded, looked glazed.

'It was a gift,' Eileen had said. 'A secret admirer just left it outside the house. Put an envelope with the keys in through the door, along with a note that said; *A love bug for my love. Drive the wild highways.* Wasn't that lovely? I never found out who it was.'

Rowan recalled the shiver of doubt she had not acknowledged when Eileen told her Beetle story. She hoped she wasn't standing listening to this recounting of Eileen's life with her jaw slack and her arms dangling limply in front of her, shoulders sagging. She felt a fool.

'It's always the same,' Ronnie said gently, 'when you hear you've been lied to. You feel a fool. Someone you liked, loved even, lied to you. She told me she was a convent girl, an orphan, who'd been taken advantage of by a priest. Told me they used to beat her at the orphanage.' He pursed his lips, looked at the wall. He could not contain how stupid he felt recounting Eileen's fabricated life. He had soaked it all up. Put his huge arm round Eileen as she cried, moved to tears by her tall tale, and patted her awkwardly. 'It'll be all right. You've got me now. I'll look after you.'

'You believed her?' Rowan said.

'I feel so stupid.' Ronnie shrugged amiably. 'There you go. You never think people are lying to you.' He crossed the room to the window. Stared out. 'I could have a look at the car for you.' Anything to get out of the room. He never was comfortable indoors. 'Terrible thing, being lied to. You never really trust again, do you?'

Rowan's face creased. 'I don't know about that. Eileen's a one-off. I think I've found out a lot about kindness since this happened to me. So how did you find out about Eileen?' she asked.

'Her folks just turned up at the garage one day. Simple as that.' Ronnie gave the car outside a look of longing. Put Sadie down on the floor. Sat beside her, started to make a small construction with her plastic bricks. Talking was easier when fiddling with something. 'They'd hired a private detective and he'd tracked me down. So one day they just arrived. I was working on a Saab. Nice car. New clutch. Kelly was up on the work-bench, I'd cleared a space for her carrycot. And there they were. Thought they wanted to take her away, but no. Their children were grown up. They'd done with babies.'

'You never saw her again?'

'She used to come back at first. Get fed. Take some money.' He found a stray something at the back of his mouth, chewed it absently. 'Used to look for her. Walked round Soho nights. West End. Never saw her. Sometimes she'd phone up, tell me about the rock stars she knew. Galleries and opening nights she was invited to. Said she was going to Iraq to live with a sheikh. Would you have believed that?'

'I probably would have at the time,' Rowan confessed.

'I got on with bringing up Kelly. Didn't think about Eileen. Her folks said she always lied. Told the school her dad was a bank manager. Told her friends he was a singer in America – one of the Beach Boys. Told her teacher her family was emigrating to Canada. Got three weeks off school before they discovered the truth. She told some of her friends she lived in a mansion with six televisions, a swimming pool and ten bedrooms. Told others she lived in a gipsy caravan with a horse and all that stuff. She said her mother had been in the French Resistance during the war. Said her sister was a model in London with her face on the cover of *Vogue* and there she was working in the local supermarket. Very red-faced. Said her brother died in a car crash with Marc Bolan and there he was sitting in the pub drinking a pint. Folk saying, "I thought you was dead." The lies go on and on. Never thought I'd hear from her again. Then a few months back, the money turned up.'

'Money?' Rowan's heart stilled.

'She sent two thousand pounds to pay for my education,' said Kelly. 'She wrote saying she wanted to help me through university. She said it was an advance for a book she'd written with a couple of friends: *Travels with Myself and a Couple of Others*. Now she's off to Rio with some millionaire she's met.'

'You believe that?' Rowan said.

Kelly and Ronnie shot her a look. 'No.'

Ronnie got up. 'I'll take a look at old Bessie.' He went from the room as awkwardly as he'd entered it.

'It was easy to find you,' Kelly told Rowan. 'The heading on the letter she wrote was a publisher. Her publisher, we would have thought if we didn't know what she was like.'

Sitting in Rowan's room, candles lit, listening to Nirvana. Sharing a spliff.

'What's that?' Eileen said. 'That's new to me. You know all these new bands.'

'Nirvana. *Nevermind*, I'll write it down for you. You never remember anything.' She scribbled it in pencil on a sheet of headed notepaper brought home from work. God, thought Rowan. You can't let a liar know anything. It'll all be absorbed, and used against you.

'I phoned. A James Frobisher gave me your old address in Islington. We went round and got your new one from there. We went to your folks' house. A neighbour told us where you were. And here we are.'

'Do you think we'll ever see Eileen again?' Rowan said.

Kelly shrugged.

'Do you want to see her?'

Kelly shrugged again. For the first time looked the teenager she was. 'Sometimes I'd like to know her. And sometimes I think about her and I'm so angry about all those lies that I just cry.'

And Rowan said, 'I can understand that. Did Ronnie bring you up knowing about her? I'm not sure what to tell Sadie. Sometimes I think I'll tell her that her mother is dead, but that's another lie. Lies just lead to more lies.'

'Ronnie never hid the truth from me. I used to lie about her, but now I tell the truth and my friends think she sounds amazing. They wish they had a mother like her. What was she like? Did you see a lot of her?'

Eileen waltzing from her room wearing little more than a daft Santa hat. 'Oh yes, I saw a great deal of Eileen. At first you think she's pretty fabulous. Then you tire of her. She rushes at you, doesn't let you breathe or think. When you stand back and really consider the things she says, they sound so over the top. Thing is, and this worries me, I think she believed them herself. She had this glisten in her eye. She was never happier than when she was telling her tales.'

Rowan looked out of the window. Ronnie had been joined by Steven. They were both leaning into the back of her car, engine-gazing, tinkering, talking. What about? Across the Square young Claudia's curious head bobbed behind the plastic ice-cream cone – who was this new person working on the car? No doubt Steven would have all the news soon enough. Then Jude would know. Then Jude's folks. After that everybody would find out. 'Oh, stuff it,' she said.

The room behind her filled with sound. Kelly put on Lou Reed. *How Do You Think It Feels* thumped out. *If only . . . if only.* 'He's not bad,' Kelly said, nodding at the stereo. She turned to look at Sadie. Since she arrived, she had avoided her.

'She won't bite,' Rowan said. 'She might give you a nasty suck though.'

'I've never had anything to do with babies. I don't know what to say to them.'

'She won't discuss the intricacies of Lou Reed's lyrics or the plot of soaps on the telly, but she's friendly. All she demands is to know you like her. You have to smile a lot.' Rowan knew what a trial that could be. 'It's tough, I know, when smiling doesn't come easy.'

Kelly shot her a grateful smile. She went and squatted beside Sadie, let her grip her finger. They eyed one another. Sadie broke the moment, a gummy grin.

'There you go,' said Rowan.

They had lunch at Raffles. 'A celebration,' said Rowan, raising her lager to Ronnie. 'It's good to discover you are not the world's only dupe. Isn't it wonderful,' she thrilled, 'when you discover that someone else is as daft as you are? You are not the only sucker in the world. So heartening.'

Ronnie agreed. He raised his glass. 'To all of us. To friendship.' He looked embarrassed at admitting this. 'We'll form a mutual dupe's society.'

They all drank to that. Lunch over, Ronnie was anxious to get back. 'Got a new gearbox for a BMW and a Renault to service. You'll find the car goes a treat.' They agreed to keep in touch. Holding Sadie, waving her hand, Rowan watched them drive out of the Square. Then she drove to Nelson's cottage.

When he came home, fishless as ever, she leapt into his arms. 'Isn't it fabulous when you discover you are not the only fool in the world?'

'Never thought you were,' he said. 'There's me. There's every single person I can think of. We've all had our moments.'

She told him about Ronnie Barr and Kelly.

'So what about the money? You didn't tell them it was yours.'

'No. I meant to, but couldn't find a moment and then it just slipped away. Sometimes you can stay silent too long.'

'You have their address. You could write.' He took her face in his hands.

She put her palm on his cheek, felt the roughness of it. 'You haven't shaved.'

'But you won't. You won't tell them, will you?'

'No,' she said. 'Maybe one day. I'll see them again.'

'Why didn't you say? It's yours.'

'They need it. It costs to go to university – lots to study law. All those books. Anyway, Kelly's family – she's Sadie's sister. I'll get it one day.'

'Saint Rowan,' said Nelson. He kissed her cheek. Held her hands behind her back. 'I'm never going to let you go. Say you love me, Saint Rowan.'

'I think I probably do,' she told him. 'But don't go thinking that means you can have your way with me.'

He lifted her up. She curled her legs round his waist. 'I will,' he said. 'I've never fucked a saint.'

'Is that what you do? Make love to a whore. Fuck a saint.'

'Well, if it's fun you're after.'

Chapter Twenty-One

'I'm not a summer person,' Mamie explained to Rowan in The Squelch. 'It's all bared bodies and bright clothes. It's sweaty. Have you noticed that?'

Rowan nodded.

'Yes,' said Mamie. 'There's people in yellow shirts and shorts revealing thighs and bits that we don't really need to see. It's a bit vulgar, the summer, if you ask me. There's always some depressingly jaunty summer hit on the radio. Nah,' she shook her head. 'Autumn's subtle. Balmier days. Lovely skies that make you feel lonely in a beautiful way. Sunsets. A good set of cinema releases. You can smell the cold coming. It makes you so glad.'

She poured tea. Happy today, despite the fact it was still July and she had a couple of months of summer to go.

She was not a rich woman. Existed on a diet of toasted cheese. Some nights had to choose between putting money in the meter, or buying a pack of cheddar. 'Will I have light? Read a while? Or will I keep warm in bed with a bite to eat?' She always chose food. 'I am so lucky,' she said, turning to Rowan, gripping her arm. 'I have known love. Some folks never do, you know. And I've seen thousands of films. Sung along with them. All those cowboys and gangsters, love songs and legends . . . I was here to see them. There are wonderful moments out there; you just never know when they are going to come to you.'

Mamie's unexpected outburst made Rowan feel dreamy. 'You sound as if you're planning some sort of something. What's up with you today?'

'I have never seen a whale,' Mamie said. 'Always wanted to be there, on a boat somewhere when a whale rose out of the water.

Great showers cascading from it. And the way it leaps, clear out of the sea, up into the air. Huge things. How do they do that? *Moby Dick*, grand film. Gregory Peck. Have you seen it?'

Rowan shook her head. 'You could go to wherever the whales are and watch them. Off the coast of Mexico. Whales go there.'

'Nah.' Mamie shook her head. 'In the morning I can walk from my front door to The Squelch here and say hello twenty times. Makes me feel wanted. I'm staying put.' She lifted her cup to her mouth, blew across the surface of her tea.' And I'll tell you what's up with me. I've got a plan. A big plan and it's cheered me up no end.' She took up her knitting. Needles worked furiously.

'What?' asked Rowan.

Click. Click. Click. Mamie seemed to go cross-eyed looking at her knitting. 'I'm not saying. I'm not thinking about it too much. If you think about plans you get scared of them. But as I grow older I've more to be scared of. Getting up in the morning. Also going to bed at night. I'm scared I won't sleep, and what I'll think about in the dark when I'm trying to drop off. And, at my age, scared if I do sleep I'll wake up dead. But I will say I'm planning a gala night. One last picture show. Glamour and wine sort of thing.'

'A last picture show? You're closing the Rialto?'

'All good things must come to an end. Likewise mediocre things. And plain old past-it things.'

'But the Rialto,' said Rowan. 'I misspent my youth there.'

'You and lots of others, judging by the things I've found under the seats over the years,' Mamie complained.

Nights, when Nelson wasn't there, Jude would come to see Rowan. She'd chainsmoke and fret.

'I'm worrying about going back to university. It's all the reading – you get a headache. And the thinking,' she said. 'I just think normally, you know, in straight lines. Maths, it's easy for me. But all these books. They let other things in. All your fears. You read something and it reminds you of what you are. I feel I'm like all the daft people in the books. Not the good ones.'

'I think a lot of people feel that,' Rowan said.

'Do they? They never say. And all these students – they're so young. All they seem to do is shag each other and drink.'

'What did you do when you were that age?'

'Same thing. But I don't think I enjoyed it as much as them. I doubt myself. I look at them and I think I couldn't invite any of them home.'

She thought they'd laugh at her collection of china animals and the gilt-framed pictures of fairies on the walls, the pink cover on her toilet seat, her blue and gold patterned carpet with the lovely fluffy rug in front of the fire. The fire! They'd laugh at her fake-flame electric fire. They'd laugh at everything she had. 'I don't like any of my things any more. The way I dress, for instance. When I worked at Snypey's it was easy. They didn't like my low-cut blouse, so I wore an even lower-cut one. What's it to you, I think. And stuff yez all. But it's not like that now.' She lit a cigarette. 'Do you have anything to drink?'

Rowan brought a bottle of wine, two glasses.

'See?' Jude pointed at the bottle. 'Wine. You have wine in a bottle, I always buy a box – if I buy wine at all. Christmas usually. I'd have brought a rum and Coke.'

'Nothing wrong with that,' Rowan reassured her.

'I have always been a bit of rough, I know that. Don't need to tell me. The worse things got, the rougher I got. Shouting the odds in the street. Not nice. I'm not a nice person. All my life I've had this feeling of foreboding.' She stopped, considered her last word. 'Listen to me,' voice softer now, 'Foreboding. I'm even starting to use fancy words. Anyway, I always thought something terrible was about to happen so I'd drink and let everybody think I'd shag anyone I could get hold of. People think I'm the town bike, but I'm not. There's only ever been Paolo and Frank. Only now I'm ashamed of letting folk think bad of me, because of Delia and what she tried to do. Before, I liked all the trouble I caused, but now I think, What are you so afraid of? Something terrible? Like what? I got pregnant when I was fourteen. My son's always in trouble with the law. My daughter tried to kill herself. It's happened. And I coped.' She stood up, twirled, arms wide, smoke spreading from the cigarette between her fingers. 'I'm here. I'm alive. But I'm still all curled up and hiding inside. I want to be fearless.'

'Fearless would be good,' said Rowan.

'You come back here with your funny hairstyle and that baby who isn't yours, and everybody's talking about you, and laughing at your hair. Turn around and they're thinking you're a saint for taking on another woman's child. Turn around again and there's half a dozen girls walking about looking like you. You're nearer to fearless than me.'

Rowan scratched her chin, blew out her cheeks. 'Maybe I'm just insensitive. Too thick to notice what's happening around me.'

Jude fiercely stubbed out her cigarette. 'I think I'll buy a jumper.'

Rowan said nothing. Raised her eyebrows. A jumper?

'One of those big jumpers like they all wear at college. Carry my books about in my hands, or buy a rucksack thing. Stop putting them in an old Tesco bag. I've got to fit in. And it'll not be a pink jumper. Black. No, grey. With a roll neck. And I'll stop saying, "What's it to you?" like I said to my lecturer when he asked about Kafka's motivation. "Stuff Kafka," I said. Then I said, "That's why I come here, getting up at seven in the morning, so *you'd* tell me all that. If he'd had to cook the tea, Kafka wouldn't have had time to write daft books about folks turning into bugs." I'll stop saying that sort of stuff.'

'You said that? And you think *I'm* fearless? Actually Kakfa worked at a job he hated, then went home to write books about folk turning into bugs.'

'Did he? No wonder he wrote them books.'

'Maybe he should've bought a jumper. Made a statement. Changed his life.'

'Yes.' Jude was getting excited about reforming her character. 'I'll buy a great big jumper. And I'll stop shouting in the street.'

Two nights later Jude stood in the Square outside Rowan's house. 'Hey, Rowan,' that nicotined voice ricocheted through the dark. 'I got it.'

Rowan opened her window. Judybonk was standing in the road carrying a bundle of books, wearing skin-tight jeans and an enormous black jumper, sleeves shoved up. 'I got it.' She whirled round on one high-heeled foot. 'Look at me. I'm a student. Ha, ha.'

Rowan yanked open the window, leaned out. 'You look great. You're fearless.'

Jude leapt into the air, clicked her heels. How did she do that, wearing those shoes? Rowan was impressed.

Mama Claudia leaned against her window, watching. 'It's that Jude, shouting in the street again.'

'Hey, Jude!' Rowan shouted. 'What was Kafka's motivation, then?'

'Stuff Kafka,' Jude yelled. Bent double laughing. 'What's it to you anyway, pal?'

Later, when Nelson came round, Rowan hadn't got Sadie ready for bed.

'I'll bath her,' Nelson said. He removed Sadie's dungarees and jersey. Took off her nappy. Went through the toss-the-nappy routine Rowan had perfected. Folding up the hideous thing and tossing it across the room to the bin.

'It's the most dangerous thing I do these days,' she said.

'Flying nappy,' Nelson called as it sailed to the nappy bin. Dropped neatly in. He took Sadie to the bathroom, ran a bath and dumped her in. Rowan could hear him singing little songs to her, playing with her toy submarine. 'Dive. Dive. Dive.' Sleeves rolled up, he brought her through wrapped in the huge bath towel. 'Here she is. All clean and smelling sweet.'

As Rowan prepared supper, Nelson put Sadie into a clean nappy. 'I'm getting good at this.' And babygro. He fed her. Then took her through to bed. Rowan did not have to look. She knew he was leaning over the cot, moving Sadie's mobile, telling her stories.

Fifteen minutes later he came through. 'She's sound.'

'For the moment,' said Rowan.

They sat at the kitchen table eating pasta.

'What about Saturday?' said Nelson. 'Would you like to do something? Go to the zoo, or to the beach? We could paddle, make sandpies. We could pretend we're a real family.'

'I don't think we have to pretend,' said Rowan.

Chapter Twenty-Two

Mamie advertised her glamour night in the *Gazette*.

The Rialto proudly presents 'A Glamour Night' 25th July, 7.30. Come posh. Or posh as you can manage. Remember the old days. Romantic film show. Chocolates and wine. Tea and biscuits. Tickets £2.50. No concessions. At that price with wine, what do you expect?

Two days before the big show, Norma and George returned from their cruise. Norma looked tired and tanned. George looked tanned.

'Look at the washing I'll have to do,' Norma complained. 'We've nothing to wear. Everything's dirty.'

'But did you have a good time?' Rowan wanted to know. 'Tell me about it.'

'There was dancing every night,' Norma said. 'Your father was never off the floor.'

'And?' said Rowan. 'What about the places you saw?'

'Athens was filthy. I liked Nice – lots of yachts. The food was good. You got a good choice. And we could sit on the deck.'

'Is that it?'

'More or less,' said Norma. 'I'll tell you more when I remember. When I've got everything sorted out. How's Sadie?' She scooped the child from Rowan's arms.

'Sadie's well. Making new friends all the time. Jude's been looking after her.'

'Jude?' said Norma. 'How did she get on with her?'

'Fine,' said Rowan. 'Just fine.'

'I don't think I'll go away again,' said Norma, sitting down in her favourite armchair. 'I like it here. There's no need to travel: I always think if you stay still long enough, the world

249

will come to you. I can't wait to get back into my old routine.'

Rowan asked if she would baby-sit in a couple of nights. 'It's Mamie's glamour night. I feel I have to go.'

Norma almost rejoiced at the suggestion.

Mamie bought a case of South African Chardonnay and hired sixty glasses from George O'Connell at the County Hotel. Sixty would be plenty, she thought. She laid them out with the wine on her dining-room table which she and Rowan had carried downstairs from her flat and set up in the foyer.

At half-past seven twelve people queued outside. They were all, Mamie noted with horror, old. By ten to eight another three had turned up. They milled about drinking wine, nibbling the canapés Mamie had spent the afternoon making. She noted sadly that only a few people had made the effort to come posh. A couple of dinner suits looking uncomfortable, fiddling with their bow ties. One or two of the women had dressed up. The conversation that Mamie had quietly hoped would be erudite and urbane was mostly about the price of margarine in the Co-op and Fred and Maisie Watson who had gone to Poland on a bus, and Fred had been so taken with the cheap vodka he'd got drunk and lost his false teeth somewhere between Warsaw and Krakow.

'Where did all these people come from?' Mamie asked Rowan. 'Have they been living here all these years and I haven't seen any of them?'

The show started at eight. Mamie planned to put on *From Here to Eternity*. People sat politely. Mamie noted that the rows of cinema seats were not anchored to the floor properly. She'd always meant to have that fixed. When one person moved, the whole row moved. And if someone got up to go to the loo, the row seemed to slip back an inch or two when the others stood up to let the loo-person past.

Halfway through the film, Mamie slipped down from the projection room to see how it was going. Several people had slipped away. Others were sleeping, heads slumped to the side. Only a few were watching, enraptured, as Mamie had dreamed. But by the end of the film they were all, they said, too tired for another. 'Past my bedtime,' a scented woman in a turquoise blouse said, heaving herself from the seat. 'Oh my,' she cried. 'These seats. I can't move.' She rubbed her stiffened limbs. 'We're not up to this sort of thing.'

People shook their heads. And left. Mamie could hear their voices drift back up the street as they headed home.

'God, that place hasn't changed in thirty years. I'm too old to sit in a seat like that for hours. My knees've stopped working.'

'I've missed *Coronation Street*.'

'I'd as soon hire a video and watch it at home. Least I'd get a decent seat.'

The night had been a failure.

'You can't win them all,' said Rowan.

'You'd think you could win at least one,' Mamie said. 'And look at my wine – they've drunk the lot. Fifteen folk have lamped through twelve bottles, that's almost a bottle each. And half a dozen glasses are missing. It's bad enough I get a bunch of geriatrics, but geriatric alcoholic kleptomaniacs, and boring with it, it's too much. These folks are so old. Is that what I'm like?'

'No,' said Rowan. 'You're nothing like that at all.'

'It says a lot for my diet of tea and digestive biscuits.'

She had planned the evening to be her big Goodbye. But maybe now she thought some goodbyes were best left unsaid. Better with a discreet wave from a distance. But then Mamie's plan was far from discreet. Nothing she did ever was.

When everyone had left Mamie took down her framed pictures of Burt and Ingrid, the hens, and gave them to Rowan. 'Keep these,' she said.

'I can't,' Rowan protested. 'They're yours.'

Mamie shook her head. 'A gift. Maybe just a temporary gift. You keep them safe.'

After Mamie had locked up they walked together down the street. From The Squelch came the yodel and holler of Country 'n' Western night, Ella Hanson singing *You Were Always On My Mind*, drunkenly sorrowful. She used a lot of h's. *Ha yew were halways hon ma myhind*. It echoed round the streets. A few young bloods were gathered outside the chip ship drinking Irn Bru. Mamie and Rowan did not merit a second glance.

'We must be past it,' Rowan said.

'Well, I am. In fact, I've been past it for so long I can't remember what it is I'm past.'

Rowan invited Mamie to come in for a glass of wine, but she shook her head. 'Nah. Thanks, but it's a night for walking.'

'Don't you go getting depressed,' Rowan said.

'I'm not depressed, I'm just melancholy. There's a difference. Melancholy's vintage depression – to be savoured.'

At one o'clock the sirens woke Rowan. She got out of bed and ran to the window. Three fire engines hurtled through the Square and into the High Street. Rowan pressed her face against the glass, trying to see what was happening. A crowd had gathered outside the County Hotel.

As soon as Rowan opened her window she heard the roar, the thunder of flames. She smelled the fury – burning maroon velour seats, old lino, ancient timbers. Huge sooty flakes floated through the night – black snow which landed on the streets, on parked cars. She did not need to call out, asking what was happening. She knew. The Rialto was ablaze.

She saw Mamie Garland standing on the edge of the crowd watching, her hands plunged deep into her pockets. There were no tears in her eyes. Her expression, vintage depression.

Paolo Rossi ran from the chip shop in boxers and T-shirt, straight from bed. He moved the beloved BMW to safety. She watched Jude watching him pad back home, barefoot. She watched him noticing her. They both looked away. They were expert at ignoring each other.

She shut the window. Checked that Sadie was sleeping, dressed and ran downstairs into the Square. Pushing through the crowd she reached Mamie. Above the crack and roar of flames, the firemen's yelling, the rush of water spewing from their hoses, she bawled: 'Mamie! Are you all right?'

'It's gone,' said Mamie. 'Best thing for it.' She did not take her eyes from the blaze. A vast billow of black smoke curved over the rooftops. The heat even several yards back was almost unbearable. Rowan pulled Mamie away.

'You've left Lavinia in there,' she said.

'I know. I couldn't take everything. I have other pictures.' She patted her pocket.

'Your flat. Everything you have.'

'All gone,' said Mamie. 'Like you said, I'm past it. I don't need anything.'

'Don't stand here. Don't watch it. Let me make you a cup of tea.'

'One of those drunken old souls must've left a cigarette burning.' Mamie did not look at her.

'Seems like it.' Rowan did not look at Mamie. She was practising her story.

'Happens,' said Mamie.

'All the time,' said Rowan. She led the old lady away. 'How much will you get?'

'Building was insured for seventy thousand; my house contents for another fifteen. Then there are these builders who want the site to put up a block of flats.'

'Who did it?'

'Bloke who did the County. He gets a cut of the insurance. You won't say?'

'I know nothing,' said Rowan. 'You weren't in there when it went up?'

'Had to be. Didn't look real otherwise.'

'You could've been killed.'

'Hardly – it was timed. What could I do? I'd no money. I'm not going to end up sitting dribbling in an old folk's home singing *Yellow Submarine*. I'm getting the penthouse at the top.'

'Was that the deal?'

'Deal?' Mamie stopped. 'What deal? I know nothing about a deal.'

'Of course you don't,' said Rowan. 'Silly me. Still, with all that money, you'll be able to make your penthouse special.'

'Don't I know it. I haven't been watching movies all these years without picking up a few tips on furnishing penthouses.'

Miss Porteous, wrapped in a blanket, evacuated from her house lest the blaze spread, and on her way to spend her waiting time treating herself to a gin and tonic, smoking a couple of extra Benson & Hedges, watched Mamie and Rowan make their way back to Rowan's flat.

Pisces: Sometimes drastic actions and desperate measures are the only

253

way forward. The only thing to do is let go of the past. A fresh start is on the way. Cancer: Knowing a friend's secret can be a privilege. Guard it well.

Mama Claudia sent out invitations to her dinner party. She wanted to do it properly. Proper written notes to Rowan, Nelson, Mamie, Miss Porteous and Jude. 'Jude?' her husband complained. 'Not her!'

'Yes, her. Definitely her. The boy and the girl are Rossis. We owe her.'

She felt, however, that writing notes was not invitation enough. She wanted to see people's faces – the anticipation of perfect food. She could not resist knocking eagerly on the shop window whenever she spotted one of the invited passing, and beckoning them in, chubby forearm waving. The invited could hardly believe their luck. They really were invited to eat at the Rossis'?

'Can I bring anything?' Mamie asked.

Claudia shook her head, arms raised in horror at this suggestion. Mamie would bring cheese sandwiches or treacle toffee. 'No. No. It's our treat. We'll eat, drink wine, chat, laugh, tell stories.'

'Sounds wonderful.' Mamie was enthused.

'It will be, believe me, a night to remember.'

'A night to remember,' Mamie told Rowan. 'We'll eat, drink, laugh.' Then, embellishing the planned festivities: 'Sing, dance and tell our stories.'

'Sing?' Rowan worried. 'I can't sing. Well, I can. It sounds OK to me in here, but everyone out there objects. I'm not singing.'

'Neither am I,' agreed Mamie.

'Stories?' Rowan went on. 'Our life stories? I don't know what I think about that. I'm not very keen on my life story. I prefer yours.'

'Mine? What have I been doing these past thirty years? Coming and going, saying hello to people. That's a swift tale. If you want a story, I prefer Robert Mitchum's life to mine. Though I wouldn't want to have lived it. Still, the food'll be good.'

'There's that,' Rowan agreed.

Next day, picking up the horoscopes for the *Gazette* Rowan told Miss Porteous that they would be singing, dancing and they'd all have to tell their life stories. 'Bare our souls, sort of thing.'

'Goodness,' said Miss Porteous. 'I'll have to make something up. I live a very narrow life, I'm afraid. Never leave town. What have I to confess? Two cigarettes a day? Hardly riveting.'

'We'll all have to sing and dance and confess our life stories,' Rowan told Nelson.

He stopped cooking, turned, pointed at her. 'Rowan! You have been gossiping. Welcome home. You are behaving like an old local.'

She covered her face with her hands. 'So I have. I've been spreading rumours. Oh my God. My God. I've got a secret. I tell tales. *I'm a local!*'

Chapter Twenty-Three

On the morning of her dinner party Mama Claudia got up before six. Lots to do. She made coffee. Ground beans, heaped them into her espresso-maker. Stood over it whilst it spat and gurgled on the flame, planning her day. Bread first, six loaves. Then, as the oven cooled, ice creams. She could do the pork in the oven, but preferred to cook it on the flame. She liked to watch it, tend it as it turned slowly golden.

Before she drank her coffee she dissolved yeast with a pinch of sugar in warm water. Set it aside to froth – her kitchen never got cold. It was raining outside. A wind whipping round the Square, crisp bags tumbling before it, scraping the pavement. She wished Paolo and Jim would marry. Goodness, she'd nagged them enough. But neither of them had found anybody suitable. She hadn't liked any of the girls they'd brought home. Recently she'd been wondering if perhaps it was Paolo and Jim that women found unsuitable. She'd spoilt them. Jim drifted in and out of relationships, and Paolo was far too old to sit on the window crooning down at young girls. They were Mama's boys. She'd cosseted them. Perhaps she should throw them out. Then, she thought, they'd marry quick as they could. They'd need someone to look after them.

It seemed to Claudia's children that she could nag from afar. Contemplating mischief, they'd experience an intense and gut-churning ESP. She seemed to be able to fold her arms and concentrate, and her children, wherever they were got vibes of fury and behaved themselves. The thing she'd noticed through the years was that nobody had ever challenged her wrath. She'd never actually hit any of her children, yet they thought she had. The more compliant they got, the bossier she got. She knew that had any of them turned on her, said, 'So what?' Or, 'What are you going to do about it?' Or, 'Stuff you,' (as she'd heard Jude's children speaking to her), she'd have fallen apart. This ferocity was a façade. Inside, she knew, her husband knew, she was as confused as everyone else.

She drank her coffee. Poured a second cup. Opened her flour barrel and scooped a mound onto the board. She'd made enough bread over the years to know exactly when the mound was the correct amount for her recipe. She added salt. With her fingers, long nails painted a defiant red, she dug a small well in the flour, poured in her yeast, olive oil and warm water. Then she kneaded. Elbow working. Young Claudia had married; her Stu was a good man. She hadn't liked him at first, but then she knew she wouldn't have liked anybody. She worried about Claudia. The girl used to be too fat. Now she was getting thinner by the day, and tired with it. She was always groaning, saying her muscles ached.

Mama Claudia stopped kneading. 'Maybe she's ill,' she said out loud. Today she would go down to the shop, and order young Claudia to go to the doctor. The dough was soft, elastic, a slight lustre to it. She rolled it in oil, put it in a damp cloth and set it on a shelf above the water-tank to rise.

At seven she gave Jim and Paolo coffee and apple croissants. Chased them from her kitchen.

Then she set about the pork. She shoved a couple of cloves of garlic deep into it, skewered holes, dropped in coriander and fennel, rubbed it with coarse salt and pepper, then browned it in butter with onions and ham. The scent of meat and garlic filled the house.

Her grandmother had taught her this recipe. When she was a child she'd visit her in Tuscany. She remembered sitting in the kitchen watching a thunderstorm gallop down the valley. Walloping rumbles of thunder, then they counted till the lightning cracked, flashed a forked streak lighting up the overcast hillside. 'Don't ever marry for love,' her grandmother said. 'Love will be your undoing. Marry for sense, for safety – for money if you like. But love? Never thought much of it. Keep love aside, as something delicious. A little *budino Toscano*. Tasty.'

Claudia poured boiling milk over the meat, watched it bubble.

She'd had quite a lot of *budino Toscano*, Tuscan pudding, in her life. It had mostly been before she came to Scotland. Affairs, matters of the heart, passion were all difficult here. Everyone knew everything. She'd been discreet, of course. Only two or three small whirls since she married. One-night stands with men she met at the hotel she stayed at in London when she went shopping for clothes. Little ego boosts, she called them. She turned down the flame. Let the meat simmer. Nobody here cooked pork in milk. 'Milk?' they'd say. 'This is milk?' 'Love,' she said. 'I miss love.' When she was seventeen she'd run away with her love, Alberto. Her father had driven after them in his Lancia and brought her back. Her mother had beaten her. 'Love,' said Claudia. 'It'll break your heart.' Taking the risen dough from the cupboard. 'My grandmother was a fool. Love is all.'

She punched the dough down. Split it into two. Rolled it flat. Lifted the loaves onto an oiled tray, oiled them, with her fingers patterned the top with tiny holes, scattered sage on top and put them in the oven. Then set about making another batch.

She leaned against the kitchen unit. 'Fish stew,' she said. 'Ice cream, toast my almonds in sugar, then the fish stew. Carrots in marsala – I *love* carrots in marsala, although they're better with lamb.' She checked her pork. 'Salads, make pasta later. Some ricotta.' She sighed. She and her love had driven through the night. She had been beautiful. She curled up in the passenger seat, put her head in his lap. She tutted. What would they have done? How would they have lived? 'We'd have managed,' she said.

Before she loved Alberto, she'd loved Marcello Mastroianni. 'Lovely man,' she said. Before she'd run away with Alberto she'd run away to Rome to stand outside a cinema where one of Marcello Mastroianni's films was being premièred. She'd squeezed to the front of the crowd. As he passed, with Sophia Loren, she remembered, she'd reached out, touched his arm. She swooned remembering. When she got home, she'd been beaten for that too. 'It was worth it.'

Her youth. My God, she thought, it was wonderful. Men – I used to love men. How many men had she had? Sometimes she tried to count, but she never could get it right. Nights, stealing from her parents' house, out to the little café where she'd drink wine and pose and flirt, and be admired. Then Giorgio had turned up with his family. They had a chip shop in Scotland. It sounded so exotic. Giorgio had courted her properly. They never met without an escort. Then before he asked her to marry him, he'd asked her father for her hand. Her father had more than agreed. He'd been overjoyed at the idea. Claudia hadn't wanted to marry. Being openly courted by a stranger from Scotland was fun, but it hadn't stopped her slipping out to the café: it just made her feel desired in a respectable sort of way. She hadn't taken it seriously. But she'd felt helpless against the fuss her mother and father made when she showed her reluctance. So she married and here she was. Spoiling her sons, nagging her daughter, getting along with her husband. But not loving. She wondered where Alberto was. Was he happy?

'We could go to bed.' Rowan put her arms round Nelson. 'You can't go fishing because of going out tonight. Sadie's sleeping; shopping's done. Let's go to bed.'

'You're insatiable,' he said.

'Don't you just love it.'

Afterwards they lay entwined, the sounds of the Square going on outside. Steven whistling. Jude calling her children. The bus rattling in; shuddering its wait. Rattling out again.

'Don't you just love that you can lie here and know what's happening without having to look? It's so comforting. Like I belong,' said Rowan. 'Love changes everything.'

He stroked her hair. One day, he expected, they would move in somewhere together. But for the moment this arrangement suited them both. He wondered what Lord Dorran, his old father-in-law, would say about his new partner. He got the impression the old man wanted him to stay single and grumpy, like he had. Lord Dorran had such a list of things he didn't like for no apparent reason – Ford Fiestas, hanging baskets, doorbells that went *ping pong*, people who wore new shoes (his own had been passed down from generation to generation), women who dressed like men, people who drank beer from tins – God, the list was endless. Nelson worried what he'd make of Rowan.

He tried to get up, but Rowan wasn't letting him. She rolled on top of him. 'Let's stay here.'

'We must get up. Take Sadie to your folks. Dress up in our party frocks. C'mon.'

'No,' said Rowan. 'I'm not getting up. Let's not. Let's stay here in bed for the rest of our lives. We'll send out for pizzas and never leave home again.' She pulled the duvet over their heads. 'Let's hide.'

They lay a moment, considering the joys of hiding. Then Nelson threw off the cover, gasping for breath. 'Let's not. Let's go over to the Rossis' and get some fabulous food inside us.'

They arrived at the Rossis' late; everyone else was already there – Miss Porteous in a dark green velvet dress, Mamie in her linen suit, Jude in a low-cut silk shirt and high-cut silk skirt. She sat cross-legged on a chair, quietly smoking. Paolo watched his father trying not to ogle. People who'd known each other all their lives, cast into a sudden social meeting, milled about exchanging banal small talk.

'Nice day.'

'Yes, nicer than yesterday.'

Rowan ate a rice ball. Sipped chilled Spumante and pomegranate juice. 'Gosh, this is good.' She picked up a sliver of bread spread with crushed olives and mint. 'We don't need to have anything else after this.'

The chip shop was closed for the evening. Blinds drawn. A long table was set up in the middle of the restaurant, with a white cloth, candles, a row of glasses at each place setting. It was groaning with food. A three-tiered cake stand layered with almond pastries and crystallised fruit. A steaming tureen of fish stew.

'My goodness,' Miss Porteous thrilled. 'Look at this. I haven't seen the likes of this in my life.'

'It's nothing. Just a little food – a small meal for my favourite customers,' said Claudia. She arranged the diners round the table. Man, woman, man, woman. Made sure Jude sat next to Paolo. Manipulating again; she couldn't help it. They fell into the silence of eating. The clatter of spoons against china. Every so often someone would exclaim with joy. 'This is wonderful! I've never eaten like this!'

Claudia glowed and shrugged. Pride and modesty. 'It's nothing.' The meal had taken over twelve hours to prepare. After artichoke

261

hearts and sweet and sour aubergine, they ate fish soup, then pasta with marinaded cod. 'Nothing. Nothing,' said Claudia. She watched her daughter. 'You're not eating.'

'I am,' young Claudia said. 'Just not as much as you.'

'You're getting too thin.'

'First too fat; now too thin. Will I ever do anything right? Anyway, I want to be too thin. Like Rowan.'

'I'm not too thin, am I?' Rowan looked down at her body.

'Yes,' said Mama Claudia. 'You're too thin.'

They started on the pork. Miss Porteous took two slices with a spreading of the sauce – grainy with bits of ham and slightly charred onion. She heaped carrots, glistening in reduced marsala onto her plate. 'I know I'm meant to eat them separately, but I like to mix my flavours. So, what about the life stories? The baring of souls? That's what young Rowan said we'd do.'

Rowan blushed.

'There has always been too much emphasis on food in our house,' young Claudia said. 'Food as gratification.'

Nobody spoke. Miss Porteous filled her glass. Her cheeks glowed alcohol. Rowan chewed slowly. Drunk, but sober enough to try to hide the fact she'd drunk too much. 'My life story's hardly worth the telling.'

'Oh, I don't think so,' said Miss Porteous. 'Taking in someone else's child. Then spending your days fretting lest the baby's mother shows up and whips her away. That's interesting, I'd say.'

The guests busied themselves eating lest Miss Porteous start discussing their lives.

Mama Claudia put down her fork. 'What does that mean, food as gratification?'

'Food,' said young Claudia. 'Always food instead of . . .' She looked away.

'Instead of what?' Mama Claudia stiffened.

'Instead of other things. Trips to the zoo. The swimming baths. Picnics like Rowan's folks. Stuff like that.'

'We did everything for you. Built up this business. Years and years of work, and you want to go to the swimming baths?'

'Yeah.' Young Claudia looked defiant.

'We did all this for you.' Mama Claudia stood up, opened her arms. Embraced the chip shop.

'Maybe I don't want it. You never asked.'

'Don't want it?' Mama Claudia was furious. 'Don't want it!'

'That's right. I don't want it.'

'Neither do I,' said Stu. 'I don't want a fucking chip shop.'

'Don't swear at my table,' said Giorgio. 'I won't have swearing at the table.'

'I don't want a fucking chip shop either,' said Paolo.

'Nor me,' said Jim. 'I never wanted to work in a chip shop.'

'I give up everything to come here to work in this place,' Mama Claudia raged. 'Now my children don't want my chip shop.'

'It's not your chip shop.' Giorgio stood up. 'It's mine.'

'I left Italy – Alberto – to come here.'

'Alberto!' Giorgio shouted. 'You're still thinking about him.'

'Who's Alberto?' Young Claudia looked confused.

The others round the table had stopped eating, except Miss Porteous. She helped herself to more pork. Refilled her glass. She liked a good argument. Especially when she wasn't in it.

'He was the man I loved,' Mama Claudia said. 'I ran away with him. My father brought me back.'

'Just like me at the Bowie gig. That was embarrassing,' said Claudia Junior.

'Who knows what you would have got up to if your father hadn't come for you.' Her mother turned on her.

'You know what she would have got up to. All the things *you* got up to?' Giorgio said. Paolo, Jim and young Claudia stared at their mother.

'You got up to things, but you never let us do anything,' young Claudia said. 'It was all chip shop, chip shop, chip shop. I don't WANT a fucking chip shop!'

Mama Claudia got up, stormed through to the kitchen. Returned with a huge glass swan filled with ice cream. Slammed it in the centre of the table. Scooped furious portions into fluted glasses. 'Pudding,' she said. 'You'll be wanting pudding, no doubt.'

'No.' Young Claudia pushed her chair back. 'No, I don't want any fucking chip shop and I don't want any fucking pudding. I'm on a diet.' She walked to the door and opened it. 'Stu. Are you coming, Stu?'

Stu gazed lovingly at the swan. He felt he hadn't eaten properly in weeks. Weeks and weeks and weeks.

'Stu.' Young Claudia sounded formidable. 'Come on. NOW!'

Stu rose, followed Claudia to the door. They left.

Her mother watched her, arms folded. Somewhere beneath her fury she was thinking, That's my girl.

'I don't want a chip shop either,' said Paolo. He threw down his napkin. And left too.

'They don't want a chip shop – I never wanted a chip shop.' Mama Claudia turned to Giorgio. 'You keep your fucking chip shop.' She stormed off upstairs.

Giorgio turned to his guests. 'Sorry,' he said. 'We argued.' He shrugged. 'We argue. All the time we argue. But eat. Enjoy the pudding.' He ran upstairs after his wife.

Miss Porteous said, 'Well, I certainly shall.' She scooped up a second helping. Nobody else liked to.

'Well,' said Rowan, thinking, There you go. 'I always wanted a big family that had huge rows and made up. Maybe it was the food. You don't get passionate over lamb chops and mash with peas.'

'My family fought,' said Jude, 'and we lived on stuff from tins. If it didn't come from a tin we didn't eat it. Mind you, all we fought about was what tin was going to get opened.'

'Not the same,' said Rowan.

Jude agreed.

'I think,' said Mamie, 'we should go.'

They all got up from the table, bade Jim good night, and left. They did not linger; did not want to be seen gossiping outside in the Square. They would gossip tomorrow, out of sight of the Rossis.

Jim sat alone at the table, considering the post-party débris. He rose, gathered a pile of plates and carried them to the kitchen. He scraped them, stacked the dishwasher. Returned for another pile. 'I don't want a fucking chip shop either. I want to buy a fish farm.'

Chapter Twenty-Four

'To think I thought nothing ever happened here,' Rowan said to Nelson next morning. She looked out of the window. The chip shop was open; Jim was behind the counter. 'Do you think they'll sell up?'

'No,' said Nelson. 'They'll carry on, eating and arguing. It's what they do best. They love it.'

Rowan left to collect Sadie. When she got to her parents' house, Norma was sitting at the kitchen table drinking tea. 'You look worried,' Rowan said, picking up Sadie.

'She was fine. No trouble at all.' Norma told her.

Rowan sat at the table. 'Is something wrong? You look sort of, well, ashen.'

'I've had a shock,' Norma said. 'I'm pregnant.'

'You?' Rowan gripped the table. 'You can't be. You're . . .' she was going to say 'old' but stopped herself '. . . my mother,' she said instead.

'I know that. Now I'm going to be someone else's mother too.'

'When did this happen?'

'On the cruise.'

Rowan said nothing. She did not like to think of her mother and father having sex. In fact, she thought they didn't any more. 'What does Dad say?'

'He's over the moon. He's full of it – he can't wait. Now that he's retired he thinks he'll have lots of time for a child. He's already planning the things they're going to do together.'

Rowan was jealous already. 'What about you?'

'I got caught. I thought I was past it. It happens.'

'Are you going to have it? You could get an abortion.'

'I could, but your father would never speak to me again. Besides, I don't know if I could cope with that.'

'I'd go with you.' She considered she was experienced at accompanying people to abortions.

Norma shook her head. 'I expect I'll go through with it, though thinking about it makes my heart sink. Waddling about. Heartburn. Oh God. Then there's broken nights. And school. Parents Day. Christ, I hated all that. Then there's George. He's fifty-eight. He'll be well past seventy by the time the baby's twenty. I'll be sixty-seven.'

'So?' said Rowan. 'The baby'll keep you young.'

'Christ, Rowan. What if George . . .' She paused. 'What if he dies? I'll be left alone, with a child.'

Rowan started. Her mother had said Christ. Twice. She didn't know her mother did that.

'Like me,' said Rowan.

'Exactly,' said Norma.

'I manage,' said Rowan.

'Just,' said Norma. 'Then there's the whole teenage thing. All these years I tried and tried to get pregnant. Then this. Out of the blue. I tell you I'm never going abroad again if this is what it does to you.'

'Let Dad cope. He's the one that's keen. You and me can run away.'

Norma smiled.

'I'll help,' Rowan offered. 'I can change nappies. Baby-sit when you and Dad want to go out on the town in your gladrags.'

'I think you're going to have to,' said Norma.

'I'm going to have a sister. Or a brother,' Rowan told Nelson when she got back to the flat.

'Your mother's pregnant? But she's . . .' he was going to say old, but didn't.

'Old?' said Rowan. 'I know. That's what I almost said, too. She's forty-seven. It happens. They must've done it – I hate to think of that.'

'Why?' said Nelson. 'I think it's good. Maybe you'll be the same – getting preggers when you're ancient.'

'Piss off,' she said. 'Not me. When I'm ancient I'll be exploring the wilds of Peru. Or driving across America.'

'Can I come?' said Nelson. 'And Sadie?'

'If you're good.'

Claudia turned up at twelve o'clock for her shift in the chip shop. Her mother was behind the counter. They didn't speak. Moved stiffly round each other. Young Claudia looked at the day's batter.

'Good batter.'

'Very good batter. I made it.'

'There you go. You make good batter when you're angry.'

'Very good batter when I'm angry.'

'Well, I'll say I don't want your fucking chip shop every day. That'll be good for the batter.'

'You do that. You're not getting my fucking chip shop anyway. I'll leave it to someone else.'

'Good. I hope the someone else enjoys it.'

They stood face to face behind the counter. Glaring. Then glaring less. A small smile. A loosening of the shoulders. A bigger smile. Then they were in each other's arms. Patting and holding, crying.

'No more fights,' said Young Claudia.

'Oh yes. Lots more fights. Painful truths. Shouting. Good for the batter.' Mama Claudia sighed. 'You still hate the fucking chip shop?'

'Yes.'

'So do I.'

They looked at each other.

'Batter,' said Claudia Junior.

'Potatoes,' said her mother.

'Chicken 'n' chips with a pickle and extra vinegar.'

'Double portion sausage,' said Mama Claudia.

They burst out laughing.

'It's hell,' said Claudia. 'Haggis and chips.'

They roared.

'What are we going to do?' Claudia wanted to know.

'Go shopping.'

'Shopping?' said Claudia.

'It works for me.' Mama Claudia nudged her. 'Next time I go to

London you come with me. I'll show you things. We'll spend some chip money.'

By late August swallows were gathering. Lining the telegraph wires, getting ready to go. Rowan watched them. Mornings she could smell a small chill in the air, cold days coming. It excited her. She liked the cold. She'd light the fire. Walk the hills watching the world on the turn.

Chapter Twenty-Five

It rained all that September. Sadie was ten months old. Crawling across the room, pulling herself upright on the red tub chairs. She was experimenting with her voice, making noises. In the supermarket she'd gurgle and yodel and reach out for things Rowan didn't want to buy. When they were snatched away and put back on the shelves, Sadie would cry. People stared.

'You're not going to be an exhibitionist, are you?' said Rowan.

The flat got messier. Rowan's life got hectic, mindlessly hectic. She'd pick Sadie up from Norma and George, take her home. Light the fire. Feed Sadie. Play with Sadie. Bathe Sadie. Then sit in the chair, legs draped over the side, too tired to feed herself or tidy up. Every night she meant to read, or paint the living room. Every night she fell asleep in the chair. Woke up shivering because the fire had died, and went to bed.

Whenever Nelson came round he'd tidy and cook. 'Two messy buggers to pick up after,' he complained after he'd dumped all Sadie's toys in the basket by the door, folded Rowan's jersey, hung up her coat and made her pasta. 'What are we going to do with you?'

'I don't know,' Rowan said. 'What do you think?' She was too involved with present problems to consider the future. Soon her mother would be unable to look after Sadie, then what? Rowan could not afford to give up work, and on her current wages she could not afford to pay somebody to look after the child. She fretted. She bit her nails. She preferred life when she was comatose in front of the fire. Sleeping kept her mind off things.

Nelson shrugged. 'We could move in together.'

269

'Don't you think a pair of messy buggers would get on your nerves?'

'Maybe I'd get on your nerves with my tidying and wiping,' Nelson said.

'Better leave things as they are, then.'

'Don't you want more than this? We could do things. Go on holiday together. Be there for each other. Meals. Breakfast in the mornings. In bed every night. You could warm your feet on my bum, I wouldn't complain.'

'That's the nicest offer I've had in my life. Don't tempt me.'

'Why not?'

'Because I'm worrying about who's going to look after Sadie when my mother's too pregnant, and when the baby's born she'll be too busy to cope with Sadie. You're distracting me from my worry.'

'OK, so it was the wrong moment. But the bum offer is always open. You are wanted.'

'I'll remember. Maybe one night when my feet are particularly cold, I'll turn up at your door.'

In bed Nelson would gently move the hair from Rowan's face and watch her sleep. He worried. What if Eileen turned up to claim Sadie? It would break Rowan's heart. He feared for her; he feared for himself. He thought if Sadie were whisked away there would be no reason for Rowan to stay. She'd go. And that would break *his* heart.

In the years since his wife left Nelson hadn't allowed himself relationships. He'd had brief affairs with women he'd met at conferences, or on holiday. No involvements; he had always held back. 'Nothing serious,' he'd told himself. Now it was as if without him noticing, something serious had happened to him. He tried to pinpoint the moment, if there was a moment. Times he'd spent with Rowan, sitting in her living room chatting, listening to music, walking with Rowan, Sadie on his shoulders, playing with Rowan and Sadie in his garden at weekends, came to him. Somewhere in there, at some moment she had become precious. He couldn't bear to lose her.

At the foot of the bed Elvis lay curled and sleeping. Like the drinkers and shouters in the Square the rain had driven him indoors. He was fat. He was happy. He was in Rowan's bed every night. Nelson envied him.

Across the Square Steven was bored. The rest of the family was sleeping. He lay on the sofa watching night television. A TV movie about a woman played by Stephanie Powers dying of Multiple Sclerosis (they were always played by Stephanie Powers), tracing her daughter. It bored him. Whenever the weeping and quality moments came on, and they came on often, he shouted, 'Shuttup!' at the screen. He smoked Jude's cigarettes, flicking the ash into the saucer of his coffee cup on the floor. Rain battered the window. It was been battering the window all week. He hadn't been out.

At last, he pointed the remote at the set and switched it off. Stubbed out the last of his cigarette. Fetched his denim jacket from his room and climbed out the window. Jude always slept lightly; if he used the door, he'd wake her.

He ran through the streets, up the hill to Elizabeth Street where Rodger Snype lived. His Jaguar was parked, unlocked, keys in the ignition, in the drive. Steven never wondered why the man never locked his car, always left the keys inside. He was always drunk. He'd sit in his office after hours thinking about his overdraft, drinking whisky. At eight, he'd lock up and drive slowly home. He didn't think it counted as drunk driving when it was only a small village distance that he knew well from his office to his house.

Steven started the car, reversed down the drive and headed for the Glen road. Window wound down, stereo blaring, wipers scraping furiously against the windscreen, he reached the Drover's Inn in twenty minutes. Grinning with triumph he punched the steering wheel. 'A new record.'

He shoved the car into reverse. Shot back into the road and headed back to the village, foot to the floor. Yelling. He switched off the lights, let out a throat-busting whoop; 'Have that, ya bastards!' And plunged, eighty miles an hour, into the darkness.

The police woke Jude at four in the morning. There were two of them – a man and a woman. Could they come in? They seemed enormous in Jude's living room. Holding their hats, they asked did Jude know the whereabouts of her son, Steven?

'In bed,' said Jude, 'through the house.'

She went to check. Came back clutching herself. Shielding herself. Wincing already at the news she was about to hear. 'What's happened?'

There had been an accident. A Jaguar belonging to Rodger Snype had gone off the road up the glen and smashed into a tree. The driver was killed. They believed it to be Steven.

Jude crumpled. She doubled over, clutching herself. 'Oh no.' Then a wail so loud it woke Delia and Charmaine; Sonia slept through everything. The girls appeared at the door in their nightdresses, pale from sleep, Charmaine clutching Harvey.

'Go back to bed,' Jude urged them. 'I'll tell you in the morning.'

The two disappeared. They knew a crisis when it came.

'Who found him?' Jude wanted to know.

'Lord Dorran.'

Coming home from his regimental reunion in Edinburgh, the headlights of his car had swept across the wreck. He'd stopped. Crossed to examine the metal heap and discovered Steven. He phoned the police on his mobile. 'Hate the things, but these days I've gone technical. Got a computer and a fax. Damn things.'

'Is there anybody we can get to sit with you?' the policewoman asked.

Ella and Bruce, her parents, lived round the corner in the High Street. Jude didn't want them.

'There's my boyfriend, Frank. But he's not speaking to me since I said I was going back to university,' Jude said. 'He gives me money for Charmaine and Sonia every Friday.' She did not need to say that. 'Paolo. I want Paolo.'

'Rossi?' said the policeman. Everybody knew everybody.

Jude nodded.

Twenty minutes later Paolo came to Jude. They spent the night sitting on the sofa in front of the fake coal fire drinking tea. They hardly spoke. And when they did Jude would repeat, 'He was a good boy. Really.'

And Paolo said, 'I know.'

Claudia Senior went round to tell Ella and Bruce. 'Are you sure?' the policewoman said. 'We could . . .'

'No,' Mama Claudia said. 'This is something I should do.'

It Could Happen To You

Six days later they buried Steven. The village went silent. Curtains drawn. Why do the young die? It was not right. It was not fair. 'Don't talk to me about fair,' said Jude. 'There is no such thing as fair.'

The Hansons, the Rossis, Rowan, Nelson, Mamie Garland, Miss Porteous and Steven's school headmaster gathered in the church for the service. They played Steven's favourite record, the theme tune to *Champions League*. 'That's what he would have wanted,' said Jude. She had to be helped down the aisle.

They gathered in the County Hotel for drinks. People spoke quietly, didn't know what to say. Somehow small talk seemed shocking. When they'd all left Jude turned to her mother. 'That's it over. Now for the hard part – getting on with things. I can't do it.'

'You can,' said Ella. 'You must.'

Three days after the funeral Jude met Paolo in the Square.

'How are you?' he asked.

'How do you think?'

They started to walk.

'I can't stand it,' said Jude. 'I think I'm going mad. If the radio's playing I can't suffer the noise. It interferes with my grief. So I switch it off. Then I can't stand the silence. How am I going to live?'

Paolo didn't know. He wanted to tell her about his guilt, but what good would that do? They walked down the hill, into the park. Passed the duck pond and the infants' trampolines, closed for the winter. Sat side by side on the steps on the bandstand.

'We were fools,' said Jude. She lit a cigarette, offered one to Paolo. He took it, though he'd given up years ago.

'Fools,' he agreed.

'You take your eyes off one to look out for another, and look what happens.'

'It's not your fault.'

'Whose fault is it?'

'Nobody's. You mustn't blame yourself.'

'That's going to take a while. Most of my life.'

They walked slowly back.

'Are you still going to university?' Paolo asked.

'I wasn't, but my mother's insisting. And I've nothing else. I'll go. All my doubts and fears about it seem like nothing now.'

'Can I see you again?'

She shook her head. 'Not like that. Not like we were. It's too late, isn't it? What would we say?'

They parted.

Lord Dorran sat in his Mini-van, wreathed in scents of wet dog and fertiliser. He saw Jude disappear into her front door, hunched, arms folded, head bowed. He knew that walk. He should, he knew, go to her. He should tell her how he found Steven. That wild grin on his face. But not now, he thought. Later. In spring when his bombing raids started up. When he drove round the countryside tossing his seed grenades from his sunroof, making things bearable, he would ask Jude to accompany him. She would go. He knew that. She would go.

Chapter Twenty-Six

Two weeks later Paolo left the village to go and work with his cousin who owned a restaurant in Glasgow. He rarely came back. Then Jim moved up the glen. He bought a house with ten acres of ground, ready to establish his fish farm. People would come, he knew, to fish where a catch was guaranteed. He would also supply trout to hotels and restaurants. Evenings he planned to stroll round his new lake, watching his fish jump. He would think and he would dream and he would never serve fish and chips again.

The two Claudias took over the chip shop. They squabbled, they fought, they made up. Every two months they shopped. Giorgio retired to polish his Rolls-Royce, Verdi playing on his tape-deck.

When Norma got too tired, too pregnant to care for Sadie, Mamie Garland took her. 'It'll keep me young.' Rowan came home lunchtimes, fed Sadie. Mamie walked the child through the park. Told her the plots and dialogue of favourite movies. She mimicked the stars. 'Of all the bars . . .' 'Match me, Sidney.' 'I cudda been a contenda.' 'I'll have what she's having . . . *When Harry Met Sally*. You wouldn't know that, would you?' Mamie said. Sadie gazed at her, wide-eyed.

During the second week of January, work started on the new block of flats on the Rialto site. Rowan and Mamie watched the foundations go down, bulldozers and JCBs groaning across the rubbled ground.

'I'll be in my flat by autumn, they say. Speed they put things up these days.' There was already a sign advertising luxury flats for sale.

'Did the insurance company pay up?' Rowan asked.

'Not without a fight. Had the police and the insurance investigators questioning me, but they couldn't find anything. It all went up in the fire – my records, photos, film posters – and they were worth a bit. Everything.' She had been staying at the County Hotel since the fire. 'It's fine. Cooked breakfast every morning. Central heating. But I like my own place.'

'Who doesn't?' said Rowan.

'I'll be up there, on top of everything. The view,' she smiled. 'The view. I'll see clear over the village and beyond to the glen. I'll know everything that happens. Though I know it already without looking out the window. Jude sitting in her living room trying to study, thinking about her Steven. Snypey worrying about his overdraft. Your mum and dad getting ready for their baby. You sitting by your fire, Elvis on your knee, Sadie asleep in your room. Nelson in his cottage listening to Mozart. Which, may I say, is daft of you both. You should be together. Someone to talk to, laugh with of an evening is a treat. It'll all be happening down there. Way below me. The two Claudias serving up fish suppers in their fucking chip shop. Dreaming of the day they'll open up a new Italian restaurant at the back. Miss Porteous having her evening sherry and her second Benson & Hedges of the day, Bach's organ music playing.' She turned to Rowan. 'I'll love it there. I can see the world from there.'

That was the day Eileen came back. She ran up the stairs shouting, 'Rowan, hello! Rowan!'

Rowan opened the door, saw her, and felt her heart stop. 'Christ, no.'

Eileen came into the house. Looked round and approved. 'Isn't this grand? You've done all right for yourself.' She wandered about, picking things up. 'This is amazing.'

'It isn't really,' said Rowan. 'But I like it. What brings you here?' Rowan wanted to know. 'You can't just disappear out of people's lives. Stealing their stuff, then come back again whenever it suits you. I don't want to see you.'

'Well, here I am. Shut your eyes if you don't want to see me.'

'I would if it didn't mean me banging into things.'

'I wanted to see my daughter. And I thought it time to return your rucksack.' She wriggled it off her back, set it on the floor.

'Is that it?' Rowan hardly recognised it. The rucksack was worn, fraying at the bottom, and stained; one of the straps was broken.

'Sorry,' said Eileen. 'It's taken a bit of a pounding. All my adventures.'

'There's your daughter.' Rowan pointed to Sadie who was sitting on the floor surrounded by plastic bricks. She gazed up, idly sucking a blue one.

Eileen crossed to her, knelt beside her and said, 'Hello. I'm your mother.'

Sadie looked at her. Blankly.

'No smiles for me?' Eileen was disappointed.

'What did you expect?'

'Dunno.' Eileen spread her arms expansively.

Rowan put on the kettle. 'You want coffee?'

'In the absence of something stronger. It'll do.'

'Coffee, then.' Rowan had no intention of offering Eileen anything stronger. 'So,' she said. 'Tell me about your adventures. Did you travel the world?'

'Did I ever. You should have been there.' Eileen always was tactless. 'You missed yourself.'

'Where did you go?'

'Paris, Rome, down to Palermo, across to Algeria. Then, you know, down through Africa.'

'I don't believe you. You gave half my money to Kelly.'

'How do you know that?'

'They tracked me down through Danny. Like you.'

'You are easy to find. I got your address. I went into the chip shop in the Square and the woman there told me where you were.'

'Claudia,' Rowan sighed. 'So what did you really do with my money?' She handed Eileen a steaming mug.

'I went to New York.'

'Then what?'

'I looked around.'

'That's it?'

'More or less. New York's huge – terrifying. I didn't like to go out at first so I stayed in my hotel. Ordered pizza.' Eileen looked embarrassed. 'I drank Jack Daniel's. I must've had too much, 'cos I slipped on a slice. It was still in the box. I pulled the ligaments in my knee.' She lifted her skirt, displaying the wounded limb.

'Is that it?' Rowan was horrified.

'Well, I went to the Emergency Room, but it was full of lunatics and junkies, so I went private. It costs a fortune over there.'

'My God,' breathed Rowan. 'My money. Fools always end up badly.'

'What!' Eileen was incensed.

'Someone told me that,' Rowan said.

'It was a tragedy. It hurt. Really hurt. I just wasn't watching for a minute. It could happen to anyone. It could happen to you.'

'Yes. I stopped watching for a minute, and look what happened to me. You stole my stuff and took off.'

'So I came back to London.' Uncomfortable with this line of conversation, Eileen changed the subject. 'Got myself together. Found a job. Cosmetics counter at Selfridges. It's a laugh.'

'You've joined the Polyfilla Sisters. Orange-faced, spraying perfume in the air. Telling folk they have oily skin, and you've got just the thing for that.'

'New place to live.' Eileen ignored her. 'A bit far out, but it's all I can afford. And here I am. Anyway, I thought I might take Sadie back.'

It took Rowan a moment. She started to shake. 'Over my dead body. You've fucked up my life once, you're not getting a second shot at it. I'll fight you. I'll take you to court.' She realised she was spitting, flecks of saliva shooting from her mouth. She hated that, but she couldn't help it. 'I'll get Ronnie to testify that you abandoned Kelly. I'll—'

'OK. OK,' Eileen waved her back. 'I was just testing you out. I don't know if I really want a baby – she'd cramp my style. I just thought I'd drop by, see how it was going with you.'

'You're not staying.'

'Don't want to – I hate the countryside. Sounds of sheep in the morning. All this open space, it isn't natural.'

'Ronnie Barr told me all about you and your endless, endless lies.'

Eileen refused to look ashamed. 'So I embellish things a bit. What harm does it do?'

Rowan looked at Eileen coldly. 'I used to think you were a Golden Oriole. A fabulous fleeting visitor in my life. Now I think you're a goose.'

Eileen sipped her drink. 'You think I'm a fool.'

'Yes,' Rowan said. 'Then so am I.'

'Oh no, you're not. You have everything. Sadie, for example.'

Rowan got up. Went to the kitchen, started to heat some food for Sadie. 'You want something to eat? There's only macaroni and cheese. You can have some.' She sounded frosty. 'I want your address. I want you to make me Sadie's legal guardian. There will be times ahead when I need to sign things for her. School. And what if she ever has to go to hospital?'

'Food would be fine.' Eileen ignored the frost. She wrote her address on the back of an envelope.

'If it's another of your lies, I'll find out. I'll track you down.'

'It's not a lie,' Eileen said.

They ate at the kitchen table. Drank a bottle of Chianti. Rowan spoonfed Sadie who sat on her high chair between them. January winds shook the windows. Snow coming.

'Can I stay tonight?' Eileen asked. 'I'm knackered. It's a long journey from London.'

'Yes. Just tonight,' Rowan said. 'Then go. I'll decide when I have forgiven you.'

'You have already forgiven me,' Eileen said. 'You have so much. If I hadn't run out on you, you'd have none of this.'

'It's time to put Sadie to bed,' Rowan said.

When she came back, Eileen was sitting draped on the red tub chair. 'This is gorgeous.'

'You're not getting her,' Rowan said. 'You made your choice. I am not letting you have Sadie.'

'I kind of got that message,' said Eileen. 'What will you tell her?'

'I've thought about that.' Rowan poured the last of the wine. 'The truth is all there is. I just hope she'll forgive me for loving her so much I kept her from her mother.'

'And me?'

'I hope she'll forgive you for not wanting her.'

'I wanted her. I just wanted other things more.'

'Jesus, Eileen. Grow up.'

'I have no intention of doing that.'

Eileen yawned. Stretched. 'So tell me about you. What've you been up to?'

'Not a lot,' Rowan said. 'Coming and going.' She decided not to mention Nelson.

'What about your old best friend? Do you ever see her?'

'Claudia. Oh yes. I think in time we will be best friends again,' Rowan said.

She didn't mention rolling down the hill. Eileen would only steal the memory. The woman was a thief. She'd taken money, a rucksack, and, worse than that, Rowan's daydreams and ambitions. She'd pilfer precious moments and squander them on strangers in bars, anyone who would listen.

'Isn't there anybody?' Eileen didn't believe Rowan hadn't met someone – a male someone. She looked too content.

'Well, maybe,' said Rowan.

'You're so lucky,' said Eileen. 'You have Sadie. You have a job. A bloke.' She looked miffed.

'You have no right to envy me,' said Rowan. 'You could have had these things. You didn't try. It could've happened to you.'

One o'clock in the morning, Eileen went to bed in the spare room that was to have been Sadie's, only Rowan liked the baby to be in her room beside her, where she could listen to her breathe, watch her sleep.

Rowan sat by the fire. For the first time in weeks she took out Walter Dean's diary. Read his final entries.

21 September. Geese will be coming soon. Legions of them across the sky. They fly along the edges of the clouds. You can hear the wind on their wings and their incessant clatter long before you see them. Speed they go. What must it be like to be a goose? Up there with your companions you open your throat to say something eloquent and all you do is honk.

29 September. Strange, the things you learn. Thirty years a postman I learned the language of cars. Walking the streets you come to know which ones are turning left, though they're signalling right. And there's ones you dare not step in front of – they'd mow you down. And cars you know will slow down for you. Wave you on.

I learned the language of houses. Just walking up to them you know them. Some are cold, sterile. You'd think nobody lived in them, though you've been delivering mail to them for years. Some are stressed – the strange cleanness of the path, the barren windows. And some reach out to you – the love that goes on inside them. I always wished for that – to be where I was wanted.

Now I have become drawn into the language of swans. They way they move. Things they say to one another, dipping their necks, floating round each other. They glide. They swim towards me, hooting curiosity. It would not occur to them to live where they did not want to be. The language of swans – I love the language of swans.

Rowan shut the book; there was no more.

She got up, looked round. This place wasn't that great, was it? She went through to her room. Packed her case. Took it downstairs, dumped it in the Beetle. Then she went upstairs, packed Sadie's clothes. Dumped her toys into a cardboard box. Took them all to the car. After that she gathered Elvis from the bed. Took him downstairs, threw him into the car. 'You're getting fat, Elvis. Just like Elvis.' The cat stared at her balefully. Started to yowl. 'No yowling. No peeing,' she ordered. 'Or it's the taxidermist for you, pal.'

Upstairs again, Rowan picked up Sadie. Finger to her lips when Sadie started to complain. 'Sssh. We're doing a moonlight. It's fun.'

Before she left she looked in the spare room. Eileen was sleeping, face calm. That sweet untroubled way she slept as if she had no worries at all. Maybe wicked people did that, slept like innocents – unaware of, not at all bothered by the pain they caused. Rowan said goodbye to her. 'I shall not be seeing you again.' She shut the door.

Car packed, Rowan got in behind the wheel, drove up the glen to Nelson.

'What are you doing here? It's the middle of the night.'

Rowan put down her case. Handed Sadie to him. 'I've got to get Elvis before he pees on the seat,' she said.

She came back, set Elvis down beside the wood-burning stove. 'I'll fetch the rest in the morning.'

Nelson stared at her.

'Your minimalist days are over,' she told him. 'I've come to get on your nerves and mess up the rest of your life. My feet are cold. I need a warm bum.'

'Just what I've always wanted. Icy feet on my arse,' he said. 'What brought this on?'

'Eileen came back. She wanted Sadie.'

'And you ran away from her?'

'No. I told her she couldn't have her. Then when she went to bed I left her. She'll wake up in the morning and I'll be gone. No note. No apologies. No goodbyes. No nothing. That's the deal. She started it.'

'You could have let Sadie go. You could have taken off yourself.'

'I know. But you're here.'

He smiled.

'Also,' she said, 'look at all the doings since I arrived. The Rialto went up in flames. The Rossis have gone their separate ways. Well, two of them. Snypey's broke. Delia tried to do away with herself. Jude's at university. And young Steven . . . well, young Steven. My mother's pregnant. A new Campbell any day now. How could I go? I want to see what happens next.'